TWO DEAD WIVES

TWO DEAD WIVES

ADELE PARKS

mira

ISBN-13: 978-0-7783-0529-3

Two Dead Wives

Copyright © 2023 by Adele Parks

Mira
22 Adelaide St. West, 41st Floor
Toronto, Ontario M5H 4E3, Canada
BookClubbish.com

Printed in U.S.A.

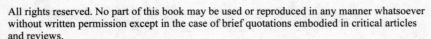

For Diana Stewart and Jonathan Douglas,
who work tirelessly to nurture the next generation of readers.

And for Annabel Spooner,
who is simply the most wonderful fun.

1

DC CLEMENTS

There is no body. A fact DC Clements finds both a problem and a tantalizing possibility. She's not a woman inclined to irrational hope, or even excessive hope. Any damned hope, really. At least, not usually.

Kylie Gillingham is probably dead.

The forty-three-year-old woman has been missing nearly two weeks. Ninety-seven percent of the 180,000 people a year who are reported missing are found within a week, dead or alive. She hasn't been spotted by members of the public, or picked up on CCTV; her bank, phone and email accounts haven't been touched. She has social media registered under her married name, Kai Janssen; they've lain dormant. No perky pictures of carefully arranged books, lattes, Negronis or peonies. Kylie Gillingham hasn't returned to either of her homes. Statistically, it's looking very bad.

Experience would also suggest this sort of situation has to end terribly. When a wife disappears, all eyes turn on the husband. In this case, there is not one but two raging husbands left behind. Both men once loved the missing woman very much. Love is just a shiver away from hate.

The evidence does not conclusively indicate murder. There is no body. But a violent abduction is a reasonable proposition—police-speak, disciplined by protocol. Kidnap and abuse, possible torture is likely—woman-speak, fired by indignation. They know Kylie Gillingham was kept in a room in an uninhabited apartment just floors below the one she lived in with Husband Number 2, Daan Janssen. That's not a coincidence. There is a hole in the wall of that room; most likely Kylie punched or kicked it. The debris created was flung through a window into the street, probably in order to attract attention. Her efforts failed. Fingerprints place her in the room; it's unlikely she was simply hanging out or even hiding out, as there is evidence to suggest she was chained to the radiator.

Yet despite all this, the usually clear, logical, reasonable Clements wants to ignore statistics, experience and even evidence that suggests the abduction ended in fatal violence. She wants to hope.

There just might be some way, somehow, that Kylie—enigma, bigamist—escaped from that sordid room and is alive. She might be in hiding. She is technically a criminal, after all; she might be hiding from the law. She can hardly go home. She will know by now that her life of duplicity is exposed. She will know her husbands are incensed. Baying for blood. She has three largely uninterested half brothers on her father's side, and a mother who lives in Australia. None of them give Clements a sense that they are helping or protecting Kylie. She will know who abducted her. If alive, she must be terrified.

Clements's junior partner, Constable Tanner, burly and blunt as usual, scoffs at the idea that she escaped. He's waiting for a body; he'd settle for a confession. It's been four days now since Daan Janssen left the country. "Skipped justice," as Tanner insists on saying. But the constable is wet behind the ears. He still thinks murder is glamorous and career-enhancing. Clements tries to remember: Did she ever think that way? She's been a police officer for nearly fifteen years; she joined the force straight out of university, a few years younger than Tanner is now, but no, she can't remember a time when she thought murder was glamorous.

"He hasn't skipped justice. We're talking to him and his

lawyers," she points out with what feels like the last bit of her taut patience.

"You're being pedantic."

"I'm being accurate."

"But you're talking to him through bloody Microsoft Teams," says Tanner dismissively. "What the hell is that?"

"The future." Clements sighs. She ought to be offended by the uppity tone of the junior police officer. It's disrespectful. She's the detective constable. She would be offended if she had the energy, but she doesn't have any to spare. It's all focused on the case. On Kylie Gillingham. She needs to remain clear-sighted, analytical. They need to examine the facts, the evidence, over and over again. To be fair, Constable Tanner is focused too, but his focus manifests in frenetic frustration. She tries to keep him on track. "Look, lockdown means Daan Janssen isn't coming back to the UK for questioning anytime soon. Even if there wasn't a strange new world to negotiate, we couldn't force him to come to us, not without arresting him, and I can't do that yet."

Tanner knocks his knuckles against her desk as though he is rapping on a door, asking to be let in, demanding attention. "But all the evidence—"

"Is circumstantial." Tanner knows this; he just can't quite accept it. He feels the finish line is in sight, but he can't cross it, and it frustrates him. Disappoints him. He wants the world to be clear-cut. He wants crimes to be punished, bad men behind bars, a safer realm. He doesn't want some posh twat flashing his passport and wallet, hopping on a plane to his family mansion in the Netherlands and getting away with it. Daan Janssen's good looks and air of entitlement offend Tanner. Clements understands all that. She understands it but has never allowed personal bias and preferences to cloud her investigating procedures.

"We found her phones in his flat!" Tanner insists.

"Kylie could have put them there herself," counters Clements. "She did live there with him as his wife."

"And we found the receipt for the cable ties and the bucket from the room she was held in."

"We found *a* receipt. The annual number of cable ties produced is about a hundred billion. A lot of people buy cable ties. Very few of them to bind their wives to radiators. Janssen might have wanted to neaten up his computer and charger cords. He lives in a minimalist house. That's what any lawyer worth their salt will argue." Clements rolls her head from left to right; her neck clicks like castanets.

"His fingerprints are on the food packets."

"Which means he touched those protein bars. That's all they prove. Not that he took them into the room. Not that he was ever in the room."

Exasperated, Tanner demands, "Well, how else did they get there? They didn't fly in through the bloody window, did they?" Clements understands he's not just excitable, he cares. He wants this resolved. She likes him for it, even if he's clumsy in his declarations. It makes her want to soothe him; offer him guarantees and reassurances that she doesn't even believe in. She doesn't soothe or reassure, because she has to stay professional, focused. The devil is in the detail. She just has to stay sharp, be smarter than the criminal. That's what she believes. "She might have brought them in from their home. He might have touched them in their flat. That's what a lawyer will argue."

"He did it all right, no doubt about it," asserts Tanner with a steely certainty.

Clements knows that there is always doubt. A flicker, like a wick almost lit, then instantly snuffed. Nothing is certain in this world. That's why people like her are so important; people who know about ambiguity yet carry on regardless, carry on asking questions, finding answers. Dig, push, probe. That is her job. For a conviction to be secured in a court of law, things must be proven beyond reasonable doubt. It isn't easy to do. Barristers are brilliant, wily. Jurors can be insecure, overwhelmed. Defendants might lie, cheat. The evidence so far is essentially fragile and hypothetical.

"I said, didn't I. Right at the beginning, I said it's always the husband that's done it," Tanner continues excitedly. He did say as much, yes. However, he was talking about Husband Number 1, Mark Fletcher, at that point, if Clements's memory serves her correctly, which it always does. And even if her memory one day fails to be the reliable machine that it currently is, she takes notes—meticulous notes—so she always has those to rely on. Yes, Tanner said it was the husband, but this case has been about *which* husband. Daan Janssen, married to Kai: dedicated daughter to a sick mother, classy dresser and sexy wife. Or Mark Fletcher, husband to Leigh: devoted stepmother, conscientious management consultant and happy wife. Kai. Leigh. Kylie. Kylie Gillingham, the bigamist, had been hiding in plain sight. But now she is gone. Vanished.

"The case against Janssen is gathering momentum," says Clements, carefully.

"Because she was held captive in his apartment block."

"Yes."

"Which is right on the river, easy way to lose a body."

She winces at this thought but stays on track. "Obviously Mark Fletcher has motive too. A good lawyer trying to cast doubt on Janssen's guilt might argue that Fletcher knew about the other husband and followed his wife to her second home."

Tanner is bright, fast; he chases her line of thought. He knows the way defense lawyers create murky waters. "Fletcher could have confronted her somewhere in the apartment block."

"A row. A violent moment of fury," adds Clements. "He knocks her out cold. Then finds an uninhabited apartment and impetuously stashes her there."

Tanner is determined to stick to his theory that Janssen is the guilty man. "Sounds far-fetched. How did he break in? This thing seems more planned."

"I agree, but the point is, either husband could have discovered the infidelity, then, furious, humiliated and ruthless, imprisoned her. They'd have wanted to scare and punish, reassert control, show her who was boss." They know this much, but they do not know what happened next. Was she killed in that room? If so, where is the body hidden? "And you know we can't limit this investigation to just the two husbands. There are other suspects," she adds.

Tanner flops into his chair, holds up a hand and starts to count off the suspects on his fingers. "Oli, her teen stepson. He has the body and strength of a man..."

Clements finishes his thought. "But the emotions and irrationality of a child. He didn't know his stepmum was a bigamist, but he did know she was having an affair. It's possible he did something rash. Something extreme that is hard to come back from."

"Then there's the creepy concierge in the swanky apartment block."

"Alfonzo."

"Yeah, he might be our culprit."

Clements considers it. "He has access to all the flats, the back stairs, the CCTV."

"He's already admitted that he deleted the CCTV from the day she was abducted. He said that footage isn't kept more than twenty-four hours unless an incident of some kind is reported. Apparently the residents insist on this for privacy. It might be true. It might be just convenient."

Clements nods. "And then there's Fiona Phillipson. The best friend."

"Bloody hell. We have more suspects than an Agatha Christie novel," says Tanner with a laugh that is designed to hide how overwhelmed and irritated he feels. His nose squashed up against shadowy injustice, cruel violence and deception.

"Right."

"I still think the husband did it."

"Which one?"

"Crap. Round and round in circles we go." He scratches his head aggressively. "Do you want me to order in pizza? It's going to be a long night."

"Is anyone still doing deliveries? I don't think they are," points out Clements. "You know, lockdown."

"Crap," he says again, and then rallies. "Crisps and chocolate from the vending machine then. We'll need something to sustain us while we work out where Kylie is."

Clements smiles to herself. It's the first time in a long time that Tanner has referred to Kylie by name, not as "her" or "the bigamist" or, worse, "the body." It feels like an acceptance of a possibility that she might be somewhere. Somewhere other than dead and gone.

Did she somehow, against the odds, escape? Is Kylie Gillingham—the woman who dared to defy convention, the woman who would not accept limits and laughed in the face of conformity—still out there, somehow just being?

God, Clements hopes so.

2

DAAN

Daan Janssen is volunteering to cooperate. He is not under arrest. A fact his lawyers tell him repeatedly (in calm, confident tones that maybe makes them think they are justifying their exorbitant fees), and a fact that the police officers inform him of at the beginning of each meeting (spat out by rote in a bored manner that somehow suggests the word *yet* is floating across the video call). It is *the* fact he reminds himself of with increasing regularity as he tries to go about his day. When he dresses in the morning. When he is eating. Cleaning his teeth, listening to music. Whatever.

Outwardly, he's striving to appear unconcerned. Unruffled. It matters. He dresses in suits when he has to speak with the British police, combined with an impeccably ironed shirt. On more casual days he wears chinos and a polo shirt, never just a T. He wants to look crisp despite the pressure of police interviews, the stress of the global pandemic and the issue of his wife vanishing.

Not his wife at all. The woman he thought was his wife but who is a bigamist. His four-year marriage to her—a stylish ceremony in the Chelsea register office, followed by an oyster and champagne reception at the original West Street Ivy—isn't worth the paper the certificate was issued on. Apparently. He plays it over and over. She was another man's wife. She lied to him, betrayed him, repeatedly. And now she is dead but is still going to ruin what is left of his life if he is sent to prison for her murder. He can't exactly blame her for that, but he can't exactly forgive her for it either.

It is important he keeps up appearances, retains standards. He will not slump, sag, admit defeat like most of the world's population. He's better than the vast majority. Although when the fact comes into his head that he is not under arrest *yet*, it puts him off the carefully prepared, nutritionally balanced meals made by his private chef. It blasts into his head when he's playing a round of golf with his father. It puts him off his game.

The tone of his internal monologue continually shifts. Sometimes he is brash, dismissive; other times the fear and dread leak in. Insidious. Threatening. He didn't kill his wife. He didn't do it. But Daan is aware that innocent men are sent to prison from time to time. Miscarriages of justice do occur. He is white, privileged, extraordinarily wealthy. People like him are very unpopular right now. It's a pity; any other time in history he would have been practically worshipped, often above the law. Look, he's not saying that's right, you know. Just that for him, personally, it would have been convenient. But now people vilify men like him, which is inconvenient. They want him to be guilty.

But he is not.

He can see that the evidence is stacking up against him. There is motive, opportunity and circumstantial data. Each meeting with the police reveals that there are more and more things to be concerned about.

"I just want to share the screen for a moment, if that's okay. I want to show you some photos," says the senior policewoman, DC Clements. He thinks of her as senior because she's a higher rank than the cocky youth who is also in the interview room, but she is still younger than Daan himself. It's a cliché, but the police are getting younger. He is turning forty this year. It sounds old. He doesn't want to turn forty in a prison. He

doesn't want to lose years and years of his life. He is too vital
for that to happen. He has too much to do, to see, to be.

The police officers are staring at him through a computer
screen. Daan is glad he's on his home turf, back in Holland,
where his influential family are known and know everyone.
He wouldn't want to be in that depressing interview room
where criminals have sat and sweated. "This is the room your
wife was kept in," says Clements.

The photos turn his stomach. The room is pocked with debris: food packages, empty water bottles, papers, plasterboard;
it radiates chaos. They show him close-ups of a radiator that
has a chain attached to it. She was chained like a maltreated
dog. There is a photo of a plasterboard wall that has a hole in
it. "We're assuming she kicked through this wall here. Probably while she was still attached to the radiator. She couldn't
crawl through the hole, but she created debris and then she
threw the debris out of the open window in the other room,
so that it would land on the street below. Some of it did, some
of it didn't." They show him photos of the second room, the
open window, the debris that had missed its target.

"Working theory, she was trying to attract attention," says
Constable Tanner, laconically. "I guess she must have been
pretty desperate. This sort of thing comes long after banging
on the door and asking for help, I'd say," he adds with a sniff.
His tone and the sniff irritate Daan. It seems disrespectful, casual. People ought to carry handkerchiefs.

"Where were you residing between Monday 16th March
and Tuesday 24th March this year?" asks the DC.

"You know where I was, you visited me there, in my apartment."

"Can you state the address?"

"St. Marina Riverview Apartments." He rattles off the full
address and postcode. He can't resist adding, "The penthouse."

"These photos were taken in apartment 1403 St. Marina
Riverview," says the police officer.

Daan gasps. "She was held captive in my apartment building?"

"Yes. Fourteenth floor. Just a few below you."

"Six."

"Sorry?"

"Six floors below me; you said a few."

"I stand corrected."

Daan blinks. He can't understand what they are saying. This is bad. Very bad. The thought of her so close for all that time, and yet completely out of his grasp. He picks up a glass of water, takes a gulp.

"And during those dates we mentioned, did you go about your usual business?"

"I was looking for my wife."

"Of course, and what did that entail? Did you put up posters to alert the public to her disappearance?"

"No."

"Did you walk the streets looking for her?"

"No."

"Did you visit her friends, ask if they had seen her?"

"I didn't visit her friends, no."

The DC obviously knows the power of silence; she lets his last negative echo. It's a technique Daan himself sometimes uses in business meetings. He's made a lot of money by judiciously saying nothing, doing nothing. Today, he counters assertively. "I called *you*. I called the police. You were looking for her."

"Did you leave your apartment building at any point from Friday 20th to Sunday 22nd March?"

Daan thinks. Where is this going? What trap is he walking into? He answers honestly, because of course they already know the answer. "Yes, I went to the local deli that is just next door. A few times. To buy food and drink."

"Alcohol?"

He sighs. "Yes, alcohol. I'm over eighteen, it's not a crime." His lawyer coughs quietly. A subtle sign to remind Daan to be careful what he says. No one likes a smart-arse.

"And when you were popping in and out the deli for your organic vegetables and single malt, did you notice the debris in the street?" asks Tanner. No one coughs to indicate that *he* should lay off the sarcasm.

Daan shakes his head. It's an automatic response. *Did* he see the debris? He'll think about it more later.

"Not even as you left for the airport?" Daan shakes his head again. "Because we noticed it straightaway, didn't we, DC Clements? Awful mess. Practically tripped over it, I did. And we arrived at St. Marina Riverview Apartments just a short time after you left there." The constable frowns to indicate that he's mystified as to how that could be.

Daan remains silent. The DC picks up the baton. "And when you were up and down the stairs, in and out the elevator and the building, you never saw or heard anything unusual?"

"No."

"And you will have been especially vigilant, I expect."

"What do you mean by that?"

The DC pulls her face into an expression of surprised innocence. "Well, only that as your wife had vanished, you'd have been keeping your eyes wide open. You'd be alert."

They show him another photo, of a filthy bucket of shit. He blanches.

"It's not pretty, is it, Daan?"

"No, it's not pretty," he repeats. His lawyer clears his throat again. Taken out of context, that comment might sound dismissive, sarcastic, cruel. He's been warned to avoid elaboration, explanations and theorizing. The thought of Kai being demeaned so—his beautiful, elegant wife—makes his heart beat faster. His heart that is aching, imagining her chained to a radiator. She was a bitch for marrying him when she was married to another man, while mothering another man's children, certainly that. But he doesn't want to think of her this way.

"Thank you for giving us permission to search your flat, Daan." As if he could have refused. His lawyers had told him they'd easily secure a warrant; it looked better if he appeared helpful. The lawyers might be regretting that decision. On their previous video call, the police revealed that they'd found both of Kai's phones hidden at his apartment, the ones she used to facilitate her double life. They also focused on a receipt from Homebase for zip ties and a plastic bucket. Daan told them he had no idea where the receipt had come from. He realizes now that they are revealing evidence to him in a particular order. They are trying to trap him. Frame him. He did not buy a bucket. He was rushing to the airport; he possibly stepped over the debris as he jumped into his taxi. He was in a hurry.

"There was some banging. I recall it now." He lights up. Pleased to show that he isn't careless, negligent. "One night. The Saturday night. I thought it was something to do with water pipes. Or at least that's what she—" He stops abruptly.

"She?"

Oh fuck. He has to tell them. It will come out. Someone might have seen her arrive or leave. "I had a friend stay over on Saturday night. I slept through the noise, but she said there was clanking, that I should get the concierge to call a plumber. She thought maybe it was trapped air in the pipes. I didn't think anything of it at the time. I had bigger things on my mind."

"Your missing wife?"

"Of course."

"And who was this friend?"

Daan turns to his lead lawyer. "Do I have to say?"

"Is there a reason you'd rather not?" asks Clements, overriding his lawyer's assurances that he's not obligated to say anything at all.

"Her name is Fiona Phillipson."

"And how friendly are you exactly?" asks Tanner with a smirk.

"Not very," Daan asserts.

Clements puts up a picture of Fiona on the screen. It's a good one. Her profile pic that she used on the dating app, which was how she first reached out to him. She must have used filters; in real life she looks her age, and her eyes are smaller. "Is this Fiona Phillipson?"

"Yes."

"Well, we've talked to Fiona, and she says you two are more than friends."

He doesn't know why they are talking to Fiona Phillipson. Nor how they might have found her. Is there CCTV in the corridors and hallways of his building? He thought that was limited to the gym and the pool. Perhaps she came forward in response to an appeal for witnesses after Kai went missing. He knows it's not good news that they've spoken to her. Fiona Phillipson is a woman he's had sex with a few times, a casual hookup. A way to pass the time when Kai was away. And you know what, he's glad he did so, considering how things had turned out. When he thought Kai was in the north of England tending to her sick mother, she was in fact living around the corner with *another husband*. Un-fucking-believable.

He still can't accept it. All he did in terms of infidelity was bend a few women over his kitchen table from time to time and bang them hard from behind. He never promised them anything. Most of them understood what they were getting. A glamorous night, a fun anecdote, a satisfying orgasm. This Fiona woman was a mistake. The timing of their latest hookup makes him look bad. He last had her a few days after Kai went missing. He wasn't thinking straight. He was confused, a total mess. He'd just heard that his wife was a bigamist, for God's sake. Fiona didn't mean anything to him, but he let her stay over. Again a mistake. She woke up clingy. She asked him if he was married. He got the feeling she left in a bit of a huff. Hurt. But Christ, is that his problem? He's got far bigger ones.

"Have you ever visited Fiona Phillipson's home in London?"

"What? No." Daan has no idea where the woman lives. It might be Highgate, it might be Brixton, north, south, east, west. How would he know? He never asked. He has no interest. Why would he visit her house?

"What about her holiday home in Dorset?"

"No. No." He shakes his head. He briefly wonders if this woman has gone missing too. Is there some sort of serial killer on the loose? Did she disappear after she left his apartment? No, that's not right; they said they were talking to her. He's not thinking clearly, he's panicking. Unless she's vanished since. God, might she have? It's insane. But is that thought any more or less insane than his bigamist wife vanishing? He feels heat pulse across his body. "I hardly knew the woman."

"You hardly knew her?"

"Know her. I hardly know her." Fuck, what's the proper grammar? He's normally careful on this sort of stuff. He's tripping up. His words are sounding shaky, imprecise. He doesn't want to think about serial killers. He doesn't want to think about Kai crapping in a bucket. He takes a deep breath. "It wasn't that sort of relationship. It wasn't *any* sort of relationship."

"Is that right?" says the DC. She looks triumphant, which worries Daan.

"I don't want to say anything else." He looks to his lawyers, but before they can respond, he hits the button that says *LEAVE MEETING* and the screen turns black.

3

DC CLEMENTS

The lockdown measures, which were just a whisper, a recommendation when Kylie Gillingham disappeared, have bloomed and bypassed the stage of being a threat and are now a fact. Immovable law. Shops, restaurants, cafés and libraries are closed. People are locking themselves behind doors, behaving like convicts serving time, grateful for a permissible hour of exercise. They've been instructed to work from home if they can. Something that, for decades, harassed mothers have begged for. Something they've argued they need to ease the burden of childcare. The concept of working from home has always been dismissed, seen as a scam for skivers. Now there is no alternative. Bosses everywhere are crossing their fingers, hoping their employees will play fair. Although nothing can ease the burden of childcare at the moment, as schools are closed and teachers are beaming lessons through laptops and smartphones. Parents are going mental.

Clements doesn't have any of that to worry about. Childcare. She can't imagine what it must be like. Trying to do your job, trying to get your kids to pick up a pen and tackle some math. Unlike some of her colleagues, she is not interested in working from home, alone. Maybe she would be safer from the virus, locked in her tiny flat, stuck at the little table under the window, but she couldn't stand it. She's always done her best thinking in the field.

She could call Fiona Phillipson, but she decides she needs to see her face. It's a matter of catching her unawares. People reveal more than they want to in their faces, and the DC has a feeling there is a lot more to be revealed yet. She and Tanner visit Fiona's house together. A well-kept terrace in Clapham. Victorian black and white tiles, a dark blue gloss door, succulents in oversize stone pots in the tiny front garden; smart, standard for a certain sort.

"This will be worth a fortune," mutters Tanner. A slight hint of resentment in his voice. People in their twenties and thirties unilaterally resent those in their forties and fifties, because a generation ago it was possible to clamber onto the property ladder, even in London. Tanner rents in Woking. It's a long commute, boring and expensive, but as close to his workplace as he can afford. Clements has arranged for him to have a car at his disposal as they investigate this case; that way he can get back and forth without being held hostage to the reduced train timetable. "Very nice," he adds, nodding toward the house, but there's no hint that he's paying a compliment. He rings the doorbell for a second time. They listen to it echo around the silent building.

Clements peers in through the window. "No sign of her."

"Taking a walk?" suggests Tanner.

"I have a hunch. Let's call in on Mark Fletcher."

She only has to ring the bell once at the Fletchers'. As she expected, Fiona Phillipson opens the door. She's flustered. Her first words are: "Mark suggested I move in with him and the boys during lockdown. Probably only going to be a couple of weeks, right? After all, I've known him and the boys for ages. I was there the day Kylie met them."

Clements nods. "Nothing illegal about that, Fiona, relax." The woman is clearly nervous, maybe even apologetic. People are just getting their heads around the new laws and rules; they don't want to put a foot out of line. Most of them.

"Do you want to come in?" Fiona opens the door a little wider.

"No, sorry, best if we stay outside. Social distancing and all that." Behind Fiona, Clements can see the younger Fletcher boy, Seb, lingering in the corridor. Her stomach contracts slightly in sympathy. He looks exhausted, blue bags hanging under his eyes. His limbs seem angular, awkward. He's holding himself in such a way as to suggest he is bracing for more sorrow. Clements has been up close and personal with tragedy before; she knows it's very possible that he will never regain the carelessness and ease that is associated with being young. He's only twelve years old, but his childhood has been brought to an abrupt halt by the actions of his stepmother and someone else. An unknown other. Adults are bastards to kids. They should take better care. He has been wrenched into a tawdry, brutal, grown-up world, and he's frightened. He should be. Clever boy.

"Have you found my mum?" he asks.

Fiona looks startled. "Have you?"

"No." Thinking of Seb, stretched taut, desperate for news, Clements adds, "Not yet, but we're following a lead. Fiona, you can help with that."

"Of course, anything."

"You mentioned a holiday home in Dorset. We'd like to take a look around there if it's okay with you."

"Do you think she might be hiding there?" asks Seb, light flooding into his eyes.

Oli, his elder brother by three years, emerges into the hallway. From previous visits—when Leigh Fletcher aka Kai Janssen aka Kylie Gillingham was first reported missing—Clements knows that's the doorway to the living room. She guesses Oli has been listening to the exchange with just as much keenness as his younger brother but less willingness to show his interest.

He pushes Seb in the chest. "Don't be an idiot." The words, the shove, appear violent, angry, and they are. How violent? How angry? Or, Clements wonders, are the words standard bro-speak? Is the shove innocent? An immature, unprocessed excuse to make physical contact from someone who won't show his vulnerability and simply hug it out. She isn't sure. She'd like to rule him out of her inquiry. No one wants a fifteen-year-old to be responsible for this mess, but she might be being too compassionate because of his age. She has to be alert to that. Careful of it. Kids can be monsters too. Does he know more than anyone? Does he *know* it's idiotic to hope? His next comment does nothing to help her decide. "She's probably dead, bro, get used to it," he mutters, as he pushes his way past his brother and heads up the stairs, feet slamming down heavily, each step a protest.

Fiona grimaces apologetically. "They're dealing with a lot. That's why I moved in for a while, to help out. Keep things calm. Shall I get you the keys to my Dorset place? I can give you directions."

Clements and Tanner drive through the deserted streets, feeling privileged to be getting out of the city. "Tumbleweed," Tanner mutters, shaking his head. He's disconcerted, a bit moody, because he hasn't been able to pop into his usual coffee shop, and while there is the occasional place selling takeaways, the queues are too long to waste time in. He's suffering from caffeine withdrawal, constantly jiggling his knee; Clements wishes he wouldn't, it's distracting. She needs to think. Piece it all together.

Somehow the empty roads and pavements are more insidious now than when they teemed with disorder. Clements isn't used to civil obedience on this sort of scale, she can't quite trust it. Take Fiona, for example, so compliant and cooperative, readily giving them permission to search her house without a warrant, handing over her key at speed. Normally members of the public, no matter how innocent, are uppity about this sort of thing. They say stuff like "I know my rights" and start quoting from TV scripts, suggesting they don't know their rights or much at all, actually. She just happened to have the keys to her country home on hand. Is that odd? Or is she, like most Londoners who can afford to, simply keeping her options open?

Planning on bolting to her second home to see out lockdown despite entreaties to stay put.

"Did you see her face?" Clements asks Tanner. "Fiona's?"

"Yeah."

"When the kid asked if we had any news."

"Right. It should have been her first question, shouldn't it?" She takes her eyes off the road for a nanosecond and turns to Tanner. "As it was Seb's. But instead she was justifying why she's moved in with them."

"She's fast getting her feet under the table at her dead friend's house, isn't she?"

"Her *missing* friend," Clements corrects, but without much enthusiasm or certainty.

"People in the States have started to call it 'forming bubbles.' For Christ's sake. I hope that doesn't catch on in the UK. Bubbles." Tanner shakes his head in derision. "As if the middle classes need to be taken any further from reality. They've always lived in bubbles, with their sourdough bread bake-offs, their quinoa and kale juicing and what have you." His disgust is palpable.

"It's not just the middle classes that are forming bubbles," Clements points out. "And I'd say Mark Fletcher and his boys have had quite the dose of reality these past couple of weeks. What with Kylie going missing, then discovering she's been living a double life."

"So you reckon it's a good thing the best friend is keeping an eye on them?"

"Maybe," Clements murmurs.

"Just saying it's very cozy," Tanner says, cocking his eyebrow, as he does to suggest suspicion. Clements wishes he wouldn't. He looks like a little boy pretending to be a detective. It makes it hard to take him seriously; surely the opposite effect to the one he's hoping for. However, the point he makes is valid.

"It is," she admits.

"She's everywhere, though, isn't she? Living with Husband Number 1, casually shagging Husband Number 2."

The same thought has entered the DC's head, but she's trying to stay open-minded. Look at the facts. Gather the evidence. Resist jumping to conclusions. The feminist in her wants to believe in the friendship between Kylie and Fiona. Twenty-three years they stretch back. "She wasn't aware that Daan was married to Kylie when she was shagging him. Or at least she says she wasn't." Feminist or not, Clements is careful about how much trust she lends anyone. True to say Fiona has had her fair share of shocks recently too. Shocks can make people vulnerable. It's possible she just wants to be around other people who love and miss Kylie; that she simply wants to be helpful and provide comfort. But shocks also make people angry, unpredictable. Dangerous. Clements recaps the facts. "She hooked up with Daan Janssen through a dating app, one that identified potential matches in close vicinity."

"She bumped into him in his apartment block, right?" chips in Tanner, pleasing his boss by keeping up.

"Correct."

"Remind me, why was she there in the first place?"

"She says she was there for work. She's an interior decorator and was pitching to redesign Mr. and Mrs. Federova's apartment."

"Which just happens to be the apartment Kylie Gillingham was held captive in."

"Yes." The two officers share a look. Coincidences do happen. More often than people think. Some people believe in fate and destiny, Clements thinks both things can be explained away through coincidence. Even good and bad luck can be attributed to something akin. But she doubts a cluster of coincidences *is* a coincidence. A cluster of them is usually a crime. So she continues to count them up. "Fiona's timeline, as she has presented it to us in her statement, is as follows. One, she finds out her boyfriend—Daan Janssen—is married. Two, she finishes the relationship. Three, her best friend goes missing. Four, she finds out her best friend is a bigamist. Five, she discovers her best friend's second husband is the very man she's been shagging." She shakes her head slowly. Maybe letting the information settle, maybe doubting it. "Of course it may not have happened in that order," she adds darkly.

"You mean…"

"One, she finds out her meaningless shag—Daan Janssen—is married to her best friend. Two, her best friend vanishes. She did admit to shagging him at least once after she knew he was married to her bestie. Said she was emotional and drunk. That she made a mistake." The accusation lingers in the air. Jealousy, fury, revenge, all create a toxicity that leads to desperate acts. "Crimes of passion have been a thing since time began."

"She had access to that apartment," Tanner says excitedly. "Probably. She certainly knew it was standing empty, but there's nothing at all to place her there, and Daan Janssen might have known it was empty too."

Clements sighs. "Let's see what we find in Dorset."

Tanner sniffs and gazes out of the window, attention once again drawn toward the relentless emptiness. Then, to fill the silence and the void, he flicks on the radio.

They are still talking about the exhausted nurse who cried in a supermarket car park and begged people not to panic-buy because after her double shift in the critical care ward, she'd gone shopping and found the shelves empty. They are also reporting that someone has suggested that people stand outside their houses and clap to show their support and gratitude for NHS heroes. Clements wonders how it can be that people are clapping for the carers and simultaneously starving them.

The world is bloody mad. A journalist describes how walkers heading to beauty spots in the Peak District are being watched by a fleet of drones and reminded that rambling sixty miles from home does not constitute an "essential journey." Clements wonders what this all means for Kylie. Is it easier or harder to hide in a lockdown?

Is it easier or harder to hide a body in a lockdown?

4

MARK

Mark can hear the police speaking to Fiona downstairs. He should possibly go and see what they are talking about.

But what is the point?

If they've found her, he'll know soon enough. He hears Oli stomp up the stairs, his bedroom door slam closed behind him. The air in the house seems to quiver. There is no news. If there was, Oli would come and tell him. He rolls over and stares at the wall. He tells himself he's not *in* bed, midmorning, just lying *on* it. Which isn't the same. Getting into bed would suggest a level of defeatism. Depression, maybe. He's not *in* bed. Mark cannot imagine a harsher agony. This is not a light claim to make. After all, he is a man who has been widowed, left with two small sons to bring up alone. He lost his first wife after six years of marriage. Frances fell down the stairs in their home and broke her neck.

He rarely admits that to anyone. For a number of reasons.

And now he is a man whose second wife is missing. Gone. Vanished into thin air. Something she's done not once, but twice. The first time when she left their home, leaving him and the boys behind. Aching, angry. The second time she vanished was from the room she was being held captive in. It's impossible not to be sardonic about this fact. It's impossible not to think, "Well, Leigh likes doing things twice." Marrying, for instance.

His wife is a bigamist.

Mark still shakes his head in disbelief when this fact punches its way into his mind. Who the hell does that? Who the hell marries two men and runs two lives concurrently? It's a rhetorical question, though, because now he knows. Leigh does. Or did. It's unclear which tense he should use.

So no, he can't imagine a harsher agony than the one he is facing now.

He's furious to have discovered he's been betrayed so comprehensively, so unashamedly. And he's terrified, heartbroken. When he discovered her bigamy, he wished all manner of vile things on her. They were just thoughts. Really they were. He doesn't want her dead, cut up into tiny pieces and fed to someone's dog. Of course not. It's just something people say to themselves. He would cross the road to piss on her if she was on fire. Obviously.

The police have confirmed that there is evidence that Leigh—Kylie, as they call her—was in one of the apartments in Daan Janssen's swanky apartment block. They have not said what the evidence is. DC Clements did let slip that she thought she had been in that room just hours before the police broke down the door. He wonders what makes her think this. What was the wisp of smoke coming from the burning cigarette that suggested recent occupancy, a chance just missed, a case nearly solved? Nearly resolved, but instead left raw and jagged, an open wound. He can't work out if they think his wife escaped from that room or was taken from it. Further, if she was taken, is she already dead? They won't tell him what they are thinking. They are staying very tight-lipped. Until there's an arrest, he's still a suspect, he supposes. Daan must be the prime suspect, since she was held captive on his property, but Mark has watched enough TV shows to know that he too must remain under suspicion for a little longer. It's always the husband. Trickier when there are two.

He has his own thoughts on whether Leigh is dead or alive, and those thoughts fluctuate all the time, depending on his mood, the weather, the news, the boys' moods. He's normally a man who is fixed and solid, but this situation has left him amorphous, liquid. He keeps clicking his finger and thumb together. Just to hear the sound, just to check he is real and has agency. He feels nebulous, imprecise. Leigh has not only vanished herself; she's made him vanish too, to an extent. He doesn't know who he is anymore. He doesn't know what he wants.

It was a mistake telling people that his first wife had died of cancer. Doing so made Frances's already tragic and painful death into something else. He made it into a difficult, messy secret. One that is proving to have repercussions all these years later. One that might hurt him and his boys. He realizes that lying about something so big makes him appear untrustworthy.

Is he untrustworthy, or is he simply doing his best? He's not sure himself anymore.

Frances did have cancer. That much is true. People were expecting her to die of it, and that was already enough of a thing at the nursery gate. People were in the habit of talking about him behind their hands, tipping their heads to one side when they caught his eye, a cartoon approximation of sympathy but really—he believed—ghoulish fascination. They pitied him, the landscape gardener, father of two, who had to soldier on as his wife got sick, got a diagnosis, got sicker, was operated on, got sicker still, underwent chemotherapy, got sick again. A woman in her early thirties dying of cancer is a tragedy. They stared at him with a look that clearly declared, "There but for the grace of God…" Some dodged and avoided him, as though he was infectious. Two or three women propositioned him. He was never sure if it was out of sympathy or perversion. Screwing the dying woman's husband was possibly a turn-on for some really messed-up types. It's a big, odd world.

So he didn't need the drama when, weak with the disease and the attempts to treat it, Frances fell down the stairs and broke her neck. She was simply trying to cross the landing of their small home, a few steps from bedroom to bathroom. She just tripped and then fell down the stairs, but a fall might have turned the tragedy into a farce.

Or worse, a mystery. A murder mystery. Because people have fertile imaginations and fast, gossipy tongues.

He heard it happen. The clatter, the recurring thump, thump, thump, then a more violent smash. The exact sound stays with him. Haunts him in the dead of night. Or when he's at work. Or playing football in the garden with the boys. Watching TV. Making dinner. It's there. An insidious earworm in his head. Just can't get it out, even all these years later. He was in the kitchen making a cup of tea when it happened. Dunking the tea bag in the boiling water. Dunk, dunk, dunk, stir. He knew instantly, at some deep level, that it was her conclusion. Her end. Thump, thump, thump, smash. Her body bouncing from one stair to another. Four bangs as she fell head over heels. Such a funny, antiquated expression. Usually associated with love. Of course she was not falling in love, but instead to her death. He ran to her immediately. Immediately wasn't fast enough.

Because they were alone, the police asked lots of questions at the time. Naturally it was their job to do so. And there was an autopsy, an inquest. In the end, it was labeled accidental death. Still, Mark felt responsible. Frances's sister, Paula, tried to comfort him. "It's not your fault, Mark. You were doing your best. You were making her a cup of tea. You were trying to look after her." Except he was making the tea for himself. He had offered Frances one, of course, but she'd said no. He'd decided to go to the kitchen and make tea anyway, because he needed space. He wasn't even thirsty. Not really. He just needed a couple of moments away from the smell of his sick wife. Away from her gray skin and the slightly fusty bedsheets, which needed changing. Away from the responsibility of it. Why did he choose to do that? He should have stayed in the room, been with her around the clock. Then, when she felt the need to go to the toilet, she could have asked for his help. He would have been happy to help her. He had done so on dozens of occasions. Hundreds. Had she sensed his need to get away from her, even momentarily? Was that why she had struck out independently, if waddling to the bathroom on unsteady legs can be thought of in such vigorous terms?

So after it happened, he decided that when talking to acquaintances or to strangers, he wouldn't admit that she'd died because of a fall, rather than cancer. He blamed himself and that was bad enough. He couldn't stand the idea of the judgment of others. He just couldn't carry it. There's only so much one man can take on.

He's never even told the boys the truth about how she died. At the time, they were too young for it to matter. The difficult bit was explaining that she'd gone away and wasn't ever coming back.

"But don't they have buses from heaven?" Oli had asked. "If they had buses, she could visit us. Or a train?"

Explaining the lack of public transport in the afterlife to a four-year-old was complicated enough. They already knew she was poorly, that she had an illness; they didn't need to become scared of stairs, for God's sake. What did it matter? What difference did it make? It was a long time ago, and it was his decision. His and no one else's. Because there *had been* no one else at the time.

When Frances died, Mark remembers a vast, gnawing emptiness. A broad and deep gap. He didn't sit in his depression. His father would have called that wallowing, even if his mother would have called it processing. Either way, he didn't indulge in it. He couldn't. Not just because he had the boys to deal with, it wasn't just that. He was scared of it. He was scared of how dark it got. How everything trembled on a point where it might so easily become nothing. And it scares him again now. Now that Leigh is gone too.

It was a lot being left with two young sons. The weight of them. Obviously back then, aged four and eighteen months, they didn't really weigh much, not physically, but by God, the *weight* of them. Ask any single parent. How much does that child weigh? That kid you owe everything to? That kid you are everything to? And they'll tell you. Your shoulders will never be broad enough.

"Pick me up, Daddy! Carry me, carry me!"

"No, carry me! I want a piggyback."

You bear the weight of the world on your shoulders. They are your world, which is frightening enough. You are theirs, which is outright terrifying.

Mark is worried that all this attention about his second wife's disappearance will inevitably mean that the cause of death of his first wife will be brought into the spotlight once again. There will be more questions coming, if not from the police, then certainly from the press, from friends, from his sons. He ought to explain about their mother's death before they read about it in the *Evening Standard*. How will they react? Will they be angry that he lied to them? Not only all those years ago, but consistently ever since. Or will they simply accept it as another weirdness in their already complicated and convoluted lives?

Mark sighs with the thought of it. The weight of it. It seems too late to tell them the truth now, all these years later. The tragedy of how their birth mother died is dwarfed in comparison to the tragedy of their vanished, most likely murdered, bigamist stepmother. A current nightmare.

It's a mess. What was it that Fiona said? She mentioned a famous Oscar Wilde quote that might prove awkwardly relevant. Mark isn't into poetry or plays and stuff. He doesn't really know anything about Oscar Wilde except that he was gay and Irish. Fiona, however, was able to quote off the top of her head. "To lose one parent may be regarded as a misfortune; to lose both looks like carelessness."

Two dead wives, what did that look like?

Trouble.

5

DC CLEMENTS

Fiona gave precise and detailed directions to her holiday home, which turns out to be helpful because the sat nav struggles to commit to a route once they are off the beaten track, and they are both city coppers, not used to venturing this far out.

"This is it," remarks Tanner, already unclipping his seat belt, practically hanging out the door he's in such a hurry. Clements is surprised as a nineties bungalow looms into sight; she was expecting something with more charm. Still, she feels her heart quicken a little. She wonders, might they open the door and find Kylie sitting there in front of a roaring log fire, perhaps holding a mug of coffee? Shamefaced—no, guilt-ridden—but alive. Alive is all that matters. Fiona mentioned that she hadn't visited here since last autumn. She commented, "Wish I made more use of the place, to be honest. Hate to think of it standing empty." Kylie would know the place was empty, wouldn't she? There was a possibility that she could have bolted here.

Clements mentally shakes herself, notes that there is no smoke coming from the chimney. Why would there be? It's a warm spring day. There probably isn't a fireplace anyhow, more likely modern central heating, considering the relative newness of the place. She is vaguely aware that she's being fanciful, and she's embarrassed by that. It's out of character, and not a tendency she should ever encourage. She gets out of the car. There is a breeze in the air; fat, pearlescent clouds race across the pale blue sky as she dashes up the path. Her jacket flies open and flutters around her in an energetic way. She feels a sense of expectancy, chance.

There is no body. Not alive or dead.

Tanner charges from one room to the next and quickly establishes as much. The beds are made, cushions plumped, towels hung neatly over the side of the bath. "No one here." He looks disappointed and mutters resentfully, "Wasted journey."

"No, look, someone has been here recently," Clements asserts. She points to a wineglass on the kitchen table. "We need to find out who." The glass has some red wine still in it, just a few drops, but if it had been there since October, the wine would have evaporated to nothing other than a residue.

Tanner carefully places the glass in an evidence bag. They will check for prints and DNA. The tips of his ears are pink. He admires his boss, but her careful approach draws attention to his more impulsive style; no one ever likes being made aware that they are trying to run before they can walk. He was so busy looking for a body, he nearly missed this. Evidence.

"Whose prints do you think we'll find on it?" he asks.

"Well, it's Fiona's property, so finding her prints wouldn't be a surprise, but why would she leave a dirty glass on the table when she locked up the house for winter? Everything else is immaculate." Clements glances about. A folded washing-up cloth hangs neatly over the kitchen sink mixer tap. Pale sunlight the color of perfume falls through the window.

"Almost suspiciously so," adds Tanner. The kitchen tiles do not have a film of dust on them as might be expected; they gleam as though they have been recently cleaned, as does the bathroom. Clements touches the cloth. It's not cardboard stiff; it still has the suggestion of malleability. It's been used since October. The glass may have Kylie's prints on it, or Daan's. Or it may be wrapped in the fingerprints of a tipsy cleaner who helps herself to a tipple as she works. The prints will reveal something. The science doesn't lie.

A thorough search of the bungalow, shed and garage confirms that it's probable that a man has stayed over, made himself at home. They find a single solid silver cuff link and male underwear. There are two toothbrushes in the bathroom, an electric one and a new-looking blue plastic one. Tanner bags up everything, commenting, "Didn't you say Fiona told you Janssen had visited just once? If these things belong to him, he certainly made himself at home on that one trip."

"Of course they might belong to someone else. Another lover, or a brother. Although Fiona hasn't ever mentioned anyone else in particular."

"Well, I think we will be able to establish if these things belong to Janssen or not. Prints, DNA on the toothbrush."

"Yes, and if they are his, things look very bad for him, since he's denied ever coming here."

Tanner and Clements grin at one another. Bloodhounds scenting something in the air. Getting closer to the stench. The kill. They take another look around the neat little house in case they missed anything. It strikes Clements that despite the expensive soft furnishings and artfully arranged furniture, the place has an air of sadness lingering about. It's tasteful, no denying it, but it looks a bit like a show home. The walls are painted warm peach and bright tangerine in places, but it still appears sterile. It could do with a bit of mess and stuff scattered about; maybe some starfish coasters or mugs with anchors on them would make it more homely. It's a house that suggests a life half lived; a place where someone waits.

Clements recognizes the atmosphere, and doing so embarrasses and irritates her. The house feels disappointed. Disappointing. She wonders if she's imagining this. If she's manifesting the vibe because she's gutted Kylie isn't here. Another door closed, another day finished. Each one reducing the chances of locating Kylie alive. And that's everything, isn't it? When it comes to it, it's not about soft furnishings, fancy clothes or houses. It's not even about the lies she's told, the men she's had. It's life and death. That's all it's about.

"What's that noise?" asks Clements. But she knows. She recognizes it. Her pulse quickens.

"A helicopter. Low-flying," confirms Tanner.

They are both out of the door in a flash. Instinct pulls them toward the coast, the same direction the search-and-rescue helicopter is flying. "Someone must have called something in," yells Clements above the roar of the blades.

As they run, Tanner calls the station. "What have they found? Why the 'copter?" he demands.

Clements doesn't try to telephone anyone. She knows the information will be piecemeal, not through any deliberate obstruction or incompetence but because the latest is unfolding in front of them. A body, maybe. Alive or dead, she doesn't know.

She's not as fit as she should be, her breath shallow and high in her chest; or maybe she's struggling due to adrenaline, fear, hope—something primal—rather than her lack of fitness. Her strides are long and firm; her feet slam into the ground, fast and desperate. Not a jog, a sprint. She can't get there fast enough. She literally can't. She strains to calculate where the helicopter is going to land. In her peripheral vision, she notices two or three other people heading in the same direction. A spike of irritation jabs her—permitted exercise doesn't include rubbernecking—but she doesn't allow this to distract her. She speeds on, only occasionally glancing to the rough ground to avoid loose stones and dog crap.

She almost doesn't stop to examine the bottle. Her mind processes it and dismisses it as litter. Left behind, no doubt, by someone drinking on the cliff edge, enjoying the view with a friend or lover. This sort of tryst is not legal, strictly speaking, but it's inevitable. She doesn't know what causes her to stop. Instinct, or less romantically but more practically, a thorough training and a lifetime of experience that has taught her to leave no stone unturned. Bugger. She doesn't want to lose a minute; she wants to run the next two hundred yards to where the helicopter is now landing, she wants to get there before Tanner. This isn't competitiveness, this is concern. She wants to find Kylie. If she's dead and decomposing at the bottom of a cliff, Clements wants to be the one who reaches her, the one to shield her dignity, posthumously. If by some miracle she's lying injured at the bottom of the cliff, she wants to be the first to comfort and reassure. She's only been on this case a couple of weeks, but Kylie has got under her skin. She finds herself admiring the rebellious woman who wouldn't accept the world's limitations, who risked disrepute and shrugged at notoriety. The police see a lot, deal with too much, know more than most. She shouldn't let it get to her. She shouldn't get so personally involved. It does not matter if Tanner reaches the site first. She's not here to play the bloody heroine, protector or savior. She's here to gather evidence. Firm, straightforward, non-fanciful work. So she stops.

She digs out a plastic evidence bag and carefully picks up the wine bottle. The science doesn't lie. Then she starts to sprint once again in the direction of the helicopter and whatever else there is to find.

JUNE 2020

6

STACIE

I wake to the sound of the sea. The noise of it—the power and thrust—is always surprising to me. Odd; since I've grown up living on the shore, I should be used to it by now. It must have lulled me to sleep thousands of times; it surely has been my alarm clock, the background accompaniment as I did my homework, when I played in the garden with my friends, when I sneaked in the back door, coming home late from parties and did not want to wake my dad and then have to sit through an excruciating fifteen minutes while he drilled my boyfriends on their intentions and prospects. Better to let them slip away undetected, their footsteps cloaked by the noise of the sea.

I ought to be used to it, but I'm not.

Since my surgery, I've found it to be louder than I expect. I believe it's generally imagined that living by the sea must be calming, therapeutic. People think of a gentle lapping that soothes and lulls. Those who live near it know that's not how it is. Even on a bright day, the waves crashing against the shore can sound aggravating, angry. Shale and shells spin and tumble in the water, caught up in the turbulence then spat out on the beach. My dad says that the trick is accepting the relentless ebb and flow, the swoosh and smash of chucked debris, and think of it as a comforting constant.

"Any sort of constant helps. Right?" he commented just last week, while we were having lunch.

"Hey, Dad, I'm thirty-seven and I'm living back in my parental home; clearly I'm a fan of consistency," I replied with not quite an eye roll but certainly a hint of exasperation. Dad laughed. Choosing to see the humor rather than the sarcasm. He's a goodhearted man. Always looking on the bright side. A happy man. He wakes up every morning thinking the day is going to be a good one, and then he sets about ensuring as much. I envy him that. I wake up every morning and drum down on the existential questions. Who am I? What's it all about?

I guess I must take after my mother.

Living back in the parental home at my age was never my plan. I'm single. I don't have a job, a partner, offspring or a home of my own; even friends seem thin on the ground. It's really depressing if you think about it, and since we've been locked down for three months, I have done little else other than think about these things.

"You have your health, though, Stacie. Thank God for that, that's what counts," Dad often says.

He's right. Well, almost. I am heading toward a full recovery—and that is the priority, obviously. But as someone who is recovering from a brain tumor and the operations necessary following that, I don't feel I can comfortably claim to have my health. I am still currently incapacitated to a huge degree. Besides the cluster of tablets that I have to take every day, there are side effects that may or may not be permanent. They are certainly expected to linger in the mid to long term—that's what the doctors said. What does it even mean? Three months? Six? A year? There is a lot that I am still processing. Still dealing with. Worse still, I can't even always remember what the doctors said, and Dad is constantly having to remind me. It's frustrating. I know, I know, I am alive. Better than the alternative, so I don't bother to argue with Dad. It seems so mean to pick at his positive assertions when they are the bedrock of his existence and he is the bedrock of mine.

I do realize that it is a hopeless, pointless, fruitless thing to do—to resent the sea for the noise it makes. I should accept the crashing waves because I can't do a thing about them; King Canute made that point, didn't he? I shouldn't get worked up by it, I shouldn't push against it. But I find I do. I am what I am, right? We're always being told to be ourselves. I've seen it written on notebooks and mugs: *Be Yourself! Everyone Else is Taken!* The assumption is that we are all pretty great.

Am I, though? I don't really know.

Here's the thing. The side effects I'm dealing with are not just a matter of headaches and lethargy, occasional panic attacks and a general sense of anxiety. The big one is that I don't have any pre-operation personal memories. Not one. I'm horrified that this is my reality and yet still awed at the drama of it all. I don't remember my father, my mother, myself. My cancer and the subsequent treatment to save my life—precarious, experimental, but essentially the only option—eradicated us. It's not easy. By which I mean it's bloody hard. Sorry to be sweary about it, but my God, how much is one person supposed to take?

I open my bedroom window. The stuffy air trapped all night in the room is pushed aside by a fresh breeze. The heat of the sun licks my face and forearms. It's only 9:30 in the morning, but it seems like it's set to be another scorcher. For all the problems this year has presented, it's some compensation that it's been unusually hot; temperatures have soared to record-breaking levels, which I'm loving. I hope the sunny days stretch throughout the summer.

I scan along the shoreline. The only people I spot are a small family: a mother with two preschool-age boys at her side. T-shirts and shorts. Buckets and spades. One child is leaping about, a jumble of skinny tanned limbs; the other is very young, maybe eighteen months, and therefore less sure-footed—that one is tottering, waddling. Other than them, the beach is deserted. I suppose if it hadn't been for lockdown, it would have been swarming with tourists and their noisy kids and barking dogs and their tendency to leave behind litter. Dad has more than once commented with a chuckle, "So that's a bullet dodged." Typical of him to find the silver lining in the fact that the entire populace is pinned to their homes like dead butterflies to a board in a Victorian drawing room. I know he's trying to make light, make the best of things, but to me it seems greedy, that we have all this to ourselves when others are clamoring for space. There are reports on the news showing entire families of four, five, six and more squeezed into small apartments in high-rise tower blocks in London's inner city. Journalists interview people leaning out of their windows three or four flights up. They say they feel trapped, that the kids are driving them up the wall. Watching those reports of families stuck and confined disturbs me, leaves me with feelings of discomfort and unease that makes my breathing a shade faster.

I lean further forward out of my bedroom window and take deep gulps of the salt-tinged air.

There are also reports on the news that incidents of domestic violence are going up. Trapped women, violent men. An age-old problem. Besides that, the divide between children's education levels is widening. It's all hideously awful. Some kids don't have access to computers and therefore are missing their online lessons that beleaguered teachers across the country beam out with hope and desperation. I feel the injustice of this pinch me in my core, as though I'm personally affected by it, which of course I'm not. I suppose it bothers me because a generation with limited education is such a depressing influencer on our global future. Maybe that's why I'm unable to shake off the thought of the misery of struggling schoolkids who are no longer being tested by exams but are now being tested by uncertainty instead.

Someone with no past to speak of is perhaps more invested in the future.

Dad is right, watching the news is miserable. *Why don't you just switch off your television set and go and do something less boring instead.* The phrase and the theme tune of the old TV show that I watched as a kid blasts into my head. Complete and perfect. I wonder how that can be. Why do I remember that trivia so clearly when many more important things elude me? I screw my eyes tight shut and concentrate very hard on recalling something more. I remember sitting in front of the TV, alone, picking at scabs on my skinny knees, no doubt the result of a playground scrape; but try as I might, I can't recall any more detail. I make an effort to think of something more recent. Last Christmas, for example. How did I celebrate? Who did I celebrate with? I wait a moment or two. The waves crash on the shore, agitated and unsettling. The blackness of my mind is a swamp and I think I might fall into it. I open my eyes; the walls of my bedroom tilt, the floor rises, then sinks. I have to stop trying so hard. Dad is always saying I shouldn't force it. "It will all come back to you when you least expect it." I have to trust that he's right about that. So far, all I have is half-formed impressions, senses, feelings that from time to time come to me fractured. They hurtle toward me and then speed right past. Taunting me.

The weirdest thing is that I remember impersonal facts. General knowledge. I'd still be okay in a pub quiz. I know that there is such a concept as a pub quiz, where little pockets of keenly competitive adults are desperate to show off their ability to recall the date a person first stepped on the moon (21 July 1969; it was Neil Armstrong). I know Henry VIII was a king with gout and six wives. I know that the UK voted to leave the EU by fifty-two to forty-eight percent. I know *Game of Thrones* is a cultural phenomenon and the final episode caused controversy among George R. R. Martin fans.

I concentrate on taking deep breaths. A day at a time. Trust. I spot Dad about fifty meters along the beach, ambling back toward the cottage. Ronnie, our bouncy, barmy golden retriever, is running alongside him, barking at the waves; dashing toward them as they ebb, retreating at pace as they flow forward. I watch as Dad stops, stoops and picks something up. It will be a smoothed piece of glass. Pearlized, shimmering, blue, green or brown. We both take walks along the coast every day. Separately in the morning as he's an early riser and he doesn't hang about for me, and then together in the late afternoon. As a result, Ronnie is a very well-exercised dog. Sometimes Dad returns from his walks with a rounded piece of glass; he will turn it in his palm, hold it out for me to admire in all its smooth iridescence. We have a pile of sea glass in the garden, a huge bed of it. Hundreds of weighty pieces that he must have brought home over the years. I visualize him holding them in his big, strong hand, offering them up to me to inspect: a delighted child, an uninterested teen, a polite woman feigning curiosity to generate chatter. I visualize these versions of me and try hard to recall them. But I can't. They are ghosts wandering aimlessly in a void.

I don't know who taught me Tudor history, how I voted on Brexit or who I watched *GoT* with. I don't remember the games I played in the garden with school friends and I really don't know if I ever did sneak home late from parties as a teen. I just want to believe that's something that probably happened, because everyone wants to think they had friends and that they were cool, right?

I don't know if being myself is a good thing.

I mean, I probably can assume I'm pretty great. The odds are with me because most of us are fair, kind, honest. Aren't we? We believe in right and wrong, law and order, actions and consequences. Most likely I'm a total delight. A sort of mix of Malala Yousafzai and Greta Thunberg. My dad acts as though I gave lessons to Kate Middleton on how to be lovable.

It would just be good to know for certain.

7

STACIE

I notice that Dad is almost back to the cottage, so I quickly dress, pulling on the T-shirt and shorts I wore yesterday. No one ever sees us, so there's no imperative to make an effort. I barely look in a mirror these days. Staring at my bald and scarred head is difficult. I'm exposed, diminished. My hair is growing back slowly; there are downy, feathery patches coming through. It's something, but it's uneven and imperfect, so I am still self-conscious. In a way, I'm glad not to be seen. I slip on flip-flops and rush down the stairs, making it into the kitchen just as Dad pushes open the back door.

"Morning, love," he says, cracking a smile. He puts a green piece of smoothed sea glass on the table as I predicted. A mermaid tear. That's what some people call them. I remember that. "How are you feeling today?" he asks.

"Fine, thanks."

"No headaches?"

"Right as rain."

"Well, that's great news. Did you take your tablets?" He always leaves them in an eggcup next to the kettle so that I don't forget.

I haven't taken them yet this morning but move to do so now. I can swallow tablets without water, I've had that much practice. He beams, obviously relieved. I'm sorry that I'm such a concern to him at this age, when I should really be off his hands. However, I'm so grateful for his concern and the safety net he provides. What would I do without him preserving my identity? I'd literally disappear if he didn't keep reminding me who I am, what I've done, what I dreamed of. I am shut out of my own life, and until that door opens again, I need him to safeguard me. It's not fair on either of us, but it is what it is. A living nightmare.

I reach for the kettle and put it on to boil. "What is it with you and the sea glass, Dad? What attracts you to it?" In part, I'm curious; in part, I'm just making conversation. Months with just the two of us for company, no outside stimulus whatsoever, is limiting.

Dad bends and pats Ronnie's back to encourage him to calm down. The dog is still circling my father's legs. Energetic, like a puppy, even though he's not. He's leaving a trail of wet and sandy paw prints on the floor; they will dry and the sand will crunch under our feet until it blows out the door or into the corners of the room. I glance around the kitchen, which is as usual in a state of chaos. Neither of us cares, neither of us values tidiness or has a particular proclivity toward it. Dad must have had fried bacon for breakfast earlier; the smell lingers in the kitchen, scalded animal fat.

"Well, my attraction to sea glass, Stacie, is to do with how it comes about. You see, diamonds and other such precious gems—you know, emeralds, rubies and the like—are mined from the earth, spat out raw and sharp. Then mankind smooths and polishes them to perfection."

"Humankind," I interject.

He chuckles. "If you like. But sea glass is the opposite way round. Humankind carelessly tosses glass into the sea or leaves it discarded on a beach, and it is nature that does the polishing and refining. It's a fine example of nature's indomitability, I think." He sits down at the kitchen table, stretches his legs out in front of him. Dad is seventy-two, with a thick head of snow-white hair, a ramrod posture, skin that tans easily. He can pass for younger most of the time. It's only after a long walk, when I see his need to rest, stretch, recoup, that I'm reminded that he's no longer in his prime, and really, I ought to be looking after him, not the other way round. He takes a moment and then carries on answering my question. "I think it's amazing, a spiky piece of glass tumbling in the waves, being lifted up, tossed about for all that time. Abrasion working at it until it's smooth and frosted, until it's beautiful." He pauses, smiles at me. "That's what I like about it, Stacie. Sea glass takes a battering but is all the more beautiful for it."

I eye him slyly. Am I reading too much into what he is saying, or is he trying to tell me something with all this talk about smoothing out rough edges, surviving and in fact being improved upon by being tossed and tumbled by nature's forces? Is he relating it to my circumstances? Or even his own? I appreciate him trying to pass on his wisdom, if indeed that is what he's doing, but it's a bit early to be philosophizing. I need coffee first.

"I've been out for the papers," he adds as he pulls them from his canvas bag and lays them on the table. "I've had a flick through them already. On the bench up at Williton Cross."

"Oh. Anything in them?"

"Not really. Same old, same old. Hospitalizations on the rise, hope for the high street declining. How can they call it news when they print the same stuff every day? I'm not sure why I buy them." He doesn't always bother; sometimes he comes home with croissants for a treat instead.

I pry open the canister of coffee beans, and as I do so, something swells inside me, a wave of yearning, my legs quiver. A memory nearly knocks me over. I recall specifically yearning for someone. I lift the canister to my nose and inhale deeply, hoping the sensation will linger, balloon. Apparently the olfactory system can help restore memories. I have a nebulous feeling that the yearning, the longing, was a perpetual state. This someone I wanted didn't give me a sense of completion or contentment. He's not about that. It is a he, I'm certain of that much.

I pause and allow the thought to swell.

The teeth of a zip, parting slowly. My dress falling to the floor. I don't care. I don't worry about it creasing. He drops to his knees and edges my underwear down my thighs. The idea makes me inwardly squeal with joy and surprise but outwardly blush, because I can't imagine that world being mine. Sexy, glamorous. So at odds with my scarred head and flip-flop-shod feet.

I've had this thought before. This sense of him doing various things to me. With me.

Then, frustratingly, the impression—thought? Memory? Call it what you will—snaps and vanishes. It feels like an elastic band has been twanged somewhere deep in my gut.

I wonder what has just played out on my face—the longing, the lust, the disappointment—because Dad asks, "What is it, Stacie?"

"Nothing," I lie. I am not about to tell my dad that I have memories about a man kissing and licking me, climbing inside me. "I was just thinking, maybe we should plant something in the back garden," I say instead.

"Like what?" he asks.

"I don't know. Roses, or sweet peas?" I'm looking for the joy of progress. I'm imagining green shoots poking up from the earth. Promising a future.

Dad shakes his head swiftly. "Won't grow. Not with the wind and the sand. Nothing much grows in our garden. You tried that when you were a little girl." He glances at me quickly, not quite confident enough to make eye contact. "Don't you remember?"

A categorical "No, I don't remember" upsets him maybe even more than it upsets me. I work around it, offering the sort of sentence that can be interpreted as a statement of fact but is really a question. "I was into gardening for a time."

"When you were about seven or eight, you had your own

patch of the garden. We turned it over together, built a little fence around it. You enjoyed painting the fence yellow. Then you planted snapdragons, phlox and a rose bush."

I am excited at the thought of this idyllic childhood. I try very hard to recall the abundance of pretty bobbing snapdragons, roses (pink?) and bright, colorful phlox. A country garden blossoming, almost overripe. I think I recall the pungent scent of blooms hanging in the air. I almost see a bed of flowers that is so full, it's somehow fleshy. But I don't feel joyful or soothed by the thought. I feel uncomfortable and cross. Perhaps this is understandable when Dad adds, "They didn't grow. It was a wet spring. The shoots drowned. The salty air, the sand, everything worked against you."

"Was I disappointed?"

"No, you didn't even notice, you'd already lost interest. Something else caught your attention probably. Gardening is not your thing, Stacie."

The memory of the blossoming garden doesn't make sense then. Another mix-up. Dad used to be a doctor. Not a specialist, a GP. Still, he's been really helpful in trying to get me to understand my unique position. After surgery such as mine, a temporary memory loss is expected. *Temporary* being the hopeful word. However, I've been warned that false memories and susceptibility to suggestibility can also occur. It's confusing. Exhausting.

"Was Mum into gardening too?" I ask carefully.

My mother is not an easy topic for my dad. That much has become abundantly clear. It's understandable, but I have to ask about her. How will I remember my past if I self-censor and avoid important subjects? When I think of my mother, I can't recall her hair color, height or smile, but I sense a keen desire to please her. Nothing particular, just an all-pervasive sense that I wanted to make her happy. My mother walked out on us, before my ninth birthday. I can't remember the specific moment, but I remember feeling abandoned, confused. I wouldn't mind forgetting that feeling, but I can't. My damned head.

Dad says, "No, she was not in the least bit interested in gardening. I was the green-fingered one."

"Here one day, gone the next," I mutter.

"It must have seemed sudden to you," Dad says, turning away from me. And to him? Was it sudden for my dad, or had he expected it? Maybe they had been fighting for months before her departure; a house whipped by hissed whispers behind closed doors. Or maybe they did not fight at all; instead were simply unhappy, disconnected. Did sullen, weighty silences drench the room after I'd gone to bed and they were alone together?

"She went far away." I struggle and stretch for the memory. It's like a tin on a too-high shelf in a supermarket. Very definitely there, but just out of reach. "Not so much as a backward glance. Moved abroad?" Dad nods. I pick up a tea towel but don't really know what to do with it; there are no pots to dry. This is a heavy conversation for so early on in the day, but our weird world, centered around a pandemic, life-threatening illness and memory loss, means we don't follow the usual conversational guidelines. I am constantly attempting to piece my jigsaw mind back together, slot things into place, so I blurt out questions whenever they come into my head. Dad tries to provide answers.

"Yes, she did."

"Was there someone else?"

"Yes."

"I see." Moving abroad, leaving your child for another man, delivers a certain message. Received loud and clear. "Did she remarry?" I ask.

Dad picks up the bottle of ketchup that's on the kitchen table and puts it in a cupboard. I realize that clearing the table is preferable to baring his soul. "I think so. I don't know for sure. She didn't stay in touch directly. Sometimes there were rumors. From time to time, an indiscreet friend we had in common would let something slip."

"Did she have any more children?" I think I remember

something about that. I can't recall if they were sons or daughters. Brothers or sisters. But I remember feeling replaced.

He nods, seeming stiff and reluctant. "Yes, I believe so."

I don't ask anything more. I've pushed him far enough on this topic for one day. What does it matter now anyway? She isn't here. She hasn't been in touch. I'm obviously not part of her life, she is not part of mine. Her leaving changed Dad. His words. He's told me that was when he gave up being a GP. He just couldn't hold everything together; taking care of me, dealing with his own broken heart and absorbing his patients' problems was too much. He became quite reclusive, prioritizing time with me above everything else, including other people's company and a career path. He took casual work that fitted around my school hours and holidays.

I look out of the kitchen window. The view to the back of the house is a gloomy field and a scattering of outhouses. There is a solid line of trees and bushes in the far distance that blocks out the light and acts as a curtain drawing a veil between us and the outside world. The tarmac around the house is framed by nettle patches and scrubby, parched grass strewn with dented drink cans and litter. I'm not sure where the litter came from. Surely not Dad. Most likely chucked over the hedge or blown through. The place has a sad, neglected air to it. It's time to change the subject.

"So gardening is not my thing. That's okay. Good to rule it out." I wait a beat. "Fairy lights then. Colorful ones. Something to bring some cheer." The back garden, which butts up against the beach, is always covered in a fine layer of sand. The grass, the stone path, even the vibrant piles of sea glass are muted.

"If you like. I'm not sure where we'd buy them."

"I bet we could get them online if we had internet." Dad chuckles, amused by the very thing that frustrates me. "We need broadband. We should find a provider," I add firmly, not for the first time.

"Oh, that's not so easy when you're out in the sticks. It's

not like living in a big city, oozing choice." He smiles at me as though he's delivering good news.

I know he isn't interested in being online in the same way I am. Dad gets all the entertainment he needs through his television. He has an enormous library of DVDs, mostly films that were popular in the nineties and noughties. He supports local shops. He reads his news in papers. He thinks constant updates are bad for our mental health, especially at the moment. That's fair enough. I can understand why he sometimes snaps the radio off and insists we think about something more pleasant. But the lack of access to the internet frustrates me. I'd like more regular updates on what is happening beyond our cottage. I'd like to see if I had social media accounts; I must have had. I certainly know that TikTok and Insta exist and are considered by many a great way to lose hours. Was I one of those many? Could my social media accounts help jog my memories? Of course, I'd have to recall my passwords first. Googling Stacie Jones would be a starting point.

I long to be back out there. To be part of it. Dad is forever telling me that there isn't anything to be part of right now. He has a point, I suppose. He keeps saying that if I'm going to be ill at all, this is the best time. I'm not missing out. I just need to concentrate on getting well. Dad is someone who enjoys taking life slowly. Naturally content in his own company, he doesn't seem to find lockdown much of a struggle. I get the feeling that he's never been one to socialize much, happy to keep himself to himself. That much is revealed by his eternally tatty clothes, which only make it into the washing machine when I nag him.

"You know what, Stacie, you've always reminded me of that princess in the fairy tale."

"Which one?" I ask, skeptically. My life seems a long way from a fairy tale.

"The one who slept on twenty mattresses but could still feel the pea that was hidden under the bottom one."

"You're saying I'm a bit of a spoiled bitch?"

Dad laughs. "You're not a spoiled bitch. I'm just aware that you struggle with the mundane stuff that others accept more readily. I'm okay without internet. All these years it's never once crossed my mind that it's a problem not having it. You're home now and it matters to you. You want more." I nod. He's right. He's identified something that feels true about me. I'm not very good at making do. I'm an unsettled sort of person. I always want to optimize, to strive forward. Dad continues, "Natural enough, you're young. Ambition is a good thing." Thwarted ambition or unfulfilled ambition is less of a good thing. It's simply difficult and painful. This goes unsaid. "You feel more than most. That's all I'm saying. I understand that it's not easy," he adds with a sympathetic smile.

"I feel more but remember less. What a crap combination."

For a moment or two there is no sound in the room other than Ronnie's claws scratching on the floor. The silence screams. "Hey, Stacie. Are you making coffee?" Dad prompts.

"I am."

"Is there enough for two?"

"Of course." I make a big pot of coffee every day. There's always enough for two, more than enough. I allow myself to be distracted, because Dad needs to think he can distract me. Dad isn't someone you'd rush to describe as in touch with his feelings, but he reaches for them when he knows it's important to me, and that's pretty amazing. He's undoubtedly a good guy. The best. Maybe that's why I'm not married. I've struggled with meeting the right man because my dad set the bar too high. I don't know. I really don't.

I grind the beans, glad of the noise that fills the kitchen, making conversation redundant. I throw yesterday's granules and filter bag into the recycling bin. Swirl the glass pot under the tap. I take another sniff of the fresh granules and will the man I can't quite remember, can't quite forget, to crawl into my head again. The sense of him settles in my consciousness. It's where he belongs. I recall his eyes meeting mine. I think I do. It feels real. And the way he looked at me. Wow. I was his world, his entire world, and yet simultaneously, it's as though he was indifferent. As though he was playing with me or experimenting with me, or simply confused by me.

What is that about? I don't know. I don't understand him, but it excites me.

I have to find that man.

8

STACIE

I spend the day sunbathing and reading. The heat is the sort that means even doing nothing becomes exhausting. I feel the sweat pool between my thighs and at the base of my back. I watch the sun slowly shunt across the sky. Our cove is deserted once again; I consider seeking out the relief of the cool sea, but lethargy overwhelms me and I stay put, it's too much effort to reapply sun cream after a dousing.

When the tide is out, a few more people stroll along the shore. There is a wooden plank walkway that stretches along the coast but stops abruptly about forty meters from where our garden meets the beach. I spot a familiar figure at that point. A woman in a wheelchair. I've seen her in the same place a few times before. She obviously follows the walkway as far as she can, then usually she turns back toward the village. Today I notice that her chair isn't facing out to sea, as you might expect, it's turned toward me. I glance behind me to see what it is she might be staring at. There isn't really anything; just our house, a run-down 1930s pebbledash cottage. Dad isn't in the garden—he's probably still napping in his room—so there's no one other than me who can be attracting her attention. I suddenly feel exposed in my bikini, judged; I reach for my sarong. I consider waving to her, and raise my hand, but squinting in her direction there is something about her expression that makes my arm freeze at my side. It's as though the sun has scuttled behind a cloud. I shiver. She's too far away for me to clearly see her face, but somehow I feel she radiates hostility. I pull myself up for having this thought. Most likely her posture has more to do with her own situation in life, nothing to do with me. She is perhaps physically uncomfortable; not scowling but grimacing. I look away from her. Train my eyes on to my book. The next time I look, she has gone. And I feel relieved.

I allow the crash of the waves to lull me. Send me into an almost hypnotic state. Something close to sleep that makes the words on the page start to slip and slide. It's hard to concentrate. I shut my eyes and feel the sun on my lids, and that's when I see it. Actually see it, not just sense it. It arrives a glorious, perfect memory.

I'm in an enormous copper bathtub. My arm is hanging over the edge, covered in soapsuds and bubbles. I'm laughing. I can't see my face, which suggests this is real, not imagined, but I can see my belly quivering with joy. I must be in a hotel, because the bathroom is so beautiful. Sensual, classy. The mosaic tiles shimmer. The room smells of something woody and dark. Ginger or citrus. Nothing like a bathroom in a normal home. He climbs into the tub too; I watch his long, strong, tanned legs. Water sloshes over the side and we laugh. Careless of the mess on the floorboards. There's a sense that there is no responsibility between us. We're playful.

There is a dress on the floor, hastily discarded, and I believe that my clothes always are hastily discarded when he is around. Tugged off me with joy and enthusiasm. A flattering impatience. I remember the dress clearly. Not just the color, the fabric and the texture. Although I do remember those things—it is burnt red, almost orange, ribbed wool. But I remember more than that about the dress. I remember how it made me feel to wear it. I remember buying it. I know I chose it because he would find it—me—sexy. He'd like to see me in it. See me out of it. I remember being in a plush changing room and having that exact thought: he'll want to strip me bare.

It was expensive. And I bought it without a second thought. I slid the credit card across the smart glass counter. Casually, not in the slightest bit concerned whether there were funds in my account. I knew there were. It's strange to realize that I once had the sort of wealth that meant I didn't care if soapy water slopped over the bathtub and splashed onto my expensive dress. Where is that money now? My memory stays with his thighs in the water, wet and attractive. It annoys me that I remember all this detail but I don't remember his name or his face in its entirety. Just his eyes and the feel of his wet hands on me, soaping my breasts. Who is he? Was he something meaningful, or a brief holiday romance? Either thing is possible. If we were in a current relationship, why hasn't he been in touch? I suppose he must be someone from long ago. Our thing, whatever it was, could have been long over before I got ill.

Or maybe he doesn't belong to me.

Married?

The thought lands like a slap. My skin prickles. Am I that sort of woman? The bit on the side? The mistress? God, I hope not. I believe mistresses are chorus girls; I'd like to think I was this man's leading lady. I just don't know.

I sit up, reach for my water. The ice cubes have long since melted and the glass glints with condensation. My memory is leaning further back, to the start of this relationship. It's steeped in something besides desire. It's a complicated play, a game of cat and mouse. A step forward and backward. I want him, but I shouldn't. I remember thinking it would weaken and disturb me if he undressed me, but it would kill me if he didn't. A rock and a hard place. And I know that even when we became lovers, I was not quite his. Why not? Why didn't I give in to him? Why couldn't he take me completely?

I'm thirty-seven; these are crucial years for me in terms of fertility. In fact, I'm already past my prime for all that. Honestly, I feel older. I've been through so much. What have I been doing with myself? Was I bothered about the fertility countdown before I got cancer? Did I ever want to make a baby with the intense man with the eyes that bored into me? Did he ever want that too? Did we try?

I look about me and see nothing other than the sea meeting the shore, the sun slipping behind the horizon. Another day closing down. I try not to think life is passing me by. Other beaches may be teeming by now; near resort towns there will be plenty of local people wanting to make the most of the unexpected heat wave. Our remote corner of the world remains empty. The emptiness does not feel peaceful; it feels like a void. I know that a woman my age ought to be out there meeting people, having relationships, scrambling up a career ladder, buying a property, seeing friends, planning minibreaks, at least attending a damned book club. That's what I should be doing, all things being even. Which, clearly, they are not.

Of course I have had boyfriends. Dad has shown me photos of Giles Hughes, a man I was in a relationship with for four and a half years; for eighteen months of those we were engaged. Apparently I called off the relationship a fortnight before the wedding, citing a nebulous "need to do more first" as my reason to break his heart. This story was recounted to me by Dad with a notable dollop of regret. Secretly I feel a flutter of pride at the decision that past-me made. It's a brave thing to call off a wedding at such a late stage and I can't imagine it was easy to do, but far easier than living in a marriage full of regrets. I guess I was quite gutsy once upon a time. I need to find that again. Channel that. The photos show Giles to be ruddy and earnest. An open, hopeful face. I don't remember him at all, but I can't believe he is the man who clambered into the tub with me; whose glance excited then dismissed me. I don't get the sense that Giles ever played cat and mouse with any woman.

Apparently, after I called off the wedding, I moved to Paris. My best guess is the man I almost remember is a Parisian. He's out there somewhere. He made my pulse gallop as though I was a heroine in a tacky paperback; he made me swell with lust, low at the pit of my body, a feeling that rushed through me and left me happily agitated.

I do remember Paris. Countless fountains, rows of elegant lampposts and grand cream buildings, wide avenues, delicious food and wine consumed at small round tables in the bustling streets. There were charming stone bridges, smartly dressed couples who regularly stopped on the pavements to kiss passionately.

I can barely speak French.

What the hell?

I can remember verb tables and that sort of stuff that you learn by rote. *Je suis, tu es, il/elle est,* but I can't string a sentence together. I can't imagine holding a conversation. Was I the idiot who lived in Paris for a decade and didn't bother learning the language? If so, I hate myself. Or did I learn to *parler français* but that is another part of my brain that has been eaten by the cancer? If so, I hate myself. Or at least, I hate my body, which has betrayed me, let me down so badly.

Dad tells me that I was a teacher in Paris. I taught English as a foreign language. I think I taught at an all-boys school, because I frequently get flashes of dark-haired, dark-eyed boys running about, or looking frustrated or bored as they pick up a pen, then proud and joyful as they finish an exercise. I must have taught a range of ages, because I get these faster-than-a blink impressions of boys of various sizes. No girls. Teaching English as a foreign language requires total immersion as the teaching method. This means I would have only spoken English in my classroom. Maybe that's why I didn't bother learning the language. That, and the haughty Parisians mocking my attempts. Still, even if that is the case, I can't help being disappointed with my past self. No language-learning and a married lover? I feel so uncomfortable with this version of me. Ignorant and deceitful, lazy and disruptive? It's difficult to wash myself in glory, and don't we all want to be the heroine of our own lives? Did I waste my time in France? That's unforgivable.

When I got my diagnosis, I moved straight back here to England, to this small coastal hamlet that I grew up in. Even though I'd been away for years, from what I can gather not even visiting my dad that often, it was the place I bolted to. The place where I could depend on someone. It makes sense. Cancerous mistresses aren't a thing really, are they? Married lovers presumably call it quits at that point. Dad has told me about the call I made from my apartment in Paris. He urged me to just get on a train and come home. He sorted out everything: having my things packed up and shipped back here, dealing with my landlord and employers over there. "None of that mattered," he's told me. "All that mattered was getting you home." My kind, reliable father. I'm grateful that he sees me in a better light than I perhaps deserve. I think I can add "daddy's girl" to my scant character profile.

I don't remember the treatment. It will come back to me, apparently. Or maybe not. As Dad points out, "There are better memories that you might want back first."

Count your blessings. Isn't that the mantra we're all supposed to live by? I have a feeling it is. I can't quite pinpoint where I am on the scale of optimist or pessimist. Glass half-full or half-empty? I think maybe I'm the sort who believes my glass is just not quite big enough. So what does that make me? Greedy?

I'm lucky, I know I am. I'm lucky that I am here. I'm lucky they detected the cancer early and that it hadn't spread to any of my vital organs. I'm lucky that they cut out all the tumors. I'm lucky that we found a consultant who dared to try this more radical, only-chance experimental treatment and that I had the operations, chemo and everything before COVID-19 created a bottleneck in hospital admissions. I'm lucky. So damned lucky.

But sometimes it doesn't feel like that. Sometimes it feels like I'm very unlucky indeed. I'm scared. My past is bleached to nothing, so my reality is terrifying, unbalanced. Liquid rather than solid, and I'm drowning. I have nightmares about drowning all the time. Water gushes into my open mouth, up my nose, drums around my ears. Everything is blurred and blunted. My clothes get heavy, bloated, and I kick hard, but the harder I kick, the deeper I seem to be dragged under the waves. I'm drowning in an absence.

A darker mood engulfs me. The sun feels as if it is scorching rather than warming or comforting. I pick up my book, slip my flip-flops back on and head indoors. Feet dragging, heart aching, and my head? My head is simply letting me down.

9

STACIE

Our lockdown days have settled into a regular pattern. Dad and I take our separate walks; when I return, I prep and cook lunch. This involves lengths of time studying recipes cut from newspapers. I try to tell myself that it's quite fun discovering what I like to eat, that I'm getting a chance to rediscover myself in a way no one else does. Turns out I'm not fond of butternut squash or sweet potato, but other than that, I seem pretty broad in my tastes. Dad is grateful for whatever I put in front of him. From what I can gather, until I returned home he lived on oven chips and frozen chicken bites. The sort of food you might occasionally (and guiltily) feed your children if you are in a hurry.

I try to serve up nourishing and tasty dishes for us both. I think I must have been quite a good cook before. I certainly find the process of chopping, slicing, grating and peeling simple and therapeutic. I'm fully aware what the differences are between blanching, browning, grilling, boiling, stewing, et cetera. How strange my memory is. So infuriatingly selective. We eat lunch, read the papers or a book; sometimes Dad snoozes in his chair. If the weather is good, I might sunbathe, but if I'm not in the mood, I amuse myself for an hour or so around the house.

There is always something that needs to be done in the cottage. When I first was well enough to start exploring the house again, I was struck by the extent of the neglect. Outside, weeds spring up through cracks in the cemented areas that connect the various outhouses: a shed, a greenhouse, a dilapidated Anderson air raid shelter and even an ancient outdoor loo. Not somewhere I've investigated. There is a lean-to bolted onto the outside of the house, a dubious home improvement that is most likely a legacy of the 1970s; the roof is made of corrugated plastic and has yellowed with age. Dad keeps boxes of things to be recycled in there: newspapers, cardboard, cans, batteries, textiles. He keeps promising to take them to the appropriate centers, but lockdown has hampered that. The stack of boxes grows ever higher, precariously balanced, always threatening to topple. There is a cracked plastic sledge propped up against the back wall, I guess it must have been mine and there for about three decades.

Inside the house, there is dated woodchip wallpaper in some rooms; others boast floral patterned papers that in places swell, have gone baggy like an old person's skin. I itch to scrape the paper off and paint the walls in solid dark blues and grays, which instinctually I know are popular and fashionable. The magnolia paintwork of the skirting boards and doors is chipped and darkened with dirt: fingerprints and lingering smoke from the open fire. The carpets are worn; dust and grime are ingrained into every surface and ornament. The air in the rooms is always stale. No matter if I leave the windows open all day, decades of sweat and smoke have penetrated the furniture.

For all his strengths, no one could suggest that Dad is a contender for any house-proud prizes, but I find it therapeutic to lose an hour or so to scrubbing floorboards until the grain and sheen of the wood reemerges. It's satisfying to paint a shelf or window frame, and it can be interesting to sort through a cupboard or drawer. Plowing through boxes and storage always offers the chance of my remembering something, so the process often has the feel of a treasure hunt. Doing chores is familiar. I have balled socks, deep-cleaned ovens, hung pictures and kept a home in the past. I sense as much. Although, I have no idea if I always lived alone or flat-shared. I was a poor communicator about such details with Dad, as he's equally clueless. If I shared my life with a significant other, it wasn't someone I thought was significant enough to introduce to my father. This thought makes me feel a little uneasy, a little shady, as it feeds into my theory that I had a married lover. Or am I being dramatic? Maybe there was nothing to hide; maybe there just wasn't anyone to share.

We eat again around 5:30, a light meal—neither of us has a big appetite, despite all the fresh air and walking—then we take Ronnie on an evening walk together. Generally we try to do a couple of miles, heading east all the way along the coastal path until we reach the most picturesque beach cove. It takes a bit of getting to; sometimes we scramble down the hillside, practically sitting on our backsides for the last few meters. Sturdy and stronger than a man twenty years younger, Dad is undaunted by his age or the lack of dignity in this, and we both always have a bit of a giggle when doing it. As we walk, he likes to recall other times we've spent there, banging on buckets with plastic spades, searching for shells, getting damp with spray. He's always hoping to jog my memory. We rarely linger. Our walks, so often repeated since my illness and lockdown, have developed an air of efficiency. There and back again. By 8:00 p.m. latest, we're usually back in our kitchen, enjoying a stiff gin and tonic or cracking open a bottle of red wine.

Then sometimes we watch TV, or if there's nothing on that we fancy, we might play cards or dominoes or we might peruse old photo albums. This is definitely Dad's preferred way to spend the evenings. I can see his excitement every time as he pulls an album off the shelf. He has dozens of them. Old-fashioned things. The photos are not great quality; faded, aged, some creased or ever so slightly blurry, many with a blue tinge. They were all developed in places like Boots. I know that's not what happens with photos now. We take snaps on our phones and keep them there, rarely bothering to print, frame or mount.

We don't give our moments that same sort of reverence anymore. I think that's a mistake. If this illness has taught me anything, it's that we should revere every moment.

Dad likes us to sit side by side on the couch, the album resting on his lap. He turns the pages carefully, keeping his eyes on the photographs, giving me space as I try to become reacquainted with my past. He slowly points to pictures of me, him, Mum. Sometimes a friend is with us. "You remember Mandy Crosby, don't you? And Jed Illingworth. He lived next door to us for years. It broke your heart when his family moved to Manchester." Often his comments are made with a forced joviality that fails to hide his longing. It's so tempting to say, *Yes, I remember.* To unambiguously take ownership of things that I don't recall. It would make him happy, and maybe it would make me feel better too. But the truth is, I don't remember either friend. I stare at images of Dad, my mother and my young, skinny-limbed, tomboyish self and don't remember any of us. I try to smile; sometimes maybe I give in and nod a fraction—not exactly a lie, but something to offer him a glimmer of assurance. Or at least hope.

The albums record my life with obvious enthusiasm until I am in my midtwenties, which is when I called off my wedding to Giles and ran away to Paris. The photos I took there must all be on my phone; unfortunately, I don't know where my Paris phone is. Dad said I had one when I came home from France; perhaps I left it in hospital at one of my many appointments. We've searched high and low for it. I've looked through the suitcases and boxes that my Parisian friends packed up and sent on as per Dad's instructions. There are several of them stacked in cupboards, under beds, behind furniture. I have yet to fully unpack; I tend to retrieve things only when I need them. I hoped I'd find my phone tucked away at the bottom of one of these boxes somewhere, battery flat, waiting for new life to be breathed into it. Obviously photos of my recent past and lists of friends in my contacts would be very helpful to me. It's another frustration that it too has vanished. Dad says he'll buy me a replacement as soon as we're out of lockdown. There's no rush. Whose number would I store?

Tonight, there's nothing of interest on the TV. We miss standing on the step, clapping into the night air, sending our gratitude to the NHS staff. That act was temporarily hopeful and rousing, but the country has collectively decided that the gesture has already had its day. Now, Thursday evenings are like every other evening. We have to duck away from the flat isolation of the horizon and seashore.

"Fancy a game of cards?" I offer.

This afternoon, as Dad slept, I searched through a couple of drawers under my bed, hoping to dislodge a glimmer of a memory. Nothing doing. I sorted through discarded makeup bags, old school books and notebooks, broken bits of fun jewelry, odd socks and tennis balls. I didn't recognize a thing. It can be exhausting. Chilling, if I allow it to be. It takes all my energy to believe in a future where things become clearer and I'm once again anchored with a past. Not adrift as I currently feel.

So I'd like a mildly competitive card game to take my mind off the blanks I'm drawing, but Dad clearly has other ideas; he glances hopefully at the shelf where the photo albums are stacked. I pretend not to notice, root about in the sideboard for the playing cards instead. Dad arguably knows me better than I know myself and will be inwardly struggling. He won't want to overwhelm me, but he's a parent; there must have been countless times when he's encouraged me to stretch myself, when he's known that persevering is good for me. It is the job of a parent to gently push, to believe in their kids even when the kids doubt themselves. If a child falls off their bike when learning to ride it, it's a parent's job to get them to hop back on. Poor Dad, I bet he thought those years of balancing cajoling with encouraging were behind us. He must long for me to place our first holiday, remember sports days and school plays. He'll want me to recall the Easter egg hunts, tea parties, sleepovers; the endless blissful days searching rock pools, bobbing on boats and all the other elements of the perfect childhood that he supplied. He weighs that hope against the outcome that experience has shown is more likely—a night of barely smothered frustration and regret as I come up blank.

It must break his heart that I can't recall all that he did for me. By not remembering, I'm sort of destroying him too. Memories are richer and fuller if shared, the ultimate affirmation. Since my mother buggered off, there's only me who can validate his efforts and experiences. My fractured, faulty memory has stolen not only my past, but his too.

Tonight, he has a nervous energy about him, and is oozing that treasure-hunt-excitement vibe I can't bring myself to douse. I nod and smile as he stretches for a large green photo album.

"Family holiday to Great Yarmouth is in this one, I think." With something akin to reverence, he opens the album. Do I imagine it, or do the stiff pages let out a sigh?

"You lived on sticks of rock," he says, chuckling. Pointing to a photo of me where I'm facing the camera and managing to smile while sucking hard on a yard of rock candy. "Your mum started to worry your teeth would fall out before the week was up. You'll recall that." He states it like a fact, although it doesn't make it one. Even if I could recall Yarmouth, I don't think my mother would have been that worried about my teeth. I look about eight in the photo; she most likely had a foot out the door by then.

"We visited the maritime museum. My choice. Retrospectively, a big ask for a child, likely you'd have been happier at the Pleasure Beach or the aquarium, but you took a lively interest. You were always so amenable." He grins at the young me in the photograph. My eyes are bright and I shine back at him, the way I must have when he took the photo; radiating love, basking in it. I would do anything to remember that feeling.

My dad paints a consistently glowing picture of me as a child. Besides being amenable to museum visits, my virtues included (although were not limited to) being sporty ("you always gave everything your best shot"), creative ("exceptionally good at art"), kind to friends, generous, thoughtful, patient... Look, maybe I *was* a model child, or maybe because I've had cancer and nearly died, he has a tendency to be a bit selective. Or— and I like this theory the best—maybe his generous description of me simply demonstrates his absolute love of me, rather than his love of the absolute truth. Being my parent blinds him to any faults: past, present or future. I find this comforting. Some parents do simply dote and only ever see the good in their offspring. Children who are subject to total devotion are so lucky. I feel this in my soul. Loved kids win the lottery. Unwanted kids, lost kids, kids of selfish, neglectful or warring parents are left with holes.

Anyway, I doubt I was as saintly and accomplished as he describes me; who could be? I wonder if secretly I was a little bugger, up to all sorts, just good at hiding it from him. Somehow, I think this is most likely, because I have a sense that I'm not a straightforward person, not like my dad. I have secrets. I just can't remember them.

"We spent a fortune in the amusement park. Hook-a-duck, whack-a-mole and the rifle range. You always wanted me to win you a cuddly toy," muses Dad. "You were so certain I could, so I'd end up sinking a fortune to secure whatever piece of tat had caught your eye." He is lost in the memories, but happily so. I'm lost in the lack of them, not happily so. I rally for him. We are a seesaw. If I'm feeling despondent, he buoys me up; if he sinks, I rush to cheer him.

"The scientists are working on a vaccine," I say. "Every brilliant brain in the world is focused on it. It's only a matter of time. Then, once they have that, we'll be out and about again and I'll start to remember things."

"You think?" Dad looks uncomfortable. Not able to hide his doubt.

"Do you fancy a slice of that coffee and walnut cake I made this morning?" I offer. Our harmony comes from knowing when to change the subject.

Dad grins and nods and I stand up and head into the kitchen.

I consider a second G&T but decide against it. I know I have to be careful with how much alcohol I drink following my op. Instead I pop the kettle on; I'll make a cuppa. I open the back door and let the fresh air run through the house. I can smell the sea, salt and sand. I leave the door open as I cut two slices of cake and put them on plates on a tray. I find mugs, tea bags and milk. As the kettle boils, something peculiar happens, swift and sure. I don't smell the sea; I can smell dank and damp earth.

I don't suppose it is Paris. In Paris, it's car fumes, perfume and red wine, right? But I remember the fusty smell of moist earth. I see a fat worm rooting its way through the soil. I wonder whether it is the plot that I briefly tended as a child, but no. This is not a garden, it's more complicated than that. I sense that there's something confusing and contradictory about this patch of earth. I'm glad of it and I'm scared of it.

Then, like a flicker in a film, I see a grave. I hate this grave. I know I do.

I stoop and place flowers. I love the flowers; I don't want to leave them at the cold grave. I will my memory to focus on the headstone. Who is lying under the earth? Who have I brought flowers to? Shudders ripple through my body as I consider that it might be him. The man I bathed with. My heart hiccups, protesting at that possibility. It's simply not fair that I'm just almost remembering him and there's a chance that he's gone already. Before he's mine fully, I've lost him.

Then I see them. Two small children. A flash, a blink. Baby teeth, flushed cheeks, hot little hands in mine. Solemn and sweet. My heart aches for them. They ooze loss and sadness. I bend at my knees so I'm level with them, balanced precariously. One of them snuggles into me. I almost topple, saved only because I put my hand out into the moist earth. Onto the grave. The child's breath is on my face. He smells of Chupa Chups lollies. He kisses me. A soft sound as his baby lips pucker up and then touch my cheek. The other little boy has his back to me. He keeps his eyes on the flowers. His skinny shoulders are stooped. I don't know which of them I pity more. Which I should comfort first. There is a man. He turns to me, his dark eyes piercing, pleading. They are kind eyes, but they hold pain and a hint of reserve. He keeps me at a distance while he's asking me to do something. What? What does he want me to do? Who is he? He is not the man I bathed with.

And then they are gone.

I hang on to the back door and take large gulps of the air. Briny once again; there's no hint of wet soil, just the salty whip of the sea. I turn to the tea tray and snatch up a slice of cake. I cram it into my mouth to stop the distress and panic spilling out; to stop me saying anything aloud that might upset my elderly father. I need to think this through. A thousand scenarios run through my head, almost simultaneously. The most obvious thought is that the boys are students of mine and I attended a funeral with them as a guardian; I'm comforting them as we're burying one of their parents. How heartbreakingly sad. But I feel incredibly close to them, so possibly they are more than students. I might have been their nanny, or they could be children of a friend of mine. Or a cousin, a colleague. *These are my children. My boys.* That's the weirdest thought to flash into my head. How could I have sons and Dad has failed to mention them? Of course not, that's impossible.

I sigh. The most probable thing is this is a false memory, not real at all. I might have seen something on TV that suggested this graveside scenario to me. There's a lot of coverage on the news that funeral attendance is being restricted. It's disturbing, and my subconscious is most likely processing that. As much as I'm desperate to get my memory back, I hope this one is a false memory, because the idea of these two grieving little boys leaves me feeling inflamed and helpless.

TEN YEARS AGO

10

STACIE

Stacie is looking for Giles. They are meeting tonight at 8:00 p.m. at his mother's house, but she wants to see him alone and they won't be left alone this evening. They rarely are nowadays. Just the two of them—cuddled up on a sofa, in the pub, taking a walk—is a thing of the past. Tonight, she, Giles and his parents will sit and watch TV together, or at least she'll try to watch TV, but no doubt viewing will be frequently interrupted with talk about the wedding. It amazes her that there is anything left to discuss; flowers, dresses, cars, food, drink, stationery, guest lists, gift list, order of service, timings have all been ruminated upon, examined and considered scores of times. Stacie wonders what they will talk about once the wedding is over.

She called Giles an hour ago, but it turns out he accidentally left his phone at the farmhouse this morning and has been without it all day. Heidi, his mum, answered Stacie's call and explained as much. "I've been taking his calls today. It's so much fun talking to his friends!" she said with a laugh. There are few privacy boundaries in the Hughes family; no locks on phones or even on the bathroom door, no qualms about opening one another's post. Stacie thinks it is cozy. Or suffocating. It depends on her mood.

Heidi suggested that Giles might be in the south barn. That's where he keeps his Tiger Supercat kit car, and sometimes, on an evening, after he's finished his work on the farm but before supper, he works on the car for a bit. Giles is a very sociable man and doesn't like being left with just his own company, quickly gets bored of it. So normally the minute he finishes work he calls one of his friends, Andy or Jim, and they meet him at the barn, maybe bring a beer along. But as he doesn't have his phone with him today, there is a chance he'll be alone.

Stacie sets off on foot because her dad is still in town and he has the car. They share a car, which isn't often an inconvenience and, even if it was, she can't afford one of her own so she has to suck it up. The quickest way to the south barn on foot is to take the coastal shortcut. She walks at speed. Hedges quickly give way to simple wire fences that pen sheep off the road, but soon all signs of humanity fall away and there is nothing other than a narrow track and rolling, rabbit-cropped fields.

She spots Prue McCullen in the distance. Prue is paused at the stile and there's no way of avoiding her. Stacie always feels vaguely uncomfortable with Prue McCullen, who was a teacher at the local primary school for over forty years. Stacie numbers among her past pupils; practically everyone in the village does. Prue might have finally retired last year, aged sixty-five, but she has retained an air of authority over the population of the village. In her company, Stacie immediately feels like she's forgotten something—her lunch money or homework—or that she has done something wrong, like giggling in assembly.

Prue starts talking the moment she claps eyes on Stacie. Her loud teacher-voice booms across the field. "I'm just drinking in the view, so familiar and yet never boring. I always say that the quality of light in this part of the world is such that the infinite variety of greens in the trees and fields means that one is offered a new masterpiece every day. Don't you agree, Stacie?"

Stacie nods dutifully. Prue McCullen is the only person she knows who can get away with a non-ironic use of the third-person-singular "one."

"I was hoping to bump into you today, Stacie. I have something to show you." Prue nudges a worn rucksack off her back, unzips it with military-style efficiency and roots around. She straightens up and holds out a length of pink ribbon for Stacie to inspect. It flutters on the wind and Stacie's heart breaks a little. "I got this from Leader's haberdashery in Williton Cross," Prue explains. Williton Cross is the nearest small town. Most locals simply refer to it as Williton; the local teens, with their natural tendency to denigrate where they've come from, abbreviate to WC. It isn't really a shithole, more of a serviceable mediocrity, with a string of shops that provide everything you might need, nothing you want. "I think it's perfect to tie the small flower arrangements to the pew ends. Gary Leader keeps plenty of pink ribbon in stock. Never goes out of fashion, does it? He offered it to me at cost when he heard it was for your wedding. Knows your father. So I took the liberty of putting in an order."

Prue beams, happy with her result. She never married and so has always had time to mother, or at least govern, the entire village, involving herself from cradle to grave in everyone's business. She passes judgment on names chosen for babies, offers advice on ways to encourage a shy child to make friends. She always knows which tradesman is reliable, available and not exorbitant. She visits people if they end up in the hospital, and if you have an old piece of furniture you need shifting, she always knows someone who is looking for just that thing. She will childmind and not charge providing your child is well acquainted with the magic words, "please" and "thank you." Most people are glad of the extra pair of hands at some point in their lives, and so despite the fact that her interest borders on interference, she brooks little opposition on a day-to-day basis.

Motherless Stacie grew up knowing that people expected her to be especially compliant, grateful for any help or attention bestowed. It is obvious from Prue's stance that she is waiting expectantly for profuse thanks for her assistance in this matter of pew-end flower ribbons. Stacie had wanted the country flowers to be hand-tied with heavy lace and she'd said that she would go to Exeter to source it herself. Prue is a good friend of Heidi Hughes, and Stacie is aware that they have shared a fair few conversations about how "poor little Stacie" knows nothing about hosting a proper wedding. She doesn't have to listen at doors to hear this sort of thing; they say it to her face. Eighteen months ago, when Stacie accepted Giles's proposal and wedding planning started, she explained that she wanted the wedding to be free-flowing, spontaneous and carefree; she said that the dress and bouquet had to reflect that. "You know, I want it to look as if I've just wandered through a meadow and gathered up great armfuls of blooms. Native wildflowers like cornflower, bluebells, daisies; also grasses because they add texture."

Prue looked concerned and commented that Giles Hughes was not a boho-wedding sort of boy. No, he was a morning-suit, carnation-buttonhole sort of boy. A traditionalist.

When Stacie first picked out a dress she liked, Heidi commented that it looked like a nightie. She said it with a laugh, but her comment found its aim and Stacie agreed to a lace dress with a high neck, a tight waist and a wide skirt. Prue and Heidi agreed that a traditional bridal bouquet, with lilies and roses and a defined structure, was what was needed, and so they spoke with the florist directly. Obviously the flowers for the pew ends must match. Prue is quite unabashed about using all her considerable energy to keep Stacie on track.

Stacie stares at the pink satiny ribbon. She thinks it's horrible. It looks like something a seven-year-old might covet, but she hasn't got the energy to say so. "Very nice," she mutters. It doesn't matter anyway. Not one bit. All she needs to do is get to Giles, talk to him. She says she's got to dash; it's started to spot with rain now, she'll get soaked. She climbs over the stile and darts along the track toward the barn.

Giles is alone. It's a relief, it's what she wanted, and yet her stomach lurches. It's the last thing she wants. He doesn't stop working on the car to jump up and kiss her, like he's in some sort of romantic novel. He doesn't passionately reach for her and take her over the bonnet of the car, like something more X-rated.

"Hiya, love," he says. Like they're an old married couple who have been together a hundred years. He glances her way; notices she is wet through. "Is it raining?"

"We need to talk." She hates herself. It's such a ridiculous cliché of a line. But what else can she say?

We think we're all so different and yet we're the same. Over the long history of humankind, people have needed to ditch their partners, and the decent ones decide to do it face-to-face. So there's nothing other than *We need to talk.*

She sees him bring her into focus. Finally. He watches her carefully. Perhaps he's noticing the fine droplets of rainwater hanging around her hairline, on her eyelashes and cheekbones; maybe he's thinking something romantic, like she looks luminous, like a mermaid. Maybe he's thinking he loves her a lot. She doesn't know what he's thinking. But she watches his expression change as the words find a way to stumble out of her mouth. It's hard. The hardest thing she's ever had to do. She manages to say that she doesn't love him enough to give it all up. This isn't what she wants. *He* isn't what she wants.

"What? Give what up exactly?" he asks, confused.

"My future."

"But *I am* your future."

She doesn't answer that. Which says everything really.

11

STACIE

Stacie thinks the only thing she can possibly do now is run. Leave immediately. She doesn't want to have to unpick the mess she's created; to stick around to hear the judgment and condemnation from nosy neighbors, concerned friends and disappointed relatives, who will all have a view. She doesn't want anyone to try to talk her out of her decision. Speaking to Giles took all the energy and courage she had. She's teetering on the edge. She wants to jump and take flight, but there's a chance she might slink back to the safety of a well-worn path if anyone really tries to persuade her to do so.

Everyone is excited about the wedding. It wasn't *her* wedding she'd just canceled, not even hers and Giles's; it belonged to the entire village. She's stolen from them. Stolen something they were looking forward to. She's aware that people have already bought new outfits for the big day. Those coming from further afield have booked trains and accommodation. How could she be so selfish? And Giles's parents. The thought of them sends a flash of angst through her core. What will Heidi and Ian say? They have paid for the drinks, cars and flowers. They will be devastated, obviously. They will be disappointed in her, furious. They'll probably just outright hate her. She is like a daughter to them. They are always saying so. Everyone is always saying so.

Except she isn't, because if she was like a daughter to them, they wouldn't hate her; they'd try to understand her, that's what parents do. Her dad is struggling with it, but she can see he is trying.

He's followed her into her bedroom. He rarely comes in here. He respects her privacy; they chat in the kitchen or living room. This is her space, but today he's stumbled into her room, tracked her down; he is wide-eyed with stress. He didn't even knock. Heidi has probably already been on the phone. Stacie has the bigger of the two bedrooms in the house. When her mother was still living with them, this was her parents' room, but after she left, her father said it made sense for Stacie to have it. Stacie thought he was simply being practical or generous—she had more toys, clothes, sports equipment, she needed the extra space more than he did. As an adult, she now understands that maybe his decision was more of an emotional one; he wouldn't have wanted to continue to sleep alone in his marital bedroom after the woman he loved had gone.

There are layers that evidence Stacie staking a claim on the room, making it hers over the years. Her old school books and notebooks laze on shelves and under her bed. Untouched for ages but not thrown away, because she isn't the sort to spend time decluttering. Broken bits of jewelry lie scattered on the dressing table, waiting for a day when they will be fixed. Bottles of nail varnish, odd socks and tennis balls languish. There are unframed pictures cut out of magazines, old birthday cards and postcards tacked to the wall. The yellowing tape is failing and the pictures droop, slip, slide. It doesn't matter. Stacie has always believed it's not what's inside this room that makes it special, it's what lies outside.

The room faces out onto the sea. The window is enormous; it's sometimes possible to imagine you are standing on the beach, being engulfed by the elements. Buffeted on a windy day, soused on a wet one, cocooned on a warm one. On extremely hot days, Stacie lies on her bed and watches the sun drip over the tiny Juliet balcony, fall through the window and pool beside her. There is no sun today, though, just a flat sky the color of a bruise. The downpour has settled into a hopeless drizzle.

Her dad watches, with obvious despair, as she darts around the room picking up clothes off the floor or urgently pulling them out of the wardrobe, then flinging them into a suitcase. She's not wasting any time folding; she's just throwing T-shirts, jumpers, jeans and pants together higgledy-piggledy. It doesn't matter to her. All she wants is as many things as possible packed as quickly as possible, and then she wants to get out of here. Ideally before a neighbor knocks on the door and says they've heard the news, demanding to know what the hell she's thinking.

"You don't have to run off," her dad says.

"I do." The words echo around her messy room. Spitefully pinching her. The very words she can't bring herself to say to Giles.

Her dad must be thinking the same thing, because color floods into his cheeks, which happens when he's embarrassed. Or angry. He does get angry sometimes. Infrequently but incredibly so. He goes red when shouting at the news; anything about animal cruelty quite naturally makes him boil, as do tourists swimming in the sea when a red flag is flying. "Bloody idiots, if they get into trouble, they put others at risk saving them." He tries to stay calm. Prides himself on remaining in control. He thinks rowing is uncivil. Violence barbaric. Stacie can remember just two occasions in her life when her father really lost it. Once when Jed Illingworth, her little friend from next door, pushed her into the road and a car had to swerve to avoid hitting her. They were only messing, he hadn't meant to put her in danger, but her dad went ape. He shook Jed so hard she thought his teeth were going to fall out. And the other time was when her mother left. He smashed plates, put his fists through paintings, tore books from shelves. He was unrecognizable.

"I thought you were so happy," he says, quietly. Not angry then, embarrassed for her. Of her?

Stacie pauses, sits on the edge of the bed and faces her dad through their reflections in the dressing table mirror. "You know what it's like around here."

"Lovely," he replies with conviction.

"Limiting," she counters.

He winces. "How so?"

"Everyone is given a role. I don't like the role I've been given."

"What do you mean?"

"Well, like Prue McCullen is the village busybody, and Mr. Baxter plays the church organ and likes to play the fool. Always relied upon for the dad jokes. Naomi Thomas is 'such a good mum' and Tanya Vaughan is 'no better than she ought to be.' Popular opinion is that she'll never be a mother, and if she is, there will be no sign of a dad. Even if Naomi literally ate her kids on the village green, people would somehow blame Tanya. Al Morgan is a solid bloke, going to do well for himself, whereas Luca Cinelli is known as a work-shy feck. No one can change or grow here."

"What's my role?"

"You're Poor Ken, whose wife ran off."

"I see."

"Come on, Dad, that can't be news."

"I'd hoped you were going to say I'm the hot divorcé." Stacie can't help but grin. Her dad is trying to make a joke, trying to understand and be on her team. "And you are...?"

"Pretty young thing about to marry her childhood sweetheart. Destined to become the farmer's wife." Her dad stifles a guffaw. "What?" Stacie demands, doubting very much that there is anything to laugh at.

"I'm just thinking about that nursery rhyme. You know, 'The farmer wants a wife, the farmer wants a wife, e-a-adio, the farmer wants a wife.' The whole village is going to be singing it."

Stacie sighs, because it's true and awful. "Well, I'm not that woman. For a start, I don't want a child, and that's how the rhyme goes, isn't it?" Giles has often said he wants to have at least four children. Stacie always nodded when he said as much. She should perhaps have contradicted him. Or at the very least raised an eyebrow, given him some indication that she wasn't buying into the big family idea. She misled him and she feels awful about that. Really horrible.

"What? Not ever?" Her dad looks shocked. He's obviously never considered this possibility. Most likely he daydreamed about grandchildren.

Four children would ground her.

Tether her.

Grind her down.

She isn't sure which.

"I don't know. Certainly not anytime soon," she says, panicked. She feels like an animal being backed into a corner.

"But you *are* a pretty young thing. That's a fair assessment."

Stacie knows she is more than that. And less. "Look, Dad, I can't think about this right now. Any of this." She stands up and closes her suitcase with an air of finality and determination. She scrambles the combination lock, then goes to her bedside table and roots around in the drawer until she retrieves her passport. "It's best if I just leave. It's the coward's way, but it's also the only way."

"Giles is a good man. He loves you so much."

"I know."

"But that's not enough?"

"It's not everything."

Her dad closes his eyes, sways back a little on his heels. His shoulders touch the wall behind him. He jumps as though startled, but then instantly seems relieved that the wall is there to prop him up. He looks broken. In some ways this feels harder than explaining it to Giles. Whatever Giles thinks now, Stacie knows he will meet someone else. The farmer will get his wife, a child, a nurse, a dog, a bone. Honestly, Stacie would put money on the fact that he'll marry the next girl he dates and that they'll marry in the local church, as he and Stacie were supposed to. They will have the reception in the village pub; he might not even lose his deposit, he can carry it over. It will be the same vicar, same order of service, same hymns and florist. Just a different bride. That is part of the reason she has called the whole thing off, because she's come to realize that she was following Giles's life plan, not her own. She felt trapped by him. She had to break away.

But her father isn't in the same boat as Giles. He will not be able to get himself a substitute daughter and gamely carry on. He depends on her. She is his everything, his world.

And in all honesty, she feels trapped by that too.

Her father is a coconspirator with Giles, Heidi, Prue, the lot of them, because he loves the idea of his daughter settling down on the farm just a couple of miles away from his house. He wants to see Stacie every day, to be part of her life. He doesn't mind sharing her—that's natural and normal—but he can't stand the idea of not having anything of her. Not seeing her. "What's wrong with settling down?" he asks. His voice is almost a groan.

"It's not just the settling down I object to, it's the settling *for*. I need to see *more*, Dad. More than the twenty square miles that we all live out our lives in around here."

"Well, yes, of course you do. That's natural. But you *have* had more. You went to art college."

"I did. Yes. And do you honestly think I'm putting my degree to good use by working in the café in the garden center?"

"You're the assistant manager. You make the cakes. People *love* your cakes, and there's a lot of creativity involved in cake-making."

"Dad, the only people who ever come into the garden center café are people I've known all my life. They are bound to say my cakes are delicious. They've been saying that since I baked for Brownie fundraisers."

"Well, that doesn't make it any less true."

"I need more."

"Well, a holiday then. That's what you need. Maybe you and Giles should still go to Ibiza, but not as a married couple. Just think of it as a regular holiday rather than a honeymoon." He is speaking quickly. She can hear the desperation in his voice; it sticks in the back of his throat. "You haven't been away to-gether for years. Not since he started saving for an engagement ring and then you both started saving for the wedding. Going away will give you time to talk."

Stacie throws him a despairing look. "Seriously, Dad, can you imagine the two of us arriving at an all-inclusive honey-moon package resort and not being married? The place will be full of loved-up couples. It will be all rose petals on the bed and champagne on ice. It would be mortifying. I need to go away on my own. Live somewhere different." She declares it as a fact. Solid. Impenetrable. Non-negotiable.

"How long for?"

"I don't know. Months. Maybe a year. Maybe longer." She never lies to her dad.

"Where will you go?" She doesn't answer him. She hasn't decided, and she knows that admitting to the absence of a plan will expose her. "You won't manage, Stacie. I know you. You're best off around here. Honestly, ask anyone you like and everyone will say the same. I'm your dad, I want what's best for you. Around here are all the people who love you, all your friends who have known you your whole life. Any one of us would do anything for you." They don't know her or understand her. She's sure of that. "You think out there there's nothing but fun and adventure, but you're wrong, Stacie. The world is a big and scary place. At least it can be." He's gasp-ing now, shaking.

She stares at him. Every word he utters proves to her that she is right. They don't have a clue. They think she's an inno-cent, rather naive child, who is throwing away her best oppor-tunity. They think she came back from art college with fancy ideas and has since been a bit above herself. With a tendency toward being haughty and distant.

It is the opposite. She came back broken. A drug habit that was veering away from recreational and toward dependency, an abortion and a third-class degree had punched the spirit out of her. She has never known how to talk to them about any of it.

Giles seemed so clean and good. Which was, at the beginning, fascinating and attractive but has become alienating and remote. She didn't actively choose to be with him; it was more a case of him being the hardest person for her to scare away. He is such a confident optimist. So she found herself dating him, then becoming engaged to him. She just sort of drifted into it; everyone expected it from them.

Sometimes it irritated her that he was so damned positive that he was unaware that anyone might be something other. He didn't seem to notice when she was rude to him, which she tried to avoid because she hated herself when she was rude to him. She didn't want to hate herself, but she couldn't help feeling sordid and unpleasant in comparison to him. On occasion, his obliviousness irritated her so much she was flat-out nasty to him. He didn't deserve that. But sometimes she couldn't stop herself. He was a sitting fucking duck.

She didn't want to fuck a duck.

It was kindest just to end it. She'd come back here to hide from the first man she'd really loved. Despite her dad's insistence that everyone around here knew her, no one knew that. She needn't have bothered hiding; it wasn't as though he ever actively looked for her. Even when they were together, he wasn't always aware she was in the room. That was what she was hiding from, really. That utter and total rejection. That sense of not being seen at all. Not mattering at all.

When she first returned, she was relieved to be seen, noted. It was reassuring. She felt more real because they noticed her: the nosy neighbors, her dad, Giles, the dog. She felt validated and healthy. It was easier to be healthy here because it was almost impossible to find drugs. At college you could hardly move without being offered boy, beans and blow. Here, you had to go out of your way, which she did sometimes, but just for a bit of hash, no pills, no powder. That was behind her. For a while, she really believed that Giles was in front of her. With his round cheeks, his Hunter wellies and his life plan.

It seemed enough. A lot. Then, unexpectedly, it seemed too much. What started as concerned interest, notice, soon felt like surveillance; her every damn move was documented. Their gazes caged her. "Be careful what you wish for," that's what they say, isn't it. The worst of it was that they were all looking at her all the time, but no one could see her. Not really. They all thought they knew her. They repeatedly insisted on it. "Oh, you've always loved pink." "You like a Malibu and Coke, that's your poison." Yes, when she was seven; yes, when she was seventeen, but they don't know who she is now that she is twenty-seven.

The scariest thing of all is that sometimes, *she* doesn't know who she is either. She hasn't had time or space to work it out.

Giles would never have given her space. And nor will her father. She has to snatch it for herself.

"I have to leave," she reaffirms with dogged determination. She drags her case off the bed and takes one, two long strides out the bedroom door. More steps take her down the stairs.

"You are just like your mother." The words are spat out.

Clearly not a compliment.

"Maybe I am." She hopes so, actually. She might need some of her mother's gumption if she is going to just go, no looking back. For most of her life, since her mother upped and left, Stacie has hated her. She's believed her to be beyond selfish, an evil, terrible, ruinous bitch of a woman. But now she wonders, was disappearing all her mum had the strength to do? Just enough strength to leave the village but not enough to take Stacie with her, even though Stacie was only very small for her age at the time and really wouldn't have been any trouble. For the first time ever, she feels some sort of sympathy for her mother, maybe even empathy. Who is to say whether their situations were that dissimilar? She feels a plan form in her head.

She opens the front door. "I'll text you my address when I have one." He knows her very well. He's probably already guessed that she has decided to head to Paris. That she's going to find her mother. She hugs him briefly; his grasp is tight, she has to wriggle out of it.

The door slams behind her.

FRIDAY
3 JULY 2020

12

FIONA

"We should do something tomorrow," Fiona says. The suggestion rolls over the breakfast table. She's using her happy, enthusiastic voice. It's not a voice that is honestly very "her." She's aware of that; she hopes they are not. She often uses this tone of voice when talking to the boys and has done for years now. Not because she's a woman without kids and therefore doesn't know how to speak to children, as some might wrongly assume. The opposite. She knows how to speak to children better than most parents. She thinks being happy, or at least appearing so in front of them, is important. Over and over again she sees parents getting it wrong, not making the effort. Parents snapping at their children, shouting at them, even ignoring them altogether because they are simply more interested in what drivel is on their phones: a C-list celebrity banging out the latest TikTok dance, a mindless meme about recognizing anxiety in high-functioning introverts. It sickens her. Honestly it does. Ungrateful, Fiona has always thought. Ungrateful and thoughtless. So she chooses to speak to kids like they are miracles, special, valued.

But it has become a strain lately, it's been a struggle to remain constantly upbeat.

Maybe it's because she's living with the boys now, and being grateful and thoughtful a hundred percent of the time is, after all, a big ask. Or maybe because of the pandemic and because everyone—literally everyone on the entire planet—is simply grumpy and fed up. Or maybe it's because Kylie is dead.

Under this particular set of circumstances it is, naturally, a strain to remain relentlessly enthusiastic, persistently upbeat. The boys don't respond. At least not all the time, not all of them and not always positively. There are a lot of "nots" in Fiona's life now that she has stepped into Kylie's shoes and "bubbled up" with Mark, Oli and Seb. A lot of negativity. She never had much sympathy when Kylie used to grumble about the boys' lack of enthusiasm. And by "boys" she meant her step-sons *and* her husband, which Fiona always thought was a little infantilizing, a little off. Before, she just wasn't able to understand Kylie not appreciating every single moment of motherhood and being a wife. She thought perhaps her friend simply wasn't good enough at either role, wasn't trying hard enough to make them all happy. Because Mark was a good husband, the boys are good kids.

But now she must admit it can be a little bit wearing.

And she finds herself using the same shorthand, "boys," to refer to all three of them. Mark sometimes acts like a lost child who needs looking after.

It goes without saying that the circumstances under which Fiona is mothering are more than trying. They are without doubt harder than anything Kylie ever faced. True, Kylie might have stepped on board when they had lost their mother, but they were tiny then. Their needs were uncomplicated. Fiona is facing a much more nuanced situation; everyone knows teens are unfathomable. She realizes she must be especially patient when Oli (or even Mark!) acts as though she hasn't spoken, or when Seb is clingy, tearful or nervous and simply won't let her have a moment to herself. He has started to literally stand outside the bathroom when she's having a pee, for God's sake. He wants to know where she is every minute of the day. Follows her around like a puppy. It's not normal. Or sustainable. She needs her space too.

Deep breath, deep breath. Of course it's not normal. She can't expect it to be yet. The clinginess is entirely understandable. Most of the time it's quite flattering, rather comforting.

But she would like to pee in peace.

She repeats the comment. A little louder and more forcefully. "We should do something." It is just possible they haven't heard. Mark and Oli are often in their own worlds. Worlds she has tried to access but can't. Not quite. Worlds of what? Grief? Regret? Anger? Fear? She's not sure. Something bad. The worlds of nightmares. "We should mark the day. Celebrate it." Their eyes stay trained on their cereal bowls. Thank God for Seb. In an instant, her frustration with his neediness is forgiven. At least he acknowledges her, responds to her. He looks up, meets her gaze. Eyes wide, dark and shining. Always shining. Sometimes with something painful, other times with hope. At least they are not dead. The other two have dead eyes. Today Seb's eyes shine with interest, curiosity. Maybe simply a desire to be entertained, distracted.

"Like what?" he asks.

"Like go to a restaurant or an amusement park." Her smile reaches across her face but has no chance of making it into her eyes. Smiling hurts. Fiona remembers the day Kylie and Mark got married, when Kylie commented that her face ached from all the smiling. She was happy about it, though. Smiling even as she said it. Fiona didn't understand. She does now, sort of. Her own face also aches with smiling; the effort it takes.

"Oh." Seb is obviously disappointed and too young to be disingenuous, even to be polite.

"What do you mean, 'oh'? Wouldn't you like to visit Chessington World of Adventures?"

"Not me. It's for little kids," chips in Oli.

"Thorpe Park, then."

Oli doesn't respond, so Fiona turns her attention back to Seb, the younger, easier boy. He mutters, "Suppose that would be good, but I just thought you meant something different."

"Well, since we've done nothing other than go for walks

for months, I thought that going to a theme park would be different."

The Fourth of July. Independence Day in the USA, and here in the UK now too. That is the date when restaurants, cafés and tourist attractions finally reopen. Life can start again. Some are calling it Super Saturday, others are dubbing it Freedom Day, unapologetically echoing the American public holiday. Quite un-British, this level of buoyancy, but Fiona is ready to embrace it. She wants to eat food someone else has cooked, and drink a cocktail that will be shaken by a smart young man, ideally with an insincere but nonetheless flattering glint in his eye. She can't understand why the others aren't being more enthusiastic.

"I thought we'd do something *really* different," says Seb.

"Like what?"

"Like look for Mum."

Fiona freezes. She doesn't know what to say. She glances at Mark, wondering if he will pick up the baton. He doesn't. He continues to spoon muesli into his mouth and chew carefully. She didn't realize how annoying Mark's eating habits were until she moved in with him. It's weird; they must have eaten hundreds of meals at the same table over the years. Aware that Fiona was often on her own, Kylie was forever inviting her to Sunday lunch, Saturday brunch or even a midweek supper if she thought Fiona was at a loose end. Over all those years, Fiona never found Mark's mastication irritating. She didn't even notice it. But now she does notice it. The deliberate, difficult way he chews each mouthful over and over again before he finally gulps it down. It's as though he finds it hard to swallow.

Maybe he does.

Death affects everyone differently. Mark is losing weight. He looks gaunt and gray. Technically he could still have worked through lockdown. A landscape gardener who operates as a sole trader could have safely carried on. He didn't do so. He moped around the house. Some days he didn't even get out of bed. As he was no longer doing the manual work that provided his physical exercise, his muscles have quickly turned slack. He used to ooze a taut, healthy strength. Now he appears flattened. Diminished. Sunken. Fiona, on the other hand, is ballooning. Since Kylie's death she has gained six kilograms, nearly a stone! She used to be a woman who watched her weight; who noted fat and calorie intake, refused desserts whilst longing for them, said no to cheese and settled for black coffee when the cream-laden lattes were obviously more appealing. Now, at this critical moment, her willpower has deserted her. Her hand seems to be operating independently of her mind; it repeatedly stretches for an extra biscuit or a second helping, it opens the fridge and cupboards and reaches for sausage rolls, chocolate, handfuls of crisps and nuts. She crams the food into her mouth; unlike Mark, she barely takes the time to chew, but gulps down the goodies greedily, desperate to satiate the pangs of hunger, to fill the feeling of hollowness. The void.

Seb is staring at her. His expression is a complicated mix of hope and embarrassment and fear. He wants to believe his mother is still alive, but his older brother has bluntly and repeatedly told him that's hardly possible; he's ashamed of appearing naive and silly, he's terrified an adult is going to tell him not to hope. That would be worse.

Fiona doesn't know what to say. She doesn't know how much hope she ought to nurture. Is it kind to allow the boy to continue to fantasize? Daan Janssen has been charged with the abduction and murder of Kylie. He has clever lawyers who have managed to negotiate that he remains on bail in Holland until the trial. Even the trial is likely to take place over Zoom. He's obviously trying to avoid extradition. But she doesn't think he'll be able to wriggle out of a conviction. There is a great deal of evidence against him. Even without a body, everyone is expecting him to go down for murder.

Everyone, that is, except for Seb, aged just twelve; he believes his stepmother—the only mother he has ever known—to be alive. Or even if he daren't quite believe it, he is still daring to hope for it. Long for it.

Fiona does not believe Kylie is alive. Nor does she hope for it or long for it. She knows Kylie is dead.

Because Fiona killed her.

13

MARK

"Can we, Dad? Can we look for Mum?" Mark is aware of his younger son's intense gaze burning into the crown of his dipped head; he is bent over his breakfast and has to force himself to straighten up and look his boy in the eye. It's an effort.

He doesn't know what to say. Mark thinks parenting is a prolonged and impossible test. Single parenting is that but with big doses of isolation. There are always so many questions and he just doesn't have the answers.

When they were little, he asked himself endless questions. Things like, should you take away that pacifier now he is approaching two years old? Should you cut back your hours at work to spend more time with them? Is he an especially picky eater? A noticeably poor sleeper? Is he shier than his friends? Is he rougher? Is he willfully ignoring you or has he got poor hearing? Will he remember when you lost it and yelled and yelled at him because he mushed his peas into the carpet?

Will your pockets be deep enough?

Will your knowledge be wide enough?

Will your advice be wise enough?

Will your love be endless enough?

You just want to bloody share it. The responsibility. The weight. Before it crushes you.

So when he met Leigh, he thought all his dreams had come

true. He really did. She was able to absorb so much of the responsibility. She wanted to; it was obvious. She slipped right
into their lives. Made to measure. And since she couldn't have
her own kids, well, she was just thrilled to step up to the plate
and mother with absolute conviction and devotion. She was
sensible, pragmatic. That first time they met, when Seb fell
from the slide at the local park and landed smack on his head,
cut wide open, blood gushing out, Mark froze. It was all too
similar to that moment he found Frances at the bottom of the
stairs. Bleeding and broken. But Leigh was just wonderful.
Obviously a trained first-aider, or so he thought at the time—
afterward she confided to him that she was acting on instinct
and didn't really know what she was doing for sure. Although
just two weeks after the accident in the park, she took herself off on a first-aid course because she said on that occasion
they had been lucky, that her instincts had proved correct, but
in the future she wanted to be sure that she could look after
them. If ever one of the boys was stung or scalded or choking
or drowning. That was what she'd said.

Leigh saw a future for them straightaway and she started to
plan for it. She was very practical that way. Willing to learn.
She also went on a few cookery courses and a "Good Parenting" one. He thought that was a bit crazy at first. A course to
tell you how to bring up your own kids. He had to hide his
amusement, but as the months went by, turned into years, he
had to admit she did make their home life calmer and happier. She always seemed to be in control, she talked a lot about
positive discipline and enabling the boys to fulfil their potential. She often spoke about equipping them with the skills that
would set them up for life. It was clear she was desperate to
do a good job. She was the best stepmother they could have
imagined, quite unlike any of the stepmothers in the fairy tales.
She oozed kindness, generosity, patience. He stopped asking
himself so many questions and Leigh was brilliant at answering the ones the boys started to ask.

Until she fucked off and married someone else, that is.

Mark stares at his younger son, who is all wide-eyed and expectant. Waiting for him to come up with an answer. Why can't the kid accept the facts and just enjoy a day trip to a theme park? He glances at Fiona, but she remains annoyingly mute. Normally she prattles on in a more or less constant manner, but apparently she's not going to answer this one. It's not her fault, she doesn't know what to say. Why should she? She's just a family friend. Ironically, Mark is aware that if Leigh was here, she *would* know what to say to Seb. She'd know which words would comfort him, manage his expectations, allow room for grief and then, eventually, acceptance. Although obviously if Leigh was here, they wouldn't be having this conversation.

The thought punches him. Deep down low. He keeps saying he's over it, he wants to move on, but—Christ Almighty—his wife was a bloody bigamist. He feels like such a fool. He still can't get his head around it. Not really.

Who could?

Fiona would hate it if she knew he thought of her as simply a family friend. He's aware she thinks she's more than that to him. Not an unreasonable idea, as they are having sex. But maybe an unrealistic notion, as they are not sleeping together. They have tight, needy, functional sex. Silently, in the dead of night, so as not to wake the boys. It's neither pleasant nor unpleasant. It's not about that sort of thing at all. They have sex so Mark can prove to himself that he's still alive, still here. It answers a need. His need, but it's not about needing Fiona. Sometimes they have sex to release tension, frustration. At least he does. He has no idea why Fiona has sex with him. They never talk about it. Afterward, he always gets up and goes downstairs to sleep on the sofa bed in the sitting room. The sex helps him fall asleep. Sleep is elusive, and so anything that helps him with that is a good thing.

Fiona has been amazing. Objectively, no one would deny that. She has kept the ship afloat. The main thing in her favor is undoubtedly that she's stuck around. Seriously, it sounds like nothing, but in the end, it is everything. The success of every relationship depends on that, ultimately. It boils down to whether a person is prepared to stay or not. She stayed when it was really hard, when everyone just cried or sulked or sat in a horrible impenetrable silence. She cooked the boys their favorite meals. Of course she knew what they were; she'd watched Leigh make them often enough. She picked up the reins on Seb's homeschooling, gently cajoling him to at least join the Zoom. He isn't that invested in doing well at the moment, but she has provided some sort of routine. She does the laundry, suggests what they should watch on TV; she made a birthday cake for Oli.

When she first arrived with her large suitcase, Mark's eyes flicked to it and somehow betrayed his surprise at the volume of stuff she was bringing with her.

"I've never mastered packing light," she said with a laugh. "Look, I don't have to stay. I'm not being presumptuous. I just thought we needed choices." Mark didn't choose, not exactly. The government did. They locked everyone down. He could have asked her to leave at any point. He could still. He sometimes thinks he should, but he never does. It requires a level of energy that he can't muster.

Yes, Fiona has been objectively amazing, and yet Mark is ambivalent about what is happening with her. Unclear, undecided. Sometimes he catches sight of her—maybe she's in the kitchen, putting dirty clothes in the washer, or it's the end of the day and she hands him a glass of red wine—and he feels so close to her. He finds himself telling her that she is his rock. That he doesn't know what he would do without her. And he means it. As he says it, he means it. Because sometimes her presence is so normal, so known. He feels like he's been taken back in time to when he didn't know that Leigh was a bitch and a betrayer. A time when Leigh was alive. Then, he is so grateful to Fiona for just providing that glimpse of normality, past or present or future. He's not sure where she fits in, but on those sorts of days, he manages to give her the type of sex that makes her come. He isn't proud of himself for this inconsistency, but he isn't ashamed either. He is entitled, considering everything; he has to make a new life for himself and for the boys.

Other times, he loathes the sight of her. Sees her, and for a fleeting insane moment imagines pushing her out the window, or bundling her up in a sack and throwing her away, in a river maybe. Insanity, obviously. He'd never actually do that. It's not a conscious thought, just his subconscious messing with him. He's under a lot of stress. On some days, her being a blatant reminder of everything to do with Leigh is just too cruelly painful.

He is divorcing Leigh. She's missing, most probably dead, but to keep things tidy he's divorcing a dead woman. A woman who was most probably murdered by her other husband. His lawyer has advised him it's the cleanest thing to do, in the absence of a body and if he wants to move on. Which he does. It's complicated and he resents this mess Leigh has brought to his door. It's a good job he has Fiona to fall back on, because his Tinder profile would be ridiculous.

Marital status: currently divorcing my (assumed to be dead) wife who was murdered by her husband. Not me, I hasten to add. The other one! Because she was also a bigamist!

What's the emoji that accompanies that? Smiley winking face? Laughing crying face?

As he's thinking of what to say next to Seb, how to answer his question about looking for his mum, Oli throws down a spiky challenge. "You mean you want to spend your first day of freedom looking for Leigh's body?"

Oli doesn't call her Mum. Hasn't for a while. A source of pain for Leigh in the last few months of her life. Or at least so she said at the time—she was always going on about it, rowing, grumbling, sometimes even crying—but now Mark wonders, who can believe a word that came out of her mouth? Either way, it turns out she only had herself to blame for Oli's sudden distance toward her. The reason he stopped calling her Mum was that unbeknown to Mark, Oli had discovered his stepmother's infidelity. Or at least some of it. He thought Leigh was having an affair with Daan Janssen. Apparently, last summer he'd spotted them on the street, strolling along hand in hand as though they didn't have a care in the world. Of course the teen didn't in his wildest dreams imagine that his stepmother was married to this other man. Who would?

Oli is a very angry young man. Very angry indeed. Mark was so relieved when the police started questioning Daan. He hadn't seriously suspected his own son of hurting Leigh, but he hadn't ruled it out either. Suspicion had billowed in every direction. Like a dust cloud, silent but tangible. It is a terrible thing to think of your own child, but apparently not impossible.

"Dad, tell him." Seb looks close to tears. He often is. The wetness sits in his eyes like a film of mist. He used to be such a cheerful, happy-go-lucky boy. Bloody Leigh, she is to blame. She ruined things.

"Tell him what?"

"That Mum isn't dead. That we should be looking for *her*. Not her body."

It is as though a bolt of lightning has sparked through everyone around the breakfast table. Fiona, Mark and Oli jolt into rigid upright positions. Stiff, yet unsure. Seb also looks brittle, as well as challenging. Another wrong word and they all might shatter. Mark has explained to the boys that Daan Janssen is being charged with murder. At the time, Seb commented, "But they haven't found her body, have they?"

"No," Mark admitted. He didn't mean to convey any hope. He was just stating a fact. Now he scrabbles around for the words that Seb needs to hear. He has to explain the bleak reality. The stark probability. Before he thinks of the right words, Seb adds, "You don't think she's dead, do you, Dad?"

Mark longs to give his son firm reassurances, but in all conscience, he can't do that. Mark does think Leigh is dead. He wishes the police would simply knock on the door and announce that they've found her body, or at the very least that Daan has confessed to murdering her. It isn't that he wants her dead; he simply doesn't want the uncertainty to stretch on anymore. He can't stand this limbo. It's damaging, draining. But Seb seems to cling to hope, even as Mark drowns under a wave of despair. Seb speaks of Leigh every day. Several times. He often starts the day commenting quite cheerfully, "I think Mum might come home today," and then ends it with a less confident but equally insistent rally at bedtime, "Well, maybe tomorrow." He obviously believes there is a chance that she will simply stroll through the door; shamefaced, possibly, but somehow expecting a welcome. A welcome Seb would give, and one he believes Mark and Oli ought to as well. He is young for his age. Most twelve-year-olds would have clocked the reality by now. Leigh babied him. A mistake, especially since she hasn't stuck around to see the job through.

The thought is unfair. Mark knows it but doesn't give a fuck. He hasn't got the emotional space to think about the things she did see through. The things that secured Seb's loyalty and love.

She saw the boys through their first days at school. Oli went in with a grim, uncomfortable fortitude, an attitude that slowly but surely won him many friends, although he was never what you'd call an impressive student. Seb bounced in believing that he'd love it—after all, that was what his brother and Leigh had promised. As it happened, he didn't really settle. Leigh spent hours with the teacher trying to ease the transition from home to school by volunteering as a class reader and helping out in assemblies so he'd see her face around. She let him trade his dinosaur lunchbox for a Captain America one, even though he'd insisted on the dinosaur one just weeks before. She spent ages helping both of them learn their alphabet, tie their shoelaces; Mark had to admit she had a lot of patience for that sort of thing.

She took them to swimming lessons and taught them how to ride their bikes. He remembers her running up the street, straining to hold the saddle as the bike wobbled precariously. She endlessly repeated words of encouragement as the boys took control of the pedals, the steering and learned to trust the road and themselves. "Yes, you can do it!" "That's it!" and eventually "You're doing it on your own! You're riding your bike!" She also stuck on the Elastoplasts and administered the magic kisses that made it all better when, inevitably, they did tumble off. "The trick is getting straight back on again," she whispered to the tearful, shocked boys as they sat at the kitchen table with bloody knees and bruised pride.

Another first was Disneyland. Her idea. Mark remembers dreading it. You are either into life-size puppets of mice, ducks and bears or you're not. Leigh was. Mark wonders how many times she insisted they must enjoy life. How many times had she made that happen? Often. A lot. Thousands.

How could she have done this to them? Gone and got herself murdered because she married a bloody psycho when she was already married to *him*. Why hadn't he been enough for her? Him and the boys. If only she had been grateful and happy with her lot, she'd still be alive, Oli wouldn't be angry and dark, Seb wouldn't be tearful and tortured, Mark himself wouldn't be sleeping with Fiona, none of them would be in this total mess. It was all her fault.

This is the first time Seb has asked his father outright whether he believes Leigh to be alive. Perhaps his hope is beginning to eke away—edged out by the sun rising and setting repeatedly on her total absence—and he's wanting his dad to bolster him. How is Mark supposed to answer? There isn't a parenting self-help book that covers this topic. Most of them are about dealing with drugs, alcohol and sexual propriety. God, those problems seem positively attractive in comparison to the one he is facing. Before he can find the words, Oli explodes.

"If she's not dead, where the hell is she?" he demands. He stands up, and his sudden and violent movement knocks over his chair. It clatters to the floor. He leaves the room without bothering to pick it up.

14

DAAN

Daan quits the daily status meeting, and as the cool, pale faces of his lawyers vanish from the screen, he leans back in his chair, stretches his arms above his head. Takes up a lot of room. *While I can.* The thought hovers in his subconscious. He envies the lawyers. They can quit this madness. Following today's thirty-six-minute consultation (they charge their time in six-minute blocks), they can move on to another client. Another mess, maybe, but always someone else's mess. He can't escape so easily. Can he escape at all?

He tries to recenter. He knows that his mother and father, possibly even his younger brother and sister, will all be in the kitchen endeavoring to pretend they are not listening in to his online meeting with his legal team. They will want to appear unconcerned, assured and positive. They are not. Like him, they are desperately worried. He must appear calm and collected. If he leads with that attitude, they might be convinced by his act and find the strength to follow. The fact is, the entire family are terrified he is going to be convicted. Their long, toned limbs, tanned bodies and glossy blondness aren't quite proving to be the shield they usually are. Primarily, the concern is for him. What will happen to him if he is sent to prison, deprived of his liberty, stripped of his reputation, housed with dangerous, desperate men? His mother has nightmares about him being beaten by burly, brutal criminals. The other day she asked him what it meant to be made into someone's bitch. Presumably she had been introduced to this phrase over a Zoom bridge party or at a socially distanced picnic in the garden hosted by her nosy, excitable friends. He hadn't known how to explain it to her. His very silence told her everything.

"Oh my God. I see," she gasped, and put her hand to her mouth. Her eyes had grown large, like dinner plates. She quickly tried to recover her poise, because the Van Janssens know the importance of composure. "Well, it won't come to that. This case will be thrown out of court. I'm sure of it." She's lying to herself or him. Both. They can't be sure of any such thing. It's a strong case. It's looking very bad for him.

His father is anxious too, yes about Daan but also about what effect the scandal will have on the share price of their business. The besmirched reputation of their family is of course a secondary concern, but it is a concern all the same. His younger siblings are scared for him too, and maybe—this breaks his heart—also a little scared of him. They don't a hundred percent know he is innocent. Only he knows that. In the whole world, only he and the person who actually did abduct and murder Kai know for sure that he is innocent. It's a lonely position to hold.

None of his family have asked him outright whether he did it. They wouldn't want to cause offense by verbalizing any doubt. They have to appear to believe him and support him entirely, because that's what has got them through PR crises in the past. A united front. A family standing together. Frankly, he wishes they *would* ask him, because it would clear the air. He'd like to say it out loud. He'd like to be believed. He did not kill his wife. He has tried to address the matter of his innocence with his father. He found it impossible to be direct; the words stuck in his throat like needles. If he blatantly insisted on declaring his innocence to his family, he could imagine his father muttering, "Thou dost protest too much, methinks."

His father is fond of old English quotes and idioms. It's a habit Daan has picked up, possibly in an effort to impress his pop.

Instead, he skirted the matter by commenting, "I think my lead lawyer might do a better job if he knew I was innocent."

"Don't be an idiot, Daan, it doesn't matter. He's not Atticus Finch," his father replied shortly. "Your extortionately expensive lawyer is the best of the best. What he can prove, disprove or even cast doubt upon is all that matters. What he believes is irrelevant." Daan felt his father's impatience.

He just wants to hear him say he believes in his innocence. For fuck's sake. His own father.

He straightens his shoulders and decides what he must do next. He won't go into the kitchen and make coffee and small talk with his family. He can't take on their energy right this moment. Or rather their lack of it. He is sad that he's brought his usually fearless, forward-propelling family to this state of apprehension and apathy, but he can't risk his own already depleted resources being further sapped. He must focus. He must stay persuasive, charming and decisive if he's going to be convincing.

He has admitted to the police that he screwed Fiona a couple of times even though he was married to Kai. Not his finest moment, but bloody hell, not a hanging offense last time he checked. At first he thought that was Fiona's motivation for ruining his life, crucifying him. Just that, right there. Simply a case of a disgruntled woman deciding to take out the wife when she discovered her existence. Extreme, but not unheard-of. But they were *best friends*. As soon as he was told that, he knew he was in much deeper and murkier waters. Obviously he'd had no idea the two women were connected in any way when he shagged Fiona. He's not an animal; he wouldn't deliberately shit on his own doorstep.

Over these past few months, he's spent some time wondering when Fiona worked out the truth: that he was not only married, but married to her best friend. A best friend she thought was happily married to Mark Fletcher. When this was revealed to her is important. Fiona must have hated Kai. She must have been convulsed with jealousy when she discovered Kai had two husbands. Fiona hasn't even one. And after she punished Kai for having an excess, who better to hang the murder on than the husband? Suspicion always pools at the door of the spouse, right? People want it to be the spouse. How messed up is that? The real end to the fairy tale that people crave isn't a happily-ever-after—at least not for others; they want a grisly end. The ultimate betrayal and unthinkable brutality. People are disappointing.

He doesn't know who Fiona hated most—him or his late wife—but he knows she has screwed them both. The police have questioned him repeatedly, and during the questioning he has gleaned some idea as to what Kai was put through in her last few days. She was bound, beaten, perhaps even poisoned, certainly drugged, most probably starved. They worked this out from blood and stool samples found in the place she was held captive. He can't think about it. It tears him in two. The thought of Kai enduring that is disgusting to him. He wants to vomit. Or punch a wall. Or Fiona. Yeah, as unmanly as that sounds, as brutal and basic, he wants to hurt Fiona. Kill her.

It is obvious to him that Fiona planted his personal possessions in her home near the sea, a place he hasn't ever visited. Why would he? He isn't the sort of man who has to drive four hours for an illicit shag. Clearly Fiona took a wineglass from his apartment, one with his fingerprints on, and then left it in the bungalow for the police to find. It looks bad for him that he said he'd never visited there, since they discovered his possessions on the property, but he could only tell the truth. Fiona had access to the protein bars that he bought and put in his own kitchen cupboard. She probably stole them when his back was turned and then fed them to Kai. He tried to explain all this to the police, but it didn't go well. He can see that his explanations are convoluted. Hard to accept and easy to dismiss.

"And how do you explain the phones registered to Kai Janssen and Leigh Fletcher turning up in your wardrobe?" Constable Tanner demanded with excited aggression.

"Fiona no doubt hid them there last time she visited." Daan's tone was less agitated. He wanted to appear calm, but he wondered whether he simply sounded like a psychopath. He was a wealthy man; the slightly gauche younger cop would be dying to peg him as egocentric, incapable of loving, lacking in remorse and shame, a grandiose sense of self-worth... Very click-bait.

"And when was the last time Fiona Phillipson visited you at your apartment?" asked DC Clements.

"Saturday the twenty-first of March," Daan admitted with a sigh. The DC twitched her mouth in a strange way; he tried to decode it. Disapproval? Disbelief? "I have an explanation for all the evidence," he insisted. He heard his father's voice in his head, quoting Agatha Christie: "To rush into explanations is always a sign of weakness." He wished his dad's voice would fuck off out of his head.

"You do. Long, elaborate explanations, but in my experience the simplest explanation is usually the correct one," replied the DC with an exasperated sigh. It was clear she wanted him to confess. She wanted clarity, certainty and closure.

That was unfortunate.

Daan had initially held quite some confidence in DC Clements. She'd struck him as tenacious, bright. The sort who prided herself on being a truth-seeker. Now she seemed to simply want this off her plate. "Why would I have kept the phones in my home? I'm smarter than that." He was aware that unfortunately when he was afraid or threatened, he had a tendency to sound like a tosser. It was his curse.

"Maybe you were planning to dispose of them but just didn't have time," said Tanner with a sneer.

"I'd have got rid of them straightaway, not left them lying around to incriminate me, obviously."

Daan's lawyer coughed at that point. Apparently stating that something is obvious is antagonistic. Detailing how you would manage a crime, risky. The lawyer later said to him, "You have to act as smart as you say you are."

Daan didn't like the comment but he saw the sense of it.

The problem is that the explanation of what must really have happened *is* elaborate, torturous even. This situation is so murky, so messy.

Fiona was Kai's best friend. She had been for years. Years before he married Kai, years before Kai married the other man even. That sort of history is dangerous. Lethal. Now he has to consider that her approaching him in the first place was not a coincidence. She said she'd first seen him in the lobby of his apartment building when she was there pitching for an interior design job, and then she'd found him on a dating app with an extremely tight geographical location search. It seemed reasonable enough at the time. Plausible. Besides, she approached him when he was feeling horny; perhaps the convenience of instant gratification made him sloppy, less rigorous or suspicious than he should have been.

He had a working theory that Fiona was in love with Mark Fletcher and had been for several years. He thought Fiona was jealous of Kai (or rather Leigh), not because she wanted Daan, but because she wanted Mark (he tried not to let his pride smart under this blow). Fiona had discovered that her friend was betraying Mark; worse yet, that she was married to someone else, and she wanted to make her pay. Could it be that way around? Or—and this theory was only just beginning to form in his mind—maybe Fiona and Mark had been in it together all along. Maybe they'd been having an affair, and when they discovered Kai's bigamy, they decided murder was easier than divorce. Or at least more profitable. It would certainly be more satisfying if they managed to hang the murder on Daan.

Daan has tried to explain all these theories to his lawyers. They admit that the scenarios he has presented are possible. "But I can't go as far as probable," one said. Daan feels sullied, morally doubted, grubby. And since the comment about acting as smart as he believes himself to be, he thinks his intellect is being doubted too. Which is disproportionately galling. He feels trapped.

So he has taken matters into his own hands.

15

STACIE

The early evening is chillier than we've come to expect, and the clouds are swelling up from the sea. We've had a run of hot days when the sun has shone with real determination, and so the coolness is a shock, even though it shouldn't be. I remember that a warm July isn't guaranteed; feeling cold and rain in the air is just as likely. Gray British drizzle that leaves everything feeling saggy and disappointing is familiar to me. Although the Crocs I wear are not. Sidebar, I can see how Crocs are practical and useful when stomping along beach tracks, into rock pools, et cetera, but I struggle to imagine the moment when I handed over hard-earned cash for a pair. They are so damned ugly. Wellingtons and flip-flops seem to have my shoreside shoe needs covered, surely, yet at some point I must have thought differently because I own a pair of red Crocs; furthermore, they are decorated with smiling daisy charms. It's unfathomable to me. *I* am unfathomable to me.

Dad and I are enjoying what we both believe to be one of the last days of silence in our little cove. We technically own the tiny strip of beach from our garden to the sea, and Dad has a sign up that says *Private Land*, but he admits it's not much of a deterrent; determined day-trippers do spread out their picnic blankets regardless. Tomorrow the vans selling chips and ice cream will reappear and park up within spitting distance

of our cove. The shops just a bit further up the coast, selling
colorful airbeds, cheap cotton sarongs and buckets shaped like
castles, will open too, and inevitably masses of tourists will
start flooding back to our tiny, tucked-out-of-the-way spot.
I'm delighted at the prospect of this rediscovery; Super Saturday seems exactly that to me, but Dad is wary and talks about
it like it's Armageddon.

"You still need to continue to be shielded, Stacie. We have
to be careful," he insists. "I don't want hundreds of people setting up camp right outside our door, bringing God knows what
with them." I understand why he is protective of my space.
I've agreed that obviously I can't go to shops and restaurants
yet—I'm not going to actively seek out the masses—but I can't
help but feel a little excited that some level of normality might
return to my life. To everyone's.

"I'm not going to lick them, Dad. I just think it will be nice
being able to see new faces."

"Yes, but if they're on our beach, it means you can't be.
You'll have to stay indoors."

"Well, I don't need to go that far. I can stay in the garden."
He eyes me warily. "I can watch them from a distance. It will
make a change from watching the waves." I turn and do exactly that right now. The waves struggle up the beach. Backward and forward. They dump a layer of fresh shingle each
time, the debris inching toward our home, the water swallow-
ing up the beach. It's the end of the day; the wind has a defi-
nite nip of salt to it. If I put my tongue out, I can taste it mixed
up with the grit of sand that is blowing about. We have about
thirty minutes before the sand vanishes. I know, as I watch the
tides every evening and have become quite the expert when
it comes to timing the ebb and flow. I am itching to get a life.
I literally can't wait to feast my eyes on something unpredictable, someone new.

Someone other than the old woman in the wheelchair.

Because every day it is the same; I watch the tides and the
old woman watches me.

In the morning, when I take my walks with just Ronnie for company, I've seen her idling in the distance. She's nearly always on the narrow plank walkway that follows the line of the beach. As she's in a wheelchair, she can't come any closer to the water's edge. We haven't spoken, which seems odd to me, but then nothing is normal at the moment, so I can't quite gauge it. I'm recovering from cancer, she's elderly; following government guidelines, of course we must keep our distance. On the third or fourth occasion that I noticed her, I did wave; a self-conscious, discreet hand gesture that I admit didn't commit to being out-and-out friendly, more of an acknowledgment that we were both in the same vicinity. That we often are. I don't know if she saw my wave. She certainly did not return it. She's not usually around in the evenings when I'm with Dad. Seeing her now, in the distance, prompts me to ask him, "Who is that woman in the chair, Dad? Do you know her?"

My father lifts his large paw-like hand and waves in her direction. His wave is broad and open; he uses his entire arm, as though he is stranded on a desert island and trying to catch the attention of a passing ship. Unmissable. The woman nods tightly in response but keeps her bony hands clasped around the travel blanket that lies over her knees. "That's Prue Mc-Cullen. She was your teacher in junior school." I look again at the old woman to see if this new piece of information causes anything to shift, to see if I might recall her features.

"Shall we go and say hello? You know, safely socially distanced and all that," I suggest.

Dad hesitates, then explains, "Poor woman. She isn't what she once was. She's often confused, used to be as sharp as a pin. She's a great pal of Giles Hughes's mother, Heidi." He rolls his eyes and throws out a funny mock grimace.

"Oh, I see. Well, maybe that explains why she's always glowering at me."

"Yes, she's always been one to hold an opinion, and a grudge," adds Dad with a grin.

"It's been over a decade," I point out, sighing.

"Well, we haven't had anything more exciting happen around these parts since you did the full-on runaway bride stunt, so you're still the talk of the town, darling. At least you are of interest to the older gossipy lot." Grinning, Dad encourages me, "Come on, don't let that frighten you off, let's go and say hello."

I pretend to be interested in playing with Ronnie. He has his jaw clamped around a stick and I play at taking it off him, causing him to prance and leap, kicking up sand as he does so. I hide behind the attention he is drawing and examine the old woman more carefully. She wears her hair in a long plait, over her right shoulder. I have recently started to dream about carrying around a pair of hairdressing scissors and chopping off people's hair. It's not just because I'm practically bald and want to even the score; it's because everyone else is so unkempt, since hairdressers have been closed for months now. Super Saturday will see them open their doors, and although I personally won't be visiting, I'm as delighted as it's possible to be. Even newsreaders on TV look a mess. Apparently they have to style their own hair and apply their own makeup before they go live. Shock horror. I suppose some people might find the stripping-back honest and refreshing. I just find it depressing. I think I can surmise from this reaction that I like glamour. I am currently very far from glamorous, but I still value it in others. This attitude most likely comes from living in Paris, where people take grooming seriously. When I watch the news, I find myself losing track of what they're saying, as I fantasize about trimming their dead ends.

I'd like to slice off this Prue McCullen's plait, which might once have been golden or ebony and a source of pride but is now white and wiry. Weight has settled on her breasts and around her trunk, although her arms and legs are skinny. She's wearing pale blue tracksuit bottoms, cheap and unsuitable for her age but I presume easy to slip on and off if she needs to get to the loo in a hurry. Her knees jut at sharp right angles, yet her gray shirt is too tight and gapes at the buttons, exposing her flesh, which is wrinkled and vulnerable. She looks angry, pale. Depleted by age or illness. As I stare at her, she catches my eye. The look she launches causes me to shudder.

"No, it's okay," I mumble. "She doesn't look like she's in a chatty mood."

Dad glances over toward the scowling pensioner. "You might be right. Another day." He looks out at the sea and no doubt reaches the same conclusion I have: the walk along the beach is almost over. It's time to find higher ground or go home. "I think I'm ready to head back now," he says.

"I might just walk Ronnie a little further on up the cliff path. I only gave him a short walk this morning and I feel I ought to make it up to him."

"Fine. Well, don't be too long. It's colder than usual tonight."

"I won't be."

Dad hesitates, and I think for a moment he's going to offer to come with me. "Should I put the kettle on, or open a bottle to let it breathe? You could have a small glass."

"The latter," I reply with a grin.

I watch Dad walk away, his head bent into the wind, and I feel a pinprick of guilt. I know he wanted me to return to the cottage with him. Ronnie doesn't really need the exercise— he has already had a perfectly adequate stretch—but the truth is I want to talk to Prue McCullen. I realize that she's likely to be a bit snippy with me, since she is a friend of the mother of the man I jilted, but after days of silently casing one another out, I think I ought to face her. I'd simply prefer to take a dressing-down on my own, rather than in front of Dad. If this Prue woman is rude to my face, Dad will get protective of me, I know he will. There might be a scene, something that escalates and causes more gossip. I can do without the aggro.

"Hello!" I yell. The old woman doesn't respond. Perhaps she didn't hear me. Maybe my voice flew away with the wind and was drowned by the sea. Or maybe she is ignoring me. "Hello!" I yell again, louder this time. I pull my jacket closer to my body and walk toward Prue McCullen, not meeting her gaze but instead watching my wet shoeprints in the sand. When I'm in front of her wheelchair, I look up.

"Who are you?" she demands.

"Stacie Jones."

She squints at me. "Come here at once," she snaps.

There's something in her voice that makes me follow her instruction despite medical advice and government imperative. I suppose as she taught me as a child, in my formative years, I had that response instilled into me. I move closer to her. Kneel so that we are eye to eye. She's clearly not only old, but unwell; most likely dementia has thrown a veil of confusion over her. She examines me carefully, her cold gaze rolling over and through me. Whatever it is she's looking for, she doesn't seem to find it. I empathize with her loss. I want to tell her she doesn't need to be embarrassed; I don't know or recognize things either.

"What are you doing?" she demands.

"Taking the dog for a walk."

"No, I mean what are you doing here, in Kenneth Jones's house? I heard Stacie Jones had run off to Paris." Her voice is a complex mix of accusation, irritation and challenge. Nothing good.

"I *was* in Paris. I've been ill," I explain, carefully. "I've come back to live with my dad while I recuperate."

She moves her head slowly from left to right. As though she is denying what I've just told her. "I've been watching you with Kenneth Jones."

"Yes, I know. I've seen you. I was going to come and say hello, but…" I don't finish the sentence.

She shakes her head again, faster this time. Impatient. "He's a good man, Kenneth Jones is. Suffered a lot."

"Yes," I sigh.

"Wife ran off, no better than she ought to be." What can I say to that? "Brought his daughter up on his own. Made the best of it, he did. Managed quite admirably."

Her vocabulary doesn't fit her disheveled state and I feel sorry for her. I guess her carers are more concerned with practicalities than dignity. Elasticated waistbands rather than a smart belted pair of trousers. My sympathy is somewhat tested when she adds, "But she turned out to be a dreadful, selfish type."

"That's me. I'm his daughter." I try not to take offense. I remember the woman is elderly; some older people do have a tendency to be abrupt. I suppose they think they've earned it. Her gaze sharpens and her eyebrows rise in surprise.

"Stacie Jones did a flit too. Broke his heart; he retired then. Damned shame, he was a brilliant GP." I don't bother contradicting her, explaining that my father gave up being a GP when my mother left. Old people do get muddled about dates. "He's been through enough. I wouldn't want to see anyone take advantage of him," she mutters crossly.

"I'm not. I'm—"

"Do you know who I am?" she demands, interrupting me.

"You're Prue McCullen, my old schoolteacher."

"He told you that."

"Well, yes. I don't actually remember you. I don't remember anyone or anything." Her teeth seem too long for her face, and they're yellow. She's not the generation who have ever considered teeth-whitening strips. It's madness for me to feel nervous of her. But somehow I want to charm her. Make her my friend, like in one of those quirky little indie movies. Bald cancer girl befriends wheelchair-bound dementia victim. Oscar contender. Miss McCullen has other ideas.

"Bullshit. You don't remember me because you've never met me before. You are not Stacie Jones."

"Who am I then?"

"You are the dead woman," she replies.

16

DAAN

He is breaking the conditions of his bail, he knows that. It's not that he doesn't care; it's the opposite. He has never cared about anything more. He is a man who has always had a colossal amount of self-belief, the sort of man who assumes he knows better than anyone else about most things, and on the whole, this attitude has served him well. He is sure he's doing the right thing, no matter what the lawyers advise, no matter what the law dictates.

Technically, he's tampering with witnesses. He doesn't see it that way; he's simply reaching out. Utilizing a resource. Fiona obviously killed Kai. He is being set up and only she could have done it. He has to prove her guilt in order to prove his own innocence. He thinks Kai's boys might help him do that. Either inadvertently or through deliberate cooperation.

He's been monitoring both boys for weeks now. They were not difficult to track. It still blows his mind that she had sons. That she was a mother. He knows she didn't have these boys inside her body, push them out into the world, feed them from her own breast—hell, he simply can't imagine all of that—but anyway, she was a mother. She mothered for years and must have wiped noses, taken the kids to school, to the dentist, to sports, all the things his own mother did for him when he was a child. It's extraordinary. In amongst all the many odd things this situation had presented, this is such a peculiar thing to get his head around, because Kai never struck him as the mothering type. She always insisted she didn't want children. Now he understands: she didn't want children with him. It would have been a complication too far. He doesn't know how he feels about that. Women usually want a slice of him, as much of him as they can get, in fact. When he was a young man, some even tried to play fast and loose with contraception in an attempt to trap him. He soon learned to never allow for that possibility.

He read all the press reports about the case and they quickly led him to Oli, aged sixteen, Seb, aged twelve. With their names, ages and locality, it didn't take long to find details of the schools they attended; the swim clubs and scout groups the younger one participated in, the local football club that the elder went to. From the latter he found details of past fixtures and team photos. The names of the players were listed proudly in black Times New Roman font; kids who were potentially in Oli's friendship group. Daan searched Instagram and found five of them with open accounts. Unguarded. One of these was a gamer, who liked to post his *Warzone* progress. His gaming name was Shoot2kil. Daan started playing *Warzone* too and became Shoot2kil's gaming friend. From there he was able to access a list of all the friends that Shoot2kil played with. Oli's gamer name was Slayr123. Soon Daan was playing *Warzone* with his dead wife's son.

Jesus, there really ought to be a law against what the papers print; far too much detail is given. His motive for finding the Fletcher boys was honest—well, honest enough—but imagine if some pedophile wanted to track them down; there are plenty of people with nefarious motives. Do parents have a clue how easy it is for their kids to be found, targeted? It makes him angry, because he feels strangely protective of Kai's boys. She is dead and can't keep looking after them, but he feels annoyed that no one else seems to be. It's clear from the press reports that their father has swiftly shacked up with Fiona. Neither of them appear to be keeping tabs on the kids.

He knows this because he is talking to both boys now. The younger one has recently started playing *Warzone* as well (certificate 18, Daan notes). Seb was thrilled to be invited by one of Oli's "friends" to become a friend of his too.

The kids don't know who he is; they have no idea who they are really talking to and even though they lie to him, it doesn't seem to enter their minds that he is lying to them. It's a convenience and a concern. Through the game chat he has led them to believe that he's a nineteen-year-old Swedish skater/gamer with ambitions to become an influencer. Which means they think he is everyone, anyone, no one. He confesses that he's living at home with his parents, that he fills his days playing games, that he likes peri peri chicken and watches *Hot Ones* on YouTube.

It feels a bit grimy pretending to be a teen to get access to their world; basic catfishing. Daan Janssen is an upstanding alpha sort, a leader, a winner, a golden guy. People look up to him. Of course, he always had secret profiles when he was married to Kai; no one could have expected him to admit to his marital status on his dating sites. That would have been madness. But that standard trickery in relationships isn't unusual. What he's doing now—this level of amateur sleuthing, with fake identities—seems beneath him. But then so is prison, and there is a serious chance that he'll end up there if he isn't careful. It isn't even a case of being careful; careful is too recessive, too apathetic. He must be proactive. He must sort out this mess and prove his innocence.

In *Warzone*, teams of four fight for survival on a vast map of Verdansk. A maximum of a hundred people can participate in one go. Throughout the game, players must work closely with each other to achieve their intended goal of surviving and winning. Parents universally dismiss video games, but Daan has started to appreciate that they can require a lot of team effort and cooperative strategy.

At first, all he and Oli talked about was game tactics.

"Using floor loot and gear works okay at first, but basically, man, you need like ten thousand dollars in cash right away. Go, go, go!"

"Always plate up."

"Jeez, man, you need to make an effort to complete contracts." Oli really knew his game, but Daan wasn't there for the kills, at least not the online ones; he knew he needed to find a way into conversations about other subjects. It wasn't easy. There were only limited opportunities because the squad was four people. He couldn't overfocus on Oli or it would be suspicious. He intermittently complained that he was bored of lockdown—hardly news or especially personal; everyone felt the same way.

During one game, when the other two squad members were dead and had quit, he seized the opportunity to ask Oli, "So, man, what is it that bugs *you* most about lockdown?"

"I miss clubs," Oli replied. Daan thought this was most likely a lie. He very much doubted that Oli, who had just turned sixteen, had been to any nightclubs, let alone enough to miss them, but of course that is the joy of technology; no one has to be who they are if they don't want to be.

"Right, a kiss-ass venue with a throbbing mass of beat-hungry clubbers," Daan responded. He had no idea where this phrase came from, how the words formed in his head and tumbled out of his mouth. Something he'd heard in a movie maybe. He didn't really understand what he'd said. Oli didn't respond for a moment, and Daan felt his breathing tighten a fraction as he panicked that his "yoof speak" was unconvincing. He'd been playing up to the fact that English was his second language, hoping any mistakes he made might be interpreted as a matter of translation, but his palms started to sweat as the silence stretched between them. The only sounds were game enemy footsteps, plating, coughing in the gas. He couldn't afford to lose the boy's trust. Then, as he listened to an enemy loadout dropping, revives, shooting, reloading, he considered that as Oli was pretending to be a couple of years older than he really was, he was maybe flailing about for the right way to respond.

Finally the boy countered, "Yeah. I'm down with hard, fast euphoric elements. Trance, techno, fast house. On me! On me!"

Daan took a shot. The enemy fell before Oli could be taken out. Daan moved the conversation on. "What else do you miss?" he asked.

"Honest Burgers," replied Oli, without skipping a beat.

"So good."

"I could live on them if I was allowed." It was a slip-up. An acknowledgment of his age and parental control. Daan decided to help him out and to appear to believe him.

"Girlfriend won't let you, right?" Oli made a noncommittal sound. "So who do you live with? You never said."

"Didn't I?"

"Are you with your girlfriend, or friends?"

"I don't have a girlfriend, like, at the moment. It's too much, right. No chance to hookup anyhow. What's the point?"

"So do you live with your parents?" Daan felt like he was attempting the verbal equivalent of a cat burglary. Stealth was all.

"Yeah, my dad and sort-of stepmother."

"What's her name?"

He regretted the abrupt question as soon as he'd asked it. It was clumsy, but he desperately wanted to know who Oli was referring to when he mentioned a "sort-of stepmother." Leigh, the missing bigamist stepmum, or Fiona, his dad's new girlfriend and a killer.

Oli didn't reply, so Daan quickly corrected himself, "I mean, what's she like? Do you get on?"

"She's all right."

They both quietly concentrated on landing a helicopter away from the highly populated spots—the hospital and the superstore—then Daan muttered, "I miss my girlfriend."

"Won't your parents let you see her? Are they like strict about the COVID rules?"

"It's not that." Daan felt hot and cold at once. His chest hurt.

"Because you could get out the house, right, meet her some-where. Most of my friends are doing that."

"No, that's not possible."

"Why not?"

"She's dead."

"Right, sorry," Oli said. He didn't splutter in shock or em-barrassment as most sixteen-year-olds might have; instead, he sounded weary. Daan allowed the thought to settle. He felt bad that he'd put this on the kid, another layer of grief. It wasn't fair of him, but he somehow had to blast past the small talk. At least he wasn't lying. Okay, so it wasn't a girlfriend who was dead. It was a wife, or a non-wife. But he did miss her. Her body, her smile, that little sound she made when she was on the edge of coming. He missed her funny habits, like keeping lists of dinner guests and seating plans, the fact that she ap-peared to be the epitome of sophistication but ate chicken legs with her fingers. He missed her telling him the plots of books she was excited about and knew he'd never read.

And he was furious with her. Why the fuck did she have to be a bigamist and cause all this trouble? Why the fuck did she have to get herself killed? He wished he hadn't met her. He'd had that thought a few times, articulated it to his family, friends and lawyers; anyone who would listen. The secret he hadn't shared with anyone was that the reason he wished he hadn't met her was because if he hadn't, then most probably she'd still be alive. He hated her for humiliating him, for ru-ining his life, but he also loved her more intensely than he'd ever loved anything and just wished she wasn't dead.

"Have you ever lost anyone?" he asked.

The beeping and shooting stopped. Oli had left the game.

Daan hasn't played with him since. If the PlayStation app on his mobile buzzes informing him that Slayr123 is playing, he hops onto the game, but Slayr123 immediately quits. It's clear Oli is avoiding him. What is not clear is why. Usual teenage embarrassment or something deeper, maybe suspicion? Daan burns in frustration.

Seb is somewhat easier to deal with. Obviously he lies about his age. He says he's sixteen but he's honest about everything else. He talks about his dad and his brother, freely offering up their names. He says his dad is probably "doing it" with his mum's best friend. This was confided to Daan late one evening when they were just hanging out together in the game lobby as Seb checked his stats and changed his loadout.

"He doesn't think I know. He thinks I'm too young to work it out. Even though I'm like sixteen and everything," Seb added hurriedly.

He isn't a convincing sixteen-year-old. He conveys uncomplicated integrity and flat desperation; both betray him for the age he is. He gets openly excited about the play, not bothering to appear chill. He talks about his teachers all the time because he's young enough to think they're fascinating. He giggles when mentioning a girl he really likes. Actually giggles. His voice hasn't broken. It's only his youth that gives him the confidence to think anyone believes he is sixteen. Daan is worried for him. He doesn't want him online, exposed and vulnerable. But then his real life is just as disturbing. At least when he is online with Daan, Daan knows where he is. When he's not online, he could be talking to Fiona, a murderer. It is sickening. Terrifying.

"I've been thinking, when we play next, we should use the gas to rotate around, rather than heading straight to the center," Daan suggested.

"Why waste time? We should go straight for it."

"It's too obvious. Let's rotate around in a pinwheel motion instead. The reason for this is so you can use the gas as a shield of sorts. It prevents enemies from taking you out from behind."

"That's smart," said Seb with approval.

"You have to watch for that," added Daan ominously. He bit down on his tongue. He wanted to scream out a warning to the boy—*Run, run, you're living with a fucking nutjob!*—but he couldn't. Where would the kid go?

"So are your parents divorced?" Seb asked. It had been a

hot day and Daan was playing *Warzone* in his childhood bedroom. His parents are too stylish to be the sort to sentimen-
tally cling to his old possessions. His sporting trophies, books
and clothes had long since been sorted into piles: "storage,"
"charity," "bin." However, the room was familiar and evoked
a long-ago time of his life when things were less complicated
and everything had seemed rosy. Just the way the light still fell
through the drawn curtains made his chest ache with yearning for those simpler times.

"No. Are yours?"

"No. Not exactly." Daan heard the aching uncertainty in
Seb's voice. His childhood had never been simple and golden
like Daan's own, and now it was totally shot.

"Where's your mum then? Why don't you live with her?"

"People think she's dead."

Daan wondered if his jagged breath might somehow cut
through the confessional air, break the sense of confidentiality,
and that Seb would stop sharing. "People do?" he asked gently.

"I don't think she is. I'd know if she was dead." Seb sounded
certain. It broke Daan's heart. A child believing in fairy tales.
"I'd feel it if she was dead but I don't feel it."

"Where do you think she is then?"

"I dunno. Hiding, I guess. Her other husband abducted her."

"What?"

"She was married to two men at the same time. My dad and
this posh banker wanker. It was in the papers. You can read
about it online if you don't believe me. I think he's still hiding
her or she's hiding from him."

"Oh, right, yeah. I did read about that. But didn't the other
husband go abroad somewhere? I think I read he was from the
Netherlands." Daan placed this fact down carefully. He wanted
the child to see sense, even if seeing sense meant losing hope.
It was cruel to let him keep hoping that his stepmother was
alive, because facts had to be faced.

"Yeah. So?"

"Well, how could he have got her out of the country? But

then if he was still hiding her when he went abroad…" Daan broke off, surprised to find that he couldn't bring himself to be more explicit with the boy.

"You think she'd be dead, right, because she'd starve if she was locked up somewhere and he'd skipped the country." Daan winced at the stark, flat reasoning. "She isn't dead, though," repeated Seb. "So I guess she must be hiding."

"But why would she need to hide from him if he's left the country?"

Seb didn't reply. He obviously hadn't asked himself this before. Stubbornly he repeated, "She isn't dead. I would know."

Daan felt like an imposter, a ghoul. He shouldn't be talking with Seb. He wasn't sure what he was hoping to find out from the boy, but the last thing he wanted to discover was this steely determination to believe an improbable thing. It was heartbreaking. He didn't want to encourage the fantasy that she was still alive, but he needed the kid to look in another direction for the killer. The boy needed to be alert. To keep safe.

"Well, I suppose she could be hiding from someone else. She'd know who she was hiding from. Maybe Daan Janssen didn't kidnap her."

Seb didn't answer. "I gotta go. My dad's calling. We're having a barbecue tonight."

17

DAAN

Right now, the app on Daan's mobile is buzzing, informing him that Oli is back online. He tries not to get too excited. This doesn't necessarily mean the boy will stick around if Daan joins the game. Most likely he'll just quit, as has been his way of late. Still, Daan hopes. What has he besides hope? He quickly reaches for his headphones. Fires up the PlayStation. The seconds lost to the blue screen are frustrating. He joins Oli's game and crosses his fingers.

Daan doesn't know the other two players in the game. They are French. Oli tries a few schoolboy phrases to establish whether they speak English. *"Comment allez-vous? Parles-tu anglais?"* His accent is appalling.

The French guys snigger. *"Tu parles français comme une vache espagnole."*

Daan is considerably more fluent than a Spanish cow, but he doesn't feel the need to prove the point. He's annoyed that they are rude to Oli, defensive for him, but he knows better than to openly defend him. No sixteen-year-old appreciates being bailed; it just draws attention to weakness. He's sure Oli will quit the game, embarrassed, but it appears he's made of sterner stuff. Maybe he was going to pack it in when he saw Daan's handle, but he can't now, as it'll look as though the arrogant French boys have scared him away. Instead he makes three kills in quick succession, underscoring his right to his handle, Slayr123. Daan hopes the French boys can't speak English well, too nationalistic to bother with another language; an attitude frequently encountered in both the countries that warred with one another throughout the Middle Ages.

"What's up? Haven't seen you online for a while," he comments. He waits a beat, unsure whether Oli will even bother to reply.

Eventually, after a brief, aggressive and effective gunfire spurt, Oli mumbles, "Nothing. As per."

Daan admires the kid's cool. His mother has been murdered, he is the center of a media storm, there's a global pandemic and his first public exams have just been canceled, and yet he maintains that nothing is happening in his life, as usual. Nerves of steel, emotionally lobotomized or a liar? Daan isn't sure.

"You play with my brother, right?" Oli asks.

Daan wanted the conversation between them to move on but hoped to control the direction; he doesn't know where this is going. Oli asking about the connection with Seb will inevitably lead to some level of unmasking for them both. Is he ready for that? So much seems out of his control nowadays. Since Kai walked in and then out of his life.

"What's his handle?" he asks, playing for time.

"GetWreckedAH."

"Yeah, I think so. Sometimes."

"He's only twelve."

Ah, so maybe this is why Oli has been avoiding Daan. He doesn't suspect him of being his missing stepmother's other husband; he thinks he is a predator. Well, that's a relief, of sorts. "Shit. I didn't realize."

"Really?"

"Well, yeah. I knew he wasn't eighteen or whatever, I thought maybe fifteen."

"You shouldn't play with him. If he asks again, you should refuse his request."

"Right, no problem. All the same to me. Left, left. On your

left." Oli's character is shot in the game. He lies in a pool of blood.

"Res me, res me!" Oli demands to be resuscitated, or resurrected—Daan is not sure what the proper term is. Neither of the French boys responds beyond muttering insults. *"Tête de noeud."*

"Sans-couilles."

It isn't the best move strategically, but Daan realizes that saving Oli in the game might help ingratiate him in real life, so he risks it. He sends his character across the deserted parking lot at speed. He's made himself an open target, but the gamble pays off. Oli mutters, "Cheers."

Once Oli is up and running again, Daan asks, "Why are you being all protective? Is your brother okay? Is there a problem?"

"I just want him off my PlayStation, right. We share it and he's always on it when I want a game."

"Got ya." Daan forces himself to wait. If he probes too obviously, Oli is likely to clam up. It's a matter of pace. They play in silence for a few minutes, the only conversation coming from the French boys, who continue to berate Daan and Oli for their play tactics. Daan is glad that Oli's French isn't up to comprehending their constant haranguing and insults, although he suspects their tone is internationally comprehensible. Oli isn't an idiot. Daan feels uncomfortable. He befriended—if *befriended* is the right word—Oli and Seb because he wants more info on Fiona, but as the weeks have gone by, he's found he feels something more for them. He's sorry for them. He wishes their stepmother was at home with them, but that's never going to happen, so he wishes at least that Oli won't be further humiliated by the mean boys. He doesn't know what to say; all he can think of is complimenting Oli's play. "Nice shot."

"I'm not eighteen either."

"Right." Daan should probably ask how old Oli is, but it seems disingenuous at best, creepy at worst.

"Nor are you." It's an accusation, but stated as a fact. "So how old are you?"

Daan wonders whether he should lie. He decides against it. There's no point; he's unlikely to be believed. Besides, if he's going to get the boy on side, he needs to do so quickly. Time is running out. He has to reveal himself. "I'm thirty-nine."

"Are you a fucking pedo?"

"No." It's not something that should be overly denied or explained.

"I thought you said you were a student."

"I don't think I did."

"But you said you were into peri peri chicken and *Hot Ones*."

"I am."

"Like as an influencer."

"No, I'm certain I didn't say that." Daan was of course subtle. No self-respecting influencer would ever say they were an influencer; he depended on that, talked around the subject and allowed Oli to draw what he wanted from the pauses and inferences.

"So what do you do?"

"At the moment, nothing."

"I know, COVID, blah blah, but I mean usually what do you do? Pre-pandemic."

"I work in the City in London. I'm a banker."

"But you decided to do lockdown with your family? Are your parents like old and sick and stuff?" Daan thinks of his virile father, his energetic, petite mother.

"No, that's not why I'm staying with them."

There's a pause. Daan doesn't see it coming, and afterward he will ask himself if that is going to be his lot in life from now on—not seeing things coming, always being a step behind. Hell, he hopes not. He'd hate that. It's so damned aging.

"You're him, aren't you," says Oli. It's not a question.

"Who?"

"You're her other husband. You're Daan Janssen."

His fingers freeze for a moment. A sniper takes him out. He lies bleeding on the floor. Oli does nothing to resuscitate him. "Yes." Daan dare not breathe.

The French boys are shouting in their own language, demanding to know what is wrong with Slayr123, why he isn't saving his friend. They call him a fuckhead and question his patriotism. *"Qu'est-ce qui ne va pas chez vous, putain de tête?"* They are not prepared to save Daan, though. In disgust, they rage-quit the game. *"Enculé!"*

Daan waits to see if Oli will quit too. He wonders what he can say to influence the situation one way or the other. Then he realizes there is nothing. It's the boy's choice. The constant sound of gunfire pounding through his headset into his brain is beginning to rattle him. The flashing explosions, the yells and footfall jar. He feels sweat bubble on his top lip. He's not usually a man who sweats.

"You must hate me, right?" he says, finally.

"I don't ever think of you," replies Oli. Daan knows this has to be a lie. Maybe the biggest lie the boy has told him so far.

"How did you work out who I am?"

"You sound old and I watched your gaming play pattern. You only play with me or Seb. At first I thought you had to be a shit-scum journalist. You said you were Swedish, but when I asked what tunes you like—besides the mainstream crap that told me you were thirty upward—you mentioned a bunch of bands I'd never heard of like Blackbriar, Heideroosjes and Sinister. I checked them out, thinking they might be cool. They are three bands from the Netherlands, death metal and punk. Weird for a Swede. My mu—Leigh always said people lie about a lot of stuff but not the music they like. She would know, right?" Daan doesn't interrupt, although he would love to know if his wife had kept separate Spotify accounts for Kai and Leigh, the way she had separate wardrobes and husbands. "Then I worked it out. An old Dutch guy. You're the man who murdered her."

There is no noise now, the game is over. The silence is deafening.

"I didn't murder your mum."

"She's not my mum."

"I didn't kill Leigh Fletcher or Kai Janssen, Kylie Gillingham, whatever the hell you want to call her."

"Whatever." Daan thinks the nonchalance has to be fake. Oli challenges, "Why did you track us down? Are you going to kill us too?"

"No! No! Of course not. Why would I do that?" Daan splutters his indignation. "I told you, I didn't kill your mum. I found you because I want you to know that."

"Yeah, but you did," Oli says, flatly.

"No, I didn't," Daan insists.

"I don't fucking care anyway. She didn't love us. She's a bitch."

"She did love you." Daan doesn't refute the bitch part. "Look, it's important you believe me. I want you to know I didn't kill her, because that means whoever did kill her is still out there."

"I don't believe you. You are a weirdo fucking worm that murdered a woman who made a dick out of you and now you're creeping around me and my brother. I'm going to the police."

"Fiona did it," Daan blurts out. "She's living with you, right? You and your brother are not safe."

"That's bullshit."

"I was framed. She framed me."

"You would say that. Anyone would say that."

"Probably, but it's true. Think about it, Oli, you're a clever young man."

"You don't know me. I might be a moron. And don't patronize me. I'm not a young man. I'm a kid." His voice breaks. He's exhausted and frantic.

Daan wishes he could help him. Even more, he wishes that Kai—or more potently for Oli, that Leigh—could wrap her arms around the boy and tell him it is all going to be okay, as she must have done on many other occasions, right? Daan wonders, was she that sort of mother? Kind, comforting, reassuring. He thinks she probably was. She was a kind wife. He'd have said her most compelling characteristics were her sexiness, her wit, the way she offered a challenge, but also, she was simply kind.

He tries again, because he wants to protect his dead wife's kids. "Just let the possibility into your head and then you can decide if you dare to ignore it. If Fiona killed your mother, doesn't she deserve to be punished for it?"

"I don't care who killed Leigh." Oli's voice is flat; he's crushed by pain and loss.

"You do, you must." Daan's voice is high, squeaky; for him, desperation and fear have trumped pain and loss. He needs this boy to understand. "Fiona is a killer. You and your brother are living with a killer."

"You don't think my dad had anything to do with it?"

Daan lets out a deep sigh. He doesn't know whether he should lie or not. Which will the boy best respond to? Which will keep him safest. "It's possible," he admits. "You are in a unique position to find out."

"But why would I do that? You're going down for it. If my dad did have anything to do with it, I don't want to know. We're all okay. He seems happy enough with Fiona, and Leigh lied to us. She was married to you. She was having sex with you for years while pretending to love us."

"Your mother wasn't pretending to love you."

"She's not my mother."

"But she is, Oli. We both know she is. She loved you so much." Daan's voice rasps with the strain of wanting to be believed. "I never saw her with you, but I know better than anyone in the world how much she loved you."

"That makes no fucking sense."

"I offered her everything, Oli. *Everything*, do you understand? A penthouse apartment in one of the best properties in London. It has a pool and a gym; you should see the views. I gave her a life of ease and wealth, where she socialized with the great and the good: actors, artists, politicians and journalists, the people who are zeitgeist." Dan is speaking quickly, not sure how much time Oli will give him. "I gave her an elegant extended family who liked and admired her. She had a life of unfettered joy, free from hardships and responsibilities, full of beautiful clothes, shoes and handbags. You know how women like shoes and handbags, right? But guess what? She couldn't leave you. If it had just been a choice between me and your dad, I'd have won. There is no doubt in my mind she loved you and your brother more than anything."

"Piss off." Oli quits, and Daan is left alone with the tragic truth of what he's just admitted.

18

STACIE

It's crazy to be unnerved by an old woman with dementia, but I set off back to the cottage at pace. What did she mean? *You are the dead woman.* Well, nothing, obviously—she has dementia—but still it's a weird thing to say. The gaps are gnawing at me now. Initially all I thought was important was surviving cancer, living. But now I feel defined by my absence rather than my presence, and it's creating intense anxiety. I am exhausted with trying to work out who I am. I should not be unnerved by the ramblings of an old woman, but I am, because I'm a house built on sand; there are no foundations. At any moment I could crumble to dust. The days without knowing who I am have turned into weeks, months, and it's terrifying.

As I dash home, I try to repeat my usual ritual that I use to calm myself. Normally I recall what I do know. General knowledge, facts about history, politics or popular culture. But that's not adequate today, and I realize I have been kidding myself pretending that it is enough to help. Instead, more ephemeral memories start to jump into my head. The few shadowy possibilities—things I dismissed as false memories or impossible dreams—jostle for attention, demanding I face them once again.

The ginger-scented bath, rich and luxurious. The expensive dresses, carelessly discarded. The sex that left me helpless, quivering. The blond man responsible for said sex. The grave that I hate. The children that I love. The garden, full of flowers and hope. The other man, silently pleading for help but also throwing me a lifeline. I sense that. It wasn't a one-way thing. Who are they all, and where are they now? I want to pull out my hair, slam my hands against my stupid head to somehow force some focus through the quagmire of these half-memories. I don't know what is real.

The sky seems to be reflecting my unsettled mood. It's looking ominous; dense engorged clouds are being buffeted by the intensifying wind, and after the weeks of sunshine, it feels especially mean and taunting. Rain starts to fall and slices into my body at right angles; it feels as though sharp needles are being thrown at me. I run the last fifty meters with my head down and so I simply barrel into him. The shock of the physical contact makes me freeze. I haven't touched anyone for months, other than the occasional hug or arm squeeze from my dad. This body is stout, and if not quite firm, then certainly substantial. I feel the soft cotton of his T-shirt against my cheek and the slip of the nylon of his waterproof jacket as I automatically reach for his arms to steady myself. I can smell the detergent his clothes have been washed in, and there is an intimacy. Unexpected and fleeting, but absolute. I feel dizzy. Our eyes meet.

Giles Hughes.

I know him instantly. His clear, bright eyes, his easy smile, his ruddy cheeks. Features that combine to make him look like a children's TV presenter; kind, in control. I wait a beat.

"Sorry, sorry, wasn't looking where I was going," I babble. I'm embarrassed, but also so delighted that I know him that I think I might fling my arms around him in relief.

"Turned awful, hasn't it?" He doesn't seem to expect an answer. His hood is pulled down low and he's barely glanced at me. He starts to stride on. Then he spots Ronnie and pauses. He glances at me again, obviously placing me now that he's recognized the dog. I try not to be offended by that.

"Hi, Giles." I smile. He squints at me, pulls his face into an expression of surprise. "Yup, it's me, Stacie," I say with faux brightness that I hope hides some awkwardness. I *recognized* him. This is really exciting for me. I want to gush and tell him so, but realize that it might be a bit much. There's a ring on his left hand; he's unlikely to welcome the news that he's the only person I've placed since my operation. It is a lot to load onto a person.

He steps further back, widening the distance between us. "Evening," he mutters. Then he abruptly turns, dashes off, head down against the wind and rain.

I watch his bent back as he shrinks on the horizon. I want to talk to him some more, but this isn't the moment. The rain is pouring, a ferocious surprise of a summer storm; I'm quickly going to be wet through to my underwear, so I sprint in the opposite direction from Giles's disappearing figure, toward Dad's welcoming cottage.

When I explode into the kitchen, the back door swings on its hinges, the gusting wind making it crash against the wall. It feels like the entire building shakes. Dad is so startled that he nearly drops the bottle of red wine he's opening.

"Oh my God, I need that," I say, practically snatching the glass from him even as he's still pouring wine into it. I glug it back like water and then hold it out to him for a refill.

"Steady," he says, and smiles. "Remember you're on medication." It's a well-meant observation, but I hate it when Dad monitors my alcohol consumption. He often mentions that the doctors say I have to "take things steady." I glower at him. "What's up?" he asks.

"I've just bumped into Giles Hughes."

Dad stares at me. And waits. "You recognized him?"

"I did!" I grin, and Dad gets it. He beams right back at me. This is momentous. "Can't say it was exactly the warm reunion I might have hoped for from the very first person I recognized, but I guess I can't expect that from him. There's obviously going to be some embarrassment between us, and the storm and everything didn't help."

"What did he say to you?"

"Not much; he mentioned the weather." I laugh at the Englishness of this. The ordinariness of it. An embarrassed ex taking refuge in small talk. It seems so normal, and as I'm generally very far from that state, it feels like a delightful relief.

Dad laughs too. "He never was much of a conversationalist." We beam at one another and clink glasses.

"It has really cheered me up. That Prue McCullen freaked me out."

"Why?"

"Oh, nothing. I decided to speak to her, but it was a mistake. She was rambling. What she said didn't make sense."

"Put her out of your head. Poor woman. As I said, she's not well. So sad." Dad sympathetically dismissing Prue McCullen and not lending her any credence is just what I need. He always knows how to cheer me, what to say. "Go and get some dry PJs on. I'll dig out some crisps."

It's a good night. After I change into pajamas and towel-dry my hair, we settle down to a game of cards. I feel buoyant that I recognized Giles, and it seems that consequently something in my mind has melted, relaxed. Or maybe that can be attributed to the fact that Dad and I drink the best part of two bottles of wine. At the end of the evening, I throw the bottles in the recycling bin and swill the glasses under the tap. Not exactly a wash, more of a cat's lick. Who said that? My grandfather? Yes, I'm sure it was. I can hear his voice. I feel the weight of lowering a frying pan into sudsy water, then lifting it out again almost immediately and far from clean. He gently ribs my efforts at washing up, but I'm very young so he's not criticizing; there's a sense that he admires that I've tried. Classical music is playing in the background.

"Did your father live with us when I was a child?" I ask Dad.

"No."

"Oh, I thought I remembered him. A grandfather, my grandfather."

Dad pauses, then smiles. "He visited in the holidays, though."

"Okay, that will be it. I remember him." I beam.

"What do you remember about him?"

"I liked him." I can't visualize my grandfather and I don't recall Dad showing me any photos of him, but I feel a sense of warmth and safety seeping through my body at the thought of him. "Like you, he enjoyed a fried breakfast, right?"

"Who doesn't." Dad waits to see if I have anything more to offer up. Retrieving a memory is like pulling on a cobweb thread. Gossamer thin. He doesn't want to yank at it, cause it to snap.

Though that's all I have, I meet his eyes and smile. "Things are starting to come back to me."

"It seems that way."

I go to bed with a mix of excitement and relief. The night before Super Saturday shimmers. I think there must be millions of people up and down the country lying in a pool of anticipation. Excited at the pull of pubs and restaurants opening, the possibility of meeting people from outside their own household, seeing old friends again. Yet I suspect very few of them are as hopeful or eager as I am. The prospect of seeing faces that might trigger memories and allow everything to fall back into place is making me giddy. I know Dad wants me to be cautious and continue shielding, but I'm not sure how I'll resist hunting people out.

I fall asleep knowing that Super Saturday will allow me to find some answers.

SATURDAY
4 JULY 2020

19

OLI

The train is packed. Like there's not a spare bit of space to move in. They are lucky to have seats; some people are standing. Mostly groups of older teens who are rowdy and drinking beer from cans even though it's only early morning. It's so hot some of these lads have taken off their shirts and Oli can smell their sweat. As usual, he tries to avoid looking at other teenagers, especially older ones; that would be asking for trouble, something he really doesn't need to do. Trouble obviously finds him. There are families too. Mums and dads with their kids with cheerfully colored backpacks stuffed with activity packs and Tupperware boxes of treats. Oli doesn't like looking at them either.

The entire crappy world seems to have decided to go to Lyme Regis, home to famous Georgian fossil collector and paleontologist Mary Anning. The words just tumble in his head. That's what Leigh always said when she mentioned Lyme Regis: *home to famous Georgian fossil collector and paleontologist Mary Anning.* She recited it in a little singsong voice. It was one of those funny (not very funny) family things that all families have. They'd all join in like a chorus; at least they did when they were younger. Now he thinks that was a bit pathetic. A dead woman fascinated with things that had died millions of years before her. Boring. Still, the tourist board make as much of it as they can, naturally. That and cream teas.

They visited here often. Yeah, over the past few years, since Fiona bought a holiday home here; but even before then, they came all the time, because Leigh said it had everything a family needed for a holiday. The sea, a beach, ice cream shops, boats and a sub-four-hour door-to-door journey, whether by train or car. She said it was ideal. Funny that Fiona chose to buy a holiday home here. Did she also love the Dorset coast, or did she do it to please Leigh? To keep Leigh close? Keep them all close? Oli doesn't know. The thoughts buzz around his head, unsettling and creating a tightness in his mind that he can't grapple with. It's like reading an English comprehension exercise at school. There's a sense that something is just a bit out of his reach, layered and perplexing. He's never thought about Fiona's motivation to buy a holiday home before. He just thought it was great that they could always go to Auntie Fi's on every school holiday. His life used to be so simple.

Leigh really had a thing for Mary Anning; she was always going on about her independent thinking and how hard it was for her in a man's world. Annoying stuff like that. Blah blah blah. Yeah, he got it. In hindsight, Leigh was stifled, Leigh wasn't happy. Well, fuck off, Leigh, because no one is happy now. Every time he thinks of her, he feels hot with fury and sick with sadness. He hates her, and he hates her most for being dead.

Seb has to be reminiscing too, possibly longing for simpler times, because he asks, "Do you remember that year when it rained and rained all week and the holiday was total rubbish and so Mum dressed up as Mary Anning and went on the beach to look for fossils?" Oli keeps his gaze above his brother's head but nods, a reluctant acknowledgment of the comment, of the memory. "That was so funny. Everyone came out on the beach, like from the other houses, didn't they? People were cheered up. Laughing and joining in." Seb's eyes are shining and Oli hates it. Hates his hope, hates his grief. Hates that his baby brother is stuck between the two things. "She kept saying Mary Anning wouldn't have been put off by a bit of bad weather. Mere drizzle. It was not drizzle. She was drenched! I wonder where she got that costume," Seb muses.

"The charity shop."

"What?"

"Don't you remember? She dragged us in there and got us to help her find the bits she needed; that was all part of the game. She bought a black blouse, a long black skirt, an old-fashioned apron thing." Oli remembers her eager face as she pounced on the apron, surprised by the perfect suitability of the find. *This is just the thing!* It kills him that he recalls this, but he does. His mum—Leigh—was determined to create some fun for them. He was about nine years old at the time. Young enough to be excited by her nutty enthusiasm for doing odd things. Of course, that was before she met Daan Janssen, before she went a step too far in terms of eccentricity and following the beat of her own drum, et cetera. Bitch.

Oli looks out of the train window and focuses on the countryside whizzing by. The trees look an especially dazzling green after months of seeing nothing other than the dull grays of buildings and roads. He can't wait to be outside in the fresh air. The closeness of other people's bodies is making him anxious. Not because of the COVID thing; he doesn't really care about all that, kids aren't getting sick from it anyway—it is an old-people problem. His angst about how close everyone is to him and Seb is that people are untrustworthy fuckers, all of them. At the station and when they were boarding the train, he kept reaching for Seb's arm and pulling him close. Scared that his brother was somehow going to be snatched away. He wishes they were younger and he could hold his hand, or younger still and he could have him in those training reins that some parents keep their toddlers on. He wishes he could strap Seb to his back. Fucking swallow him whole or something, just to keep him close and always know where he is.

Fuck, that's mad.

He is losing his mind.

Oli rubs his eye sockets with the heels of his hands. His breathing is too fast, his palms are sweating. Seb doesn't seem to notice; he is just so thrilled that he's been invited along.

Oli doesn't think Fiona is a killer. That is mad. Just mad. She makes them chili con carne in tacos. Still, Leigh was also a good cook and a bigamist at the same time. Culinary skills don't rule out being a total bitch. The whole thing is such a head-fuck. He is exhausted by it. And frightened. He just needs to get away from them for a bit. From the house that holds Leigh's ghost in every corner, from his dad and his stupid depression, from Fiona and whatever threat she might be. Obviously, even the slightest possibility that Fiona killed Leigh meant he couldn't leave Seb in London; he couldn't leave him alone. He wouldn't let Seb wake up and find him gone. Not him too.

Honestly, Oli doesn't have much of a plan at all, beyond keeping Seb safe. Seb is extra. He'll slow things down and ask a lot of questions. He will go on and on about being hungry or thirsty or hot or cold or tired. He's like that; he thinks his physical comfort is of interest to everyone and so always gives a running commentary. Leigh used to encourage that crap, pander to it, strive to fix it by having a constant stream of snacks and drinks and layers of clothes. Seb should now get used to the idea that his updates on his bodily comfort are of interest to precisely no one.

This morning, Oli woke up literally at the crack of dawn to a chorus of birds squawking and crowing outside his open window. Birdsong is supposed to herald happiness at the start of a new day, but the noise sounded more like an alarm bell—disturbing, like the wail of an ambulance siren. He packed them a bag with food and drink, suncream, caps, because although he doesn't want to pander to Seb, he can sort of see what Leigh was doing all these years—just, like, making things easier. He packed their passports too. He has no intention of going abroad, couldn't even if he wanted to, but it never hurts to have your passport with you. If he needs to speak to the police, for example, he'll have to prove who he is. Look, that's not his plan. He doesn't expect things to turn out that way.

He sneaked into Seb's room and gently shook him awake. He held his hand over his brother's mouth so he couldn't yell out any surprised questions, then put a finger to his own lips. Seb nodded his understanding. Eyes wide, he quickly, quietly hopped out of bed. Oli threw a T-shirt and a pair of shorts at him, whispered that he had to keep completely silent as he got dressed. Downstairs, they found their dad asleep on the sofa bed in the living room. They crept past him, eased open the front door. Left. Oli only let Seb put on his trainers at that point, then they rode their bikes to the station. They pedaled fast. Got on a train to Axminster. It never crossed Oli's mind to leave a note.

"Are we looking for her?" Seb asks. Pathetically hopeful.

It annoys Oli.

"No. She's dead."

Seb shakes his head a fraction, the way he does every time anyone tells him this, or even implies it. An act of defiance, or maybe just shaking off what he doesn't want to hear. "So why are we here?" he asks as they finally dismount at Axminster station.

They stand on the small platform as everyone around them streams with purpose and certainty one way or the other, toward town, the taxi rank or a bus. Oli is frozen. Usually Leigh drove them to Lyme Regis, but they have been to this station before, a few times. Sometimes they would head to the coast by train if Fiona was already staying in her second home, then she'd pick them up from the station in her car. Other times, the three of them would take a cab to her place when it was empty, and then their dad would join them at the weekend, bringing the car. If he is honest with himself, Oli has to admit they have had great holidays here; holidays where they visited the Jurassic play park, rode on the Seaton tramway, searched for fossils, mucked about on Fiona's little boat and then warmed up again by drinking hot chocolate and feasting on salty chips. He allows himself to recall these happy days. Sometimes with his dad. Sometimes with Fiona. Always with Leigh.

"Think of it as a holiday," he tells Seb. The station empties out; crowded buses full of excited families pull away. The longed-for space now seems too much. The boys feel deserted. The familiar place made unfamiliar without a guide or a waiting lift.

"Dad is going to kill you," mutters Seb.

"You think? I think they'll like having the place to themselves."

"So they can shag and he doesn't have to sleep downstairs pretending they're not." Seb is trying to sound nonchalant and unconcerned; he fails on both counts when he turns pink. Oli is aware that they are starring in their own grim fairy tale. It has all the elements—they are alone, they have an indifferent father, a wicked stepmother, it's the classic setup. He just isn't sure which woman is the wicked stepmother.

He isn't sure either why he's come here, what he's hoping to find. Not Leigh. He knows she's dead; unlike Seb, he's accepted as much, and he knows that the police have already searched Fiona's property for clues, for a body. They didn't find a body. So what is it that he's looking for?

"I think we'll find her here," says Seb confidently.

Oli pities him. And sort of admires him at the same time.

They both gaze around the empty station. It's a hot day, but a wind is blowing through, buffeting them. Across the road is a builders' yard and a giant pet store. There's a supermarket a hundred meters away. These are solid, normal things that should offer some level of reassurance; they are not in a different world. They are not in the same one either. Oli takes a deep breath, fills his lungs with the country air, checks the bus timetable, then fishes out a ham sandwich from his bag and hands it to Seb. They wait fifteen minutes and then hop on the next yellow bus, which takes them into town.

"I can see the sea," mumbles Seb as they approach Lyme

Regis. Oli nods, acknowledging the long-established game they've always played.

What the hell is he doing here? What is he hoping to find?

20

STACIE

I just can't resist. I know Dad is concerned about shielding, so I plump for the path of least resistance. I don't tell him I've decided to go into town. But how can I not go, after the breakthroughs yesterday: recognizing Giles, remembering my grandfather? I'm on a roll! Damned COVID has stolen enough from me—and everyone, come to that. I have to seize the opportunity of doing everything I can to maximize my chances of remembering more as soon as possible, which means I have to take myself to familiar places, hopefully meet more people who know me.

My plan is that when Dad takes Ronnie for a walk, I'll grab my backpack and set off along the road. I won't take the beach route, because I'd have to pass him. It seems a little cloak-and-dagger, considering I'm a grown woman in my late thirties. I should perhaps simply stand up to Dad and tell him this is what I need to do, but somehow having cancer and more specifically losing my memory has temporarily infantilized me.

It's only as I am leaving the house that it crosses my mind that I don't have any money. I haven't had use for a handbag, wallet or bank cards during lockdown. Going into town without a bean isn't a sensible move. I need enough to buy a cold drink and maybe lunch, depending on how long I'm there. The past months of rummaging through drawers and cupboards means that I know where to find some loose change. I unearth eight pound coins and pick up a tenner that's been propped behind the mantelpiece clock for weeks. That's plenty.

It's a hot day, and although it's not even 9:00 a.m., the air feels still and sticky, the tarmac on the road shimmers. I've brought an Ordnance Survey map with me, because while the countryside feels generally known to me, I'm not totally certain of the exact route into town. This is galling, as I obviously must have done it hundreds of times before. The roads are narrow, room for only one car at a time. Mother Nature has flexed her muscles during lockdown, and a number of robust tree branches—gangly, bold and verdant—reach, bend and drip over the road, causing the few cars that are trundling this way to swerve and dodge. Grasses growing from the verges whip my legs, and I have to keep vigilant to avoid stinging nettles.

According to the OS map, the journey into town is just over four miles. I don't come across any other pedestrians; this route is the most direct, but it isn't as picturesque as the beach and field trails, and not many people opt to travel this way on foot. A few cars pass me, and there are slightly hair-raising moments every time a bus trundles by and I need to swiftly scramble onto the bank at the side of the road, but all in all the walk is a success; it has an undeniable sense of excitement and independence to it.

As I approach Lyme Regis, my excitement builds. I feel I am being wrapped in a huge welcoming hug; the town is perfectly, reassuringly familiar. I see the sea. I recognize the stone walls, the curve of the road and the Georgian and Victorian houses, most of them white but some painted lemon or blue, the same shade as sugared almonds. The joy I feel causes my heart to speed up a little. I approach from Langmoor Close and am delighted as I correctly predict that there is a bookshop on my right and a fudge shop on my left. Knowing what to expect to see is wonderfully reassuring. My constant anxiety and sense of isolating uncertainty recedes a little.

It's a small town, but made to feel bigger today because it's rammed with joyful tourists. They move like bees swarming around a hive, industrious, purposeful. Dad was right to be concerned about social distancing; it's impossible to keep, so I wear my mask. Many other people do the same, as face coverings are required indoors and those who are popping in and out of shops presumably can't be bothered with repeatedly putting them on and taking them off. I, like almost everyone else, migrate toward the coast. I suppose a lot of these people will have come from inland towns and cities and are desperate for a paddle. I've had the luxury of being by the seaside throughout, but head in that direction anyway, hoping that there will be more opportunity to spread out on the beach than there is on the streets. Then I can make a plan as to how best utilize my time here.

The moment I see the beach, I realize my mistake at thinking there would be more space; every spare inch seems to be covered with a picnic blanket, a windshield, a deck chair. I drink in the sight of groups of buoyant teens, loved-up couples and families, nuclear and extended, sprawled over the pebbles, laughing, chatting, flirting, reading, bickering, sulking, shouting and even—in one case—singing. Dogs are barking, music is blaring from people's phones and speakers; the place teems with life. Over and over again I am reassured by things I find familiar: the mini golf, the amusements and the antiques center. I recognize the Dinosaurland Fossil Museum, although I can't think it's likely I've been there since I was a child. Coming out today was the right thing. I feel confident that my memory is going to return to me. It would most likely have done so before now if only we'd been living in a more usual way. The absolute isolation of these past few months has hampered my rediscovery.

I realize that milling around with the ice-cream-eating populace is not necessarily the best use of my time. I thought I'd pop in and out of shops to see if any of the staff recognize me. However, as masks are necessary and it seems many of the shops are staffed by teens, I'm not sure that plan is likely to be fruitful. I decide to visit the library to use their internet. I'm ready to look up my Facebook and Instagram accounts. The thought sends adrenaline carousing through my body. The idea of discovering more about who I am is like unwrapping the ultimate surprise gift.

21

STACIE

The library is an oblong redbrick building, most likely built in the 1970s. I don't have to check on a map to know where it is. I am able to recall its location, which sends a little thrill through me. I imagine I spent hours here as a child.

There are three mothers with children waiting outside in a queue. One of them turns to me and explains that there is currently a system that allows just two families inside at a time, "to keep everyone safe." I resist commenting that nothing can really keep us safe—how could I have avoided cancer?—and instead nod with what I hope looks like understanding. She glances at her watch and sighs, a theatrical display of impatience. "Closes at twelve thirty, though, so I hope Naomi Thomas and her mob aren't going to be much longer. Hogging all the books, hogging all the time."

Naomi Thomas. I play the name around in my head to see if it's by chance one I recognize.

"Bleedin' von Trapps," the woman goes on. "Five kids between the ages of fifteen and five. One more than the queen, just to make a point. Although I can't imagine what lockdown must have been like in their house." She sniggers, obviously delighted at the thought of someone else's domestic trials.

This woman has just one child with her, a girl aged about seven who is sitting on the grass nearby, contentedly making a daisy chain, leaving her mother the job of keeping a space in the queue.

"I'm not being funny, me and Naomi have known each other since school, so obviously I'm saying this with affection, but my God, she makes a huge deal of everything." She rolls her eyes in mock despair.

I nod, trying to show a polite interest. I'm not sure what the normal response might be to this sort of gossip. Somehow it feels familiar. I think it's a universal default setting: one mother gossiping about another to a third party. I believe it happens at every school gate; I must know this from my teaching. I didn't realize the model might be re-created anywhere. The thought of a supposedly innocuous queue outside a library oozing entrenched rivalry somehow exhausts me. Still, what can I do other than let the woman talk?

"This is her first time outside our village since lockdown began. She took the stay-local thing to heart. Scowled at other people's kids if they were out longer than the hour of permitted exercise. Daft bitch. Some say she's a paragon of virtue, the best mum in Williton Cross. I let my Violet play outside all day if she wants. Fresh air is good for them."

"I'm from Williton Cross," I interrupt excitedly. "Well, close by. I went to primary school there. My dad lives by the sea." I am surprised and delighted at the connection. "Stacie Jones." I pull off my mask and beam.

For a moment, this woman stares at me blankly; then her entire face shifts into a wide-eyed expression of astonishment.

"Oh my God, Stacie! I haven't seen you for years. It's me, Tanya. Tanya Vaughan. Well, Tanya Cundliff now. Has been for eight years. Name lasted longer than the marriage. How are you? Didn't you go abroad?"

"Yes. Paris."

"Oh my God, yes, you jilted Giles Hughes, didn't you? Talk of the town, that was!" She laughs as though this is the funniest thing she has ever heard. I feel a small flare of irritation reverberate through my body, but I let it go. I'm just so thrilled to be with someone who knows me. I chase her name around my head, hoping it will spark something, as Tanya starts to give me a potted history of her life since we last met. She met an "out-of-towner," got pregnant, got married, got divorced. "There's been a few fellas since, but they all turn out to be bastards in the end, don't they?"

Like everyone, Tanya must have been short of company over the past few months and has forgotten the art of conversation, where not only is one person supposed to inquire after the other, but they're also meant to wait for a response. Instead, she rambles on about herself. I don't mind. It's great to be inside someone else's head for a while.

After about ten minutes straight of Tanya speaking, an elderly woman leaves the library and it's Tanya's turn to go inside.

"Bloody Naomi is still in there. No doubt picking out the classics and pushing them at her kids. For all her hopes for Mother of the Decade award, she's oblivious to the fact that her eldest smokes weed in the bus shelter."

Tanya winks at me and then disappears into the building. I want to keep talking to her, and hope to take her phone number, but she's in and out before Naomi Thomas and her brood emerge. The strict one-way system means we can only wave at one another. I have to go inside or lose my place. I look forward to the opportunity to connect with Naomi, but I'm disappointed that once inside, we're kept at a distance from one another by an officious school-age volunteer librarian.

It takes a bit of negotiating to be allowed to use the library computer. One librarian says it's simply not possible, not hygienic. A second suggests plastic gloves would be the answer and says she has a pair in her handbag. "What on earth are you doing with a pair of plastic gloves in your bag?" asks the first.

"They come with the kit for dyeing your hair, but I never bother with wearing them, I thought they might come in useful. Proper boy scout I am."

I gratefully don the gloves and excitedly turn on the computer. My optimism is immediately tested when I search my name. There are over four hundred Stacie Jones profiles on LinkedIn, seventy registered in the UK People Directory—192. com, and countless Instagram and Facebook members with my name. I take some consolation in the fact that it's a name for winners, clearly, because there are pages of articles about Stacie Joneses throughout the world. The various incarnations include (although are not limited to) women in the film industry with IMDb entries, a famous basketball player, a professor of pediatrics at the University of Arkansas, a VP of exploration at Golden Planet Mining Corp and the star of the second season of NBC's *The Apprentice*. This Stacie Jones has a jewelry and accessories range; apparently it's doing very well.

My own achievements have of course been significantly more modest. I'm not expecting to feature in news articles; the searches on social media are going to be most fruitful for me. It's a blow, therefore, when I can't access the Stacie Jones profiles on Facebook, Twitter or Instagram because I'm not registered on any social media; or rather, I'm sure I am, but I don't recall my passwords. I go through a frustrating process—if I had any hair, I would most certainly be pulling it out—as I try to guess at the passwords that will give me access to my accounts. I eventually admit defeat and so try to reregister. This is an equally confusing and complicated process, because every time I try to make a new account, I'm reliably informed that I already have one and am asked for my password—the passwords I can't remember. I go around in a Dante's hell of ever-decreasing vicious circles, clicking on pictures of bridges and traffic lights to prove I'm not a robot. I finally set up my new Instagram account just as the sweet librarian who gave me her plastic gloves says she's very sorry but the library must close. "We do a half day on Saturday."

"But I'm just getting somewhere," I groan.

"You can come back on Monday, dear. Can I suggest you write down your passwords somewhere? I know they advise us not to, but I've watched you struggle. I've a terrible memory, so I sympathize."

I nod and write down the password for the Instagram account I've just managed to open, without bothering to go into details as to exactly how terrible my memory is and why. I also don't confide my belief that my dad will veto any more trips to the town until they've discovered a cure, or at least a vaccine, for this virus. Of course I'm exaggerating, but I do believe he might be a bit noncompliant. I'm itching to start searching all the Stacie Joneses and find my old account. The idea that relatively recent photos of my friends and possibly lovers are just a few clicks away is so infuriating. I know I'm close to discovering who I truly am, getting my memories back. I feel it.

Just as I'm leaving, I impulsively check. "Can I take a book out?" At least with a loaned book, and the threat of a fine if it's not returned hanging over my head, I might have an excuse to come back into town.

"Are you a member of the library, dear?"

"I was, a long time ago. I think my membership will have lapsed."

"Well, let's have a look, shall we. What's your name?"

I tell her my name and address and she types it into the computer behind the desk. "Yes, here you are, we have you." I feel a surprising sense of delight, and relief too. "Oh, you're Kenneth's girl, aren't you?" I can see the wheels turning in her head. She beams at me. "Oh, my dear, I am so happy to see you doing well." I realize Dad must be friends with this woman and she is aware I've had cancer. "Of course you must take a book. You can have up to four. You go and pick and I'll start wiping down the tables and chairs. It's just so wonderful to see you well." She pauses, her face flooded with sympathy. I wonder what my chances of recovery were, whether my father ever sadly speculated with his friends about whether I would survive the big C. The librarian reaches out and squeezes my gloved fingers.

Moved by this intimacy, I blurt, "Did we know each other before? You know, when I was a child." She looks confused.

I point to my head. "I can't remember everything clearly," I explain.

"No, love, I only moved to Lyme four years ago. We've never met before." I nod. "Do give my best to your dad, won't you. I'm so glad you came home eventually. He's missed you so much. Dreadful circumstances, obviously, but so nice to have you back in the community, Stacie."

22

SEB

It has been sort of a good day. They are at least doing something. After months of doing nothing, Seb feels the relief of this. Oli keeps saying he isn't looking for their mum, but obviously he is, because why else are they here, in the town center where *living* people are? If she was dead, her body wouldn't just be lying around Lyme Regis. That's just stupid, someone would have found her by now. So they're not looking for a dead body.

Anyway, if she was dead, Seb would know. He's sure of it.

He misses his mum so much that he feels a hole inside his body. He aches from the inside out. It feels like he's a Halloween pumpkin and he's been hollowed out. His innards are probably lying in a big gloopy mess somewhere. That's stupid. He knows it. He's just saying, it's how it feels. He can't tell anyone that. Can't explain it without sounding like a pathetic kid. He could have told his mum, if she was here. She understood him when he tried to explain complicated things like that, and she never laughed at him. It's embarrassing that he misses her so much. He knows she lied to them all and liars are bad people. She was always telling him not to tell lies. Yet she was a liar. He knows that but he misses her anyway. Oli says he doesn't miss her but that just makes Oli a liar too, because he has to miss her. Maybe he's lying to Seb or to himself, but he's definitely lying. People do.

Oli keeps talking about going to Fi's house.

"Do you think Mum will be there?" Seb asks.

Oli sighs. "No, because she's dead."

Seb turns away from his brother, looks out at the sea. He hates it when Oli does that. He doesn't think his mum is at Fi's house, because the police have been there already and she'd know it was being watched. If she is hiding, that would be the last place to go, so he isn't in any rush to get there either. He doesn't want to leave the town yet. He feels close to his mum here; the memory of her and the possibility of her.

"We could walk there; it's a few miles up the coast," says Oli. He looks doubtful, though, as neither of them are big fans of walking. They both used to hate their mum and dad's enthusiasm for a Sunday afternoon walk to "settle lunch."

"Yeah, but there's the really steep bit at the end," points out Seb. It is a sticky, hot day. At the end of the route, they'd have to do a basic rock climb. He can't imagine how they're going to do that. To discourage Oli from that plan, he adds, "Probably, if we go there, Dad and Fiona will be waiting for us."

Oli considers this. "Maybe we'll just stay in town tonight. Get a room somewhere."

"How would we pay for that?" asks Seb.

"I've got money."

"Where from?"

"A friend gave me it."

"Which friend?"

"Shut up, Seb." Seb tries not to appear hurt by the curt dismissal, but he probably doesn't do a good job, because Oli looks impatient and regretful at the same time, then offers, "You hungry? Shall we get some fish and chips?"

They sit on the pebbles, facing out to sea, and gobble down the hot, greasy, vinegary food; they don't bother using the little wooden forks that have been provided. Then they agree that an ice cream is needed. There is a shop that sells about a million flavors; over the years they have tried them all and established that cookies and cream is Oli's favorite, mint choc chip is Seb's. Today, though, they can't be bothered with the queue that snakes right around the corner, so they buy cones from the van, which has a slightly shorter queue. They also have a cream scone each and buy some sweets. Oli pays for everything with a quick tap of his bank card.

Most of the afternoon they spend on the beach. Everyone around them has brought beach towels. Oli remembered suncream but not towels. The pebbles are uncomfortable, but it doesn't matter; neither of them tries to lie back and sleep or read, the way the people around them are. Both of them sit bolt upright, alert. Oli is staring out at the horizon. Seb is more interested in who is on the packed beach. His eyes scurry across the tangles of families, the clusters of people tightly crammed together as he looks for her.

When the heat of the afternoon starts to slacken and the first whisper of evening approaches, they move on to a café where they can buy Cokes and then sit at a table outside. The table wobbles, but Seb likes the view. The café is on Broad Street, perched above the Marine Parade. He glances about. The streets are as busy as the beach, even now. People walk up and down, dragging their flip-flopped feet, directionless but just glad to be out. It might be better if it hadn't been quite so hot today. Fewer people would mean she would have been easier to spot. Seb feels sweat under his baseball cap, but he keeps it on, because the peak allows him to look around better.

"Who gave you the money?" he asks for the second time that day. He has been thinking about it and can't imagine any of Oli's friends handing over cash, let alone transferring funds into his account. Grandparents do that and his dad and mum. No one else just gives you money. Why would they?

"None of your business."

Usually, if Oli says something like this, Seb accepts the close-down, doesn't dare fight him, but things aren't usual between them. They are more like partners now—partners in crime, as they've run away together—so he persists. "Tell me." The condensation on his Coke glass glints in the amber glow of the sinking sun, but his throat feels dry and scratchy.

Oli sighs. "Daan Janssen."

It takes Seb a moment to place the name. "Her other husband? That knob?"

"Yeah."

Seb feels his skin prickle as though he's been stung. "How do you know him? How has he given you money? Isn't he in prison?"

"He's still in the Netherlands. He's on bail, so he's allowed to live at home." Oli pauses and then adds, "You know him too. You're talking to him."

"I am not." Seb is furious to be accused of this. He'd never talk to that man. He hates him. That man stole their mother.

"He's Golden Warlord."

"What?" But the outraged one-word question is hardly out of his mouth before he comprehends. People are never who they say they are, least of all online. Teachers are always going on about stranger danger on the internet. He is stunned that he hasn't made the connection before. "Why did he give you money? Do you know something, has he paid you to keep quiet?" Seb's eyes widen in panic. "Oli, if you know something you *have* to tell the police. No matter how much he's paying you."

"No, I don't know anything. Least, I don't *know* know anything."

"So why did he give you money?"

"He wants me to find things out. He says he didn't do it."

"And you believe him?"

"No, not really, but I don't *not* believe him." This is where the boys sit a lot of the time now, in a quagmire of uncertainty. "Anyway, what does it matter if I believe him or not? He's a rich twat, right? Free money. He owes us a holiday, wouldn't you say?" Oli shrugs. "When he asked me to help prove his innocence, I told him I couldn't go anywhere or do anything as I'm just a kid and can't afford it. He got the hint. He asked for my Monzo number and sent money."

"When? When did all this happen?"

"Last night...well, this morning. I texted him at about 4:00 a.m." No one is getting much sleep.

"What does he want you to look for? How are you supposed to prove his innocence?"

Oli shrugs again. "Dunno."

"So why did you come here?"

"Dunno."

"There must be a reason," Seb insists, infuriated with his brother for not letting him in, not quite. Oli is scared. It doesn't help Seb knowing this, but he's his brother, he knows everything about him. Like different branches of the same tree or something. He did that in French at school, had to draw a family tree. It was just a stupid way to remember *grand-mère*, but also it wasn't totally stupid, because it made Seb think how he and Oli are connected and always will be, even when Oli says things like he wishes Seb hadn't been born or had been born without a tongue, something he says fairly often. Seb knows Oli is scared because of the way he holds himself. Sort of stiff, as tall as possible. He juts out his chin purposefully and repeatedly brushes his hair off his face, and he glowers as though he wants to see more, stare extra hard, spot anything that might be heading their way. As if. They never saw any of this coming.

Oli is definitely hiding something. "Nope, just a holiday really. Something to do." He stands up abruptly, reaches for his mask. "I'm going inside for a pee. Don't move." What a stupid thing to say, thinks Seb, where would he go?

He recognizes her instantly. It is so weirdly perfect and stupidly unexpected at the same time that he finds himself acting like someone off a comedy TV show; he literally jumps up from his seat. He jolts the table, and one of the empty glasses that held Coke wobbles over.

"Mum! Mum!" he screams, really loudly. Loads of people look his way. They probably think he is just some overdramatic kid saving a table for his mother and trying to get her attention. The glass rolls to the edge of the table and then falls to the ground; it smashes, and the slivers of glass skitter across the cobbles. There is a dog under the table next to them; its owners look really pissed off. Seb doesn't care. "Mum, Mum, it's me, Mum!" he yells again. He waves his hands in the air. She doesn't turn toward his voice, even though everyone else is staring quite openly now. She is on the road beneath him. Just about ten meters away, but down the steps, and there are about a million people between them. Stupid people, just standing around eating ice cream, drinking beer, chatting and laughing and stuff. Seb hates them. They need to move. They need to get out of his way. He starts to push toward her.

She is arguing with an old man. Well, not arguing exactly. She isn't saying much, but she is giving him filthy looks and doing that heavy exasperated sigh thing that she sometimes used to do to Dad; her shoulders would go up to her ears and then basically slump to about her waist. It is such a well-known gesture to Seb. He wants to laugh out loud at its familiarity, even though, in the past, it used to make him feel a bit uncomfortable and sad when his mum did it to his dad. Now he celebrates how known, noticed and particular it is. Although his father never seemed to notice it; was that a problem? Should his dad have spotted when she was pissed off?

He has all these thoughts as he runs down the steps toward her, as he shoves through the bodies of people who smell of sweat and sea and suncream. He pushes against their backs and elbows, stands on his tiptoes to get glimpses of her. It is unbearable, losing sight of her even for a second.

"Mum, Mum!" It is a noisy street full of chatter and drunk laughter, but surely she can hear him. Why doesn't she turn to him? Instead she gets into a car; the old man slams the door behind her, then quickly gets in the driver's side and drives away, swiftly. He moved really fast for such an old bloke. Seb starts to run after the car; his feet slam down hard on the pavement, his breathing is ragged and stays in his chest. At one point he is only a couple of meters away from them, but he has to keep dodging around people milling about who are just idiots and can't see how he needs them to get out of his way. The car revs and accelerates up the hill. Seb keeps running, but the gap between them widens.

"Seb! Seb! What the hell, Seb?" Oli shouts.

Seb is bent double, resting his hands on his knees, trying to get his breath back, trying not to cry. The disappointment throbs through him. He thinks he is going to be sick. He feels Oli put his hand on his back, hot and heavy; he wants to shake it off. "Run after that car, Oli," he gasps.

"Which car?" Oli looks up the road. The car is out of sight now. Seb wants to cry. He mustn't cry. He can't.

"A gray Honda. Old-looking."

"What? Why? Did they nick something?" Oli looks around frantically, probably searching for their backpack. Seb knows he left it at the table; he hopes someone will have looked after it for them, but he doesn't really care that much. There is nothing in it that he values. Everything in the world that he values is in the Honda. He feels his stomach roil and his bowels clench.

"Mum is in the car." He stands up straight and stares at Oli; eye to eye, he might be believed. They are brothers. Seb still sees Oli as an extension of himself, although he is never certain this is a two-way thing. It is possibly a younger-brother thing. But he needs Oli to believe him. Help him. Help their mum.

"What?"

"I saw her. I saw her get in the car."

"No you didn't." Oli's response is flat, devoid of any emotion.

"I called out to her."

"Did she respond?"

"Well, no, but…"

Oli sighs, looks at his trainers, then puts both his hands on Seb's shoulders. "You imagined her. You want it so much you imagined it. You've thought of nothing other than her since we arrived and so you've seen someone who looks a bit like her and imagined it's Mum, but it's not her, Seb. I'm sorry, but it's not."

Seb shakes him off and starts running up the street after the Honda, although it is long gone and he knows it's pointless. He stops halfway up the hill, admitting that his efforts are futile.

"She's cut off all her hair," he yells.

"She would never. She was really vain about her hair," replies Oli quietly.

"Do you think she's hiding from someone? The person who took her?"

"For fuck's sake, Seb, Mum is dead. How many times do I have to tell you?"

"She's not. She's really not. I saw this man put her in a car. She didn't want to go with him."

"What, he forced her? Lifted her into the car?"

"Erm, no, not exactly, but he took hold of her arm and sort of marched her toward the passenger door."

"Marched her?"

"Kind of led her. She didn't want to get in."

"Did this woman scream out? Did she protest at all? Why isn't anyone else chasing this car if a man just kidnapped a Leigh look-alike?"

Seb can't explain it. A blank opens up inside him, eating his words, his reason, his ability to expound. He has felt this happen before, a number of times since she left. It seems like in his life there is a massive crevasse. He's scared there always will be this feeling. He has to find her. If there is always this emptiness, he'll fall into it, he knows he will, sooner or later. He's too young to avoid it without her, without his mum. He needs her.

He starts to cry. It is the worst thing he can do. It makes him seem like a kid. Then Oli puts his arms around him and that is worse still. He feels his own body quake. Oli will assume he's crying because he is sad, but he's not. He's howling because he is not being heard. Because he is frustrated and because it is unfair. The whole bloody horrible, bloody stupid bloody thing is unfair and a nightmare. And he wants to scream and scream and scream. Crying is actually an act of self-control.

He struggles to free himself from his brother's embrace and heads back to the café. A server is on her knees with a dustpan and brush sweeping up the pieces of broken glass. Seb thinks of the last time he saw his mum. She'd been cleaning the kitchen because their cat, Topaz, had got at the Sunday lunch chicken that was on the counter in a greasy baking tray. Topaz had made a load of oily footprints everywhere. Seb was worried she was going to choke on a chicken bone. His mum had got scratched when she tried to get the chicken carcass from the cat, and then she'd washed the floor. Seb, Oli and his dad had gone out, left her to it. He remembers looking back over and seeing her kneeling next to a bucket of hot water. Later that night, they came home and she was dancing in the sparkling clean kitchen. He tries to remember her dancing, but usually when he thinks of her he remembers her plunging her hands into the sudsy water. It makes him feel weird. His tongue sticks to the roof of his mouth.

A group of women in their twenties are hovering around the table Oli and Seb were sitting at, waiting for the glass to be cleared up so they can swoop into their seats. A couple of them are holding the backs of chairs purloined from other tables. One of them is holding Oli's rucksack. She hands it to him. It's all really embarrassing. Seb keeps his head down, but he can feel their sympathetic gazes burning into him. He knows Oli will be glaring at the young women. Fury burning from his eyes. Oli hates people feeling sorry for them. Seb doesn't care. He feels sorry for himself. He wants people to feel sorry for him. They should. He has just watched his mother disappear for a second time.

23

OLI

Coming here, to this place where they spent so many summer holidays when they were young, was a mistake. He'd triggered his brother, who is in a really fucked-up state, which was not his intention. He is trying to keep him safe. Even though Seb is as annoying as hell, on some molecular level they are attached in a way that is different from everyone else in the world. Even when they experience different things, think different things, they are in some weird way connected. And Oli's the oldest, so he's responsible. He is doing his best, but the whole thing is so fucked up, he doesn't know if a best is even possible, and if it is, he sure as hell doesn't know what it might look like anymore.

He swears a lot in his internal monologue. As he does so, he imagines Leigh telling him off for it. "You're cleverer than that, Oli. Use the vocabulary I know you have. Show the world you are brilliant and articulate." She was the only one who thought he was brilliant. He is dyslexic, and his teachers sometimes just think he is a fuck—an imbecile. He self-corrects. Not that Leigh can hear him or anything. But he does it anyway.

What was the point of coming here? He stubs his toe into the pavement, grinds the end of his trainer into the curb as though hoping to make an imprint, an impression. Why is he here? He just had to get Seb out of the house; that was the important part really. He could have gone anywhere. Once he had the cash, he could have gone to Scotland or Manchester. It's most likely banging up there. He won't acknowledge that he feels sentimental about Lyme Regis and that he was perhaps drawn here because it is a place where he used to be happy. Maybe it is simply habit that brought him here. He found his way here on autopilot because this is where they always came; it isn't a stretch or a challenge. He's simply here because he's lazy.

Or maybe it is more than that.

The thing is, he can't shake off Daan Janssen's words. He doesn't trust or believe him exactly, but he decided to test him. Just in case, because this isn't a situation where he can risk not checking every possibility, no matter how off-the-wall the possibilities seem.

He had sent Janssen a message via the PlayStation app and said that he and Seb would look for evidence to prove Janssen's innocence and that Fiona was involved with Leigh's disappearance, but they would need money to do so. Like resources. Daan sent a thousand pounds to Oli's Monzo account in just minutes. It was unbelievable. A thousand pounds. Why would he do that if he was guilty? Just give away cash trying to prove something unprovable. He wouldn't. So he had to be…well, not precisely innocent, but maybe something in between.

And if Janssen didn't do it, someone else had to have. Because she didn't chain herself to the radiator, did she.

Oli shakes his head. He doesn't have a clue and it is almost too much to think about. He just wanted to have a day off. Really, the only good thing coming out of this is the fact that he's had an all-expenses-paid day at the beach; or at least it was a good thing until Seb started hallucinating and then having a breakdown in the street. WTF?

They are sitting on a bench now. Oli has bought them both hot chocolate. They don't need warming up exactly, but sweet things are good for shock. He remembers Leigh giving him tea with about eight sugars when he fell off his skateboard once during a particularly complex trick and needed stitches. Seb isn't drinking the hot chocolate; he's just staring at it. Oli hates Leigh for leaving him all the parenting. Really hates her. But he isn't being totally fair. Then again, why should he be? What is fair about this? Truthfully, he isn't doing *all* the parenting stuff. Fiona is washing their clothes and making meals.

His scalp seems to shrink as he thinks two things simultaneously. One, his father should have taken over the parenting. Two, Fiona should not have.

Oli looks about aimlessly. There is a young family sitting on the bench next to theirs. A mother with a baby in her arms and a dad with a sleeping toddler on his lap. The toddler is sprawled, exhausted no doubt after a brilliant day making sandcastles and getting high on seaside sugar treats. The dad is managing to drink from a can of beer above the kid's head. There is a carton of chips wedged between the parents; now and again the dad feeds one of the steaming, greasy chips into his wife's mouth, or his own. He does so silently. The wife never requests or refuses a chip, just chews them down happily. Her hands are full holding the baby, which is feeding from a bottle. The mother is playing with its toes and keeps murmuring, "There, there." Just a moment ago, the baby was screaming its head off, hungry or hot or a combination. There are still tears on its cheeks, but now it seems really content, stretched out in the mother's arms; trusting that she can and will fix everything. Always.

Oli aches.

He wishes someone would just walk up to him and take over, fix everything. Obviously he is too old to sit on a parent's knee, to have his feet stroked, but he longs for someone to pat him on the back and say whatever the equivalent of "there, there" might be when speaking to a teenager. "I got this" or "over to me." The weight of it is extraordinary. He feels his life bearing down on his back like a physical load. Exhausting.

Oli starts to wonder about Fiona. Could she be responsible for Leigh's abduction and murder? It is unimaginable. Auntie Fi a killer? He's known her practically his whole life. She was Leigh's best friend even before that. Would she, could she have hurt her? It is a thousand times harder to believe than

blaming a stranger. Harder, but not impossible. If Fiona did
have anything to do with it, how can they prove it? He doesn't
know exactly, but he supposes starting at her house is as good
a place as any. The police have searched it, yes, but they don't
know the place like he and Seb do. The two of them might
see something the police have missed. Like what, though? He
doesn't know. It is all mad. He doesn't believe it. Daan Janssen
is fucking with him.

His dad will go mental.

The sun is totally over itself now, drooping behind the
clouds, just a sliver on the horizon in the way that a day-old
party balloon drops behind a sofa. Day-trippers are slowly
packing up, reluctant to leave the good times behind them.
Oli watches as they file off the beach and head to their cars or
the bus. He envies them their sense of purpose. Somewhere
to go. The air is beginning to cool. The night feels unsettled,
unsure. The plan to get a room somewhere seems unrealistic
as the time to do so grows closer. Oli starts to wonder whether
he actually dares to walk into a guest house and try. Won't he
draw attention to himself and to Seb if he does that? Two kids
booking a room without parents is weird, right? He's never had
to do anything like it. Besides, since he's said that's what they'll
do, all he's seen are signs in the window saying *No Vacancies*.

The streets are still full of people eating and drinking. There
are more drunks now; loud and leery. He isn't scared or anything. He lives in London and knows when trouble is likely
to land. These coastal drunks aren't looking for fights, they're
looking for hookups. It is just a different vibe from earlier and
he doesn't want Seb to get scared. He glances at his brother,
who is still crying. Silently now, but with a sort of irritating
determination to be sad. He isn't the only one who feels like
crying, but he is the only one who ever gets to do it.

This stupid obsession with thinking Leigh could still be
alive is boring, and now Seb has completely lost it, imagining he's seen her. Although, if Oli is being totally honest with
himself, he might admit that he went through a stage a bit

like that. The first month after she disappeared, he'd think he'd seen her at the end of the street, or jogging, or walking a dog, but the woman he thought was her never was. Obviously Leigh didn't jog, and they didn't have a dog. It was just a case of mistaken identity. Loads of women had long brown hair like hers. Close up, the other not-Leigh-after-all women always had funny teeth, or eyes that were too close together, or something else not quite right.

The thing is, he doesn't think Leigh is alive. But he does think the right person should go down for killing her. He lied to Daan Janssen about that when he said he didn't care. The eternal default setting for teens. In fact, he does believe in justice and people paying for what they've done. Loads of his mates jump the barriers on the Tube all the time, but he always pays his way. He is the sort of kid who owns up if he's done something wrong at school, and he thinks others should do the same. There's this one kid in his year, a total shit, Thomas Dobbs, who's always doing sneaky-as-fuck stuff and letting other kids take the blame for it. Sports equipment stolen and sold, the smell of weed in the classroom at lunchtime, homework he's copied, ideas he's plagiarized—that sort of stuff. He's a straight A–grade student, though, so teachers never think he does any of this crap. He never owns up to anything, even if it means an entire class is put on detention. It doesn't sit right with Oli. Do crap, yeah, but own it.

"We should go to Fiona's after all," Oli says to Seb. He has to have a plan of some sort; sleeping on the street isn't an option. He points to Seb's mask, a dingy blue disposable one, lying forlornly on the bench.

"You should keep it on."

"No way. Why would I?"

"People will be looking for us. Dad will have called the police."

"Really? You think so?" Seb checks the time. It's 9:00 p.m. "I feel bad." Oli is unsure whether Seb feels bad because their dad will be worried or because the layers of treats feel heavy and sickly in his belly. The matter is cleared up when he adds, "Maybe we should ring him and say we're fine. Tell him where we are."

"No."

"Then send a text message, at least."

"No."

Oli has brought the key with him. When the police returned it, Fiona hung it up in the under-stairs cupboard, where there is a wooden wall-mounted key holder with the words *So Good to be Home* painted across it. Leigh must have bought that. Fucking hilarious if you think about it. As Oli took Fiona's house key (easily identifiable because it was attached to a fossil key ring), he noted that Fiona had three pairs of trainers and a pair of heels, some sliders and two pairs of sandals in the cupboard too. That's, like, loads of shoes. The recent days have smudged into weeks and months. Many of them hot and heavy, all of them empty and endless. He can't remember, did Fiona move in when they were still looking for Leigh? Wasn't the deal that she was coming just to keep them company while they waited for news? When did she bring her enormous suitcase? Her Kardashian-worthy selection of shoes? He isn't sure. The shoes suggest she knew she was staying awhile. Forever? Does she know they're never going to find Leigh?

The thought makes his blood slow, leaves him clammy. But his next thought is worse. The next thought makes him want to find a toilet. What has his dad got involved with this time?

24

DC CLEMENTS

Mark Fletcher is frantic. His boys are missing too. Clements's gut response is "this bloody idiot man," but she works swiftly, automatically, ever the professional; it takes just moments to conquer her gut response and bring her reason to the forefront. She has to establish whether she should pity him or distrust him. A missing wife, now two missing sons. Other people limit their carelessness to car keys or their reading glasses. Has someone taken the boys, or have they run away? No matter which, the two minors are in danger. That is Clements's priority.

"They've run away," Mark asserts; he must know this looks bad.

"Is there a note?" asks Clements.

"No."

"When did you last see them?"

"Last night when they went to bed, or at least when they went up to their rooms. They were playing video games."

"What time?"

"About nine thirty."

Twenty-three hours ago. It's 8:30 p.m. now. Clements waits a beat. "You haven't seen them or heard from them all day?" She is aware that she sounds exasperated. She is. Many, many parents will have lost track of their teens today. Thousands, probably. Kids are desperate to flex, to hunt out some fun, some contemporary companionship, some rebellion. A lot of beat bobbies have spent the day breaking up drunken spats, encouraging worse-for-wear revelers to go home, sleep it off.

When Mark says, slightly apologetically, slightly defensively, "It's Super Saturday. When we got up this morning, we just assumed they'd gone out early to make the most of it," Clements has some sympathy, but FFS, his kids are not like everyone else's naturally curious and buoyant teens. His kids are in the eye of a media frenzy, they are grieving, they are mixed up. He should have taken more care. She tries not to be judgy, but truthfully, it's her default setting. Her job would be much easier if people weren't so damned irresponsible. She possibly ought to feel sorrier for Mark—he too is in the center of a media frenzy, he's grieving, mixed up—but she finds she's just a bit irritated with him. Stupid, careless man, never quite noticing what is under his nose. What isn't.

"We?" she challenges. She knows the answer but wants to make him say it.

"Me and Fiona." He sounds cautious. Clements recalls one of her earliest conscious snap judgments of this case. Mark Fletcher—family man; Daan Janssen—ladies' man. How does that sit now? She has the ladies' man under arrest, awaiting trial for the abduction and murder of Mark Fletcher's wife. But the trial hasn't even come to court yet. As the parlance goes, Kylie Gillingham isn't cold in her grave. In fact, there isn't a grave; they haven't even found her body. Clements is aware that the grieving process might not be straightforward in this case—when is it ever?—but she feels the family man's behavior is a bit shoddy. Cozying up with the best friend at such a speed is, at the very least, confusing for the kids. Cozying up or shacking up? Fine line. "Separate beds, obviously," Fletcher says with a forced laugh. Why did he feel the need to add that? Clements hadn't asked for clarification. And she doesn't have to now. He's clarified something he probably was hoping to hide. More likely than not, they are sleeping together.

So Fiona's behavior? Clements has to consider this too. Fiona's actions don't quite add up. If she's moved into the Fletcher household to care for her missing friend's boys, as she repeatedly reiterates, shouldn't she be doing a better job of it?

From the moment Clements picked up Kylie Gillingham's case, she's cared a little bit more than she should. She is aware of that. She cares for all the incarnations of the woman. Her entire, messy whole.

Mark gave her a photo of Leigh Fletcher when he first reported his wife missing; a woman with big, soulful brown eyes. She was beaming in the snap, a broad, determined smile, but there was something about her eyes that made Clements wonder from the outset. She looked weary. Drained. Done for. More tired than most working mums, who generally are set to exhausted. Maybe she knew on some level where this was all heading. She must have known she couldn't get away with it forever. Although she could never have imagined she'd end up chained to a radiator, starved, beaten.

Dead.

Not many people die for their crimes. Even murderers brought to court might expect a matter of years. Life doesn't mean life in the UK. Clements wishes it bloody did. But Kylie hadn't murdered anyone. She was just a bigamist, a crime that carried an average sentence of two years.

Clements also cares for the other version: sleek, groomed, ostensibly indulged Kai Janssen. The woman who kept a logbook detailing who came to dinner when, and what they were served. That level of organization (Control? Paranoia?) fascinates her. It's clear that Kai Janssen did not sit comfortably with the great and the good that her husband brought home to eat with them. Her meticulous notes about entertaining, her obsessively neat wardrobe (clothes cataloged and hung by color), her lack of contacts in her phone, all suggest a tightly controlled life, one that was clipped, pinched and measured, despite the abundant wealth and the obvious resources that should have meant possibilities. Clements thinks that perhaps Kai refused to take advantage of all that was on offer; perhaps the weight of her position—the fact that she was cheating her way into the opulence—sat too heavily and she couldn't quite enjoy it. Although she couldn't quite give it up either, could she? Maybe the sex was wild and abandoned. Maybe that was the irresistible draw to the other man, the second life. Clements hopes so. She wants Kai to have had as many good times as possible. Considering how everything turned out.

Yes, Clements likes every version of Kylie Gillingham, the woman who spat in the eye of convention. She can't see the criminal in either incarnation, and she loathes the fact that the woman has been turned into a victim, a statistic. It's the hardest part of the job, having a front-row seat to the filthy underbelly of humanity and keeping count of those who suffer at the hands of others. At least Kylie managed to defy convention for a time. Until the burning-at-the-stake mentality—or whatever the hell it is that always seems to win the day—reasserted control. It seems convention has it that rebellious women must be punished, brought into line. There is no patience or space for those who refuse to conform in this world. Sometimes Clements finishes that sentence with the word *yet*, other times she finishes it with the word *still*. It depends on how her week is panning out.

The fact is, the moment when she and Tanner ran into the destroyed apartment room where Kylie had been held, and found it empty, was one of the worst of her career. She was so close. So damned hopeful. For a fleeting second she allowed herself to believe they would find Kylie alive. That they'd save the day.

Tanner wants a body or a confession.

Clements wants more.

She hardly dares think it; certainly won't articulate it, because they have a case. All the evidence points directly at Daan Janssen. Basically open and shut. Basically.

But something still nags at her.

It's as though someone is breathing on her neck. Not breathing down her neck, not accusing or watching her as such, just reminding her of their presence. She doesn't believe in ghosts, but she does believe in her gut and she does believe in doing a good job. A good job in a murder case means finding the correct culprit, obviously. A case being basically open and shut is an oxymoron. Yes, all the evidence points to Daan Janssen, yet Clements has started to wonder about something in particular. As she lies awake at night staring at the ceiling, she finds herself asking why Daan Janssen reported his wife missing in the first place. If he murdered her as revenge for her bigamy, he would have known that even though her life had been lived in duplicate, there could only ever be one body. He did not have to associate himself with her going missing at all. Kai Janssen could have simply vanished, and her disappearance could be explained to Daan's friends and family as a sad but not unusual marital breakup, the subsequent lack of contact justified through a desire for a clean break. Kai didn't seem to have any friends of her own. It was unlikely anyone would have vigorously pursued the matter of her whereabouts. If Daan had killed her, the clever thing would be not to report her missing. It would have been a less risky move, a less humiliating one as well. If a body had ever turned up, that body would be identified as Leigh Fletcher. Daan did not have to make himself known to the police.

Mark was not in the same position. Leigh Fletcher had friends, children, family. She would have been missed. There was no way he could have killed her and then pretended she'd simply walked out on them. Mark Fletcher had no alternative but to go to the police, whether he was the killer or not. Mark Fletcher, who is now living with his wife's best friend and whose sons have vanished.

Should Clements be concerned for Fiona Phillipson or concerned *by* her? She allows the thought to roll around her mind. It's brutal to think that women live in a misogynistic world with the dice weighted against them, the cards dealt unfairly, often with nothing up their sleeves, encountering insults, prejudice and violence at male whim with horrific regularity. That is hard to swallow, but there is something worse still for feminist Clements to contemplate: the fact that men are not the only enemy. They have a case with a lot of physical evidence, but she can't quite dismiss the thought that the evidence is... What? Circumstantial? No, not quite that. Convenient? Maybe. *It's always the best friend* doesn't have the same ring to it as *it's always the husband*, and yet...

She shakes her head. She is conscious that she is often told she has too much imagination for a cop, that she ought to keep it in check. It is a fair point perhaps, although only ever made by the unimaginative. Sometimes she secretly congratulates herself on this particular character trait. She views problems through a different lens, and that is often a good thing in life. Still, she has to admit, it's perfectly possible that she is reading too much into the home-share arrangement.

Clements knows that she can't think about Kylie Gillingham's case at this moment. What is most important right now is the whereabouts of the boys.

"What have you done to find them?" she asks.

"We've called their phones. They are both switched off. Seb often turns his off, he's not so dependent on it, but Oli never does. It's definitely out of character."

"And you've left messages in case they turn them on again?"

"Of course. Voice and text. No response."

"Do you have any sort of tracking on their phones? Find My iPhone, that sort of thing?"

"Yes, but as they've turned them off, the last place they're registering is here at home."

"Have you called their friends?"

"Of course, and their aunt Paula. I've called everyone I can think of. No one has seen them. It's not like them to go off without telling me what they're up to. We're all quite careful with each other, you know."

"I can imagine."

Clements knows there are set questions to ask about children who have potentially run away. For instance, has there been any upset at home? Obviously, she already knows the answers to this. Are the children under any pressure? Have there been any changes in mood or behavior? Are they speaking to strangers? Maybe the boys are just making the most of Super Saturday. It's not late. The night is young, in fact. They could be hanging out at a cinema or bowling alley, doing something wholesome. Maybe. Hopefully.

Possibly not.

She tucks her phone under her chin and starts to fill out the missing persons information log. She confirms the boys' full names, asks for DOB, height, weight and whether they have any particular identification marks.

"What clothing were they wearing last time you saw them?"

"Pajama shorts, I guess. I don't know."

"Well, they're unlikely to have left the house in those. Is there any chance you can work out what's missing?"

"Not really. I don't keep track of their T-shirts. They both have loads."

"Check to see if rucksacks, water bottles, bikes, et cetera have gone." She creates a crime reference number. She's supposed to go off duty in ten minutes. She's never off duty. "I'll come over now and take a full statement. We'll get eyes to start searching the areas the boys are known to frequent. We'll check local hospital admissions and start reviewing CCTV footage. We can look at their computers. See if we can get an idea who they're speaking to."

Clements sighs as she hangs up. She feels the weight of this latest development. She speedily briefs Tanner.

"Your initial thoughts?" he asks. She's surprised he hasn't just dumped his own, as per. She realizes that he's beginning to respect her experience, her instincts.

"Obviously I'm hoping they've taken themselves off, rather than this being another abduction, but nothing can be ruled out at this stage."

"But if we do assume they're runaways, do you think they're running toward or away from something?"

"That's one of the things we have to find out."

"Maybe they know something we don't, or at least think they do," suggests Tanner. "About their mother or her murderer."

"Possible. All I know is that happy kids don't run away."

25

FIONA

Fiona can't understand why Mark is fretting. To her it is obvious where the boys have gone. How has he not thought of it? Her hunch is confirmed when she checks the rack in the cupboard and discovers the key for her bungalow is missing. Mark has nothing to fear. The boys know the area, Oli is sixteen now; he has done the train trip quite a few times. He's a responsible brother, he'll look out for Seb. They will turn up sooner rather than later, most likely when they are hungry. They can't have much money on them; neither of them is a saver. They'll soon discover that Lyme Regis isn't the holiday resort of their imaginings once they realize they don't have an adult with endless pockets on hand to pay for ice creams and hours in the amusement arcades. They'll most likely call and ask to be picked up at some point soon. Mark keeps muttering about it being like Leigh all over again. Which is crazy. The boys haven't been abducted. They aren't going to be pushed off a cliff. There really isn't anything for Mark to be concerned about. Nothing bad will happen to them in Lyme Regis.

Fiona, however, has a lot to be concerned about.

Not only is it really annoying that her first day of freedom has been commandeered—no shopping or haircut for her, as it would have looked callous if she hadn't demonstrated some concern for the boys' whereabouts. But more importantly, Oli and Seb dashing off like this is unpredictable. Something she hasn't accounted for. The more she thinks about their unpredictable behavior, the more uncomfortable she is. By late afternoon, she would go so far as to say she is actively agitated. She has to concentrate very hard to think clearly. She needs to be a step ahead. She needs to have thought of everything. That's how a person gets away with murder.

Most likely the boys are looking for nothing more than somewhere to let their hair down; they probably just want a break, to get away from London. After all, they have been locked down for months, and, she'd guess, they simply don't have the imagination to think beyond the holiday destination they've frequently visited in the past.

She repeatedly tells herself that is what is most probable. However, it is impossible for her not to be aware that she murdered Leigh at said frequently visited holiday destination, so she doesn't like the thought of the boys snooping around there. She doesn't like it at all.

She can't imagine they will find anything that might incriminate her. She's been careful. The only things to find were the things she planted for the police to discover, which they duly did. In Fiona's experience, people tend to see what they want to, which worked against her when she trusted Leigh—believed her to be her best friend and so was blind to her treachery and lies—but worked to her advantage when the police were looking to pin Kylie's abduction and murder on one of her husbands. They quickly reached the conclusions she'd hoped they would.

Still, she doesn't want the police to go back to the scene of the crime and snoop further. If they work out where the boys have run off to, they might pursue them. The thought makes her uneasy. She has to consider all possibilities, even the inconvenient or distasteful ones. What if she and Kylie were seen by a neighbor or a stranger back on that night in March? She doesn't think they were. No one has ever come forward and said as much, but memories are intricate, capricious things. People might remember more if they recognize the boys. They may recall seeing them with their stepmother on a past holiday, or even with Fiona herself. That sort of connection would be dangerous, because then someone might remember seeing Kylie with Fiona that final time. It is possible that they were spotted. Fiona doesn't recall seeing anyone, but it was dark and stormy, and she was distracted, obviously. Killing a person takes a lot of brain space. She accepts that there might have been an individual forced out of their house despite the inclement weather, out walking their dog, for example. A witness who may have remained cloaked by the dark sky.

Her head is pounding now. A loud, distracting banging that pummels her reason and nerves. It is tricky to think clearly, something she absolutely must do. She can't deny it, sometimes she is frightened by how things have turned out. Scared and surprised by what she has become and what might yet lie in front of her. She doesn't sleep well, even with the use of medication. She never imagined she'd become a murderer. Who does? It wasn't her plan. She just wanted to punish Kylie, teach her a lesson. Things simply got out of hand, went too far.

Fiona repeatedly reminds herself that it was Kylie who became a criminal first. Kylie who set them both on this path toward such vile darkness. Fiona really wasn't left with any other choice. All she wanted was some acknowledgment of the chaos caused, an apology maybe. But Kylie was so damned smug, so unrepentant. Besides, once both Daan and Mark were aware of her disgusting duplicity, her casual cruelty, what sort of life could she have ever gone back to? Neither of them would have wanted her once they knew what she really was. Her lives were over before Fiona killed her. Fiona couldn't be blamed for that.

Sometimes, though, Fiona thinks about the early version of Kylie. That woman fights her way into Fiona's fitful sleep and her waking subliminal mind. She doesn't want Kylie there; persistent, noisy. Sad. Her presence is annoying, irritating, and yet sometimes she finds a strange comfort in seeing her old friend. The woman she once loved. Before she hated.

They met not long after they both graduated. They were

looking for their first jobs and had signed up to the same re-cruitment agency. Just a chance encounter in a waiting room, but it shaped both their lives. Fiona doesn't want to get too sentimental about that; after all, what is life other than a series of chance encounters that people grab at and try to grapple into meaning? The two young women instantly clicked, and they became really close. There was a point when they were totally there for one another, no questions asked. Inseparable. Thoughts, aspirations, cravings all aligned. They were each other's people. Although even at the time, neither thought that was the ideal situation; both wanted to find a husband and then have kids that they could love more than they loved each other.

Of course it only happened for Kylie.

Twice.

The thought burns Fiona. As though someone is holding a match to the soft fleshy bit of skin on her upper arm. Kylie betrayed Mark and Daan, everyone gets that, but she betrayed Fiona too. Way back before the bigamy, she betrayed her when she married Mark and left Fiona alone. Fiona had to suffer end-less blind dates without even the comfort of returning to their flat and knowing that Kylie would be there, ready to laugh at the night's antics, the way they often had when they were both dating. She was doomed to creating humiliating inter-net profiles alone; she endured countless meaningless shags, morning-after rejections, ghosting and catfishing. Without help or companionship, she faced the conundrum of whether she ought to present as a "cool girl" who didn't expect com-mitment, exclusivity or even decent communication, or risk being labeled insecure and clingy. Supportless, she negotiated the many weird stages that were part and parcel of the run-up to being in a relationship nowadays: texting, talking, seeing each other, dating non-exclusively, then exclusive but not ac-tually in an official relationship, and all of this in the hope of finally reaching the nirvana of a full-blown relationship. Peo-ple could be so damned mean.

Of course people do fall in love. People do marry. Fiona gets that. That wasn't the issue. Fiona believes the ultimate betrayal that Kylie committed against her was not that she fell in love and married Mark; no, the treachery was that she didn't consider Mark enough. In Fiona's opinion, Kylie didn't split herself in two, Leigh and Kai; she had in fact doubled. Gobbled up two men. She should never have done what she did, considering all that she'd had with the first. If being married and a mum couldn't make Kylie happy, what the hell was Fiona striving for?

There's no point in romanticizing her now, just because she's dead. Fiona recalls that Kylie hadn't had much idea or drive back in the beginning, when they first met. Her ambition was limited to a desire not to be a server in a coffee shop forever. She mentioned that an office job would at least mean she had an excuse to buy decent clothes. She used to present her early career as a textbook approach to resilience and persistence; Fiona thought it was more of an example of chaotic indiscrimination that eventually led to Kylie stumbling into an unwarranted opportunity. If you throw enough mud, some sticks. Fiona watched as Kylie wormed her way up to an undeniably impressive management position in a global consultancy. She was delighted for her at the time, of course. She took her out for champagne to celebrate every one of her promotions.

Yes, delighted.

And also a tiny bit irked, because the truth was, everything always sort of landed in Kylie's lap, and that just didn't seem fair.

It was always the same with Kylie. Often as not, someone would take a liking to her and just offer her something she hadn't really earned. Like free food at the restaurant she was working at when they met, or a tip-off as to where a decent flat was being advertised, or a hint as to what might be a wise next rung on the career ladder. People just seemed to want to help her. Mark did the same thing, when you think about it. He'd just taken a liking to her and offered his ready-made family. Fiona was in the play park when Mark and Kylie first met. It could just as easily have been her who caught Mark's attention, who he welcomed into his family, his bed, his home, but somehow—as always—the good fortune landed at Kylie's feet. Just because she was the one to dash up and perform first aid on Seb after he fell off the slide. She didn't even know any first aid; she said later that her response had been instinctual rather than expert. It was really rather risky of her. Some might say she just poked her nose into another person's business. Made herself important.

Kylie didn't really value the high-flying position she'd hustled her way into. She chucked it in the minute she inherited off her father, because she was running a double life and couldn't hold down a job as well as two husbands. She must have been delighted when her estranged dad unexpectedly came through for her and afforded her the opportunity to deceive both her husbands. A lifetime of neglect made up for in one fell swoop. The luck the woman had was unbelievable! Kylie always landed on her feet.

Fiona allows herself a small internal smile at the subconscious choice of metaphor. There is no way that Kylie fell on her feet when she tumbled over the cliff. Her luck had finally run out. Well, all good things come to an end. Eventually.

Fiona herself always had a much clearer idea of what she wanted out of life, and she worked hard to achieve it. She had to. It's unfair to think things never panned out as easily for her. She was never handed anything on a plate; no one ever rushed to help her. She hasn't inherited a penny. Both her parents are still alive and still together, insisting on living their "best lives," which means they seem pretty determined to spend all their money before they die. Kylie was always going on about how lucky Fiona was to have two loving, adventurous parents, but there will be no unexpected windfalls fluttering Fiona's way; she has always known she'd have to make her own way in life.

When the two women met all those years ago in the recruitment office, Fiona had a clear passion to work in fashion. She envisaged herself as a buyer for a decent-size department store, going to catwalk exhibitions where they showcased the new seasons, ultimately setting the trends as to what people might decide to wear, perhaps through writing for a magazine or working as a consultant in one of the big fashion houses. However, fashion turned out to be an incredibly competitive industry. The best roles went to the anorexically thin women with trust funds or the gay guys who all stuck together. Fiona wasn't either, it wasn't fair. So she diverted her creative talent, her colossal ambition and her work ethic toward interior design. No one could call her a quitter. The interiors industry tends to be dominated by middle-aged women with wealthy husbands and a little bit of flair but no ambition to speak of, so she cleaned up. But it is all her own hard work.

She sighs. Thinking about Kylie is uncomfortable for her. She wishes she could simply put her out of mind. But considering everything, she knows that is never going to happen. She recalls every moment of their last encounter in lurid detail. The narrow, winding path, the ground wet underfoot, having to shout to be heard above the wind and the sea. Making Kylie finally decide.

"Tell me which one of them you loved the most."

"I don't know why it matters. It's not as though I'm going to get to choose between them."

"Just pick one!"

"I took immeasurable risks for Daan, I lost friends for him. That shows I love him."

"You don't know what love is."

"But I do. Twice over. I love them both."

"That's not allowed."

"I know, but who decided it wasn't?"

"Pick one!"

"Mark. Mark, Oli and Seb outweigh Daan. I guess they always did. I was never able to leave them. I choose Mark."

"Right, good, I'm glad we've got that cleared up. Finally."

She remembers the feel of Kylie's body through her clothes as she brought up her hands and shoved hard. It was solid, yet soft. Not at all resistant; she folded into the fall. Accepted the inevitability of it. Her face was so white, it was almost transparent. Her features spun through a myriad of emotions in that split second. The initial shock as she tumbled over the edge was almost instantly replaced by horror, but then—and Fiona is almost sure of this—she looked glad. Relieved it was over at last, most likely.

Fiona likes to think that on some level her friend knew she was doing her a favor. Sorting out the mess Kylie had created. She shakes her head, tries to dislodge the thoughts. Difficult, since everything around her belongs to Kylie and is a reminder of Kylie's life with Mark. Maybe she ought to redecorate. She has no intention of moving out; that would be such a backward step. Unthinkable after everything she's gone through to get to this point. Could Mark ever be persuaded to sell this house and make a fresh start? It would be a good move for everyone.

She swallows down a couple of tablets. She doesn't bother with water. She has been taking a lot of medication recently and can knock tablets back like shots. Even so, these painkillers aren't doing much to combat the pounding in her head. Or the rage that seems to flow through her blood, poisoning her. Truth is, the fury against Kylie hasn't subsided, even though she has been dealt with. Even though she is dead. It sometimes settles in Fiona's throat, growing there like a cancer. It feels like there is a tie around her neck, a tie that is pulled too tight. She is choking. She needs to hold her shit together. Stay calm, stay a step ahead. She has a lot to play for: the husband, the house, the boys. And she has a lot to lose. The thought of prison makes her freeze.

She doesn't want the police tracking the boys. It's best if she deals with them herself.

"Mark, I'm going out to look for Seb and Oli."

"Should I come with you?"

"Didn't the police suggest it was best that you stayed here, in case they show up? Which, by the way, I'm sure they will." She smiles at him, risks putting a hand on his arm, squeezing. She's never certain how much physical contact she should ini tiate. She's careful about that; lets him take the lead. She never knows when he'll knock at her door at night, peel back the duvet, climb between her sheets. She always readily submits whenever he does, shows clear enthusiasm. There will come a time when she approaches him in that way, she has to believe that, but she's not certain when that time might be.

"Where are you going to look for them?" he asks. He has no ideas of his own, and that irritates Fiona, to be frank. He should have.

"I thought I'd start at the skate park on the South Bank. Oli likes hanging out there. I'll have my phone on and I'll keep in touch. Don't worry about me."

Mark nods and turns his attention back to his phone. Checks his messages for the hundredth time. Fiona smothers the thought that her last instruction was unnecessary. There is nothing about Mark's demeanor that suggests he has ever spent a single moment worrying about her.

26

STACIE

It is starting to get dark, as the journey home takes far longer than it should. Traffic curls around every winding road. The lanes are soon clogged. On three occasions, a stream of vehicles are forced to reverse on a single-track road to give way to oncoming traffic. Some drivers appear flustered or incompetent; there's a lot of posturing. My dad manages all the maneuvers steadily and skillfully, but the atmosphere is still charged. Tension rolls through the car like a sea mist. It smells of us, bodies that wash in the sea more often than in the shower, dusty plastic dashboard, feet. I press the button to open a window; nothing happens. "It's broken," Dad mutters.

These are the first words he's said since I got in the car. I glance his way and catch his gaze. Cold. Cross. He's furious with me for slipping out of the house and going to a crowded town where I might become infected. When he found me in Lyme Regis, he was purple in the face, incandescent. He repeatedly spat out the words, "All these people, Stacie. So many people." I am equally furious with him because he forced me to abandon my research trip. I feel like a naughty teen who has ignored her curfew and whose parent has crashed the party, turned off the music, switched on all the lights and exposed the teenagers who are smoking dope and having sex. It's mortifying.

Because of the traffic jams, we're driving incredibly slowly; in fact we're often completely static. I could get out of the car at any point and walk back to the town that was gifting me some memories. I'm not trapped. I'm not being restrained. Yet somehow it feels like I am, because considering Dad's worry for my health, acting independently leaves me feeling selfish.

Eventually the traffic loosens and falls away, and in the last stretch homeward Dad puts his foot down and travels at speed. Too much speed, in fact. He takes the bends aggressively, no doubt as a way of venting his frustration at me. I wish he'd slow down. If the cancer doesn't get me, a head-on collision with a tree most certainly will. At one point my head almost touches the car's roof as he takes a bump too fast; the car is old and the suspension does little to cushion the impact. The headlights bounce on the road ahead and startled animals scamper out of danger, their eyes glinting with terror. I hope to hell no child of a holidaymaker strays out in front of us like the rabbits, foxes and mice have. A child wouldn't be as quick or knowing about getting out of the way.

"Slow down, Dad." I grip my library books and my knuckles turn white.

"Oh, *now* you want to be sensible," he snaps back with uncharacteristic sarcasm.

I turn my head away from him and study the farmhouses in the distance. These homes are filled with people living ordered lives; lives they understand and control. They will have pasts, presents and futures, memories, purpose, ambitions that they will quite naturally take for granted. I feel envious. It's perfectly possible that the people in these houses were once great friends of mine, but their lives are unknown to me now; not surprisingly, as I am only just beginning to know my own life again. Hope bubbles up and even my father's furious disappointment in me can't pop the excited swell of possibility. Today I met a school friend and I recognized the geography of the streets. Real progress.

As we approach our cottage, Dad's profile is illuminated by

a light on the corner of the property. He's waxy, yellow, like a corpse. There's no hint of his usual warmth. His eyes are black, like bodies of treacherous still water. I don't think now is the time to tell him of my triumphs. He pulls up close to the house and switches off the engine. My legs feel heavy. I don't want to go inside. I'm not done with outside, only just starting. His protectiveness of me is veering into something annoying, restrictive. I want to yell at him for picking me up and forcing me to come home, but I can't. I know he's worried about me and means well. My protest manifests in a silent mini sit-in.

He sighs, gets out of the car. "Come on, let's be having you. You need bath and bed. You need to take things easy, Stacie." He opens the back door, ushers me inside. He oozes a sense of ownership and "father knows best" that irritates me.

Ronnie bounces about, his claws scratching on the wooden floor, his tail wagging so enthusiastically it beats my leg and the kitchen units. Thump thump thump. He nuzzles our hands and I pat him. I realize that meeting Dad's fury with my own irritation is pointless, so I am about to offer to put the kettle on, but Dad turns from me, reaches for the whiskey bottle and pours. He seems to pause as though considering whether to include or exclude me. I watch his back bent over the glasses and am relieved when he eventually turns and hands me one. He drains his quickly and flops into the armchair.

"Have you eaten anything?" I ask.

"I haven't eaten all day," he snaps. The onus of his omission swells in my conscience.

"Should I make supper?" I offer.

Dad looks at me for a long time, as though I am a puzzle to him that he is trying to solve, which I suppose I am. He chews the nail on his thumb. "I'm not hungry." His attitude is unbecoming and honestly fairly annoying. As I don't remember our life before, I have no idea if he has a propensity to sulk or how long it might last. I don't know if it's a case of waiting it out or whether I can coax him back into a better mood.

Even though it is a warm night outside, the cottage is nearly always cold. I drop to my knees and start to build a fire in the hearth. I scrunch up newspaper into balls, add kindling; once that's taken, I carefully layer on sticks, then logs, crisscrossed and increasing in bulk. By the time the fire is roaring, Dad is asleep in the chair. I suppose today has exhausted him, and once again I feel a flare of guilt flash through my body. I wonder how I'm going to manage his concern and my own need to explore and reintegrate, because somehow, I must. However, that feels like a question for another day.

I put the guard around the fireplace and sit in the chair opposite Dad's, sipping the large whiskey he poured me. The amber liquid dances and catches the light from the fire; when I sip, it burns my throat. His mouth is slack and his forehead has a sheen to it. Sweaty panic. After a time, his head falls forward and I can see his pink scalp beneath the slick of silver hair. I study him, as he studied me earlier. He's not a puzzle exactly. In some ways, he's an open book with large, easy-to-read print. He's simply a man who loves his daughter dearly, above everything and everyone else. Yet he is unknown. I keep hoping that if I look at him for long enough, I'll remember us.

I sit for the longest time, and then I stand and lean close to him. I put the tip of my nose to his head and inhale, because I think heads smell quite distinctive. I think I will remember him as today I remembered the smell of freshly baked pasties, slick with fat, drifting up Bridge Street, and the briny air near the flotilla of small boats bobbing close to the shore. I take two or three deep inhalations.

Nothing.

27

DC CLEMENTS

"What are you doing?"

"Jesus, Tanner. You made me jump." DC Clements almost knocks the box she is rooting through off the shelf.

"What are you doing in here?" Tanner's tone is cold, suspicious.

The evidence room is a prosaic place. Less glamorous than the name suggests. More of a cupboard really, painted in a vanilla tone, rows of shelves that house boxes that hold lives. It's not especially prepossessing, but it is sacrosanct. It has gravitas. This is where a deal might be sealed and a criminal trapped, something they collectively work for. They all have hunches and theories and thoughts, but evidence is what it boils down to. There are procedures to get access; electronic and physical signing-in is necessary. Visits are generally only made in pairs. No one wants to be accused of tampering with evidence. Clements is alone, late at night, rooting through the boxes of evidence that pertain to Kylie Gillingham's case. She knows she looks shifty.

"I'm looking for something."

"Yeah, obviously. What?"

She is impressed that Tanner is challenging her. Pleased with him. Other senior officers might take offense, but Clements feels a swell of pride. She is as straight as an arrow, but there are bent cops, and it is up to the good ones to root them out: the not so good, the bad, the downright evil. She respects the fact that Tanner is prepared to challenge her, that he distrusts her a tiny bit; it also makes her think his instincts are a bit off. Daft bugger.

"Nothing bad, Tanner, although nice call-out." His jaw remains jutted, his teeth set. "No, seriously, well done. Always ask what a copper is doing in this room after hours. There is cash and drugs, and police officers aren't saints. Often far from it. However, I was looking for this." She triumphantly holds up a wine bottle in a plastic bag. "It was never sent to forensics."

"What is it?"

"A wine bottle."

"Ha bloody ha. You know what I mean."

"It's the bottle I found that day we searched Fiona Phillipson's house."

"I remember a wineglass, not a bottle. The glass had Daan Janssen's prints on."

"Correct. But this bottle wasn't in her house. It was on the clifftop."

"So maybe not anything to do with the case. Anyone could have left it there."

"They could have. That's what we thought to begin with. That's why we didn't send it away. Why waste the resources when it was a long shot? We thought maybe we'd send it if the other evidence didn't cough up anything."

"Which it did. As I say, the glass had Janssen's prints on it, which placed him at the seaside place he insists he's never visited."

"Correct again. Great recall." Tanner looks uncertain. Clements has seen him wear this expression before. The one that says he isn't sure what his boss has up her sleeve but he is sure there is something. They both know she is always a step ahead. He likes it about her and it exhausts him at the same time because he wants to keep up. She likes that about him. "As you say, this bottle could have been left on the cliff by anyone. I'm just wondering if anyone is *someone* in this case. I want to send it away and have it checked for prints. I need you to pull in favors, get someone to push it through asap. Tonight, ideally."

"You think they'll get a read on the prints after all this time?"

"If we're lucky. Depends what elements the bottle was exposed to before we bagged it up. I'll leave that with you. I need to get moving." Clements is almost out the door as she says this.

"Where are you going?"

"To look for the boys."

Tanner doesn't need to ask which boys. He knows that his boss has been consumed with this case for months. "Where do you think they are?"

"Everyone likes to be beside the seaside, beside the sea, Tanner," says Clements. "At Lyme Regis you can still find ice-cream sundaes, sausages, artery-clogging pasties."

"I want in on that. I'll get on it with our mates in forensics and I'll meet you at the bungalow."

"Good lad." Clements smiles to herself as the door bangs behind her. She doesn't need backup, but she'd like him there all the same.

28

OLI

It takes ages to walk to Fiona's place. About a million times Oli wonders whether they're making the right call by bothering to go there at all, but he can't think of what else to do or where else to go, so he puts one foot in front of the other and plods on. Not exactly committing to a plan; not exactly rejecting it either. He's beginning to think that's what life amounts to. Plodding on. He hopes not. Probably Leigh would have laughed at him if she'd ever heard him say as much. Thrown her head back and barked out an enormous guffaw, insisted that he was too young to be so sapped and cynical. She was always challenging him on what she called "morose teen stuff." She maintained it didn't suit him, insisted that life was for leaping into, charging at. She would have insisted on being all positive and motivational; she almost always was. She'd maybe have said that he'd come across a few dead ends but there would always be wide avenues and open fields to dash toward, mountains to conquer. It is sort of weirdly helpful imagining what she might have said if she could. Funny, because Oli used to find it hideously embarrassing and awkward. She hoped for so much for him, and for Seb; she believed their lives were going to be brilliant. He used to find it intense, and most often he just left the room when she got that fervent look in her eye. It was too much.

Now he sort of misses it. Her confidence. Her assurance. Her belief in him.

Part of him regrets treating her like crap for the six months before she died. Well, specifically he regrets seeing her with Daan Janssen and knowing that she was a lying bitch before everyone else did, so feeling compelled to treat her like crap. It made things harder for him. Sometimes he wonders whether things might have turned out differently if he'd just challenged her back then when he first saw her strolling along the South Bank holding hands with that prick. Maybe if he'd called her out then, things would have ended differently. Yeah, there would have been massive fights, consequences at the time. Probably a divorce, and he'd been so scared of that then. But now he sees that wouldn't have been the worst thing. She wouldn't be dead.

Is it his fault?

The thought flashes in his head and he longs to hear Leigh's voice. She would be annoyed with him for blaming himself. He tries to imagine her saying something like "Damn straight it isn't your fault, Oli. I made my own mistakes, don't take this on." He knows she would have said that because sometimes when he caused a fight between her and his dad (say, because he wanted to stay out late for a party and she thought it was okay and his dad didn't), she'd tell him it wasn't his fault that they were disagreeing. "Your dad and I decide what we want a discussion about, it's not all about you," she'd joke.

They did fight about him, though.

Like when he wouldn't call her Mum anymore. She begged his dad to intervene, which he didn't. She still didn't blame Oli; in fact she went to quite some lengths to avoid him hearing the disagreements that were about him. Those usually played out in hissed whispers, late at night; he listened to them through walls or from the top of the stairs. His ears burn now when he remembers that he liked hearing them argue. That he got a sense of satisfaction from it. The morning after, he would always make a point of asking Leigh if they had been arguing, trying to get a reaction from her, trying to make her feel bad, but she always said everything was fine. She'd smile at him, tell him not to worry. At the time, he thought she was just trying to protect herself, avoid discussing anything that might expose her as an adulterous bitch, but now he wonders whether there was another reason she always pretended everything was okay. Like maybe it was possible that she was trying to protect *him* from anything upsetting. His hands feel sweaty and his mouth dry thinking this.

He keeps thinking too about what Daan Janssen said. Not just the bit about Fiona being a killer; clearly he absorbed that on some level, or why else is he here? But the other bit, the bit about how much Leigh loved him and Seb. The fact that she couldn't leave them. Was Janssen right about that?

He shakes his head. It doesn't matter. It's too late either way. She's dead.

But if it is true, if she did love them in a way no one else did, then that's... Oli can't pursue the thought. He doesn't know why that is. It makes him feel so, so sad and yet somehow relieved. If she loved them that much, it's...well, it's something. His dad loves him, obviously, and his auntie Paula does too. But if Leigh loved him—them—like a mother, is that better or worse because he hates her so much for dying? For being a bigamist. For letting them down.

Seb doesn't whinge once as they slog up the cliff path toward Fiona's place, which is surprising. When they used to walk on Sunday afternoons with their parents, both boys voiced their discontent repeatedly, batting complaints between them like a game of ping-pong. Oli wonders whether Seb is also thinking about Leigh's rallying calls. Her stupid motivational stuff is deeply embedded, hard to shake. Or maybe he's still sulking because Oli wasn't prepared to indulge the fantasy about him seeing Leigh alive and her being kidnapped by some old geezer. WTF was that?

They quietly let themselves into the bungalow. Sneaking about as though they fear waking anyone, which is mad because they're alone. Very much so. The place feels stuffy and neglected. It smells of burnt dust. Oli thought it would feel familiar and maybe even comforting, so he's disappointed. He turns on the immersion heater so they can have showers, if not now, then in the morning. He looks in the pantry and finds some tins.

"Do you want tuna and sweetcorn mash or baked beans?" he asks Seb.

Seb turns away, refusing to show any interest. Oli opens the beans, because it's marginally easier than opening two tins and mixing the contents. He doesn't bother to heat them up; they eat straight from the tins, rather than creating washing-up. They eat in silence. Afterward, they collapse onto the beds in the spare room that they always thought of as theirs. Oli on the left, Seb on the right, no discussion; it's just habit. It takes a matter of minutes before Seb's breathing settles and Oli knows he's asleep. Exhausted from the walk, the emotion, the crying and ultimately, he supposes, the disappointed hope.

Oli is surprised to find he can't fall asleep as easily. He feels oddly jittery, something like he does before a big football match or before he tries a new trick on his board but not as good. He's not sure what to do next, what he'll do in the morning. He doesn't know who he trusts or believes. He doesn't know why he came here. The whole thing is a mess. His father is going to be furious, or worried, or hurt. Something bad.

Thinking about his dad makes him turn on his phone, even though he knows it's a risk. He can see that there are a number of messages from him. He doesn't open them; he can't face that right now. Just as he's about to turn the phone off again, it flashes announcing a message from Daan Janssen. Wanker. The insult drifts into Oli's head without malice, just through habit. He doesn't feel any focused loathing toward Janssen anymore; it's more of a general frustration at his existence, simply a wish that the man had never been born, because his existence has ruined everything.

How's it going?

Oli isn't sure what to reply. He has to say something to justify taking Daan's money.

We're at Fiona's.

The response is almost instantaneous.

Find anything?

No. Oli thinks that whilst true, that response is perhaps a bit discouraging. He *is* discouraged, but feels a responsibility not to pass it on, so he adds, Not yet.

Keep looking.

He resents being given instructions, especially from Janssen. He switches his phone off, rolls over to face the wall, his back hunched like a shell. He lies there for a while but just can't get to sleep. How is it possible to feel so exhausted and yet so alert at the same time? Exasperated with himself, he gets up and starts to snoop around the house. Directionless but somehow believing he might as well.

The walls are all painted pink, peach or orange. He recalls Leigh saying it was like the sunset could be inside and out, that it was warm and cocooning. Oli thinks that at night, the place looks like a bad trip. The orange is more of a threatening bloodred and the walls close in around him. More claustrophobic than comforting. He moves from room to room looking on shelves, rooting through drawers. It's hopeless and pointless; he's unlikely to find a signed confession from Fiona or indeed anything that incriminates her. If there was anything here, the police would have found it already. It's easier to go back to hating Janssen and trusting Fiona. He should just pocket the money and not think about it anymore. It seems like an easy solution, but nothing in Oli's life is easy really. He worries whether it's legal to take the money if he's not using it on legit expenses to investigate. Whatever the hell that might mean. Should he tell his dad about it? But then, does it matter, as Janssen is most likely going to prison for years? The whole thing is a mess. His life is a mess and running away has just made it messier.

He roots around the kitchen and finds a big bag of crisps. Salt and vinegar flavor. He flops on the enormous couch and stares at his own reflection in the large window opposite him. It usually affords great views, but in the black of night, all he can see is himself as he shoves handfuls of crisps in his mouth.

That's when he spots it. It's not exactly a case of finding evidence. It's a little less than that. But it is something. He's found an absence. There was always a whole selection of framed photographs on the coffee table, all in different not-real silver frames. Oli remembers because he has always thought it was a bit annoying. The frames were in the way if you wanted to put your feet up on the coffee table when you were stretching out watching TV. Whenever they wanted to play a game of Monopoly or cards on a wet day, they had to carefully move them all to one of the shelves. Fiona was really into taking photos; she had loads of them all around the house.

Oli had often idly looked at the pics, vaguely wondering about other people's good times, or good times he was part of but could only loosely recall: Christmases, holidays, birthdays. Many of the photos were of the Fletchers. Most of them, he realizes now. He hasn't given that much thought before. Never questioned where photos of Fiona's family and other friends were. There were some really old photos of Fiona and Leigh, from before Mark, Oli and Seb were part of their lives. In those, the two women looked drunk and skinny and were smiling like loons, arms flung around one another. There were some of him and Seb when they were really young and at various milestones of their lives: first day of school, collecting football trophies, that sort of thing. Thank fuck the end-of-year prom was canceled, because otherwise Fiona would have insisted on taking like a hundred photos of him in a suit, which would have been mortifying. There were photos of them with their dad; in TGI Friday's, where Seb was wearing a hat made of balloons; messing about on Fiona's boat here in Lyme Regis.

Oli gazes at the familiar display and realizes it is no longer that. The photos of his mum and Fiona are gone. The ones of them skinny and smiling and the one taken on Fiona's fortieth in Paris. In fact, all the photos of Leigh are missing. There was one of her toasting marshmallows on the beach, silhouetted against the sunset, a sleepy Seb propped next to her; Oli always liked that photo. He knew it was taken the first time he tried cider. There was one of his mum and dad's wedding, a formal one, taken by the official photographer; Fiona was in the shot too, because she was the bridesmaid. His dad was always making that lame joke about a thorn between two roses. Pathetic but memorable. And there was a photo of Oli himself with Leigh, perched on a branch of a tree they'd both climbed. He was thirteen at the time. Seb tried to follow them up but just didn't have the height. Oli recalls sitting on the branch and enjoying the feeling of sneaky triumph; he had his mother to himself for a few minutes.

But where is Leigh now? He stands up and swiftly moves around the house to check the other places where he knows Fiona displays photos: the fridge, the dressing table in her bedroom. There are no photos of Leigh. She's disappeared. She's been eradicated.

It's possible that Fiona took down all the pictures of Leigh because it made her sad to look at them. People do that and other strange things when they're grieving. But when would she have had the opportunity to do that? She told the police that she hadn't been here since October; he remembers hearing her confirm that to the woman police officer who put him in mind of the small terrier that lives next door; tiny but punchy. It's possible that someone else took down Leigh's pictures; possible but not likely. Because who? No one has been allowed to leave their house from the week after she went missing until today.

Oli is trying to be calm and logical. To use the clever brain that Leigh believed in, to prove her right. He doesn't want to be an impetuous kid, too ready to jump to fanciful conclusions. All that said, he is sure that Fiona made his mum vanish. He reaches for his phone, switches it on and then quickly types.

Got something. Got her.

He's so sure and the thought terrifies him but also lights him up. He's solving this for his mother—well, for Leigh. Whatever. The ticks do not change from gray to blue, which is frustrating. Oli feels alert, agitated, pumped. He waits for another twenty minutes and the ticks stay resolutely gray. Eventually he accepts that as they are an hour ahead in the Netherlands, Daan Janssen is probably asleep. His own eyelids are getting heavy. He yawns and goes back to bed, pulling the duvet up to his chin. He can deal with this in the morning.

29

FIONA

Fiona stands outside the bungalow and considers what to do next. The curtains are drawn, suggesting her hunch was correct: the boys are most likely inside. Probably asleep now, because it's almost two in the morning. They've no doubt made themselves at home. They know where the sheets are kept, how to switch on the immersion heater.

Her eyes scan across the lump of mud-colored beach. She doesn't like the bungalow. Never has really. She bought a place here because Leigh liked this part of the world, and the boys did, and Mark. She reasoned that if she had a property in the area they wanted to holiday, she would become central to their plans. Their lives. And her strategy worked. Kylie and Mark would never have been able to afford a second home. Some years they could hardly afford a holiday. That's why this place became useful; they always jumped at the opportunity to holiday for free here. By buying the property she avoided feeling like a spare part. She was integral.

God knows why Leigh liked this spot so much. The beaches on this coast are sand or pebbles in most places, but right where Fiona's bungalow is situated, it's more of a case of fifty shades of mud. Spring, summer, autumn and winter, all year. The coastal bit, a paler mud; the clifftop, darker mud. The sea sometimes looks like mud too; liquid mud, like brown sauce, slow and gloopy. But Kylie could never see it. She thought being here was joyful. There was nothing she liked more than walking along the beach, searching for shells, getting damp with spray and then insisting that they warm up again by drinking tea from a flask and eating tasty sandwiches that she'd prepared that morning before any of them were even out of bed. Fiona remembers how much of a fuss she made peeling back the tin foil and announcing, "Ham and mustard!" or "Egg and cress!" as though she was revealing the lottery numbers. The boys and Mark would indulge her, act as though eating a few sandwiches on the beach was really something special. The fuss they made when she brought along sausage rolls. The whole thing was ludicrous. Disproportionate. They were all in her thrall.

Kylie was spoiled.

Fiona remembers the time when Kylie suggested they build a fire pit on the beach and roast marshmallows. The boys drank hot chocolate, the adults drank cider. Oli begged for a sip, and when Mark wasn't paying attention, Kylie allowed him to have one. He then proceeded to act far drunker than could have been possible after just a couple of mouthfuls, playing to the crowd. They all laughed a lot, then he picked up his guitar, something he was often shy about doing. Maybe the alcohol had emboldened him, or maybe just Kylie's encouragement. They listened to the waves accompanying the music and eventually Seb was lulled to sleep. Mark carried him back to the bungalow, all the way up the steps.

It was a wonderful night. There was a lot of laughter. Fiona remembers that and the thought makes her want to kick something or someone. Because it isn't fair. It isn't fair to have all that and want more. To mess everything up for everyone else. Truthfully, there hasn't been much laughing since Kylie went missing and died. Technically, Fiona knows that is her fault, but really the blame lies with Kylie herself. It should have been enough for her. She should have been grateful. Fiona is the one carrying the load here. She is the one left to pick up the pieces.

She knows that she needs to make the boys smile again,

laugh. They have to trust her and like her if she is ever going to replace Kylie completely.

And why shouldn't she?

It isn't unreasonable to think that one day she might become their stepmother. Mark and the boys need her. She *is* needed. They just don't necessarily know how much they need her yet.

She sighs at the enormity of the task. First she has to get them to go home. Get them away from here. This place gives her the creeps. It is impossible not to think of that final night. Not the happiest of things to recall, obviously. Details keep smashing into her head. Kylie's bruises, her blistered mouth, her filthy body. Fiona is not a monster; she doesn't want to think about that sort of thing. About Kylie's last moments. Better to think about the kindnesses Fiona showed her. She made a pasta supper, poured bath salts into the bath, warmed a fluffy towel for her. She didn't have to do any of that, but she did.

Kylie got what was coming to her, her just deserts, but still, it was uncomfortable dwelling on it.

Fiona tries the door. It is locked. She keeps a secret spare key in the shed. Something she's never told anyone. Not even the Fletchers, despite all the occasions they've stayed with her. There has been no need. It's a matter of security. Privacy. Her senses are on high alert, and as she eases open the shed door, she is hit with the smell of bagged manure, rust and dust, with a heavy kick from the tar on the roof, still warm from the day of sunshine. She retrieves the key from under a pile of plastic plant pots and quietly lets herself into her house. She nearly trips on the boys' trainers, which have been kicked off and abandoned at the door. She recalls the hundreds of times Kylie yelled, "Shoes off, boys, don't trail sand and mud everywhere." They listened, which Fiona ought to be grateful for, but somehow this act of obedience niggles. She feels Kylie's influence stretch like a shadow late in the afternoon.

She locks the door behind her and then pockets the key Oli and Seb used, which they have carefully placed in the fruit bowl on the hall shelf; another practice instilled by Kylie's nagging.

Even though she hasn't put her head around the spare bedroom door to check on them, she sends Mark a WhatsApp message.

Found the boys. They are totally fine and happy. Just having a day out. We're all shattered so will come home tomorrow. Get some sleep. Leave everything to me.

She sees the double blue ticks pop onto her screen. She waits a little longer, hoping to see that Mark is typing. It feels like a long time before he responds.

Thank God. OK.

She tries not to acknowledge the flare of irritation that ripples through her body but settles for suppressing it. Mark is always succinct. She doesn't need to be thanked as such.

It would be nice, though.

You should get in touch with the police and tell them everything is fine. Maybe it's best to say it was a miscommunication, that they left a note saying they were going out for the day and we've only just found it.

She inserts a blushing embarrassed emoji and hopes that makes her look like fun. Mark doesn't respond. Fiona sighs with impatience. It's been a long drive. She has a lot to deal with. She really doesn't want the police knocking at her door. She has to up the ante a fraction. Mark responds to a sense of threat and impending doom. His history has shown him that worst-case scenarios are a genuine possibility. She types another message.

We don't want to look incompetent or cause any more problems. Last thing we need is social services getting involved.

This time she adds the upside-down smiling emoji. She has no real idea what that one means, but she hopes it conveys that she's totally benign, on his side, and maybe something like *Gosh what a crazy world we live in, as if!* She's relieved when he responds.

OK. Will call Clements now.

Fiona takes off her shoes and sneaks silently into the spare room. As quiet as a mouse. The boys are asleep. She watches their bare chests rise and fall. They are sleeping in shorts; maybe the clothes they've worn all day. She's noticed they don't seem to have a strict code about what to wear when, but instead are led by an unfathomable sense of reasoning that is only logical to teens: sometimes they wear the same pair of tracksuit bottoms for three days straight, sometimes they change clothes four times in one day. Both things slightly irritate her. She doesn't like it when they get a bit whiffy, but nor does she like washing and ironing multiple outfits. Once things settle down a little more and life goes back to normal after lockdown, she plans to introduce some rules of her own to the Fletcher household. They shouldn't take her for granted. They need to appreciate her a bit more.

Seb's phone is on the set of drawers next to his bed. Fiona silently pockets it. Oli is clasping his. Carefully, a millimeter at a time, she eases it from his grasp. She isn't planning on hacking into the boys' phones. Not as such. She's only taking them away because she wants to oversee the narrative a little, for a while, that's all. She will give them back when she thinks it's safe to do so. But it just wouldn't do if they contacted their father and contradicted what she has told him. Revealed that they are not "totally fine and happy."

She has to talk to them alone first and just double-check that coming here, to the place she murdered their mother, is simply a coincidence. If it's not, if they suspect her of something, then she needs to... Her thoughts falter. She hasn't really considered what she might have to do if that was the case. Tell the boys they are mistaken? Talk them out of their suspicions? Silence them? She doesn't know what that means; she just knows that she will do whatever she has to do to deal with the situation.

She doesn't want to wake them at this hour—they all need their sleep—so she quietly sneaks into her own bedroom and closes the door behind her. She'll surprise them in the morning when she announces her arrival.

30

DC CLEMENTS

Clements accepts the incoming call from Mark Fletcher. She keeps her eyes on the dark road but feels her heartbeat increase a fraction. She gave him her mobile number months ago, and urged him to use it if he had any questions or information. If there was an emergency. In all this time he has never called her on this phone, but instead waited until she's brought news to his door or phoned her at her office. She's only ever served up tragedy and disappointment; she wonders what he's going to flag to her in return.

She thinks of Seb's face peering at her from behind the door Fiona Phillipson held open, last time she saw him. He wore an expression of simple desperation, but that wasn't what moved her as such. He also looked hopeful. He believed in her. The police are vilified more often than not nowadays. Spat on, sworn at, punched quite regularly. The boy's faith was sweetly old-fashioned, and she wants to deserve his trust. She isn't doing a good job of that. She wasn't able to return his mother to him, and now he is missing too. She wants him and his brother to be safe. Apprehension pulses through her body.

Mark launches straight in. "We've found the boys."

The apprehension dissipates. Thank God. It's like peeing after waiting to find a loo for hours, a physical relief. "How are they?"

"Fine. Good. Really great."

She wonders which it is. That's quite a range. "Are they home?"

"No, not yet, but they're fine." His reassurances have the opposite effect to the one he intends.

"You've spoken to them?"

"Fiona is with them."

"Where?"

He pauses. When he does speak, he doesn't answer. She wonders what he is hiding from her. "Thing is, they just wanted to let their hair down after the months of restraint. Understandable. No harm done. I'm calling so you don't waste any more time on the matter. I'm sure you have a hundred more important things to attend to."

She does have a hundred things to do. She always does. She doesn't know how she might prioritize the boys in among all her responsibilities. Technically safe and well, that's what their dad is saying. "Well, there's a case number. We'll have to follow up tomorrow. Pop in on the boys, see how they are. You know, just procedure."

"I don't think there's any need for that."

"Just procedure," Clements repeats with determination.

"We're thinking of going away tomorrow. Having a little break. We won't be around."

Clements is frequently lied to. She usually knows when it's happening, and right now she believes this is something Mark Fletcher has just made up on the spot. The question is why. Maybe the totally innocent response of a concerned dad who has just had a shock and wants to do something nice with his kids. Maybe a man who is hiding something. "You are? Have you got somewhere booked?"

"No."

"I'd say you'll be lucky to find somewhere. All the hotels and B&Bs in the country are booked up if you believe the media hype."

"I don't as a rule," he mumbles. Clements feels crass. Fair

point. The man has been on the wrong end of media specula-
tion and sensationalism. She hears him sigh down the phone.
He's not happy. Of course not; that would be a lot to ask considering everything. He sounds exhausted. "I'm just saying we
might take a run out. We need a bit of family time."

"Right."

"You can understand."

"Of course."

"So don't waste a journey coming to see us. I'll get the boys
to call you if you like."

"Mark?"

"Yes."

"Are you sure everything is okay?" He laughs. It's a hollow,
mirthless sound; she corrects herself. "I mean as okay as it can
be under the circumstances."

"We're fine." He ends the call.

Clements doesn't know what to do. She's been driving for
over two hours already and there's at least another couple to
go before she reaches Fiona Phillipson's beach house. Why
would she go there now she knows the boys are safe? This
isn't an investigation. She'd have to arrest herself for wasting
police time, her own. Her eyelids feel heavy, though, and her
body is stiff. She can't face driving back to London right now.
She should pull over, have a nap in the car. Think what to do
next after that.

She finds somewhere to do just that, then sends Tanner a
text to keep him in the loop.

Mark Fletcher called. Boys found and safe. Don't bother coming. See you tomorrow at the station.

She doesn't even wait for a response, but instead winds her
seat back as far as it will go and settles down to sleep.

31

FIONA

Fiona lies on her bed. She's going to take a quick glance at the phones now, otherwise she'll never get to sleep. She just needs to see who they have been texting and talking to. Seb's is not locked, but then nor does it reveal any secrets. It's a jumble of gaming and football apps, with a constant stream of pointless memes on his social media channels that she doesn't understand let alone find funny. Unsurprisingly, Oli's phone *is* locked. She knows that after six failed attempts to enter the passcode, the iPhone will disable for just a minute. The seventh incorrect attempt locks her out for five minutes. She googles to check whether there is a limit to how many guesses she can make. Her search suggests that after the eighth failed try she will be locked out for fifteen minutes, and that the punishment increases the more attempts she makes. She's so tired, if she has to wait fifteen minutes she'll most likely fall asleep.

She wonders whether there is a finite number of attempts that can be made and what happens when that number is reached. She imagines the phone blowing up like in a Bond movie or something. She has already tried 123456, 654321, his birth date forward and backward, prime numbers, and 280085, because when he was a little boy, he thought spelling *two boobs* on the calculator was hilarious. None of these combinations lets her in. She feels frustrated and is aware that there are a million numerical possibilities. She has no idea what Oli might have chosen.

Holding the phone in her hand, feeling like she is wading into deep water, she sneaks back into the boys' bedroom. Seb has rolled onto his stomach, but Oli hasn't moved since she was last in here. *Dead to the world*, that was what her mother used to say of heavy sleepers. Oh, so gently she holds his finger to the pad on the phone. Eases it carefully from one side to the other until the screen springs to life. Messages and reminders flash up. She is nervous that the bright light will wake him, and quickly rushes out of the room.

She doesn't feel proud of herself. Reduced to sneaking about. Spying on the boys. Boys she wants to think of as sons. It should be beneath her. But if ever there was a case where the end justifies the means, this is it. Oli is completely untrustworthy. He's talking to Daan Janssen, of all people! A man he has sworn he hates. A man who is accused of murdering his stepmother. Janssen has been pleading his innocence to Oli, casting suspicion elsewhere. He's even given the boy money, apparently, so he can investigate.

Fiona feels fury slither through her body. She can't believe Daan has had the audacity—and the ability—to turn Oli's loyalty and trust into hate and suspicion. He has placed a spy in her camp. It's so typical of the man, arrogant and determined never to lose. She thinks of their encounters and feels so filthy she wants to scrub her skin. She used to consider what they had to be a relationship, but now she knows better. He was just another married man who lied to her. He had sex with her when his wife was away and he felt horny. He used her. Bent her over the kitchen table, made her come and then said, "See you again." It confused her. They were playing a game, but she wasn't aware of the fact so had no idea about the rules. He's not the only man who has toyed with her in this way, but he was certainly the proverbial straw that broke the camel's back. She's not prepared to lose to him again.

Then she reads the last message from Oli to Daan and her

blood slows. Daan talking to Oli is not the worst of it. Him giving the boys money and inciting them to snoop about her business is not the worst of it. The worst of it is that Oli has found something that he believes proves her guilt and he's told Daan as much.

What the hell?

Fiona throws the phone against the wall.

SUNDAY
5 JULY 2020

32

STACIE

I wake up and the fire is dead. There's nothing colder than gray ashes. My mouth tastes like I've licked said ashes; I should not have poured myself that second whiskey. In fact, I should probably try to drink less generally, but bloody hell, without alcohol, what is there for me right now? The glass is on the floor on its side, and I get a slightly shamefaced feeling that I dropped off whilst holding it; the heat of the fire and the sound of Dad's light snores obviously had a soporific effect. I'm lucky it didn't break. Dad is not in the chair opposite mine. Most likely he got up in the middle of the night and went up to his more comfortable bed. I check my watch. It's 6:00 a.m. I never sleep late after alcohol. It's my curse. I look about for Ronnie but can't see him. Maybe Dad had a really early start and is already walking the dog; he often gets up with the sun, irrespective of how much he has had to drink the night before.

I head upstairs. We share a bathroom, Dad and me, which strikes me as oddly old-fashioned. Not just the bathroom, decorated with graying, peeling linoleum that I think was once cream, but also the very fact that I'm sharing my intimate space with a parent; it is undoubtedly a regressive step. The bathroom here is nothing like the one I recall (or have imagined). This one is damp; there is only one window in the sloping ceiling, and we leave it open all the time to allow the staleness a chance to escape. It never does, though, and I can't get used to the perennial musty smell. The shower is inside the bath, a handheld number, not even wall-mounted. Whenever I take a shower, the slightly moldy curtain determinedly clings to my body like a small fussing child who refuses to be put down. This means that no matter how many times I try to rearrange things and be careful, I always find that water splashes on the floor.

Still, I do quite value my time in the bathroom. On the days when I really can't get my act together, I come here to be alone. Obviously there's a lock on the door, and so this is where I hide. I hide from Dad seeing how hard everything is, how overwhelmed and lost I sometimes feel. The thing is, though I can hide my fear from Dad if I need to, I can't hide from myself. The horror of my own exhausting shape-shifting, my blanks and fractured states follows me into the bathroom. So over these past few months there have been a number of times when I've cried hot, fat, silent tears in the bath and emerged blotchy-faced, red-eyed. I always pretend to Dad that I got shampoo in my eyes or took my bath a fraction too hot. He pretends to believe I'm very clumsy. We have a number of coping strategies that we share to protect one another from the harsh reality of our situation.

This morning, however, despite the furry mouth and nagging headache, I feel quite excited. I want to get an early start, freshen up, and then talk to Dad about the progress I made yesterday. I know he found it less than ideal that I sneaked out of the house, but I'm sure once he hears how successful the trip was in terms of helping me recall, he'll endorse another jaunt. If I promise to wear a mask and socially distance, et cetera, what possible objections can he have?

Despite my optimistic mindset, the bathroom seems even less appealing than usual, as surprisingly the window is closed and so the air is especially torrid. I would have to precariously balance on the side of the bath to reach up to open it, and I haven't the energy, so I decide to simply breathe through my mouth as I take a very quick shower. I emerge from the bathroom wrapped in a towel and dash to my bedroom. It could be my hangover, but that room feels stuffy too; it needs airing. I pull on underwear and a T-shirt, then open the blinds. This window is also shut. I wonder whether I slept through heavy rain last night, which might be why Dad closed all the windows. Or did he perhaps close them when he set off to find me in Lyme Regis, knowing he was going further afield than usual and feeling security-conscious?

I attempt to open the window, but it's stuck. I'm slow processing because of the hangover, and it takes me a second or two of straining to understand that it isn't stuck, it's locked. They are ugly white plastic window frames, a questionable "home improvement" that must have happened in the nineties because it was fashionable then. Again I marvel and despair that my memory knows this but has lost all the important stuff. There are locks on every window in the house, but I've never seen a key, or even thought about it before. I try the second window in my room. It's also locked.

It's peculiar, but my body reacts faster and more violently than my mind. I don't know why, but I immediately start to sweat and shake. My palms and under my arms feel clammy despite the fact that I've just emerged from the shower. My mouth is dry; my breathing is thin and rapid. I actively try to slow it down, but I can't. I gasp and gulp like a fish out of water. I feel I'm suffocating.

I pull on shorts and stride onto the landing. I try to open the window there. It's locked. The one in Dad's bedroom is too. I rush downstairs, my legs shaking so badly now I fear they might give way beneath me, like when you have severe pins and needles. My jaw is chattering, I feel my top teeth bang against my bottom teeth and I push my tongue to the roof of my mouth in an attempt to stop that. I have no idea why my body is responding in this disproportionate way to Dad becoming security-conscious. It's not a big deal. I assume he has been spooked by the hordes of rowdy holidaymakers he saw last night. Now that he has become aware that they are just a few miles up the road, maybe he fears marauders and intruders. Perhaps he believes someone might break in, although I'm not sure why he's especially worried, since we have nothing of value to pinch.

I try the front door, as it's the first in sight. It's locked. I rattle violently at the handle. I rush through the kitchen, almost slipping on the floor in my haste. The back door is locked as well. I hammer on it and force myself to swallow back demands to be let out. That's ridiculous, but it also feels instinctually like the right thing to do. I think I have been locked up before. The thought is terrifying. I check the windows downstairs, but even before I do so, I know that they will all be fastened tight, and I'm proved right. I tell myself I'm just frustrated, but I feel stunned by a sense of terrifying claustrophobia. The thing is we've slept here without locking the doors for as long as I can remember. Why are they locked now? My mind is spinning. An out-of-control rocket hurtling not toward the stars but toward a dense, infinite oblivion. A black hole. Another one.

I start to root about for keys, flinging open kitchen drawers and scrabbling through cutlery, elastic bands, stray pens and random lids for plastic tubs. My heart is pounding. Where is Dad? Why has he left me locked up and alone?

What the hell is happening here?

I don't know exactly, but it's nothing good, that's for sure.

33

STACIE

"Hey, love, I'm home." Dad's voice shatters the solid silence. In an instant I am on my feet, striding the few paces across the sitting room into the kitchen. The back door swings wide open, fresh air floods into the house. I dart to the door and hang on to it. Ronnie leaps about, almost knocking me over, as my legs are still quivering. I am half in the house, half out. I could run. Just go. Now.

What am I thinking? Run from what? Run to what?

"You all right, love?" Dad looks concerned.

I take enormous gulps of air. Try to steady myself, try to sound sane and reasonable. I fail. "You locked me in," I yell, my tone a hundred percent accusatory.

"What?" He seems confused.

"You locked all the doors and windows. I was trapped. Why did you lock me in?" I don't step back into the kitchen, but instead am set like a runner on the blocks. Ready, steady, go.

"Oh, sorry, love. God, how silly of me." Dad playfully slaps his forehead. "I didn't plan to, obviously. I locked up last night before I set off to find you. I forgot I'd done so. I locked this door behind me when I left this morning without giving it much thought. You were still asleep. It's only eight o'clock now. I didn't even expect you to be up." Ronnie is licking my hand reassuringly. Dad looks concerned. I tell myself that everything is as it should be. "I'm so sorry. You're as white as a sheet. Did something happen? Why were you so worried? I wasn't out long."

"All the windows were locked." I'm already beginning to feel foolish, but try to explain my panic. "We never so much as close windows, let alone lock them."

"There are more people hanging about now that things are opening up. Innocent holidaymakers maybe. Strangers definitely." He smiles. "You have your own key, don't you?"

"No," I snap. Then I realize I sound like a sulky teenager and so try to be more reasonable. "At least, if I do, I can't remember where it is."

Dad looks sheepish. "Sorry, love. I never thought. We'll get you a new key cut as soon as we can. Today, if we can't unearth the original one. You're shaking. Sorry. I'm home now." He smiles, his broad, kind smile. The only thing I know and trust. Right? "Do you fancy a cuppa?" he asks. I nod. "Have you had breakfast?"

"No."

"Leave it to me. You rest up."

I sit down on the stoop, lean against the back door. Dad makes the tea and toast without another word. Then he potters about the garden while I eat and drink. I watch him pick up the odd piece of litter that has blown in onto the pile of sea glass. He brushes the stones with a long-handled broom and then gets out the hosepipe and washes them. The water splutters, then forms an impressive arc that catches the sunlight and glistens.

I feel a need to normalize things and make conversation. "You tend those as though it was a rose bed," I observe.

He grins. "Damn sight easier than any plants."

I'm not certain, but I think I recall Dad once bragging he was green-thumbed. I can't be sure about anything, apparently. The seagulls are entitled and curious; they swagger around about a ruler distance from me. It feels too close. They're waiting for me to share my breakfast toast. I break off a corner and toss it at them. The sense of claustrophobia hasn't quite subsided. Screeching, they fall on it and start to tussle, reminding me of fat boozed-up men falling out of a pub door when someone calls time. They don't have any grace or sense of decorum. The pigeons come right up at me; one of them pecks a crumb off my Croc. I crush my instinct to flinch and scare it away. It feels like a moment when I need to hold my nerve. I know what I have to do.

"Tell me more about my illness, Dad."

"Oh, what a topic. I'd have thought you'd had enough of talking about that." Dad straightens, looks up at the sky. "It's going to be another beautiful day."

I am not going to let him avoid the subject. I force myself to grin at him. But it's hard, I don't feel like smiling. "I know you've spoken of it before, but the problem is, I keep forgetting what you've told me. I've forgotten the treatment."

He nods at me. "They said you might."

"Did they?"

"Yes."

"Who are they?"

He laughs. "Well, the doctors and nurses, obviously."

"And the specialists, the consultant?"

"Well, yes."

"They said I'd forget my treatment?"

"Yes, that's right." Dad stares at me, trying to figure me out. "What's up, Stacie? What in particular is bothering you? Are you still feeling weird because I accidentally locked you in?"

"What's his name again? The name of the man who was in charge of my treatment."

Dad turns off the tap. The water from the hose slows, splutters, then stops, before he finally replies. "Now, let me think. There was a Dr. McDougal, for a start. He was the main consultant, and then along with him there were a number of other doctors and nurses. Off the top of my head, I remember Rosie, Deja and Jamal were the nurses' names."

"Were they all nice?"

"Nice?"

"Well, I realize they're heroes, saved my life, et cetera, but were they nice? Did I like them?" Why can't I remember them? You'd think they'd be a big deal to me, right?

"You liked them all, except for maybe Dr. Brookfield; she could be a bit cautious and that depressed you. You always wanted to hear just the good news."

The sun falls on my thighs. Tingles. It's going to be a scorcher. "Tell me a bit more. Give me some details."

Dad sighs and starts to coil up the hosepipe. "Frankly, I've no idea why you want to dwell on this morbid subject, but if you insist. The anesthetist was rather dour. He was in charge of your tracheotomy. You didn't like the EEG cap, but it was there to measure seizures. Your sleep wasn't solid."

I try to imagine the situations he's describing. I try to recall the feel of the cap.

"When did my hair fall out?" I touch my head; there is a uniform covering now, just a couple of centimeters long.

"What?"

"Did it come out bit by bit, or did I cut it all off before the treatment?"

Dad looks awkard. "I can't recall."

"You can't recall that?"

"Can you?" He laughs. It's a joke, but I don't find it funny. He catches sight of my expression and then says, "Sorry. I think you cut it off. Yes, you did. I remember now."

"Did we keep it?"

"What, the hair?"

"Yes. Did we keep the hair?"

"No. No, you donated it to a charity for kids with cancer who needed wigs. Yes, that's right, it's all coming back to me now." He smiles broadly. "It's growing back well, though, isn't it?"

I nod. "It's growing back darker than I was in the photos."

"A little, perhaps. That happens."

I stare at him for a long time. "When did I visit them last, the consultants, the hospital?"

"Oh, I'm not sure."

"Before lockdown?"

"Well, obviously. You've seen the news. They aren't exactly keen to bring vulnerable people into hospitals. Thousands of people are dying, Stacie."

"I understand, but I'd have thought there would be online consultations."

"No internet." Dad shrugs. "Besides, you were at the end of your treatment for now. God willing, forever. You're in remission. You don't need to see anyone at the moment. You know all this, Stacie." A muscle in his cheek is quivering. It looks like he's chewing a moth.

"Are there letters?" I probe.

"Letters, what sort of letters?"

"Appointment notifications from when I did go in. Details about my treatment and consultations. You don't have internet, so nothing was emailed. There must be letters. Physical ones." I can hear my voice tightening. I try to remain calm. I don't want to sound as though I'm accusing him of anything. Although I am. But what exactly? A terrible thought is beginning to seep into my mind. Did he abandon my treatment? Maybe the hospital called me in for further appointments during lockdown, but he decided I shouldn't attend because he's so afraid of damned COVID. It sounds odd, but something is not right. I'm not in control of my treatment, or anything, come to that.

"Well, yes, of course there are letters."

"So where are they?" I should have asked this before, this and so much more. How could I have not asked? I should have taken more interest in my condition, treatment and prognosis. I've spent my time thinking about my past, but obviously the most important matter is my future.

"I've shown you the letters. You've just forgotten them

again," says Dad with a sigh. His patience seems less abundant than usual.

"I thought the operation took away *past* memories; are you telling me now that my memory *since* my illness is spasmodic too? Am I supposed to live with this going forward?" I rattle the questions out at the speed of gunfire. Dad bends his head; he won't meet my eye or answer me. In frustration, I stand up and stride past him.

"Where are you going?" he asks.

"For a walk."

"Are you taking Ronnie?"

"You've just brought him home," I point out.

"We didn't go far."

That doesn't ring true; he was out for over two hours and Ronnie is settled on the sofa in the sitting room, bathing in a shaft of sunlight that's flooding through the window, obviously tired. I bristle, because there seems to be a level of control that comes from the suggestion. It feels restrictive. Everything Dad does feels like a rope is being wrapped around me, and even if that rope is made of silk, I want to snap it.

"Show me the letters again."

"What?"

In all the times I've tidied the house, and today when I searched through drawers, boxes and cupboards looking for the keys, I've never come across a single medical letter. "Where do you keep the letters from my doctors? I have a right to see them."

"In my room." He blinks, once, twice.

I turn back into the coolness of the cottage. I can't storm off; I need to get to the bottom of this. I need to understand my treatment. He follows me, and the moment we are both in the kitchen, I hear the back door bang closed and the key turn in the lock. I feel like I'm climbing on a bouncy castle. Walls sloping, floor sinking, everything trembling and moving, nothing solid. I turn and see an expression on his face that I haven't seen him wear before but somehow I still recognize.

Betrayal.

34

STACIE

"Who are you?" For months I've been asking *Who am I?* I now realize that was the wrong question. So terribly wrong. My mind starts galloping at a hundred miles per hour. I see, and sense, and feel, and maybe even remember so many things at once that I feel sick and dizzy. "Open the door." He shakes his head sadly. "Give me the key."

"Darling, you look terrible. I'll get you some water. I wonder if you've picked up something in town. We need to check your temperature. It could be COVID." His face is a picture of concern. An expression I've melted into for months but abruptly no longer trust. The strange thing is, my father calling me darling was something I wanted in the past; I know that, I recall that. But this man calling me darling doesn't feel right.

"Who are you?" I ask again. My voice rattles around the house. It seems to ooze through the scruffy furniture, the dusty books, the ornaments and the mug tree. I focus on these things, telling myself that I have grown up with these objects, that they are familiar and known, but they are not. Not really. My mind is racing in and out, over and through, as though exploring. Looking for the answer, which is hidden just out of sight. It pushes at the locked doors and locked windows. Unable to escape.

"I'm your dad, silly. Are you having an episode? Is your

memory playing up again? Don't worry, darling girl. This happens. You've been very ill. Remember?" I shake my head. He takes the gesture to mean that I don't remember, so he repeats things he's said to me before. "You had brain cancer. You were operated on before lockdown. You have no long-term memories. You can't recall anything that happened to you before the cancer, and sometimes you get confused about events that have happened since. You lose some short-term things too." He squeezes my shoulder; a little too long, a little too hard. It feels awkward.

I have longed to wake up from the living nightmare of not remembering. I've actively wished for as much every few minutes of every day, for months. And now I *am* waking up, becoming fully conscious in every sense, and I fear my reality might be worse than the nightmare I was living. I breathe deeply. My mind is processing dozens of things all at the same time. I fight through the mishmash. I examine the idea that my father stopped my cancer treatment because of his fear of COVID. On some level it makes sense. My lack of memories about the treatment, the lack of letters detailing consultations... Something doesn't add up. My mind swirls with more thoughts and, yes, memories. I allow them space.

My memories will create me, I know that for sure, because the lack of them destroyed me. But will my memories fix me or damage me further? I have no idea, but I have to accept whatever it is that unfolds. It feels like I am coming round from an anesthetic or sobering up the morning after a big session.

The ease with which my brain makes the leap is a surprise. Every thought I've had for these past few months has been such a struggle, so it is on one level reassuring to feel so certain, yet on another level horrifying, because in that instant I know Kenneth Jones is not my father.

I don't know who the hell he is.

That can't be good.

"Darling?" He holds his hand out toward me. I edge further back, move my arm out of his reach. I have a sudden conviction that being called darling by my real father never felt right or safe. I believe it was a tool he used to control me into collusion. *And, darling, obviously as that woman was nothing, we don't need to mention this to Ellie. It's between us.* Who is Ellie? I know my father said this to me. My father trained me to have secrets. Kenneth Jones is not my father, although it appears he has secrets of his own. I did not enjoy the carefree childhood that has been described to me, captured in photos. I didn't grow up by the sea, eat rock candy and visit the maritime museum in Great Yarmouth. I didn't have a patch of garden that hosted an abundance of pretty bobbing snapdragons, roses and phlox. This delightful childhood doesn't belong to me.

My childhood was desperate, difficult and divided. My parents insisted I split myself in two. The truth of that thought is absolute. It is the root of who I am. What grew from that root? I sense the answers are in my head now, no longer a black hole. The absence has been filled by a darker, denser threat. Reality. Whatever grew from that root wasn't good.

Why is Kenneth Jones lying to me? I remember the first time he told me this story about my cancer, offering it as an explanation as to why I woke up in bed, bruised, confused, my head shaved and stitched. He's right, I didn't have any long-term memories, and his explanation seemed reasonable. He filled some of the terrifying holes that were gaping wide in front of me. Holes I thought I might fall into, disappear into. These past few months have been dreadful, not knowing who I am, unable to recall my childhood, friends, lovers, family or colleagues. This man was all I had to depend on, to believe in. He was so patient and kind, and I readily accepted what he told me, happy to embrace the identity he provided for me. I rushed to be engulfed by it.

What he created was not a perfect life. It was one that was blighted by illness, but it was not an altogether unattractive life. I inhabited it happily, accepted it as my own. Stacie Jones, as Kenneth Jones depicted her, was an independent woman who lived in Paris, taught English and had enough confidence to

walk away from a wedding to her childhood sweetheart because she believed her fulfilment lay elsewhere. Confidence
that I admired and that I was proud of. I believed that confidence came from being a much-loved child, because my God,
for all the lies that I'm now confronted with, I do believe Kenneth Jones loves his daughter, Stacie.

But I don't believe I am Stacie.

I don't know who she is or where she is or why he is pretending I am her. But I know I am not her. It's too much to
compute. It seems crazy. I think of the clothes upstairs in cases
and boxes. They fit me, but I understand now that they don't
belong to me. It's not just that I can't remember wearing them; I
can't imagine wearing them. The garish Crocs, the vintage fes-
tival T-shirts advertising bands I don't recall. The clothes never
felt like mine. I never found the expensive burnt-orange dress.

I look at the old man in front of me. He is tall and lean. Normally he walks with a lengthened back that suggests he had
ramrod posture as a younger man. His light eyes are bright and
intelligent. His eyebrows and hair unkempt, as white as snow.
There's something about his jaw and the ease with which his
face falls into a smile that seems dignified and yet playful too.
I thought I loved this man and that I could trust him. I feel
something gush through my body.

Loss.

I thought he was my father, but now that I know that he is
not, it hurts to lose him. To lose *her*, even. Stacie Jones. The
identity I have owned these past few months. I loved the idea
of being an adored daughter, having a devoted father. It felt
like something I could lean into, something I always yearned
for. I remember now. My relationship with my father was not
at all like the relationship Kenneth had with Stacie, the one I
have temporarily enjoyed believing in.

My head is pounding, and I can feel my breakfast in a lump
in my throat, threatening a reappearance. I don't try to run.
What is the point? The doors are locked, and besides, I have
nowhere to go.

Stacie's mother walked out, but her dad picked up the pieces. I know that; I have seen the photos, the look of love beaming between father and daughter. I now remember that my father left me and my mother when I was very young, which I suppose is why I could believe the story that I was once abandoned by a parent; somewhere deep in my subconscious, I must have felt it to be true. The difference being, when my father left, my mother didn't rally; she fell apart completely. I can recall her crying, wailing. I see her dark head dipped into her hands. I see her frame, the angles of her body sharp and spiky. It's a clear, precise memory. She's not the woman in the photographs that I've been shown.

My parents didn't have much in common, but one thing they did have was their indifference toward me, the embodiment of their shared past. A past that my father wanted to run from, a past my mother grieved for so intensely that she couldn't imagine a future for us. From a young age I was shuttled between the two of them. I remember a small brown plastic suitcase and a bustling waiting room at a station that I often lingered in, apprehensive and vigilant. My childhood was sad and difficult. Scarred and chaotic. Neither parent provided the necessities or the niceties of family life. I was often hungry. I recall opening sticky Formica cupboards and the door of an old fridge, aware even before I checked that they'd be empty. My father had money but didn't make room for me; instead he moved on and had more children. Sons. I have brothers somewhere. My mother had no money; we shared a bed, we were so poor. I grew up feeling hopelessly overwhelmed with being responsible for her happiness. A happiness that was impossible to deliver.

I recall all of this with total clarity. Kenneth Jones was not part of my childhood.

The room is airless. There is no escape. I stay in my head, pursuing the memories that are now tumbling, abundant and vibrant. No longer vague, stilted or forced. I know the truth. As an adult, I battled with the longing and the hunger to be loved. I wasn't engaged to Giles, the open, hopeful-faced farmer, nor was I the sort of woman who might have had the confidence to walk away from an unfulfilling relationship—more's the pity. I was the opposite. I accepted whatever was tossed my way. It's painful and shaming to recall that as a teenager and young adult, the ravenous lacking controlled me. It pelted its way around my mind and body, eating up my confidence and trust, shredding and destroying conviction, poise and any hope I had at future intimacy. I never gave a name to the anguish of being unwanted. Identifying it would have imbued it with more power than I could allow. Better to leave it as a wordless curse. I vividly remember a number of faces; boys and men who I desperately tried to accommodate and impress. Always an extreme people-pleaser, I was in the habit of molding myself to their ideals. A chameleon, putting on a show and only revealing the part of me I knew they would find palatable. I never gave the whole package. I always held something back.

I would present myself as straightforward. Men adore straightforward. But I am very complex. I was then and I'm more so now. I managed. I grew up the way many women do, accepting what was offered, not believing I deserved or could demand more. The longing to be loved was contained to a throb or a pulse, a dreary, austere lacking.

It comes back to me in one overwhelming tsunami. *Oh my God.* I feel my body turn to liquid and I think I might be swept away altogether. I know who I am. I know *what* I am.

I am a bigamist. I am a fugitive. My name is Kylie Gillingham.

Their specific faces come to me. One man, dark, tanned. He wears T-shirts and works outdoors. He's muscly and solid. Solid emotionally as well as physically. He rescued me. It sounds oddly old-fashioned and anti-feminist, but it's okay, because I rescued him too. I sense he needed me. Although I can't recall exactly why. My brain won't cooperate with that.

And my other man. The second husband. He is the epitome of sophistication, tall, blond, rich, young—at least younger than I am. Ambitious, determined and eager to live his own life, he doesn't demand much at all. He looks after me. He treats me well. He makes reservations and introductions; he gives me holidays and jewels. He somehow senses that I'm just out of reach and he likes my elusiveness. I'm a challenge.

And I liked it that neither of them knew me completely. It felt safer. But now it doesn't.

Neither of them knows me completely, so they won't know where to look for me, and I am lost. No, I am more than lost. I am being hidden. The memories carouse, crash and tumble into my head. They are unbelievable, but absolutely true. I know it. I was kidnapped, drugged and held captive. I recall being chained to a radiator. I force myself to look at Kenneth. Did he do those things to me?

It's too much. The room swims, blackness starts to climb into the edges of my vision. My blood pounds in my ears.

Then there is nothing.

35

DAAN

Daan has sent a number of messages to Oli. They have been read, but Oli has not responded.

What did you find?

What is it that proves she's guilty? Call me.

Are you safe?

He's phoned several times too, but Oli has not picked up. Why not? Daan is concerned. He starts to consider more carefully what he's asked the boys to do. This isn't a bit of boy scout snooping; he's embroiled them in a murder investigation with a ruthless, dangerous woman. He didn't want to put them at risk. That was what he was trying to avoid. He sighs to himself, examines his thoughts. He's a clear, logical thinker. He's known for it at work; it's made him and others buckets of cash in the past. Unimaginable—some might say obscene—amounts of money. He's good at being logical.

He doesn't have to lie to himself; he knows his main motivation for contacting the boys in the first place was to get his own arse out of this trouble. That's why he feels so bad, possibly worse now than he did before. Going to prison for a murder he didn't commit would be hell enough to endure; putting two boys in peril, being part of the chain that led to them being harmed, would unlock a whole extra level of personal demons. Has he done that? Led them to harm? Of course, it's perfectly possible that Oli is messing with him. Off spending his cash and having some careless fun somewhere. But Daan doubts it. The kid is more serious than he likes to admit. Life has made him so.

Maybe Oli isn't responding to him because he has his own crap to deal with. Perhaps he's considering the possibility that his father is involved with the abduction and murder too. Daan doesn't believe that, but then he's not a stressed, vulnerable and desperate sixteen-year-old. Oli might be imagining that Mark was having an affair with Fiona. His life is so fucked up that nothing is unthinkable. It most likely depends on what he found. Daan needs to know what that is. Might it be enough to prove his innocence? Enough to prove Fiona's guilt? All he really needs is enough to cast reasonable doubt. There is a sliding scale when it comes to law and order. Justice is an arbitrary, shadowy concept; he's come to learn that.

Since Kai's disappearance, Daan has experienced a myriad of emotions. He resents them all. None of them are good emotions, and besides, he isn't a great one for feeling; he'd always rather think, or better yet, act. Even so, he's been hijacked by feelings of devastation, resentment and frustration. Guilt is the latest unwelcome contender to join the litany. He believes Kai would have expected him to take care of her boys; ironic considering she never told him about their existence. But he knows she found him dependable, expected him to deal with things, have solutions and plans. That was their dynamic. At least he thought it was, but what does he know about anything anymore? She was clearly capable of making solutions and plans of her own. Quite the expert. Although she was notably lacking in the dependability department.

The whole thing is a murky quagmire of lies, secrets, suspicions and fear.

He does know that his concern for the boys—which may have originated from his mixed-up feelings of responsibility toward his batshit-crazy ex-not-quite-wife—has now stabilized into something more personal. Oli and Seb have been screwed over too, and they are possibly in danger. This time it is his batshit-crazy ex-occasional-shag who is to blame. He can see that he is in the thick of this situation. He is not one to shirk responsibilities and he feels a level of personal responsibility. Something has to be done.

He could call the police. He probably should. But he weighs it up. If Oli is okay—say his battery is simply flat and he's looking for a charger—Daan will regret involving the police. Anything Oli has found is likely to be challenged in court and refused as evidence if Daan's involvement is revealed. Tampering with witnesses is obviously a big no-no. It is better if someone else calls them.

On reflection, Daan does not believe Mark is involved in Kai's abduction and murder. Yes, he has shacked up with Fiona quite speedily, but Daan doesn't think they were shagging before Kai's disappearance. He thinks it's a petty and ill-advised act of revenge. Mark needs to prove to himself that he's desirable. It's a bit pathetic, but he tries not to judge.

Daan believes that Kai's abduction and murder and him being framed is all Fiona's work, and hers alone. He doesn't know that for a fact, but he trusts his own judgment. His confidence is such that even now, even after being duped by a bigamist wife, he thinks he can make a savvy guess at people's characters. He has met Mark only once. Just after Kai first went missing, Mark turned up at Daan's apartment looking for answers. Daan was curious at the time, suspicious too. He allowed Mark to roam around the flat opening doors and cupboards, checking out each and every room. He gave Mark the freedom to study his wife's second incarnation because he felt sorry for him.

He saw the man's grief; it was absolute. Mark is not in love with Fiona. Daan secretly watched him in Kai's dressing room. Mark took a dress off the hanger, held it to his body and draped the sleeves over his shoulders as though the dress was embracing him. Then he slowly swayed from side to side, clearly imagining he was dancing with her. It was a moment of almost shocking tenderness. Daan was stung by an intense hatred of Mark at that point. He hated him for loving his wife so much. Dancing with her dress after she'd gone missing was not the action of an adulterous coconspirator. Mark is a prick, though. Because despite Daan's generosity in allowing him to see Kai's home, when he asked if he could see Mark's house, the one Kai lived in when she was Leigh, Mark flat-out refused. He said it wouldn't be fair on the boys. It irritated Daan at the time. It felt uneven. Mark wouldn't play ball. But then maybe Daan wasn't the sort of person people felt sorry for. He wouldn't want to be.

He wonders now whether the second thing he's ever asked of Mark will be granted or refused. He hopes for everybody's sake that Mark is in a more cooperative mood than he was at their first encounter, although it seems doubtful. Mark has less reason to trust Daan now than he did then; more reason to hate him. But Daan must do something.

Mark is even easier to find than his sons were. His mobile number is detailed on his landscape gardening website. Daan is surprised that he hasn't taken this personal detail down. He must have had countless unsolicited calls from journalists, but then maybe he's had an upturn in business too, Daan thinks cynically. People like a bit of notoriety; it's the next best thing to celebrity. As Daan hits the numbers, he realizes there's a possibility that the phone will be disconnected, or that Mark won't pick up, or that he'll hang up as soon as he knows who is calling.

Still, he has to try.

He is pleased that Mark is either trusting or stupid. The number rings, the call is answered.

"Hello."

"Mark Fletcher? This is Daan Janssen calling. Do not end the call." Daan uses his most imperious voice. The one that has clients and colleagues, employees and even employers sitting up, taking note. "You need to listen to what I have to say."

"Fuck off. I don't need to listen to a word from you."

"Oddly, you do. I really want to help you."

36

MARK

Mark wants to say it again. Fuck off. Again and again and again, actually, because he wishes this man would just fuck off out of the world. He wishes he'd never been in it. What is Daan Janssen doing calling him? Surely that's breaking some parole stipulation. At a very basic level it is off-kilter, callous. Mark wants nothing to do with a brutal murderer. The man who has killed his wife, destroyed his life, ruined his boys' lives. But he bites his tongue. He finds he's more curious than he is furious, or even scared.

He answered his phone in a hurry, assuming it would be Fiona or one of the boys with an update as to when he should expect them home. He's called all three of their mobiles this morning and sent texts, but he's heard nothing from them. It's only ten o'clock, though, it's very possible they are all still asleep. Teen boys can sleep as though it's an Olympic sport.

Hearing Daan Janssen's voice when he was hoping for Oli's or Seb's is especially jarring, disturbing.

He is talking to a killer. He wonders whether it is possible that Janssen is going to reveal where Leigh's body is. He's read about murderers doing just that. He has found himself drawn to such stories on the internet; ones about abductions, murders, missing persons, missing bodies. It's obviously not healthy. What obsession is? Of course, his immersion in such dark vileness also means that he has read about murderers doing the exact opposite instead. Some, famously, go to their own grave without revealing where their victim's remains might be found. The final power kick over the grieving family, over the police and even the general public. So far, Daan Janssen has insisted he is pleading not guilty. Mark wonders whether he is going to change his plea, but even so it is unconventional of Janssen to call him directly to tell him as much. What does he want?

"I did not kill Kylie Gillingham."

The cool, confident, foreign voice irritates Mark. It makes him feel less. Everything about Janssen makes Mark feel less. No shit, Sherlock. Daan Janssen is the literal embodiment of the fact that his wife didn't think he was enough. Mark thinks it is interesting that Janssen uses that particular name. He doesn't claim her as his Kai, he doesn't admit she is Mark's Leigh. Is he trying to neutralize her? Maybe it's nothing more than the fact that Kylie Gillingham is the name the police use. As Janssen is under arrest and in constant touch with the police and law-yers, he has probably heard her referred to that way officially so is simply used to the impartial, original name.

"Where are your boys?" Janssen demands.

Again Mark wants to respond, "Fuck off." It's basic of him. Pathetic. He knows that, but he's so damned furious. Furious with the world in general but Janssen in particular. He hates him with every fiber of his being. He's blistering from the in-side with how many unjust things have happened to him. He really means that; he imagines he feels ulcers, lacerations, welts inside his body. The pain is so intense. "None of your fuck-ing business," he says.

"I think maybe it is. They are not at home, are they?" Jans-sen asserts. Mark wonders how he knows this. He looks about him. For one crazy moment he wonders if there is a nanny-cam trained upon him; if Janssen is spying on him. Perhaps even his privacy isn't his. Then Janssen explains how he has this inside knowledge. "I gave them money to run away."

"You did what?" Mark's voice lifts and cracks; it's undignified, embarrassing, but he doesn't care. Outrage is creating fissures.

"No, not that exactly. But to get to safety."

"What are you talking about? You've been in touch with my sons?"

"Yes." Daan efficiently describes his interaction with Oli and Seb. He doesn't sound regretful, embarrassed or apologetic. He sounds like a man who feels he is entitled to reach out to two traumatized and grieving boys for his own convenience. Mark is stunned at how easily he infiltrated their lives, won their trust and then gave them the funds to go on an ill-advised wild-goose chase, apparently to somehow prove Janssen's innocence. What the hell? He feels the man's determination and selfishness; he feels his own despair and passivity.

"I should call the police, say you have been tampering with witnesses. Juvenile witnesses at that," Mark splutters.

"I realize you could do that. At least what you accuse me of is true." Mark wonders how he keeps it up. How does he manage to remember to profess his innocence at all times? Janssen continues, "I am aware that I'm taking a risk calling you. I could just be making things worse for myself. Look, I hope I'm wrong. I hope Oli and Seb are safely at home with you right now. Are they?"

Mark doesn't want to answer this question. He owes Janssen nothing at all, not even a response. Besides, his sons are okay. Last night he called the police and told them that the boys were, "Fine. Good. Really great."

Janssen sighs; he sounds stressed, urgency creeping into his voice. "I am not the threat here. I told you I did not kill Kylie Gillingham."

"And I'm just supposed to take your word for it, am I?"

"Fiona killed her." Janssen's accusation is flat and assured. It's all the more chilling for its lack of hysteria. He continues, "Fiona killed her and then set me up. Where is she now? Is she with your sons?"

Mark wonders if Janssen is insane and believes what he is spouting, or sane and just devilish.

"Well, yes, she is, but…" He wants to explain that Fiona has been a marvel. She's kept them all going. She cooks, cleans, shops, fucks. He talks to her, gets drunk with her, he trusts her. But Janssen cuts him off.

"I believe your boys are in serious danger. Really. I'm trying to help you."

Mark hears the words but can't make sense of them. Why would Janssen be trying to help him? Janssen is the murderer. "Bullshit," he splutters.

"Oli and Seb went to her holiday home on the coast. The place where she left my possessions to be found by the police. I have never been there. I told the police that. She told them the opposite. It is the place I think she murdered Kylie. Oli and I were messaging. He said he has found evidence that looks bad for her."

"Why should I believe you?" Mark asks.

"Because it's too dangerous not to," Janssen snaps. Mark doesn't know what to say to that. Janssen seems to lose patience completely. "Forget it. If you won't call the police, I will call them myself. I think they would believe anything you say more easily and therefore act quicker. With me they will think I am trying to save myself, but I will call them anyway. I don't care if this backfires on me and they charge me for speaking to witnesses. This is too big. It is too much of a risk to do nothing." Mark still doesn't know how to respond. This can't be true. Janssen adds, "You are a prick who can't see what's in front of you because you are so wrapped up in your anger and because you are getting to screw someone new."

All at once, Mark realizes that Janssen's fury, fear and confusion is immense. It matches his own. Janssen has exposed himself as someone who is not in control, not as together as the endless dark suits and crisp shirts might imply, and he has also exposed himself as someone who cares. He is right, Mark does not want to believe this latest twist in the bleak tale of his family life. But he must consider the possibility. He starts to think quickly. Run through the facts. Weigh them up.

Fiona did not say where she and the boys were when she messaged to say she had found them. Was she at the skate park, the place she'd mentioned originally, or is Janssen right, did she find them at her bungalow? If so, why didn't she reveal as much? Considering the time she messaged, it is possible that she had traveled as far as Dorset to look for them. He didn't speak to the boys himself. Was that odd, or was it perfectly normal considering the late hour? Probably they were shattered and in bed when she texted. He doesn't know. Shame sloshes into his consciousness as he recognizes that he should have asked to talk to them. He was so relieved that they'd turned up and that she was dealing with it. He hasn't got it in him to always be dealing with everything. Fiona suggested he call off the police search, though, which of course he duly did.

Mark thought the worst thing that could possibly happen to him already had. Twice. He had lost two wives. But now he considers that there is a possibility of something more dreadful. Daan Janssen is right. He has taken his eye off the ball, he has slumped into the easiest option, that of Fiona taking the reins. Is it possible that option is not convenient but dangerous? Toxic? He let her move in and take over because he didn't have the energy or the courage to parent on his own.

"They are with Fiona, she messaged me to tell me," he confesses. "I don't know where they are exactly."

"She killed Kylie, and the boys are with her in her holiday home in Lyme Regis," Daan reasserts.

"No, that's ridiculous. Fiona loved Leigh."

"You are screwing her, right? If she loved her best friend so much, how come she is sleeping with her husband just three months after her death? A little quick off the mark, don't you think?" Mark doesn't say that in fact there wasn't even a grieving period as respectable as three months; they started having sex almost immediately. He was so angry and confused. What was *her* reasoning? He's never thought about it. "Fiona had motivation to kill Kylie. She was jealous. Probably, she was in love with you, or me, or both of us? There is precedent for that particular model," adds Janssen wryly.

Mark can't see how Janssen finds it in him to make cool wisecracks at a time like this; he must just say that sort of thing as second nature. He probably never has to think about coming up with something funny or witty or quick. Those thoughts clearly just tumble freely into his mind, off his tongue. Mark wonders if that was what attracted Leigh to him. Did he make her laugh? Did he challenge her intellectually? It was bad enough thinking the attraction was that he was rich and handsome. He realizes now that none of this matters. Leigh is dead and gone. He has to snap out of his despair and sharpen up. For his boys. Still, he is struggling to process it. He can't accept more pain. He wants to deny it.

"But even if you are right and she did kill Leigh, she would never hurt the boys. She's known them for years and I've watched her with them these past months. She cooks for them, cleans their rooms, she's done all of Seb's homeschooling with him. She's so patient."

"Yes, that was when she wanted to be their mother and thought there was a chance of that. What if they've discovered something that proves her guilt? What if she knows that they have that evidence and now they are a threat to her?"

"Then they are in danger," admits Mark. Cold dread settles in him. His blood slows, freezes. Time slackens, his life shrinks. He feels trapped. His world is hanging by a thread. Everyone's is.

37

FIONA

It's getting very bad. Fiona sees that matters are out of her control. Other people are doing things, thinking things, finding things. That bastard Daan Janssen is repeatedly messaging Oli. Asking what he's found, if he is okay. He was never so persistent in trying to reach *her*, she thinks bitterly. She wonders, should she respond to Daan as Oli to get him to go away? She drafts a response.

Just messing with you. Found nothing. Because there's nothing to find. You did it, you fucker.

She wonders, does that seem like the sort of response Oli might send? She isn't sure. Maybe she needs to be a little less careful with the grammar and spelling.

Just messin wif u. Found nothing. Nothing 2 find. u did it, u fucker.

She's unsure. She's frazzled. Wired. She needs to sleep but it's out of the question; she can't even sit still but instead paces up and down. She can't make a decision. Even if she sends this message and it stops Daan pestering Oli, will that be enough? That will only solve the problem of Daan.

Oli knows something. What?

She considers running. Just giving up on the whole thing and getting out of here. But could she leave everything behind? Her homes, her car, her business? She could, she supposes, if she had to. But she doesn't want to leave Mark and all that he offers; the possibility of a family life. Over these past few months they've had something really special going on. She feels it, believes it. She's never had anything like it before and she isn't ready to give it up. Why should she? Doesn't she deserve a bit of happiness? Finally? After everything she's done to earn it? Yes, she does. Besides, running would make her look guilty, and though obviously she *is* technically guilty, no one has actually accused her yet, and so she would be escalating the situation by running. No, running is not an option.

But then nor is going to prison.

The only solution is to find out what the evidence is that Oli has uncovered and see if it does incriminate her. It's perfectly possible that she can convince him it's not evidence at all. She simply has to stick to her story. There is so much evidence pointing to Daan's guilt. It's always the husband. No one should be looking her way.

She doesn't want to scare Oli, or Seb, of course not. She loves them both, but she has to put herself first in this instance. She isn't being selfish; this is more a matter of self-care. Her Instagram feed is always full of affirmations on the subject.

Put your own life jacket on first before helping others.

Remember you deserve the care you gift others.

You are the hero in your own story.

She has a sticker on her makeup mirror that reads: *I am working on fully loving and accepting myself.* She really is. She needs to take deep inhales of oxygen. It is in everyone's interests for her to get away with this, because then she can be a mother to the boys. Help them deal with their grief. She'll be no use to anyone in prison.

Oli can be stubborn, though, she knows that. And he is physically intimidating, as he is taller than she is. She wonders how she might control him, at least until he hears her point of view, accepts reason. Seb is still a boy. He has to be lighter than Kylie and she managed to manhandle Kylie when necessary. He is the key to controlling Oli.

She sneaks into the boys' room. They are still sleeping; they no doubt had a long and busy day yesterday and they would probably sleep all day if she let them. She would like to, but she has to get on. She puts her hand over Seb's mouth. His eyes immediately open. In an instant, he jerks from deep unconsciousness to a panicked presence. It's a pity; he's been through a lot, but that is not her fault. She is just cleaning up Kylie's mess really. She whispers, "I have information about your mum that I can only tell you if you trust me. Do you understand?" Her mouth is very close to his ear. She can smell his hair, salty and sweaty; he obviously didn't shower last night. He really does need a mother.

His big brown eyes are the same color as melted chocolate in a pan, glistening, rich. He blinks and then nods. She knew he wouldn't be able to resist that. It is all he longs for, news about his bloody wayward stepmother. It infuriates her. Kylie was so undeserving. She whispers, "You have to stay absolutely silent, agreed?" He nods again. She smiles at him and takes her hand away from his mouth. He doesn't shout out to wake Oli; instead he smiles at her. A broad, hopeful grin. "Come with me, don't make a sound," she whispers. Silently they sneak out of the room, down the corridor and into the kitchen.

Only once they are there does he ask in an excited whisper, "What do you know?"

"I have to take you somewhere," she says. Seb looks thrilled. "Have some breakfast first. We'll drive." She watches as he eats the pain au chocolat and drinks the milk: both are laced with liquid MDMA, left over from when she held Kylie captive. She'd brought it with her because it was always better to be prepared. He really is well behaved; even when she is locking the door behind them, he doesn't say another word. Momentarily she wonders whether she needed to drug him at all. Maybe she could have just asked him to do her a favor and climb into the boot of her car, but in the long run, it's better for him if he doesn't remember anything.

"You can sit in the front," she says.

He grins and scrambles into the car as quickly as he can, puts on his seat belt without her having to ask. Slowly she edges the car into gear and sets off along the narrow road. They've only been driving for a couple of minutes before Seb starts to look lethargic. He repeatedly blinks his eyes and shakes his head, no doubt trying to ward off dizziness, numbness in the arms and legs, drowsiness that he probably thinks is down to tiredness after a late night. "Are you taking me to see my mum?" he mumbles. He's smiling. "I knew she wasn't dead. I said she wasn't. I said I saw her."

"What do you mean?" Fiona asks sharply.

But before he can answer, he loses his ability to speak. There is a fraction of a second when he looks scared. Well, terrified really. Probably at the moment when his heartbeat sped up and he realized that he couldn't speak even if he wanted to. At that moment he might have wondered whether he could trust Fiona. But then, almost straightaway, he falls unconscious, and Fiona reminds herself that he won't remember any of this after it's all over. It's better now he's given in to sleep and closed his eyes. The way he was staring at her was disconcerting. The way his head lolls forward over the seat belt at a peculiar angle looks a bit grotesque too. She wonders whether she has possibly given him too big a dose. She needed it to work quickly; she didn't have the luxury of time the way she had when she drugged Kylie. She wasn't sure whether increasing the dose would mean it would take effect faster, or make the effects more severe, or equally severe but more enduring. She didn't have time to look it up on the internet. She's working a little on the fly here.

Whatever, she can't worry about that now. She has to tie him up and then bundle him into the boot of the car. She uses her scarf to gag him. She hopes he doesn't dribble on it. It's not designer, but it is rather lovely. She'd rather it didn't get ruined. Once he is safely stowed, she turns the car around and drives back to the bungalow to wait for Oli to wake up.

The two of them need to have a really good heart-to-heart.

38

KYLIE

I am lying on the sticky kitchen floor. Kenneth Jones carefully props my feet on a pile of books so that the blood flows back to my brain, and then dabs a cold, wet tea towel to my forehead. I accept his care as I have done since we met; frankly I'm not conscious enough to reject it. Still in a shocked, fugue state, I can barely speak, but when he suggests fresh air, I see the opportunity to be out of the house, out of his grasp, so I nod my agreement. He helps me up and I limp outside. I'm leaning most of my weight on him, but, physically hale, he doesn't seem to mind. I drift in and out of full consciousness. Aware of a cool breeze, the bright sun, then shade again. When he lets go of me, I slump to the ground.

I come around for the second time in the small, dank outside loo. I'm sitting on the cement floor and the stench of pee turns my stomach. My feet are tied together and attached to the bowl of the toilet and my hands are tied to a beam above my head. "You can't be serious!" I scream my frustration.

Kenneth is standing at the open door; he looks embarrassed but determined. "You'd run away otherwise. I don't have a choice." His eyes dart about. I wonder how I ever thought they were kind eyes; now all I see is the instability they betray. I look carefully to see if I can identify its root. It's important, I know. I see pain, anger, maybe embarrassment?

"Did you drug me?" I demand. "The tablets I took every day, what were they?"

"Mostly vitamins."

"Mostly?"

"Okay, I have been medicating you for a while. It really is for your own good."

"Jesus." I'm obviously dealing with an out-and-out madman.

"I've brought you some reading material. You'll understand what I'm trying to do if you read these first." He drops a pile of newspapers on the floor and then carefully spreads them out around me and across my legs so I can read them even whilst bound. He slams the door behind him.

I quickly gather that these are newspapers that fill in the gaps from the days when he returned home and said he hadn't bothered to buy one. I realize now that he was censoring what I read. I also recall him turning off the radio in a hurry; I suspect that too was so I wouldn't hear what was being reported. Because it appears that I am infamous. My eyes skim across the papers and quickly land on photographs of me. The story of my bigamy is big news. Huge. A public starved of anything other than death tolls from COVID has clearly enjoyed soaking up the lurid details of my private life.

I read all the articles carefully, a spectator of my own life. I'm watching the understudy perform. My memories are correct. I am a bigamist. I split my life between two husbands for years. I had two identities, two names, two different sets of friends and family. The two men I recalled were not past lovers. I was—am—married to both. I am a criminal. I broke the law and I broke hearts. What the hell is wrong with me? Now that my reality is finally pulled into tight focus and the fuzziness of these past months has been shed like a skin, I am left with a sharp, cruel, frightening reality. I thought not remembering who I was presented a challenge; now I realize that my challenge is actually *understanding* who I was.

It's horrifying, and yet irrationally I'm awed at the drama of it. I read about a life that is unimaginable but at the same time feels entirely real. More real than the memories Kenneth tried to foist upon me: the photo albums, the stories of school friends and jolly jilted fiancés. I guess I only thought I recalled Giles Hughes when I bumped into him because I'd seen so many photos of him and I was looking to make the connection. My real life is torrid, complicated. The reporters gleefully slouch into the scandal, roll in it, pigs in muck. I'm horrified yet perversely fascinated by my own daring. A woman who broke all the rules. Part of me wants to sink back into bleached, fuzzy unreality, but I can't. I can only move forward.

The case depicted by the press is made all the more scandalous and salacious because my second husband is not only slightly younger than I am (side note, I am forty-three, not thirty-seven like Stacie Jones, which is another uncomfortable surprise but feels truer), he is also from an extremely wealthy, influential Dutch family who appear to be friends with the likes of Richard Branson, several minor royals and the billionaire Heineken family. There's nothing journalists like more than pinning scandal on the wealthy, watching them fall from grace. I married him four years ago in the Chelsea register office; he works in the city, earning a salary that seems unimaginably large, and we live in a penthouse in an exclusive apartment block. I recall it now in detail. Expensive art hangs on the walls; it is sparsely furnished, impeccably clean. I remember the magnificence of wealth, the occasional uncomfortable otherness of it. We've lived a life of privilege and indulgence, avoiding public attention until I disappeared. Now Daan Janssen is under arrest for my abduction and murder. He is awaiting trial.

As I read this, I automatically try to stand, but I fall back down, banging my knees on the filthy porcelain toilet, while yanking at my tethered arms just jars my shoulder awkwardly. His arrest is unfair, wrong. I am not dead, there is no murder; but apart from that, while I recall being held captive—yes, as the papers report, in the very building we lived in—I do not believe Daan was responsible. I remember being chained, hungry, gagged, beaten. I don't believe it was the man I bathed with, the man who massaged my feet, playfully threw Tiffany boxes my way when he'd earned a bonus at work; a man who told me repeatedly that I was beautiful and brilliant. Someone I ate fresh crab and lobster with at Martha's Vineyard after the boat we'd chartered had docked—because yes, he could afford to hire a crew so that we only ever played at being sailors but didn't have the responsibility of navigating. He could also play tennis and golf; he even fenced when he was younger. A regular James Bond. The memories are glorious and glamorous. Daan is that man.

I married Mark Fletcher ten years ago. He is a landscape gardener and a widower. The papers have not tried to condemn him as a murderer as they have Daan, but nor have they been kind to him either. They paint him as a clueless cuckold, a gullible idiot who (they hint) couldn't satiate me sexually, and so I betrayed him in the most remarkable and complete way possible. It isn't true. I recall now that Mark and I had a great sex life. He always satisfied me that way. The papers imply that he is depressed, emotionally unstable, a loser. There is an early article or two hinting at the fact that his first wife died under mysterious circumstances; clearly at one point the whiff of suspicion did blow his way.

My heart aches for him. My gentle, dependable Mark. The man I remember creating a warm, cozy, chaotic home with. The soft furnishings were shades of gray and beige, the various tables a light rustic oak and always lost under the clutter of family life: magazines, newspapers, books and ironing piles. There were cheap but fun prints on the walls, and in the kitchen, a cork noticeboard heaving under the weight of pizza delivery flyers and money-off coupons. With Mark I painted walls until my arms ached, and we once laughed that no one ever behaved like they did in adverts when they were decorating; no one wasted time or resources adorably painting cute messages on the walls or spotting paint onto each other's cheeks. Then one day, he did write words on the wall. He wrote *WILL YOU MARRY ME*. He forgot the question mark. It didn't matter.

I'd said yes by the time he'd got to the second R. The memories are wonderful and comfortable.

I recall both homes clearly. Both men clearly.

Both the men I loved have suffered so much because of my actions, and a deep sense of shame and regret burns inside me.

But that is not the worst of it.

My boys. I have two stepsons. Oli and Seb. Mark's boys by his first wife. The memory of the graveside, and me trying to offer comfort and support to two little boys, was real, not a false recollection as I convinced myself. They are much older now than they were in that image. Oli is a young man now. I brought them up. I was their mother for years. This feels right and honest at the innermost part of my core.

It's fascinating how my brain is revealing things to me. Yesterday I started to recall the layout of a seaside town, and that was all I had. Today it has all come tumbling back to me. My parents and childhood, my men and marriages, and now my boys. I guess they were buried most deeply in my subconscious because they are the ones I most regret hurting. Children ought to be protected. I believe that completely and ferociously. They have a better chance in life if they are cosseted and cared for at the beginning; it gives them a chance to establish who they are, what they want. Something that I was deprived of but longed to deliver. I've failed.

I find I am wiping away tears. The air is rough and visceral. I want to throw up. I want to scream or run. My mind is spinning out of control as I remember everything and see how ridiculous it is. The life I lived was impossible. I was selfish and crazy trying to run two parallel lives, but I was trying to avoid the boys having to face the trauma of me leaving. Now I see that I have hurt them in an immeasurable way. Children get over their parents splitting up, divorcing; if things are handled carefully, the pain can be minimized, people can recover. But this? My disappearance, what they believe to be my violent murder, the exposure in the newspapers, their father being gossiped about, the lurid details of my sex life, how do they get over this? I remember my fingers combing through dark curls, comfortably tangled. My heart breaks. I think I actually hear it crack and disintegrate. And it's not over yet. Not for them or me. They are still alone, no doubt confused, angry at my betrayal. I have to get out. I have to find them and fix what I can.

However, whilst a lot of my past is coming back to me with blinding clarity, there are still a number of unanswered questions. Why did Kenneth Jones take me prisoner? Did he abduct me in London? Is it because I look like his daughter? Where is the real Stacie? How did I get from that room in the London apartment to here, the Jurassic coast? And why do I remember Lyme Regis so clearly? Some things must still be too traumatic for me to deal with. My brain is protecting me, allowing me to remember only what I can cope with. But now that so much of my memory has come back to me, I'm sure the rest will follow.

Anyway, all these questions are about the past. And though my past is important, it dawns on me that the most crucial thing right now is the future. So the biggest question of all is: How do I get out of here?

Because know this, I *am* getting out. I am having a future. I will return to my boys.

39

OLI

He wakes up and instinctually reaches for his phone to check the time. When he was a little kid, he slept with a blanket from his cot. He did so until he was about seven, then Leigh finally weaned him off it. She used to joke that the phone had taken the place of the blankie, that clasping it gave him confidence. But it wasn't an especially mean joke; she delivered it in a way that was sort of indulgent, as though she thought it was cute to recall his early years. He can see that now, although he used to growl or roll his eyes when she said it.

He feels around the bed for the phone. But it's gone. He flicks his eyes to Seb's bed. He's also gone. He wants to believe that his little brother has got up first and stolen his phone because he's run out of data on his own and wants to play Candy Crush, but he doesn't believe that, not even for a nanosecond, because that's not the life he leads. A life of innocent explanations and ordinary scenarios is not his lot.

He senses her outside the door. Sort of feels her presence before she opens it wide. "Morning, Oli." Her voice is singsong. He's heard her use it before over these past few months, especially when she thinks she's being patient and kind, and he really detests it. It's so fake. He can't believe he was ever taken in by it. She's carrying a breakfast tray; he can see a bowl of cereal, a jug of milk, a mug of tea. Unbelievable.

"Where's Seb?"

She places the tray on the bed in front of him. He doesn't touch it but eyes her warily. He's known her for as long as he can remember, he's been on holiday with her, spent birthdays and Christmases with her, he's lived with her since March, but everything has changed now that he knows she is a murderer.

"Seb?"

"Yes, Seb. Where is he?"

She pulls her face into a tight smile. It looks like an effort. "Well, yes, we need to talk about Seb and so many other things. Don't we?"

Oli wants to get out of bed. He's taller than her and that, somehow, will help. When she's towering over him and he's lying in bed, he feels like a kid. He starts to move. She reaches out and places her hand on his chest. "No, just stay where you are. It's best for now. So shall we just get all our cards out on the table?"

"If you like."

"Okay. I know you've been talking to that murderer Daan Janssen." Oli wasn't expecting that but tries not to react; it's important to keep a poker face. "I know you've got things a bit confused. You are very upset. You've been through a lot. An awful lot. No one can blame you for getting muddled." She pauses and smiles at him again. It still looks like an effort. She reaches forward and with apparent tenderness sweeps his hair out of his eyes. Leigh used to do that all the time. Fiona has never done it before. He automatically jerks his head away from her touch, lets his hair fall back down over his eye. "So, you think you've found something that makes you believe I'm involved in your stepmother's death." She shakes her head in a manner that suggests she's mystified.

"How do you know that?"

She doesn't answer him but carries on. "Okay, so that's silly, of course. You can't have found anything that would connect me because I didn't have anything to do with her death, so..." She breaks off and shrugs. He hates the word *silly*. He's not seven. He's not silly. "Now then, tell me what it is you think you've found and I can explain. Whatever it is, I'll have a to-tally innocent explanation, because I *am* totally innocent."

"Where is Seb?" he asks again. It's all that matters. "Seb! Seb!" he yells, but no one answers.

"Seb is just resting. You can see him after we've finished our talk."

Oli leaps out of bed. He isn't planning on pushing the break-fast tray at her as such, but he overturns it in his haste. She swears at him and reaches to grab his arm, but he shakes her off and gets past her. He's out of the room in seconds, bolting along the corridor toward the back door. "Seb! Seb!" he yells repeat-edly. His heart is beating so hard and fast, it feels like it's in his throat. Fiona follows him slowly. She doesn't appear to be in a rush. He tries the back door, but it's locked. He turns around, his eyes scanning left to right looking for the keys. They are not in the fruit bowl as usual. They are not on the table. Fiona stands in the doorway from the hall to the kitchen; she folds her arms across her chest. Oli starts to root around in the kitchen drawers, pulling them out, not even bothering to close them. He flings open cupboards, although it is unlikely he's going to find the keys under the sink with the bottles of bleach. He hates it that she is taking her time and he's frantically running around, heart racing. He knows that means she's in control and he's in danger. Hell, he's terrified. She killed his mum. Where is his brother? He stops darting around the kitchen looking for the keys; obviously she has them. He turns to her.

"You took down the photos," he says. "I know you killed her because you took down the photos. You wanted to make her disappear. You wanted her life."

Fiona shakes her head, sadly, slowly. "You are too clever by half, Oli." She doesn't deny it, and his legs quake. He thinks it would have been better maybe if she was still pretending to be innocent. "We need to strike a deal here," she says icily.

"I'm not making any deals with you."

"But I have something you want."

"You don't have anything I want."

"Oh, but I do. I have Seb."

40

KYLIE

The rope that ties my hands together is wrapped around a rough beam above my head. I wonder, if I move them left and right, can I create a sawing motion that will snap the rope? It's hard work; I have to move my arms and shoulders a considerable distance to create just a couple of centimeters of movement at the point where I am tied. Swinging them backward and forward is exhausting, but I persevere. I know shouting is unlikely to draw any attention, as we're so far away from our nearest neighbor. Even if there are tourists or dog walkers on the beach, happy, carefree families and couples, my voice will be drowned out by the crash of the waves. I'm on my own. I have no idea when Kenneth will return or what he will do to me when he does. How can I predict the actions of a madman? All I know is that I have to do something. I can't just passively sit here and wait for what happens to me next. For weeks now, months, I've been aware of my mental well-being—or rather lack of it; now my physical self dominates. I'm a trapped animal. I will chew off my own leg to get out of the jaws of a metal trap.

This desperation and determination to escape are both completely familiar. I recall struggling to escape from the room where I was held captive in London. It's not just the newspaper reports that are informing this. I clearly recall that I kicked a stud wall over and over again while chained to a radiator. I remember watching as the plasterboard started to crumble and cave in front of me. Then I was only tied by one hand, and so I managed to throw the bits of debris out of an open window in the adjoining room, trying to attract attention. Sometimes my aim was off; other times the debris sailed satisfyingly, gratifyingly through the gap.

It didn't work, though.

No one noticed my efforts and I stayed chained up. The thought stings, and I feel panic skitter through my body, but I force myself to stay calm and focus. The takeaway from that memory must not be that I failed to escape then; it has to be that I am still alive and I am here. My attempts to get help were very possibly what made Kenneth bring me to the country to isolate me. I have agency. If he is reacting to me rather than carrying out his own plan, I have some sort of control, don't I?

I think of Oli and Seb. Oli an angry teen but with the potential to become a good man, I'm sure of it. Seb just a child still, with so much growing up to do. They both need me. I don't doubt they are furious with me. Perhaps, like the papers report, they hate me, but I am their mother and I need to stem the flow of confusion and pain in their world. I need to apologize and try with every ounce of energy I have to make things a bit better. Mark won't be managing well on his own. He never does. He needs me too. He is unlikely to want me as a wife, but he needs me not to be dead; he needs me to help save his boys from that at least. And Daan needs me. He is being falsely accused of my murder. If I die here, no one will ever know the truth and he will be sent to prison for life. He doesn't deserve that simply for falling in love with me. For me falling in love with him. I have to find my way back to them all. I need to find a way back to my weird, unconventional life. I need to fix what I can. So I refocus my energy and pull sharply on my bindings. I'm a bigamist, yes. And according to the papers, I'm a bitch. Well, maybe. I'm certainly a mother, and I'm definitely not a quitter. Never that.

This outside loo is made of brick. I can't kick it down, so I continue to patiently and repeatedly swing my arms left and right, pulling on the rope as I do so, hoping that the strands of yarns will begin to fray and eventually snap apart. Freeing me. My wrists are bleeding where the friction from the binding scratches, my shoulders ache, but I push on and am grateful when I become numb to the pain. These sorts of escapes always look easy on TV and in movies, but the reality is bloodier, slower.

"Are you hungry?" His voice through the door makes me jump. I freeze and pray he hasn't heard my escape attempt.

"Yes," I admit.

"I'll make you something."

"Just bring me a bag of crisps or an unopened packet of biscuits."

Kenneth chuckles. He sounds benign. Part of me wishes I could turn back the clock, live in blissful ignorance where I believed he was my loving father, when I didn't know I was in the care of a madman. "You think I'm going to drug your food," he says.

"Not unreasonable under the circumstances," I snap back.

He opens the door, and I panic that there is evidence of me sawing at the rope.

"I have administered sedatives now and again. Needs must," he confesses. He shuffles and looks at his feet. I wonder if he is ashamed, or at least regretful. If so, he quickly shoves those emotions aside and starts to justify his actions. "I had to, though. I had no choice."

"You are insane," I mutter.

"I suppose that would be the easiest explanation, but I'm not. Not really." He pinches the top of his nose as though he's trying to stem emotion, then swiftly drops to his haunches to be closer to me. "I'm desperate. I'm lonely," he states flatly. "I know you're not her. I know you're dead." He slaps his hand on his forehead and corrects himself. "*She* is dead, I mean. I know *she* is dead."

So Stacie is dead. I thought that was most likely, but now I consider what it means that he has confirmed as much. How did she die? *I know you're dead.* Was that a slip of the tongue or a threat?

He looks me directly in the eye and says, "I know you are not her." He loved Stacie intensely, there is no doubt about that. Was I safer when he was make-believing that I was her? "I knew that as soon as you remembered one thing it would all come back to you quickly and everything would be over. I'll go and get you something to eat." He stands abruptly and leaves.

The moment I think he's out of earshot, I start to swing my arms again, frantic to escape before he decides how he feels about Kylie versus Stacie. My life is apparently doomed to be one of duality, choices. I freeze when I see him returning along the garden path toward me. He is carrying two packets of ready salted crisps, a banana and a can of Coke. None of these things could have been tampered with. He opens the crisps and starts to hand-feed them to me.

"I'm thirsty," I mutter.

He opens the can and carefully holds it to my mouth, tilting it at an angle to allow me to drink. His tenderness confuses me. I recognize it, and until recently, I wholeheartedly believed in it, but now I know he tricked me, so I don't know how to respond to his care. I eat and drink in silence for a while. Sad, scared. He starts talking again.

"The thing is, you look just like her and I thought that meant something. You know?" He meets my gaze, eager, excited. "I just wanted the chance to take care of you because I didn't get that chance with her. You were a second chance. Who doesn't want one of those?" I let him talk. Providing he's telling me the truth this time, any information he can give me will be useful. "I missed her, so much. So much. You can't begin to imagine. I simply thought maybe I could play a game, that I could pretend. Nothing more. Who would be hurt by that?"

I want to interrupt and say, *Me, I would be hurt.* I have been. I was taken from my life, and however complicated that life appeared to be, it was mine. I have a right to know who I am. There is no excuse or reason that would justify him forcing a new identity on me, unbeknown to me. It's not just kidnap. He stole more than my physical body; he stole who I am. However, I bite my tongue. I pull back from saying any of this for fear of riling him.

"You needed me," he insists.

Maybe, but what I need now is answers. "What were you doing in London? How did you get access to Daan's apartment block?" I ask. "Why did you keep me there? Were you planning on framing him all along?" I have so many questions that they tumble out, a barrage of confusion.

Kenneth stares back at me; he looks as bewildered as I feel. "We didn't meet in London," he says. "I found you on the beach."

"What?"

"I just wanted to help you."

"I don't understand. I remember the room. Being chained to the radiator, just as it's described in the papers." I nod toward the articles. "I know that happened."

"Yes, it did. But it wasn't me who held you captive in that hellhole." He looks offended that I've suggested it. Ironic, considering my current predicament. "You don't remember it now, but after you went over, you were washed up just a couple of miles along the coast from here."

"Went over?"

"The cliff." He rushes on, "You were unconscious, near death. I saved your life. You have a lot to thank me for," he adds self-righteously.

My head is spinning again. Everything I thought I'd pieced together from the newspaper reports falls apart. Once again I am on quicksand. Kenneth Jones, if he is to be believed, did not hold me captive in London; he did not bring me here to Dorset. So who did?

On a number of occasions over the past few months I have believed this man could read my mind. I thought it was largely charming, a natural by-product of us living in such close and constant proximity and having such a tight father-daughter bond. Now I know that isn't true, so I am disconcerted that it appears he can still guess what I am thinking. He answers my unasked question. "*She* did it. The friend. Your *supposed* friend," he clarifies.

I glance at the newspapers. Recall the reports and remember the comments; who was commented upon. "You mean Fiona Phillipson?"

"I saw her do the deed. It was dark and wet. Awful night. Ronnie still wanted to pee, though, so I was taking my usual walk when I saw her shove you over the cliff."

His words fall like a physical blow, because in that moment, I see her face. I can feel her presence. Fiona. A woman who loved me and then hated me. He's right: my best friend of over twenty years, pushed me forcefully over the cliff edge. And in the moment she did so, I saw in her expression a kaleidoscope of emotion: satisfaction, triumph and hate. I know he is telling the truth. I was betrayed. Punished. Whatever she thought she was doing, it was horrific. Disproportionate and vicious.

I recall the two of us walking up to the top of the cliff. It was pouring down; we were soaking wet. The waves smashed, the wind roared. I felt exhausted and frail, unused to exercise after the captivity she had kept me in. Now, I am sure that she was my captor, but back then I was ignorant of that; I thought Daan was responsible for my abduction. I was so grateful, believing her to be my brave and brilliant rescuer. Despite feeling physically challenged, part of me found it completely exhilarating to be outside, no longer locked up. I remember I was a bit drunk, but I gladly stumbled up the hill. I recall that she kept asking me which man I would choose if I had to pick one. She doggedly pushed for an answer. I was bewildered by that, but I trusted her. Eventually I said I'd pick Mark. Mark and the boys. I believed that was the right decision to make. It was, in a way, the decision I had made every day by not leaving them for my new love. Suddenly I felt her hands on my chest and my feet coming off the ground. Round and around I spun, plummeting. I remember hitting the icy water. The pain was extraordinary. Ten times as awful as the most inelegant belly flop.

Kenneth saw all of that? We weren't alone?

He elaborates, "I scrambled down the cliff. Keeping out of sight of that madwoman. She didn't hang around. Had to get away from the scene of the crime, I suppose. By the time I reached the bottom, you'd disappeared. Gone under. I went into the water. It was brutally cold. I had to dive for you but couldn't see a thing. It was pitch-black. I knew that every minute mattered, that running for help would have been a waste of time. I kept flailing about, desperately searching for you."

I think of this old man, wet, cold, scared but determined. His actions seem a lot like bravery. A lot like compassion. The man who is now holding me captive once risked his own life to save mine. It seems unfathomable, but I, better than anyone, know that none of us are one thing alone.

"I walked up and down the coast for hours, repeatedly going in and out of the sea, hoping to find you but thinking it was hopeless. Then, just as the light was coming up, I heard Ronnie barking from a spot not far up the beach. I didn't know if you were just unconscious or already dead. I lunged toward you, barely able to stand myself by that point, I was so cold and tired. You were bleeding and unresponsive. I started chest compressions to keep the blood pumping around your body; it helps to keep the vital organs, including the brain, alive. You would have died if it wasn't for me."

So I owe him everything and I also resent him for everything. "Why didn't you call an ambulance or the police once you'd done the emergency care? Why didn't you report finding me?" I demand. It's not that I am still unsure if this account of events is true. Finally, I believe this is what happened. It feels raw and unwanted, yes, but authentic. What I'm trying to establish is Kenneth's thought process.

"I was going to, of course. But the immediate priority was

to get you warm, avoid hypothermia. I was planning on taking you to my house, calling an ambulance from there. But I got home and my phone wasn't charged. It just seemed to make sense to tend to you myself. I had to shave your hair off so I could sew up your wound. I was out of practice, but it's like riding a bike, you never forget. I dressed you in dry clothes, put you to bed. I'm a doctor first even after years of not practicing. I have to preserve life. That's the oath."

"And then?" I nudge him.

"You have to understand, the moment I clapped eyes on you, I noticed it, the fact that you looked so much like her. And as you slept, I started to think that was a sign. All I wanted to do was look after you. Well, her, Stacie, I suppose." He shakes his head, bewildered. "I reasoned that you needed someone to take care of you, and I needed someone to take care of." He grabs at my knee and urgently squeezes it. Wanting me to buy into his warped logic. "It seemed like you'd been sent to me. We were meant to find one another. There had to be a reason that I was the one who witnessed what was done to you and that you survived the fall."

"It's just a coincidence that I look like her," I say sadly.

He shakes his head firmly. Like a terrier with a bone. "You woke up confused. You didn't know who you were or where you were. Your story hit the papers the next day. All the gory details. The two husbands. One of them a suspect in your disappearance. They said he'd skipped the country. It became very ugly. I'm not sure how they got the story so quickly. I've thought about it since. I suppose that was Fiona Phillipson too. She probably leaked it. You were confused and exhausted. You slept most of those first few days. You'd been through a lot. Then people stopped looking for you. *They* didn't want you. I did."

"No, you didn't. You wanted Stacie."

"I deserved you. They'd given up on you so easily."

"They thought I was dead."

"Yes, they did," he says eagerly. "And wasn't it for the best that the troubled Kylie—a discontented woman who couldn't accept the limits of life—just stopped being?" I gasp inwardly at that thought. No, never. It is never for the best to be gone, to be done. "Then, when you started to get well, the similarities between the pair of you became more apparent, not less. Your eyes are the same color, the shape of your face. Same height, weight. All those obvious things, but there was more. Many of your mannerisms were similar. There were moments when you yawned in a certain way, stretched, threw a ball for Ronnie, and it was as though you really were becoming her." I suppose this was why Tanya Vaughan believed I was Stacie when we met at the library. Enough of a resemblance to convince a long-lost school friend. Kenneth pushes on with his weird train of thought. "It was easy enough to believe that I wasn't doing a bad or stupid thing; I was in fact giving you a new persona, a new opportunity. I was doing a good thing."

His eyes shine and I marvel at his self-delusion, but at the same time I understand it. We all tell ourselves a lot of lies.

He continues, "If I had called the authorities, they would have arrested you. I felt sorry for you. You've read the papers now. You've seen it. You were the most hated woman in the country. Pitied one day, when you were two missing women, loathed the next when it emerged you were a bigamist cheat. That hasn't really gone away, even though many of the great British public think you died for your crimes. They still hate you." He shrugs, acknowledging the way of the world. "At one point I thought things would settle down, that you could get better, stronger, and then turn yourself in, argue your case. But your memory didn't come back. I suppose there was an element of your subconscious that was acting in self-preservation by suppressing your crime, your complex life and the captivity. Think what you like, but I just saw an opportunity." I nod slowly. His grief for his dead daughter is so intense that he's stopped thinking clearly. He's not a bad man. He's a sad one. "We were both so alone," he states finally.

"Tell me about Stacie. What happened to her?" I ask carefully. Kenneth Jones is grieving for his child. I can't judge that. I want to understand it.

"Oh, she was everything to me. I was devastated when she died. I missed her so much, I ached. And the gap inside me… The pain gnawed a hole that grew and grew; I was being eaten up from the inside. I just wanted to bring her back. Was I so bad? You like being different people. We were made for each other."

"But my boys. They must miss me. They must be so scared," I point out gently. I hope that he respects the parent-child bond enough to empathize with their loss. Enough to see he can't keep me here.

My hope is blown away when he says with a cynical chuckle, "Oh, I don't think so. I imagine they hate you very much. What you did was quite terrible."

"So what's next?" I ask carefully, unsure that I really want to know.

"Well, that's up to you. You could agree to stay here with me. We're okay, aren't we, Stacie? Not as close as we once were, but there's a warmth. We can work on that."

"My name is Kylie." I regret saying it immediately, as I note his lips pull together a fraction. His body hardens and he turns to stone in front of me.

"Stop being silly, darling. There's no place for Kylie. She's dead and everyone thinks good riddance. You and I know who you have to be in order to stay safe. No one loves Kylie." It is impossible not to hear the threat.

"How did Stacie die?" I ask gently. "Was it cancer? Did she have the cancer you told me I had?"

Kenneth looks at me with a slightly puzzled expression, as though he can't quite comprehend how slow I am being. "Oh no, darling, I killed her."

"You…" The words stick in my throat. "You killed her."

"Be sensible. Kylie hasn't anywhere to go. No one wants her. No one would miss her. But Stacie has a loving home here. I'm happy for her to continue to live here with me. I would have to get rid of Kylie, though." Kenneth squeezes my knee. His touch is torture. I try not to shrink from him, I know it will annoy him, but my reaction is instinctual and I furl into myself. "Think about it," he says. Then he stands up and walks back to the house.

41

DC CLEMENTS

The sound of her phone ringing wakes her up. It takes her a moment to orientate. The car clock says 11:15. Damn, she's slept far longer than she intended. She should have set an alarm, but she assumed the sun coming up at 5:00 a.m. would wake her. She rarely sleeps well, and can't believe that bedding down in her car at the roadside resulted in such a deep slumber when most nights in her little flat she spends hours tossing and turning and staring at the bedroom ceiling. She planned to be back in the station by now, or at least in the shower at home. The car stinks; it reminds her of that first breath when waking up in a sleeping bag, in a tent that has caught and trapped a night's sweating, farting humanity. She used to enjoy camping, but after she trained as a police officer, she started to associate this particular smell with a stale cell or a long night's stakeout rather than the great outdoors, and it put her off. When would she have time to go camping anyway?

Her back and neck resist as she moves to reach for her phone. It's Tanner.

"Where are you?" he asks.

"Spent the night in my car. I'm about halfway between London and Lyme Regis."

"Sleeping on the job. Slacker." His tone is buoyant. She doesn't mind his teasing, but she really wants a coffee. She glances around the car; the only sustenance she can see is a dusty packet of mints. Not exactly a nutritious breakfast. She's glad of them all the same, and pops one in her mouth.

"What is it?" she asks.

"Just got the results from forensics."

"The bottle?"

"Yup."

She rubs her eyes with the heel of her hand and rotates her head to bring movement to her neck. "And?"

"Two sets of prints."

"Known?"

"Damn straight."

"Okay, Tanner, stop being a tease."

He waits a beat. "Kylie Gillingham and Fiona Phillipson." The two names come out in a triumphant rush, and Clements's mind bangs into focus. "That means—"

"Yeah, it does, Tanner." Clements rarely interrupts anyone, always mindful that in her job it's better to listen rather than speak, you learn more, but this time she can't resist. "It means that most likely Kylie and Fiona were together at some point on that clifftop. And there were no other prints?" She can feel her heartbeat. She has to rule out the possibility that Daan Janssen, or anyone else, took the wine bottle from the house and left it on the cliff. The science never lies. People, though, well, they're unreliable buggers.

"No. None."

"Well, that's interesting." She wants to punch the air.

"What do you think, boss?"

"Well, it's possible this wine bottle was left on that clifftop eight months before we found it." Fiona and the Fletchers confirmed that the last time they visited the holiday bungalow together, with Kylie, was July 2019. "Possible but not probable."

"Very unlikely," agrees Tanner. "Pre-COVID there was a group of volunteers who spent every Saturday afternoon picking up rubbish in the area. I found a website. They are quite vocal about litter being left behind. They photograph big piles of the stuff they collect, and post about it to try to embarrass the tourists into being a bit more careful."

"Genius."

"Yeah. I imagine it has a bit of an effect."

"No, I mean genius police work, Tanner. Well done."

"Right." She can sense his delighted smile down the phone, even though he appears to have taken the compliment in his stride.

"And when did they last post?"

"The last time this group formally got out to clean up the area was Saturday the fourteenth of March 2020. They comment that they had a lot of volunteers, that everyone did a good job. It seems unlikely this bottle was left there before then. If it was, it would have most probably been cleared away."

"I think we need to talk to Fiona Phillipson."

"Should I go and bring her in? Meet you at the station."

"Try it, but I don't think she'll be in London. Not if my instinct serves me right." Clements turns the engine on, slips into gear. Mirror, signal, maneuver. "I think I'll carry on toward Lyme Regis after all." She's about to pull away when her phone starts to beep. "I have another call waiting. Got to go." She doesn't bother with niceties. Tanner doesn't expect them. They are both focused. Close. Bloodhounds on a scent. She picks up the second call.

"It's Mark Fletcher here. There's something I need to tell you. It's about the boys. I'm not sure I was totally honest with you last night, and I'm worried."

42

KYLIE

Time passes. I have no idea how much or how little. I can't see if I'm making any progress with sawing the rope, which is discouraging, but I have no choice but to push on. Suddenly my hands flop to my sides. The rope has finally snapped. For a moment I'm so shocked I don't have the capacity to move. My hands are numb and my arms are dead weight. Then I wiggle my fingers as I do in yoga when I come round from Savasana, and run my hands up and down my arms, encouraging feeling back into them. As soon as I have control over my movements, I start to untie the rope around my legs.

In just a few more minutes I am able to stand up. I wiggle my toes and resist crying out as a pins-and-needles sensation shoots up my legs. I straighten, and then try the door. I'm expecting it to be locked or barricaded. It isn't. Slowly, silently I edge it open. I expect to see Kenneth Jones sitting guard outside, maybe even with a weapon in his hand. He is not. Clearly he had confidence in his bindings. The door creaks as I carefully close it behind me. I don't want to leave it gaping, which he might notice from the kitchen window if he is keeping a lookout. And then I run.

Silently, swiftly. I don't think about where I am going. I just run. Somehow my legs seem to know where I must head even if my mind is still struggling to catch up. Fiona has a house here. We holidayed together. I remember that now. That's why I recalled Lyme Regis in such detail. I feel drawn toward the house. I am needed there.

43

KENNETH

Kenneth watches Kylie Gillingham run down the path. She has made her choice then. She is refusing to be his darling Stacie. Refusing to give him a second chance. He isn't that surprised. Women are always running away from him. He doesn't deserve it to be so, but it is. That's life. Lots of people don't get what they deserve. He thinks about the women he's loved. Who have left him.

First there was his wife. Terrible, ungrateful woman. He loved her so much. He was very devoted. Admittedly not in an overly romantic way; he might not have been one for the big gestures. He was not the sort to send Valentine's cards, and he was more likely to buy a slow cooker for a Christmas gift than a sparkling piece of jewelry, but he consistently provided for her; gave her a comfortable home, worked around the clock to do so. That wasn't enough, apparently. She fell in love with some bloke from Exeter. All those trips to the city to attend art classes were just a cover for their dirty little affair. Yes, she did go to the art classes, but so did he. That was where it started. They got into a habit of going out for a drink together after class. Initially coffee, which progressed to a glass of wine; soon they were sharing a bottle and then, inevitably, a bed. She gave Kenneth most of this detail when she was packing. Spitting out her thoughts as she filled her suitcase. She didn't hold back. She seemed to want him to know how completely and utterly in love she was with this middling would-be artist; she was insistent that Kenneth should know that she just couldn't live without this new man, that she had no choice but to leave him and Stacie and her home and go with this waster to Paris.

There's nothing as selfish as a person in love.

She said she hadn't been looking to fall in love but she was powerless to prevent it. She simply couldn't resist. He let her reel out all the tired clichés. Nodded when she asked him if he understood that it was simply beyond her control. But he *didn't* understand. Surely there must have been a point when she could have said no. A moment when she might have recalled Kenneth at home taking care of little Stacie. A moment when she could have refused the second glass of wine, fastened up her blouse, got up from the bed.

Whore.

But as the years have passed, he has come to understand love bigger than reason. Love bigger than logic. Love bigger than anything. Not romantic love, but parental love. The love he felt for Stacie was everything.

His wife recognized that he was a devoted father. That was why she was able to just walk away without so much as looking back. She said the art scene in Paris wasn't a stable place to bring up a child and that Stacie would be happier here in Dorset with him. Stacie liked the local school; she had friends here. The whore didn't want to be too disruptive. Kenneth thought that most likely she simply didn't want Stacie cramping her style. So she left with barely a backward glance. Her subsequent contact was limited to the occasional phone call, postcards and birthday presents. Within five years, even that measly effort at parenting dried up. Stacie became entirely Kenneth's concern. Kenneth's responsibility.

He embraced being a single parent better than most. He was a devoted father before his wife left; after she left, he was practically a martyr to his role. He somehow managed to juggle his work as a GP with bringing up a child, prioritizing Stacie's well-being above everything. He never so much as glanced at another woman, let alone dated. He focused entirely on his daughter, poured all of his love into her. He made jokes during dentist appointments to ease her fear, he saw to it that she joined Brownies and Girl Guides and learned to play tennis and swim. He hand-stitched costumes for school plays along with the mothers of other kids, he turned up to every sports day and cheered on the sidelines with the fathers. He set up playdates with Stacie's little friends. He challenged teachers who said she was a chatterbox, basked in the praise of those who said she was particularly creative and talented. He cooked, cleaned and shopped for her; talked, listened and read to her. And he did all of that with joy, never resenting the sacrifices he made. They were happy. Or so he thought.

But it turned out Stacie was more like her mother than he could have anticipated. Nature overwhelmed nurture in the end. He'd thought that after all his loyalty, devotion and sacrifice Stacie would turn out like him. Dependable and dedicated to him. That seemed fair. But life isn't fair. Stacie went to art college and came back altered. A different person. Discontented, dissatisfied. Like her mother. He used to catch her staring longingly out to sea, a faraway look of yearning in her eyes. It was as though she was forever imagining escaping, leaving. He remembers her commenting once, "Funny, isn't it, how the foaming sea sometimes looks like blue dragons are firing out white fire, while other days it looks like soapy suds in a plastic washing-up bowl."

"I've found it best not to over-romanticize," he replied stiffly. Scared for her.

He pretended not to notice her restlessness, hoped it was a phase, and indeed he thought she was going to be okay when she started dating Giles Hughes. For a time she seemed more settled, calmer. It was the happiest day of his life when she accepted Giles's proposal. He imagined her living just down the road. He dreamed of a brood of grandchildren waiting in the wings.

But then that wasn't enough for her either.

Before he knew it, she wanted more. She wanted to follow her mother to Paris. They hadn't seen each other for nearly twenty years; it didn't make sense. It was an insult to him. Stacie was basically spitting in his face when she called off the wedding and declared that she was running away, after all he had done.

She turned out to be just another woman who did not appreciate him or want him. He loved her so much and she patronized him. Implied that he and his life were small, not enough. Another woman running from him was unbearable.

He didn't mean to kill her.

God, no! Never. He loved her more than he loved himself. It was an accident. The worst, most horrific accident imaginable. He would never get over it. Never forgive himself. She slammed the door behind her, and my God, he wished he'd just let her run. He has wished that a thousand times over. Hundreds of thousands of times, probably. But he didn't let her run. He yanked open the door and started off down the path after her. He was just reaching for her shoulder, trying to get her to turn around. To face him. He was perhaps heavy-handed. He hadn't intended to be. He simply wanted her to pause for a second. Think about her decision. But he unbalanced her. How many times had he seen her fall over then get back up again when she was a kid? Dozens, hundreds. How many times had he washed her grazed knee, kissed it better, popped on an Elastoplast? But this time she fell backward over her suitcase and he didn't catch her. His reflexes were just too slow. He was worked up. Not thinking clearly. She fell awkwardly down the garden steps. There were just three steps, but he knew the moment she hit the paving stone that it was not going to be something he could put an Elastoplast on. Not something she was going to get up from. He heard her head crack, her neck snap.

She was dead.

He tried everything to resurrect her. Obviously as a doctor

he knew all the proper procedures, but to no avail. No matter how many times he compressed her chest he couldn't get a wisp of breath from her. He was just a doctor, not God. The difference had never been so starkly apparent. He saw her spirit leave; her energy drifted upward and he was left with a husk. Nonetheless, all night, he continued to try to resurrect her. He probably broke her ribs doing so. She wouldn't have been able to feel that, of course. Still, he wept.

He should have called the police. Explained what had happened. He knows that now. He's often thought that in these past ten years or so. He wonders how different his life might have turned out if he had. There would have been an investigation, an autopsy. It might have gone to court, but a judge and jury with any sense would have realized he wasn't a killer. It was an accident. He didn't call the police, though. It was not because he was afraid of facing justice, it wasn't that; he just couldn't bear her being taken away from him, taken to a fridge in a morgue. He couldn't stand the idea.

He stayed up all night with her as she turned cold and stiff in his arms. He wasn't thinking clearly when he started to dig. He just dug and dug. They say *six feet under*, but no one has any idea how deep that is until they try to dig a grave. He dug the whole of the next day and late into the evening; even so, he doubts it was ever quite six feet. He thought someone might come along. A neighbor, perhaps, who had heard that the wedding was canceled, or Heidi and Ian Hughes, Giles himself. He thought someone would come looking for her, for him, and if they had, they would have stopped him. Helped him make a healthier choice.

But no one came. No one stopped him.

She lies under the pretty sea glass. The mermaid tears.

When, after a week, Heidi Hughes finally showed her face, he told her Stacie had gone to find her mother in Paris. It was what he wished had happened. It offered him some comfort, pretending she was still alive. The weeks turned into months, into years. No one looked for Stacie. Kenneth was initially concerned that Giles would grow a pair and decide to follow her to France, try to track her down, but he never did. He married someone else within two years. A young woman from the next village. The wedding was held in the church that Giles and Stacie had been planning to marry in. Kenneth was invited but didn't go. He heard it was lovely, very traditional. Pink flowers on the pew ends.

No one missed Stacie as much as Kenneth. As much as they should have. He resents that.

He does sometimes wonder: Would it have been so bad if it had gone to court and they had sent him to prison? He imprisoned himself anyway. He gave up his general practice after she died. He just couldn't find it in him to care, to try, to listen to other people's problems. Shingles, arthritis, sore throats all seemed so trivial to him. He no longer went to the pub or mixed socially. He became a recluse. He didn't deserve to be happy, and besides, he didn't like going out and leaving her alone in the garden. He preferred to stay close to her. From time to time he allowed himself a trip to Lyme Regis, if he needed something specific, like chicken wire or a new pair of glasses, something he couldn't get locally. Whenever he was there, he popped into the library.

A few years ago, he told the librarian that Stacie was ill, that she had cancer. It wasn't a pre-planned lie. It was just something that popped into his head. The librarian had never known Stacie, but she was a nice woman, chatty, and so she always asked Kenneth a question or two, just to be polite, just to make conversation. One time she asked if he had children or grandchildren. A natural enough inquiry. He admitted to having a daughter and stuck to the story that she lived in Paris. There was something about how she nodded her head when he mentioned Stacie that revealed it wasn't the first she had heard of her. No doubt she'd heard the gossip about his beautiful daughter jilting Giles Hughes nearly a decade before, and she probably wanted to know if Stacie had moved on, if Stacie thought the decision she'd made was the right one. There was little you could do about the perennial nature of idle gossip, the scourge of a small town, other than lean into it. The problem was, Kenneth couldn't imagine the grandkids that the librarian was expecting to hear of. He wanted to gift them to Stacie because she deserved a dignified happy-ever-after, but he just couldn't picture little chubby babies or boisterous grandchildren kicking a football about. So he told the librarian that his daughter was ill, gravely ill, with cancer. He wasn't sure where the lie came from, but once he'd told it, he realized it was the right route. Maybe it was time to let Stacie rest. He could allow her to die in Paris; a tragic early death. But not as tragic or early as her death had really been.

Over the next eighteen months, whenever he spoke to the librarian, he gave a fictional account of Stacie's illness. He implied that she wasn't responding to treatment, that her decline was accelerating, her demise inevitable. He was on the cusp of letting her go. Allowing her to rest in peace.

Then Kylie came along.

He's tried to explain it to her. That he was so alone, so lonely. That he missed Stacie so much that he sometimes wished his heart would stop. Kylie was his second chance. Sent so he could redeem himself. Mend her, keep her safe. He isn't a bad man.

But he saw her face when he was honest with her. She was scared. Terrified. And now she's running from him too. Why do the women he loves always run away?

Well, he isn't going to let this woman escape. He can't. He'll have to bring her back.

44

DAAN

The moment Daan finishes speaking to Mark and hangs up, he calls his lawyers. He doesn't trust Mark Fletcher to do the right thing. He doesn't trust him to do any bloody thing. The man seems shocked to the point of incapacity. Depressed, most likely, but Daan's not going to sit back. He's not that sort of person. Never has been and never will be. For good or bad, he has to act.

"I need to get to England," he tells his lead lawyer. He's careful not to ask for permission or guidance. Not to ask for any damned thing.

"We'd advise against that."

"Of course. Nonetheless, I need to get there today."

The lawyer suppresses a laugh, but in a way that communicates he is doing so; he wants Daan to know he is laughing and that he thinks Daan is foolish. "You are in a stronger position fighting this from the Netherlands. We've talked about that."

"I am aware, but I need to get to the UK."

His lawyer sighs audibly, and then, as though he's talking to a slightly confused child, he says, "It's impossible. Even if your bail conditions allowed you to travel, which they don't, there are hardly any flights. All governments are operating policies of essential travel only."

"It *is* essential," Daan responds tersely.

"Well, as I mentioned, the conditions of your bail don't allow it."

"Tell them I did it."

"What?" Daan can hear the energy being transferred from him to his lawyer, who must be blindsided by this turn of events. Daan has been vigorously protesting his innocence for months.

"Tell the police I murdered her and I will show them where the body is. That should tick the essential travel box."

"Did you?" the lawyer asks. His voice quivers, and Daan dislikes him for it. He doesn't bother to respond. Eventually the lawyer says, "Well, they might put you on a plane in the next day or so if you say this is the case."

"I need to get to England today," Daan insists.

"I'm not sure that can be done."

Daan thinks of how much this man and his company are paid by the hour. "Get me on a fucking helicopter by noon or you are fired. Tell DC Clements we'll meet her in Lyme Regis."

Daan knows that when he gets to Lyme Regis, he will not be able to show the DC where Kai is buried. He knows he's going to be in a lot of shit for this. There is a risk his theory is wrong and that Fiona is not a threat to Oli and Seb. If that is the case, he will be charged with wasting police time, and since he'll be on UK soil, they will most likely make him see out the time before the trial in a British prison. If he is condemned there, he won't be able to wiggle. Everyone knows playing a game on home territory is best; playing an away match puts you at a disadvantage.

Oddly, considering all of that, he thinks the best-case scenario is one where he is wrong and Fiona isn't a threat and the boys are safe. The thing is, he believes the worst-case scenario to be more likely. Fiona is completely mad and threatening. The boys are in great danger. He might be able to help them. Someone has to. He is not leaving those boys alone.

45

OLI

"You are going to let me tie you up, Oli, because you are very big and that's dangerous; we both know you could overpower me," says Fiona.

"I wouldn't do that."

She looks bored and disappointed that he is bothering to lie to her. "Yes, you would," she asserts with a deep sigh. "Remember, I have your brother."

He holds out his hands in front of him. She shakes her head and roughly pulls them behind his back, binds them there. Honestly, he doesn't know if it's the right call to give in to her. Should he punch her in the face and make a run for it? Maybe. But she has Seb. Not here in the house. Somewhere else. He can't leave his little brother with her. He can't risk her never revealing where Seb is, as she has with Leigh.

"Sit," she commands.

He obediently flops into the kitchen chair and she ties his feet to the legs. He wants to kick her in her stupid face, but he doesn't. He can't lose Seb.

She doesn't behave like the baddies do in movies, not DC and Marvel ones at least. She does not reveal her entire sick plan. She leaves him guessing.

"Where is Seb?" he asks.

"I don't want you to worry about that right now." She sounds like an annoyingly bossy schoolteacher. He really hates her, like a thousand times more than he's ever hated a teacher. More than he hated Leigh.

"Is he okay?"

"Yes. At the moment."

The threat is loud and clear. "What are you going to do with us?" She doesn't respond to that one. She begins to move around the house, packing a rucksack. She takes some of Seb's clothes from their day bag that Oli packed yesterday. He can't believe it was just yesterday; it seems such a long time ago. She looks delighted to find their passports. She takes Seb's, leaves Oli's on the kitchen table. He feels a sharp, illogical sting of rejection—he's being left behind—but it's almost immediately consumed by overwhelming horror. "Where are you taking Seb?" he demands in panic. "What is your plan?"

"You are asking too many questions," she says with an impatient tut.

He regrets giving in to her now. He opens his mouth to scream for help, but as though she's anticipated this, she lunges in with a tea towel and his screams are swallowed as she roughly, and far too tightly, gags him. He resists, moves his head violently from left to right, but he's too firmly bound to do much now. He's an idiot, a total idiot to have let this happen; he's let Seb down. He brought him here to protect him, but now he's put him in greater danger.

Oli thinks he's going to cry. The thought fills him with dread and shame. He doesn't want to cry in front of her. He's not scared, he doesn't want her to think that. He's frustrated and furious with himself, that's what is pushing him to the brink of tears. He had the upper hand for a brief moment, and now he's a bloody victim. She carefully closes all the blinds and draws the curtains, as he's seen her do when they leave here at the end of a holiday. No one will be able to see into the house. Is she going to leave him here alone? Will he starve? Die? Where is she taking Seb?

She doesn't even turn to look at him as she opens the kitchen door, walks out, and then closes and locks it behind her.

Oli has never felt so alone.

46

FIONA

Seb is still unconscious, and that is for the best. Fiona swings up the garage door and is hit by a sense of things scuttling into the dark corners, spiders or mice. She never keeps her car in here. It's full of the usual beach paraphernalia: punctured inflatables that she always plans to fix because she feels bad about adding to landfill but never gets around to (the road to hell is paved with good intentions!), deck chairs, windbreakers, parasols. There's also an assortment of tools, the lawn mower and several half-empty pots of paint. Her little aluminum boat takes center stage. It's mounted on the trailer, ready to go. As she sweeps away cobwebs that hang low and catch in her hair, her gaze is pulled to the five wetsuits hanging like headless bodies on the pegs on the wall. Hers and one for each of the Fletchers. The suits haunt her, reminding her that they were once like a big happy family, or so she thought.

She considers suiting up and decides it's worth taking a couple of minutes for her to do so, but dismisses the idea of trying to wriggle an unconscious Seb into his suit; it would be an impossible task. The little family boat can be rowed or driven by an outboard engine. Fiona is glad she decided to equip it with a combustion engine. It's not like she could row to France. And France is her plan. Yes, it's considerably further than she's ever sailed before. Normally she bobs around the coastline, limiting herself to calm waters and short stretches of just a few hours tops. However, she's a good sailor—she's taken exams—and she has an iPhone and a compass; how hard can it be? People cross the English Channel all the time; people who don't have passports or any sailing skills. She has both.

Seb might stay unconscious throughout. That would probably be for the best, because Fiona hasn't quite thought through how she might explain to the boy what they are doing. When he wakes up, if they are already in France, she can tell him they are on holiday. That will do, won't it? In the short term, at least. He'll believe what she tells him, won't he? Her plan is vague and on the fly, she knows it, but she can't think about it right now. She has to get going. No time to lose.

She hitches the trailer to the car and pulls onto the road. Then she glances in her rear mirror and realizes that an open garage door is as obvious as a missing front tooth. Infuriated, she stops the car, gets out and dashes back to close the door.

47

KYLIE

I run harder, faster and further than I have ever run before. I develop a killer stitch and my lungs feel as though they are being stretched like overinflated balloons and might burst. Sweat is pooling in the small of my back, my feet are slick in my shoes, a blister is forming on my right heel. I don't care. I run on.

My feet lead and I try not to think about the direction they are choosing. If I overthink it, I might lose my way. Better to let my subconscious remain in charge. The moment I turn the corner and set eyes on the small but well-kept 1990s bungalow, I instinctively know I am in the right place. Fiona's second home. Not somewhere I consciously knew existed until a few minutes ago, but that I can now identify with one hundred percent assurance. There is no time to marvel at how cunning and interesting brains are. I need to work out why I instinctually came here.

Because I do believe I should be here. I am needed, but it isn't clear to me why. The papers all reported that Fiona is in London; one or two of the tabloids revealed the detail that she is living with Mark, Oli and Seb. They ostensibly praise her kindness for stepping in and caring for her friend's grieving husband and sons, but I get the sense that they are hinting at a more scandalous situation. The implication is that Fiona is living with Mark as a partner. Is that possible? It seems so soon. Has she been in love with him for a long time? That would explain her crime; she may well have been motivated by jealousy. Or maybe she is just being opportunistic; maybe she's moved in with Mark not because she loves him passionately but because she hates me viciously and wants to dance on my grave. That would explain why she was so insistent on knowing who I would pick if I had to choose one of my two husbands. If I'd said I wanted Daan, she might have moved in on *him* and framed Mark. I shake my head. It doesn't matter anyhow; I'm not going to waste time trying to understand the brain of a would-be murderer. The important question is: What does all this mean for the boys? I am unsure, but I doubt it is anything good.

It's incredibly disappointing that the bungalow seems to be deserted. There is no sign of a car; the blinds and curtains are drawn. I was so sure my subconscious had brought me here for a reason. Now I don't know what to do next. Should I head to Lyme Regis and turn myself in at the police station? Or should I go to the nearest house and knock on the door, explain who I am and ask if I can call the police from there? Frankly, that doesn't appeal. Whoever's door I knock at will most likely have a view on both me and my case because of the extensive, lurid media coverage. It's unlikely to be a favorable view. I realize I will have to face the police, press and public very soon, but I think it would be better to control the narrative of my return to life rather than have some stranger privy to it. A stranger who might very well sell the story to a tabloid. So I guess it makes sense to set off toward Lyme Regis and place myself in police custody.

But something stops me. It is a strange twang, a fluttering of anxiety.

Oli, Seb.

I've had this feeling before, many times. Whenever I waved them off to school knowing they had to sit tests or exams that they were nervous about. When Oli had his tonsils out and was under the anesthetic, and every time either boy was worried about playing in a sports fixture or performing in a school production. I carried their anxiety. Mark used to laugh and say I was a witch. "A good one," he'd add. I'm not a witch. I don't believe in superstitions, ghosts or anything paranormal. But I do believe in a mother's instinct, and I am a mother. I decide to take a closer snoop around the bungalow. I don't know what I expect to find, if anything, but I know the importance of being thorough. Fiona tried to murder me and this is Fiona's home, reason enough for a poke around before I set off to the police station.

There are no gaps in the sitting-room curtains at the front, and the only way to peer through the kitchen or bedroom windows is to climb over the five-foot fence and into the back garden. I'm so weary, but I drag the bin to the fence and clamber onto it, hoisting myself up and over. I land heavily on the other side.

The blinds are closed at the kitchen window; nothing can be seen. I check the bedrooms, but the curtains are drawn tight there too. Then I recall the tiny bathroom window at the side of the bungalow, which doesn't have a curtain or a blind. I've always thought that was a bit exposing and the only room that really needed either, but now I'm grateful. I peer through. It's a piece of luck that the door from the bathroom to the hallway is open. It is just possible to see past the tiny hallway, no bigger than a coffee table, and into the kitchen. At first I don't spot anything of interest. The kitchen is tidy to the point of sterile; it doesn't look as though anyone has been in there for a while.

Then a miracle happens. Oli shuffles into view. My boy. My son. He is lying on the floor, his arms and legs tied to an overturned chair; he's moving like a caterpillar toward the kitchen unit. He is gagged and red in the face, obviously panicked, scared. I bang on the small window and yell, "Oli. Oli darling, it's me."

He lifts his head. Our eyes meet.

48

FIONA

As Fiona drives along the narrow country lanes, overhanging branches whip the car, her tires kick up loose stones and she racks her brains trying to come up with a convincing explanation for Seb as to why just the two of them might stay in France long-term. She'll have to think of something believable and compelling, as the boy is twelve, not two. It might be possible to string him along for a while. Initially she can tell him his dad and Oli will be joining them, that they're all going to spend the summer abroad. She can easily justify a holiday by pointing out that they've all been under so much stress. She can argue that they need to get away from the press and recuperate somewhere out of the spotlight. A little later down the line, she can then say that the COVID restrictions mean Mark and Oli can't get out of the UK to join them. She'll say that they'll have to manage, just the two of them, for a while.

She can spot flaws in her own plan even as she is forming it. For a start, how will she explain the fact that they arrived illegally on the boat? Even if she can fob him off with some "special circumstances because of COVID" guff, he'll want to FaceTime his father and brother. How will she negotiate around that? Plus, she can't have their true identities revealed to anyone; how will she convince him to adopt a pseudonym and give a different story to any acquaintances they make? She can't realistically expect to isolate the boy from everyone. Perhaps she can tell him that they are using fake names to leave behind the gossip about his bigamist stepmum. Lies, lies, lies. So many of them and so hard to keep track of. Fiona's head is reeling; she can't discern what might be possible and convincing because she's desperate and panicking. The explanations she's coming up with sound viable one second, ludicrous the next. She opens her mouth and screams with frustration. Her plan is a mess.

This annoys her. She spent months working out the details of Kylie's abduction. She thought of every scenario, every risk, every potential consequence. She is angry with herself for ending up somewhere so chaotic and faulty. It was an incredible act of hubris to remove the pictures of Kylie from the bungalow. Unnecessarily dramatic. The sad truth is, Oli was right; Fiona just wanted to rid herself of every reminder of her former friend, but look where that one impetuous act has led. She thought she'd considered everything, but she never thought that Oli and Seb would run to Dorset and start snooping, or that Oli might be so observant and actually notice the photos had gone. As neither of them has any money, she didn't think they would be able to independently strike out in this way. Damn Daan Janssen and his deep pockets to hell.

She is on this path now and there is nothing she can do about it but rush on, she thinks as she puts her foot down a little too heavily. The roads are narrow and twisty; normally she takes them at a snail's pace, but now all she can do is push through. This part of her life is out of control; she has to get past it, find a more even keel. Things have to get better. Part of her is already regretting that she acted so hastily. It would perhaps have been more sensible to let Oli tell her what he'd found before she drugged Seb. Then she could have told him he was mistaken, that the photos were removed long ago, months before Kylie went missing. Maybe she could have said that Kylie herself took them down, that she didn't think they were flattering or something. She should have just insisted that he was reading something into nothing. After all, when they were taken away isn't something anyone can categorically prove. It would have been his word against hers, and besides, what did it prove anyway? Even if he'd gone to the police with his suspicions, she could have argued she was grief-stricken about Kylie's disappearance and didn't want sad reminders of her friend around the house. The removal of the photos doesn't prove she's a killer. The "evidence" is circumstantial at best.

She should have held her nerve.

She curls her hand into a fist and hammers the steering wheel in exasperation. She does so with such vigor that she hurts her wrist, but it doesn't ease her frustration, so she knocks hard on her own skull, trying to bang a solution into being. "Think!" she yells at herself.

The problem of course is bloody Daan Janssen lurking in the background, persistently, vehemently insisting that he is innocent; now going as far as infiltrating the Fletcher household. Really that is what has caused her to panic. She's intimidated by Daan. Intimidated by his confidence, his wealth, his indifference toward her. When they were together, she always knew he had the upper hand. Briefly, when he was arrested, she thought she was beating him. Defeating him. But is that possible? Men like him rule the world. She thumps her head with her fist again. "Stupid, stupid," she tells herself. She should have sat tight. She could have reported Daan to the police; he has tampered with witnesses, broken the conditions of his bail, unduly influenced and harangued children. She would have been wiser to turn it all against him.

Yes, she should have paused to reflect a little more, because sailing across the ocean with a drugged child, hoping to disappear in Europe, seems like a risky, flaky, flawed plan.

Should have. Could have. Would have. Stupid, helpless, hopeless words.

Thoughts bounce in and out of Fiona's head like fireworks in the sky now. Bright and vivid one moment, lost to a smoky blackness the next. It's hard to stay focused, to remain calm.

She doesn't know what jurisdiction the English police have in France. Might she be extradited? Will she have to go deeper into Europe? Disappear altogether? How will she get to her bank accounts? How easy is it to travel across borders at the moment? She has so many questions and no answers. She is not a criminal mastermind, someone with access to fake passports and such. How will she manage?

The one thing she does know is that after all she has endured, she is not going to come away from this empty-handed. That is not fair. Not acceptable. That is why she could not run away on her own. She will not accept being alone again. At different points in recent history, she has been the lover of both of Kylie's husbands. There has been a chance for her with both men. She isn't greedy like Kylie, she never wanted them both at the same time; she was happy to take one or the other. She would have been delighted to be Daan's girlfriend; way back when, in the beginning, that was her hope. Until she discovered that he was married. It was a bitter pill, but if she was being totally honest with herself, it was not one that was altogether impossible to swallow. Women do become mistresses; some settle for that, others hope in time that their status will change. But then she discovered he was married to her best friend. Now *that* stuck in her throat. *That* she choked on.

She has been Mark's lover for months now. She's lived in his home, cooked meals for him, washed and ironed his clothes; they've played cards, and watched *Normal People* and the latest season of *Better Call Saul* on TV together. They are a couple. Besides which, she has been like a mother to his sons. She's tended them with fastidious care. She's glimpsed a life where she has a family of her own, and she is not going to give up on all of that. She won't. It just wouldn't be fair if she lost everything.

She is surely entitled to at least one boy. Oli can be moody and sullen; Seb is by far the more pliant. Besides, it's better for Seb if he is with her. He is still young and needs a mother. He hasn't got one. He needs Fiona.

In the final analysis, she's killed a woman, for God's sake; she is not going to come away from this with nothing to show for her trouble.

She has had to leave Seb in the boot of the car, which isn't ideal. She considered strapping him into the back seat; she almost did so, telling herself that anyone they passed on the country roads would probably just assume he was snoozing, but then she decided it was better to be cautious. She couldn't risk someone recognizing him and calling the police. If Mark hasn't done as instructed and told the police the boys are safe and well, they might still be looking for them. For all she knows, the search might have escalated by now. She thinks Mark most probably did follow her instructions, because he tends to. He isn't especially good at thinking for himself right now. Other women might find that irritating, a little weak, but Fiona has seen the advantages. She's been able to make herself useful to him, indispensable really. She does believe he will miss her, which is somehow satisfying. Most likely he will have done her bidding, but she hasn't been in contact with him since swapping texts last night, so she can't totally depend on it. She knows it's impossible to depend on anyone. A mistake. So it's safest if Seb stays in the boot, and as he's asleep, he'll have no memory of the journey. No harm done.

When she arrives at Lyme Regis harbor, she parks the car at a careless angle across two spaces, then reverses so that the trailer is in the water. She jumps out, rushes to open the boot. Her next problem is getting Seb out of the car and into the boat without drawing too much attention. She is shocked at the sight of him; he looks so pale he is almost transparent. He appears smaller than usual, as though the ordeal is making him shrink. He's still unconscious, which is a bonus, as he doesn't panic when she throws a rug over him or feel it when his head bangs against the boot of the car as she hastily scoops him up and carries him to the boat. She drops him unceremoniously on the floor. It's not that she means to be callous, but while he looks slight, he is still hefty to carry any distance, and she's not only exhausted but in a hurry.

Returning to the car, she picks up her rucksack and throws that on top of Seb. There's nothing heavy in it. Just clothes, some food and water. Okay, so the full water bottle might cause a bit of discomfort, but he doesn't stir, so no harm done. Next she flings in buoyancy aids, boat gloves and boots. She hopes that if anyone is watching, they will imagine she's simply moving supplies, and not think too long and hard about what might be under the blanket. There's no more room for anything else; it's a squeeze as it is. She'd best get going.

The sun is searing. It scorches, and she feels further irritated that she didn't pack suncream. She's not thinking clearly. She's not prepared, and the more she admits this to herself, the more cross and, frankly, afraid she becomes. She looks at her phone. Google Maps gives the time it takes to cover a distance by car, public transport, bike, foot and plane; she makes a mental note to contact them after this is all over and say that they need to include boat travel too. She has no idea how long it might take her to get to France or where exactly she should try to dock. She supposes she'll have to sail up the coast until she finds somewhere appropriate. She refamiliarizes herself with the compass app and then turns on the engine. The aluminum boat slips out of the harbor.

49

OLI

His mum is quite the badass really; he'd forgotten that. The moment she spots him, she springs into action, doesn't hesitate. She dashes back to the kitchen window. "Move away from the window," she instructs. He can't call out to her to tell her he's following her instructions, as he's still gagged. He wriggles as far away as he can, scoots back so he is facing the wall, hunched like a tortoise. She must trust that he's protected himself as much as possible, because she doesn't hang about. He hears the window smash. Glass splinters shower in every direction, some flying through the air, loads of it slithering across the kitchen tiles. He feels one or two pieces tap against his back.

Almost immediately, he feels her hurriedly undoing his gag and the rope round his wrists. He wraps his arms around himself and rolls his stiff shoulders as she unties his legs. Neither of them speaks while she does this. She's concentrating, all her energy focused on setting him free, while he doesn't know what to say. He notices that her arms are cut and scratched. She took less care of herself than she did of him. There's a big stone gnome on the floor, the paint on its red hat chipped and the fishing rod snapped; she obviously used it to smash the window. He remembers her buying it as a tongue-in-cheek gift for Fiona last summer. She howled with laughter as she handed it over. "It's so bad it's good, don't you think?"

All of a sudden he is clinging to her and she's clinging to him. And he's crying. Proper bawling like a baby, but it doesn't matter, he's not embarrassed, because crying in front of your mum is totally okay. She would never judge him. He feels the warmth of her hug, the strength of it, and he forgets all the things he hates her for.

He's just so fucking glad she's alive.

50

KYLIE

I pull my son so close to me that I can feel his heartbeat. I squeeze tightly, clinging to him as though there is a danger he might slip from my grasp. He won't, not ever again. I won't let that happen. "It's okay. I'm here. I'm here," I whisper. If he wants to challenge me—and my God, he'd be within his rights to do so—he finds the courage or tact to somehow resist.

"You're not dead," he mutters, clearly amazed.

"Right, yes." I realize this must be a huge shock for him. I am back from the grave. I don't want to let him go, not even for a moment, but I have to break the hug to ask, "Where's Seb?" I'm up on my feet and moving toward the hallway, broken glass crunching underfoot. "Seb! Seb!"

"She took him," Oli replies. His voice cracks with pain and panic. I freeze. Turn back to him.

"Fiona did?"

He nods. "It's all my fault. I should never have brought him here."

I dart back to his side, pull him to his feet. As he gets up, he towers above me. I reach up and take hold of his face in both hands, then tilt it down to mine. He tries to avoid my gaze, but I keep my eyes locked on him. I know he will meet them eventually. He's taller than I recall, and maybe even a fraction broader. I feel a pinch of sadness that he is a physical embodiment of what we have lost. Time has passed. It does. It always will. It seems ludicrous that Oli is taller than I am but still a child, still in need of reassurance, care. "None of this is your fault," I say firmly. "Do you understand?"

"You're not dead," he repeats. "Seb was right." Now he allows himself to look at me properly. "Here you are, a skinhead version of you, but you all the same." He gives in to a grin.

I smile back. "Good news, I hope." He laughs, and because he's been crying and is full of snot and emotion, the sound bubbles out of his nose. He seems so young. "We definitely have a lot to catch up on," I say as I wink at him. He lunges at me and hugs me tightly again. For a moment the world has stopped, spun backward on its axle. This feels like our very first moment of connection; a private moment that I recall with crystal clarity. It was the day I met Mark, Oli and Seb. A traumatic day that ended up with a trip to hospital after Seb took a tumble off the top of the slide in the play park. While Mark tended to Seb, I—then a complete stranger to them— took care of Oli. I remember gaining his trust by feeding him chocolate-covered raisins and reading him stories as we sat in the hospital waiting room. There was one particular moment that will stay with me forever. He rested his head against my shoulder and then asked if he could climb onto my knee. He *chose* me. He felt safe with me. His instincts were right then and are right now. He *is* safe with me. He can trust me. His eyes shine and I know my boy so well; I know he is excited, jubilant. "Okay, tell me everything you know," I instruct.

"I haven't seen Seb since last night, when we both went to bed. When I woke up, he was gone and Fiona was here. She said she had him. Then she left in the car. I didn't see her go because I was tied up, but I heard the engine. I guess Seb was in the car too. He must have been gagged, because he didn't call out. I suppose he might be somewhere else. She could have taken him somewhere last night."

"Let's assume she kept him with her. She might have given him something."

"Drugged him, you mean?"

"She drugged me," I say carefully, apologetic that I have to articulate this. I know I'll be adding to Oli's apprehension, but I have to be straight with him. I can't protect him from this reality. "Did she say anything at all about what she plans to do next?"

"No, but she took his passport."

The words ricochet through my body, but I know it's vital that I appear in control for Oli. "Well, she can't get far during a pandemic. There are restrictions everywhere. Where's your phone?"

"She took that too."

"Okay, well we need to get to a phone to call the police." I race to the back door, but it's locked. I make toward the broken window.

"No, climb out of a good one, you'll cut yourself," yells Oli.

"You go through the front room one," I say. I'm already halfway out, but he's right, I do cut myself. But I'm only thinking about Seb now.

I rush to the garage and lift the door. It's unlocked, so I know what to expect before I see it. The Buster Mini boat is gone. "No!" My objection splits the air; the entire garage seems to quiver under my fury. I feel futile and hopeless as I imagine Fiona hell-bent on getting to France in her tiny, insecure little craft. She has always overestimated her sailing skills. I count the wetsuits. Hers is missing. Seb's is still there. She hasn't bothered to keep him warm.

Oli is now at my side. "We need to get to the harbor," I tell him.

"You think she's going to try to sail to France?" he asks. "That's insane."

I'm about to point out that Fiona is most likely certifiable, but at that moment a car comes around the bend and pulls onto the drive. It's Kenneth Jones. He edges the nose halfway into the garage, obstructing our exit, meaning we have no choice but to move closer to the back wall. "I attract nutters, Oli. I'm sorry." I don't want to panic him, but before Kenneth can get out of the car, I say, "Run, go now." He'll have to squeeze his way past the car, but I want him to get away while he can and not end up trapped in here. Being trapped is hell. Seeing *him* trapped would be worse.

But Oli does not run; he stares at Kenneth as he slowly gets out of the car. I see the old man through my son's gaze: scruffy, lanky, disheveled. Crazed. His bright blue eyes flit manically around the garage. He could be mistaken for someone who is high on speed. That's when I notice that Oli's attention is trained specifically on Kenneth's hand. He is holding a knife. I recognize it as a kitchen knife I have used often in these past few months. It's funny that in all the domestic chaos we muddled through, the one thing Kenneth was always fastidious about was keeping the kitchen knives sharp.

I know that I can't risk Oli pushing past him. I step in front of my son; Oli jostles with me and tries to get in front of me. I don't allow it. After a few seconds, I realize I'm wasting my energy, and we stand shoulder to shoulder.

"So this is one of the lads, is it?" says Kenneth. "One of the kids Leigh Fletcher abandoned."

"I'm her son, yes," says Oli. "And she didn't abandon us. She was taken." His loyalty breaks my heart. I ache with longing to be out of this mess. All I want is to find Seb and give us all the chance the boys deserve, but looking at Kenneth gripping a knife, knowing Fiona has Seb, I wonder whether I will ever get that opportunity.

Kenneth seems struck by Oli's comment too. He tilts his head to one side and looks quizzical. "What are you doing here?" he asks.

"We came to find her."

"We?"

"Me and my brother."

"I'd like to meet him too."

"You can't." Oli looks Kenneth straight in the eye. He speaks in a calm and assured voice, although I know he must be terrified. I am in awe of his ability to appear composed. "Fiona Phillipson has taken him."

"I see." Kenneth's face collapses into an expression of concern.

"Who are you?" Oli demands.

"I'm her..." Kenneth pauses for the longest time, then eventually says, "I'm her friend."

"Why are you carrying a knife then?" Oli demands.

The airless garage smells of dust and creosote; it is tight with fear. Kenneth looks down at his hand and seems shocked to see the knife there, as though he'd forgotten he had it. He gives a small sort of shrug. "I brought it along just in case."

"In case of what? Are you going to hurt my mum?"

"No, I—"

"Don't you fucking dare."

Kenneth looks surprised, and then confused. "I...I wasn't thinking clearly. I've had a very difficult day." His eyes moisten. "I'm sorry." His shoulders seem to melt into his chest; he looks vulnerable, manageable. His apparent docility might not be real, and even if it is, it might not last, so I must try to manage him while there is perhaps opportunity.

"Will you put the knife down?" I ask. "Will you let us go? We need to get to a neighbor; we need to call the police. Please. I'm begging you. Fiona has a boat and Seb. He's in danger. I know you are a good man, Kenneth." I know nothing of the sort.

"I could help," he states.

How can I trust him? He's confessed to killing his daughter. A daughter he once loved above everything. He locked me up and drugged me. He's obviously unstable, unwell, and he's literally blocking our exit from the garage. He doesn't seem in any way helpful. He reaches out a gnarled hand, but it's the hand holding the knife, so both Oli and I instinctually pull away from him. He must see our fear; it crackles in the air.

"Really, I can help," he insists, reassuring no one as he instantly appears agitated. "I have a car. I can drive you to the harbor. Going to a neighbor, calling the police, that will all waste time. She's most likely already in the water." He tosses the knife into the back seat of the car. "I see now that you were right, Kylie. They did miss you, your boys. They came here for you. You do have a life of your own."

"Just like that? You're suddenly seeing sense?" I ask skeptically.

"I thought you had nothing. I thought I was giving you something. I shouldn't have tricked you and I certainly shouldn't have locked you up. I see that now. But before then, these past few months, have you had anything to complain about? Didn't I take care of you?"

"What happened to Stacie?" I ask. I know I am testing him.

"It was an accident. And I'm sorry. Sorrier than is bearable. I hope you never have cause to be this sorry. When you came into my life, I really believed you were my second chance. Well, perhaps you are. Not because I get a second chance at being a father, but because I might be able to help save a loved child. What are you waiting for?"

Honestly, I don't know if I can trust him. I've seen such tenderness from him over these past few months, and then today, such desperate cruelty. I wish I could just call the police right now and believe that they will get a boat in the water to give chase before it's too late, but I don't imagine that will happen. The explanation as to who I am and what is going on is convoluted and complicated; it would most likely take hours to convince anyone that Fiona has Seb and for them to pursue her. Hours I don't have. I don't have many options right now.

Oli looks at me, waiting for me to make a decision. He's poised like a lion ready to pounce. If I give the nod, he could tackle Kenneth to the floor. A strong young man versus a weakened old one. No contest now that Kenneth has dropped the knife. But I don't want to watch my son overpower him. I don't know if I can trust him, a self-confessed killer, a man who has lied to me, imprisoned me, but he is right: time is of the essence here. We don't have a moment to spare. Every second that

Seb stays in Fiona's grasp is potentially lethal. Kenneth Jones
is grief-stricken, lonely, misguided. He's desperate, depressed,
deranged. But he was a father. *Is* a father, because even death
doesn't change that status. Whatever he's done, he understands
what it means to be a parent and values that above everything.
I believe him when he says he'll help me find my son.

51

DAAN

Daan doesn't speak to the pilot or his lawyer as he climbs into the sleek-bodied helicopter. A friend of his father's was able to supply his private aircraft at short notice when the authorities, the lawyers, the police, failed to do so. Money talks. Shouts, actually. He told his dad he's going to the UK to prove his innocence. He's told the police he's going there to prove his guilt. It hardly matters what he says to any of them. He's going because he has to do everything in his power to protect Kai's motherless boys.

The rotor blades start turning, and they are deafening. He and his lawyer are handed intercom headsets so they can hear the pilot. The rotors whir and it seems to take an age to get up to speed. The pilot asks air traffic control for permission to take off, and finally clearance is given, Daan sits back and lets the overwhelming physical vibration take over his body. The speed of the vertical takeoff is such that he feels as though he is being pushed down into his seat.

He's glad of the thunderous sound of the blades, which drowns out the possibility of making any sort of conversation. What have they to say to one another? His lawyer has already confirmed that they are heading to Lyme Regis. His request inevitably led to raised eyebrows and raised heartbeats. It has been agreed that he will be taken into police custody the moment they land. He doesn't care; his goal is getting the police to where he believes the boys are. His confession was apparently greeted with relief and delight, according to his clearly disgruntled lawyer. Daan imagines that the responses are Clements's and Tanner's respectively. He keeps asking for information about Oli and Seb, but no one will tell him where they are. He isn't sure if they don't know or if they are simply refusing to give him that level of peace of mind.

He gazes about him. Helicopters afford great visibility, which will be useful. He swivels his head, looking out of the front, the sides, down below his feet. He is determined to find those boys.

52

KYLIE

Kenneth drives at a dangerous speed, considering the route is one of narrow hairpin bends and tight tracks. I'm already aware of this after our journey home from Lyme Regis yesterday, but this time, I am glad of it. Even though for most of the journey we jolt in and out of potholes or seem to just narrowly miss hitting livestock and fences.

When we arrive in the town, the streets are jam-packed with milling tourists and the roads are so busy that traffic is virtually at a standstill. I can't imagine ever finding a parking spot. "Oli and I should get out. We could run faster," I say to Kenneth. I tense for a moment, scared that he might not agree to my suggestion. That he'll once again flip from someone trying to help me to someone trying to control me. However, he immediately pulls onto a stranger's driveway. I am expecting that just Oli and I will get out of the car, but Kenneth climbs out too, and simply abandons the vehicle. I don't have time to argue with him.

We push through the crowds, causing people to grumble and tut. One or two seem to purposefully jab their elbows into me as I run. What is wrong with them? Clearly I'm in trouble; why won't they get out of the way? I don't bother to explain or apologize. There will be plenty of that ahead of me and I'll happily face it, but first I need to find Seb.

"There's her car!" Oli yells, pointing toward the water.

I recognize it too, and my heart sinks. It's parked badly, right up at the water's edge, the boat trailer still attached. It's clear that my worst fear, that she's leaving the country, has been realized. A few obviously irate people are standing close to the car, grumbling because it has been inconveniently abandoned on the harbor ramp. It's causing an obstruction for others who want to launch small craft. I would kill for that to be my problem right now. A normal life, what a luxury.

"What shall we do?" asks Oli.

"We'll take a boat and follow her," says Kenneth.

"Like steal one?" asks Oli, somewhere between impressed and shocked.

Kenneth shakes his head. "I was once a trusted doctor." He must clock Oli's expression, because he almost laughs. "I know, hard to believe. But people used to tell me where they hid their boat keys, in case I ever needed to get to a patient in Charlton Undercliff or Charmouth Beach in a hurry. You saw the tourist traffic today. The roads are often blocked." I try to imagine Kenneth as he's describing himself; a once dependable member of this community, respected even, now ruined through grief. "That one over there belongs to a former patient of mine. There will be a spare set of keys in a plastic box strapped underneath the bench in the hull. People round here don't change much."

He sets off to the far end of the harbor at speed. I follow, no longer bothering to question whether he can be trusted or not. Despite everything he has put me through in the past months—all the lies, trickery and deceit—I will accept any port in a storm, and undoubtedly this is a Category 3 shitstorm. He dashes toward a small flotilla of boats that are bobbing on the water and leaps confidently onto one. When he straightens up, he is brandishing the keys in triumph. "Hurry up," he instructs.

I step onto the boat, then turn to Oli, who is hot on my heels. "No way. No. You have to stay here," I instruct firmly.

"I'm coming too."

"No. It's dangerous. There isn't enough room and you need to call your dad and the police. Tell them what's happening." Oli looks torn, outraged at being left behind but sensible enough to see that calling the police, getting help is a priority. He glances up as he hears a helicopter. I use his momentary lapse of focus to shove him off the boat. He falls onto his backside, landing on the jetty. Kenneth starts the engine and we move away before Oli can get up. "I'm sorry," I yell. He stares at me with shock and disappointment. I hope that soon he will find a level of understanding. I need to keep him safe. I can't trust Kenneth, Fiona or the sea. I wish I had time to hug him again. "I'll bring him back," I yell. In my head I add, *Or I will die trying*, but I don't articulate that bit.

Kenneth is already pulling out of the harbor, cutting through the dark blue sea. I watch Oli turn and start to run back toward the crowds. He stops everyone he meets, obviously asking for a phone. The third person he approaches hands him one.

Kenneth draws my attention away from Oli as he tosses me a life jacket.

"Where's yours?" I ask. I have to yell to be heard above the engine and the waves.

"There's only one. Put it on." I hesitate. "Don't waste time, I want you to have it," he snaps. There's something about his tone that feels similar to mine when I yelled at Oli just now. It is born of concern. "Please," he adds more reasonably. His hair is blowing about in the wind, his face is creased with worry. I feel like a child. But not the child I was; constantly worried and old before my time. A child who is protected. Adopted, after a lifetime of neglect. I put the jacket on. "Good." He nods, satisfied. "I think there might be some binoculars in that plastic box if my memory serves me."

I dig about for the binoculars and retrieve them. Then I start to scan the horizon.

53

DC CLEMENTS

Clements listens as the helicopter clatters above her head. A deafening, disconcerting sound. She remembers hearing the same sound last time she was near these shores; back then, against her better judgment, she allowed a flutter of hope to beat in her chest. That time, she and Tanner had come to Lyme Regis to search Fiona's bungalow and they had been doing so when they heard the helicopter. They had run toward the sound of it. Tanner had immediately called the station, he excitedly demanded to know what was happening. They had thought that…maybe.

She recalls gasping with dread, hope—something primal. She had allowed Tanner to get ahead, as she stopped to bag up the discarded wine bottle. She recalls being irritated that her thorough training had overridden her desire to race to whatever it was the helicopter had been called out for. Damn her good-girl instincts; she had wanted to be the one to find Kylie first. She'd been prepared to discover a decomposing body at the bottom of a cliff, she'd wanted to protect Kylie's dignity, posthumously. And if by some miracle she had been lying injured at the bottom of the cliff, Clements wanted to be the first to calm and comfort. But she had stopped to bag up the bottle because it was the right thing to do and Clements always did

the right thing. It had only been a bloody dog in the end anyway. She hadn't missed anything.

A bloody dog.

She wouldn't want you to get her wrong, Clements is as
much of a dog lover as the next person. She is glad they'd rescued the overly adventurous labradoodle from the cliff side,
but the disappointment that the 'copter was out for a dog, not
the missing bigamist, had been like a physical blow. Back then,
she'd only been on the case a couple of weeks but Kylie Gillingham—rule breaker, lawbreaker, law unto herself—had got
under the officer's skin.

And now here she is, months later, standing in a field just a
few miles away from that clifftop, waiting for a different helicopter to land. Daring to hope again. For something different this time. Something not as illustrious. Not a chance of
recovering a woman, a wife, a mother—that was snuffed out
but at least a chance of closure. Daan Janssen is going to show
her where Kylie's body is. She sped here, blue lights flashing,
siren howling. Her obsession with the Kylie Gillingham case
has in no way abated over these past months. If anything it
has intensified.

This morning she believed Fiona Phillipson to be the killer.
She was convinced that finally the answer she had was the right
one. She felt sure of it in a way she had never been when placing Daan Janssen under arrest. She had arrested him because
it was the correct thing to do; there was a body of evidence
that pointed to him, it would have been irresponsible not to
charge him, take him to trial and put him in front of a judge
and jury. But something always nagged her about the evidence;
it seemed a little too neat for her liking. A little too complete.
Yes, initially she was delighted to discover Daan's things at
Fiona's place, especially after he had denied ever being there,
but on reflection, it struck her that the items he had supposedly left behind at his love nest were too emphatic. Too convenient. Boxers, a cuff link? Who wears cuff links at a beach?
How do you leave one behind but take the other with you?

Clements has been trained to be logical and practical. The evidence was enough to create a case, but the nagging disquiet had not gone away during all these months when dealing with Janssen. Yes, he could come across as an arrogant tosser in interviews. Privileged, entitled and overly confident. He definitely presented a number of unlikable and unpopular traits, but she didn't think of him as a vicious killer. He seemed so exasperated, so insulted by the charge. Interestingly, his indignant insistence that the police were idiots for suspecting him—which made Tanner furious and determined to send him down—had the effect of convincing Clements that he was indeed innocent of this crime. Not innocent *per se*—the man was far from that—but not a killer.

Then this morning, Tanner called with exactly the news the DC had been hoping for on some deep level. The bottle that she'd stopped to pick up on the clifftop, turned out to be gold. It had Fiona's and Kylie's fingerprints on it. Win. And forensics had also discovered traces of MDMA in the sediment in the bottom. There had been just a few drops of wine remaining but enough to categorically define this beverage was something much more insidious than a friendly tipple at a picnic. Then Mark Fletcher called and confessed that his boys might not actually be safe yet; that he hadn't seen them for himself—only that Fiona had told him they were okay and with her, but that he'd begun to doubt her honesty, her trustworthiness. Clements felt at once horrified and vindicated, certain that Fiona had killed Kylie.

But how does that fit with Daan Janssen's lawyer calling just after Mark and saying Janssen had confessed to the murder and that he wanted to charter a helicopter to come to Lyme Regis so he could show the police where he'd buried her body?

It doesn't, obviously.

Clements feels disconcerted. These people! They are so damned tricky, so eternally slippery. One minute she is sure she has the measure of them, the next she is blindly stumbling around in a dense fog of uncertainties again.

"Why would Janssen confess to killing Kylie after all these months of denying it?" she asks Tanner.

"Guilty conscience," he replies with a nonchalant nod. He is bouncing on the balls of his feet. He reminds her of a grey-hound in a trap waiting for the off. Dogged, tenacious.

Clements shakes her head. Not disagreeing exactly, but certainly finding it hard to wholeheartedly acquiesce. "I don't know. What if he didn't do it?"

Tanner looks confused. He likes to deal in certainties. "But he's said he did."

"And why did he insist we meet him here in Lyme Regis?"

"To show us where the body is buried, apparently."

"But he could have just *told* us where he buried it."

"Clearly he has a penchant for the dramatic," says Tanner, pulling a face that communicates he thinks the phrase "penchant for the dramatic" is contemptible, let alone the act. For the avoidance of doubt, he adds, "Twat."

"This man doesn't need to fight his way into the spotlight, it tends to find him," points out Clements. Tanner tuts impatiently at that. All men are, on some level, jealous of Daan Janssen. They envy his wealth, his height, his charisma. Clements is aware of that, even if Tanner isn't. "And where does Fiona fit in? Mark Fletcher called to say he doesn't trust her."

"Fletcher has just become anxious. He's overthinking things. I tell you, we'll get a call from the local copper soon saying he's at Fiona's place and that she and the kids are there, safe and well. I bet all three of them are eating ice cream or doing something equally innocuous."

"I hope you're right."

Tanner nods. He daren't say *I am*, although he wants to. "Janssen is the killer, he's confessed as much. End of. Fiona is just a daft mare who wants to make herself indispensable to the grieving widower but has actually caused him added stress. We're so close now, boss, I'm telling you. Nearly there." Tanner is shouting above the sound of the helicopter's blades as it gets nearer and louder. "Soon all will be revealed."

"Just put a call in to the local station, will you? Ask how they're getting on with the home visit?" Clements regrets delegating that job. She was on her way to Fiona's house herself when Janssen's lawyer called and said that his client insisted that she meet him here. She had to prioritize. Janssen said he wouldn't deal with anyone else. Clements hates herself for feeling fleetingly flattered that he asked for her. She keeps telling herself that she is pleased because she's won the trust of the suspect, built a relationship with him, and that will help her solve the case once and for all; it's not that the hot villain is making her feel special. Still, she should have sent Tanner to Fiona's place, not outsourced it to the local copper—it would have been better to keep it in the team—but Tanner is so obviously keen to have his moment. He wants to be there when they find the body. She doesn't have it in her to deny him that. He has worked on this case almost as hard as she has.

Tanner makes the call to the local bobbies. He turns his back and walks away from the noise to do so. The moment he walks back to her, she knows from the expression on his face that something is up.

"What is it?"

"They were just about to call us. There's been a break-in."

"At Fiona's?"

"Well, they think it's a break-in. The kitchen window is smashed."

"The boys?"

"No sign."

"Fiona?"

Tanner shakes his head. He pulls his mouth into a thin line, clearly unnerved. This info muddies his theory that everything is finally clean-cut.

"Any sign of a struggle? What did they see?" asks Clements.

"I've asked them to send photos through so we can take a look ourselves. I suppose Fiona might be on her way back to London right now. The break-in could be a completely unrelated matter."

"Do you believe that?"

Tanner sighs and admits, "No. I wish I did, but I don't."

"We've called her several times today. Why hasn't she answered her phone? Why haven't the boys?"

The officers stare at one another, concerned, confused. The helicopter lands behind them. They start to run toward it, still hoping for answers.

54

KYLIE

"Can you see anything?" Kenneth asks.

I shake my head. There are countless yachts, dinghies and motorboats racing, wending and scooting about, but I can't see Fiona's. I've often stood on the shore and stared through binoculars trying to spot her, Mark and the boys—or any combination—in her aluminum boat. I'm good at picking it out. Often the sun glints on it, the reverse of a lighthouse, a beacon on the sea assuring me of safety. I recall happily waving to them from the harborside, my only concern then whether or not they had applied suncream. The sea is a whirl of silver and shadow and unfathomable depth and breadth. It terrifies me. The plan of chasing Fiona now seems ridiculous. "Where might she head?" I ask him.

"If she's thinking clearly, perhaps she'll follow the coast down past Dartmouth, maybe even through to Salcombe. Then she'll cross, heading toward Tréguier. It's a quiet route, away from the containers and naval boats. It's probably the easiest area to cruise in the English Channel, with day sailing between ports available at all states of the tide. It's easy to navigate, straightforward pilotage," says Kenneth confidently.

I doubt Fiona has that level of knowledge about the sea paths, so I ask, "And if she's not thinking clearly?"

He gives my question due consideration. "Well, she might

decide she wants to stay away from the coast in case she's spotted, so she might attempt a more daring crossing. As the crow flies, she'd be heading somewhere near Cherbourg. Southwest and she'd be at Lannion; if she's prepared to sail a little further due south, she might go to Saint-Brieuc."

"Basically, you're saying we have no idea."

"Is she a very good sailor?"

"Adequate. She sailed as a kid and then picked it up again when we started holidaying down here." Kenneth wrinkles his forehead.

"What? Tell me," I demand.

"Can your boy swim?"

"Yes. He's a good swimmer."

He nods. "Well done. Good parenting making sure of that."

Right now I think most people in Britain would vote me worst mother in the country, so I feel the intention of his kindness, but I can't ignore what he's saying to me. I know enough from the small amount of boating I've done on holiday to realize this is a perilous trip. It's warm now, but what if the weather changes? It's already late afternoon; it will be dark in a few hours.

"You don't think she'll get to France. You think the main danger is her capsizing, don't you?"

"Well, while things look busy right now, it's mostly just day-trippers and pleasure-seekers, so we'll leave them behind in a mile or so. COVID and lockdown means there will be far fewer ferries and ships coming and going, so the shipping lanes will be less challenging than usual. That's a good thing." I sigh. "Look, I don't think they're far ahead of us. The busybodies at the harbor said the car had just been abandoned. We have to hope to spot her."

I appreciate he is trying to stay positive.

"Have you crossed the Channel before?" I ask.

"Yes, many times when Stacie was young."

"So not for a while."

"Not since she died. I haven't done anything much since then, but I'm confident enough I can keep you safe."

"I'm not worried about myself."

"I know you're not, but all the same…"

I nod, grateful. The boat slaps against the sea. People talk about boats bouncing along, as though the experience is akin to a child's jolly romp on an inflatable castle at a fairground, but the impact feels harder to me. It feels like the sea is flexing its muscles, reminding me how powerful it is. How endless. I shiver and blanch as water sprays up. I'm not dressed for this. I'm wearing a T-shirt and shorts. I'm already freezing. Why didn't Fiona make Seb put on his wetsuit?

I constantly scan the horizon, concentrating hard, hoping to will the little boat into sight through the sheer force of my longing. On a couple of occasions I trick myself into believing I've spotted it, but then realize it's a family of four or a lone male sailor in the craft. So when the moment finally happens, I barely trust myself. "I think that's her. That's her boat! Look, look there." I hand Kenneth the binoculars and steer for a moment or two while he takes a look. He spots the boat, nods and then takes back the wheel.

"Can we catch up? Did you see Seb? I couldn't see Seb!"

"We just need to keep them in view. That's what's important now."

"Please tell me you have a phone on you, Kenneth." He shakes his head. "A radio, then."

"Your boy Oli seems like a sensible, reliable kid. He'll have the police out here soon."

"How will they know where to find us?"

"You have to trust your luck," says Kenneth.

I glare at him. "News flash: I have issues with trust, and luck come to that. I'm not what anyone would describe as lucky."

He smiles at me slowly. "You have a great sense of humor,

Kylie. That's a lovely thing, but I beg to disagree. Many would say you have the luck of the devil."

I don't respond. I don't know if he means that's a good thing or a bad. Surely it would be better to have angels on my side.

55

DAAN

Daan has spent the entire journey scouring the scene below. Land, then sea, then land again. Watching as houses the size of Lego bricks take on some sort of individuality as the helicopter flies lower. He becomes particularly absorbed in what he can see as they near Lyme Regis. Of course he is not a whimsical man; he doesn't expect to spot the boys dashing across the hilltops, darting from Fiona's evil clutches, but he wants to familiarize himself with the layout of the area. It will be useful to know what they will have to search. He sees countless barns and outhouses, stretches of dark woodland and jagged cliffs. There are a lot of places in which two boys could be hidden, then lost. They have about four and a half hours before the sun will set. He's already checked, it sets at 9:26 here tonight. Searching in the dark will be harder, obviously. So they do not have much time. The question no one can answer is how much time do they need?

They land on a field above the beach. Daan leaps out of the helicopter with a show of confidence. If deep inside he has any misgivings about the course he has chosen, he does not betray them. He walks directly to the gaggle of police and officials who are waiting for him. He searches out Clements. Tanner is by her side, holding a pair of handcuffs. He is wearing what can only be identified as a notably gleeful expression. Fuck him, thinks Daan.

He does not bother to make eye contact with the junior officer as he says, "I won't be putting those on."

"You don't get to call the shots," responds Tanner. "Not anymore. You confessed to a murder. You'll do as you're told from now on."

Daan stares through Tanner as though he hasn't spoken. He waits for his lawyer, who was slower to get out of the helicopter and had to dash to catch up. He's puffing. Of course, Daan's experience is that people are slower than him at most things. Daan speaks directly to Clements. "I didn't kill her. I can't tell you where her body is. I lied to you to get you here."

"What the hell?" says Tanner. He throws back his head, a picture of exasperation and disbelief.

Clements doesn't move her face or body a millimeter. Daan admires her composure. She asks, "Why did you want to bring us here?"

"Fiona did it."

"So you keep saying."

"She has the Fletcher boys. They're in danger. And she's here somewhere. It's my fault. I asked Oli to spy on her for me. That's why he ran away from home."

"Stop talking, we need to have a private conversation," barks his lawyer.

"When did you speak to Oli Fletcher?" asks Clements.

"We've been talking for a while now. Some weeks. Different forms of chat. I told Mark Fletcher to call you, but I didn't know if he would. I couldn't take the risk that he wouldn't believe me. He's involved with Fiona. He hates me. He might not see things clearly."

"I need a private word with my client," Daan's lawyer insists.

"No, you don't," replies Daan dismissively. "I got you here the most efficient way I knew how."

"By lying again," retorts Tanner.

"By lying for the first time." Daan holds Clements's gaze.

"Here's my phone, you'll see all the correspondence between me and the boys. We game-chat too. Oli is Slayr123, Seb is GetWreckedAH, I am Golden_Warlord. I can help you find records of all the conversations. That's not what's important now. What is vital is that Oli has found something that proves Fiona's guilt. He told me he has incriminating evidence."

"What evidence?" asks Clements.

Daan is relieved she is listening to him, that she hasn't instructed her lackey to put on the cuffs and send him away for wasting police time. He was banking on the fact that she's clever enough to know he's not the sort of man who wastes time; least of all his own. However, he regrets having to admit, "He didn't say exactly what he'd found. After telling me that much, he cut all contact." The police officers exchange a look. It's brief, and Daan can't quite identify it. Skepticism or concern? "I firmly believe Fiona has Oli and Seb. I am here to look for them."

"Swooping in on your big white charger, are you?" asks Tanner, rolling his eyes. The helicopter is black; Daan thinks it's beneath him to point that out.

"Mark Fletcher rang us," says Clements. "I was on my way to Fiona's house when your lawyers called. Far from helping inquiries, you've complicated them. She might have been in my custody by now if you hadn't pulled this stunt." Daan has had enough women swear at him in his lifetime to know Clements is biting her tongue.

"So go to her house now," he suggests.

"She's gone."

"The boys?"

"Gone too."

"Well, what are you waiting for? We should be looking for them."

"There's no *we* in this," comments Clements with a frustrated sigh. "We are the law and you are a suspect. We're not on the same side."

"I think we are," says Daan.

Tanner looks like he wants to punch him, but then, unexpectedly, his face breaks into a wide grin. "Well, you've wasted your time doing the action-hero bit, mate, because it looks like we've found them without you." He points behind Daan, who turns and sees a police car stopping at the field edge and a boy emerging from it.

"Oli." He is so relieved to see him, he doesn't even register Tanner's smugness. He immediately breaks away from the gaggle of officials and runs toward the lad. Clements and Tanner are hot on his heels, charging toward the teen. "Thank God. I thought Fiona had you. I'm so happy to see you, Oli," Daan shouts. He looks about excitedly for Seb. He's waiting for him to climb out of the police car too. "Where's your brother?" The relief that has just swamped his body starts to recede. Hope is like a faltering power source; easy to switch on and off.

"Fiona has Seb. She has him and she's sailing to France," Oli yells. His entire being oozes anguish.

"Take a moment. What can you tell us?" asks Clements.

"They're on her boat. She's trying to get to France. She drugged him. Tied me up. She's totally lost it. *He* was right." Oli jerks his head toward Daan. His expressions are mercurial. For a moment his face was alert with the importance of the task of delivering the news; now it collapses in fear. "But what if she can't get them there? She's in a crappy little boat. She's never sailed to France before. What if they capsize? What if he drowns?"

"We've got the coast guard on it already," says the police officer escorting Oli. "The lad called this in fifteen minutes ago and we did that first, even before bringing him to you."

"Good work," comments Clements.

"And my mum is out there too, chasing them with some old geezer. I don't really know who he is."

Daan's world judders. Slows down, maybe even turns backward. All the laws of physics dissolve. "What?" he demands, in unison with Clements and Tanner.

"She's not dead," Oli announces.

"You're sure?" Daan daren't believe it. Not quite yet. He heard the boy's words, but he just can't allow his mind and soul to trust the news yet. He has to be sure. "You saw her? Kai? I mean your mum, Leigh?"

Oli rolls his eyes, acknowledging even in this extraordinary moment that his mother isn't an average mum. "Leigh Fletcher aka Kai Janssen, yeah. I spoke to her. She rescued me. Fiona had me tied up. Mum smashed a window to get to me. She climbed across broken glass."

"That would fit with our local officer's report," chips in Tanner.

The euphoria now freely bounces through Daan's body.

She is alive.

He wasn't aware how much he was longing for this until now. He had not allowed himself to consider this possibility. Over these past few months, he thought his only desire was to avoid going to prison. In the last twenty-four hours his sole hope has been that the boys were safe. He had not realized that on a deep level, in the fiber of him—the heart and soul—all he desired, all he hoped for, was these three words. *She is alive.* He didn't dare think he could be this lucky. That such luck existed anywhere. He is surprised at himself and the world.

She is alive but at sea. Giving chase in a boat. Oli is staring at him, waiting for answers, wanting help. "You can have my helicopter," Daan says to Clements, "but I'm coming with you."

"I should come," says Tanner.

Clements looks torn. She swiftly takes Tanner's arm, moves him to the side. "Did you see his face when he heard she was still alive?"

"Well, his charge will be reduced."

"Come on, don't be a prick," Clements teases. "You're a married man. He loves her, you saw it." Tanner looks irritated. He knows what's coming. "You stay with Oli, get a full statement. Stay in constant touch. I'll go with Janssen."

Daan and Oli are listening in to the conversation, though pretending not to. Oli glances at Daan when Clements states her belief in his love. He looks curious. Daan tries not to react. Kai is married to the boy's father after all. What is the proper reaction? He has no idea. But as he and Clements sprint toward the helicopter, he acknowledges that the DC is a bright, intuitive woman. He wants to punch the air.

56

KYLIE

"We're gaining on them, aren't we?"

"Yes, we are a little, I think. Slowly does it."

I initially urged Kenneth to give chase. He refused. "Too risky. We don't want her doing anything stupid and putting Seb in danger. We just need to keep them in sight and not be noticed by her if at all possible. We should wait for help."

"But what if it doesn't come?"

"It will."

"The sun will set and it won't be possible to keep tabs on Fiona's boat when the light fades." Kenneth didn't respond to that; just glanced at the dusky sky. He knows I am right.

Now he says, "Have a look in the box, see if there is a waterproof or a jumper or something. You're blue with the cold."

My fingers are numb and I struggle with the little plastic device that locks the storage unit. I suck my fingers to try to warm them up. I can taste the salt. I look around me. The sea is always described as blue, but it is not that alone. It is green, black, gray, silver; all the colors of the iridescent sea glass that lies in a pile in Kenneth's garden. I wish it was just one color; that would make it seem more benign, more manageable. But it is not a color; it is just a fractious mass that can absorb anything.

"How much fuel do we have?" I ask. Kenneth looks uncomfortable. I don't know how he managed to fool me for so many months into thinking that an entirely other person's life was mine; now he strikes me as utterly readable. "How much?" I demand.

"Not enough to get us all the way across the Channel," he confesses.

"Oh my God."

"I didn't have time to check when we took the boat."

I want to yell at him, accuse him of being careless, but I didn't check the fuel either, and so the responsibility isn't his to own. Besides, what is the point of blaming? Distributing blame in the middle of a disaster seems like a waste of energy; better to think of strategy, next steps. "Well, we can't stick with this plan then. If she has a full tank, we'll lose her and just end up drifting about, waiting for rescue."

"She might not have a full tank either."

"And that's what you're counting on? No, we have to be more proactive. We have to try to rescue him. I'll hide on the floor and you can get close. She doesn't know who you are, she won't be alarmed."

"Then what will we do?"

"I don't know. Please, I just need to see that Seb is okay." I think when we are close, I will yell to my son, clamber into Fiona's boat, throw her to the damn fishes, but I don't say this to Kenneth because he might point out that it's unrealistic.

He considers my suggestion. "It might work," he agrees. "It would be good to check in on the boy." He accelerates and I grab the side of the boat. No longer cold, but lit from the inside by determination.

57

FIONA

Seb has not moved. She wishes he would come round now, even if it leads to awkward questions. She didn't account for how lonely and frightening the journey would be. She thought her seafaring skills were good enough, but now she thinks it would be nice to have someone reassure her that this is the case, someone to tell her that she is most likely going in roughly the right direction. That she is doing the right thing. Even a kid. Seb is the sort to always stay positive. She could do with a bit of his optimism right now.

With her foot, she moves aside the blanket that is covering him so she can see him while still steering. His lips are blue. He looks very pale. If he wakes up, he could have something to eat or put on some clothes. Maybe she should turn off the engine and take a few minutes to dress him in more layers. She didn't realize quite how cold it would be out here—and she has a wetsuit on. She didn't bring trousers for him, but that isn't her fault; Oli hadn't packed any in his day bag, silly boy. She could only take what was there: a hoodie, a couple of spare T-shirts and a cap. They will help; a lot of heat is lost through the head, everyone knows that. She would have taken the time to dress him earlier, but she couldn't risk being seen. This far out, that isn't likely to be a problem.

When she first pushed off, she was irritated by the num-

ber of other boats in her way. She was nervous that someone
might get a good view of her, so she put on her own cap and
pulled it down low. But as she got further out to sea, the boats
started to fall away, and now she's very aware of her isolation
and conscious of how small the boat is. She's always thought
of the English Channel as a sorry apology for a body of water,
not as impressive as an ocean—the Atlantic or Indian, for example—or even the Mediterranean, which is always warm and
inviting. She's regarded it as a grimy pathway that for centuries
facilitated cruel wars and grubby trade, then more recently as
an ephemeral chance for desperate illegal immigrants. She's
never thought it grand or challenging. Now it seems plenty
big enough. Too big, in fact. With the engine off, all she can
hear is the sea hitting against the boat; not even the sound of
seagulls or an airplane overhead.

She kneels next to the rucksack and digs about for Seb's
clothes, then wrestles him into everything she has packed,
which she can see now is not much. Not enough. The thought
of starting all over again, a new life in France, scares her. They
will need clothes, a house, food. His limbs are unyielding and
it's an awkward process dressing him. She recalls helping him
dress as a little boy when they all went swimming together in
the local pool, or when he'd spilt something down himself;
little kids seemed to eternally be in need of a fresh change of
clothes. Then he would wriggle and chatter as she popped a
T-shirt over his head; now, his silent, stiff state is unnerving.

As soon as she is in France, she will need to move her
money from her bank to an offshore account, before the police freeze her assets. She has no idea how to open an offshore
account. She'll have to google it. Of course, she can get a job,
but doing what? Her French is passable, but not fluent. She'll
probably have to work in a restaurant or clean. It doesn't matter what she does, anything to pay rent. They will be okay. In
the absence of a conscious companion, she has to answer the
questions she asks herself. Her mind bounces from bravado to
doubt and back again every few minutes. She closes her eyes

for a moment, tries to steady her thoughts, but it's impossible to think clearly. She's cold and hungry too.

What will Seb do while she is at work?

Well, he'll be at school.

New schools are always hell.

He's a nice kid, he'll make friends.

How will he make friends? He doesn't speak French.

She'll get him lessons.

How will she pay for lessons?

She'll teach him herself. She will be solely responsible for him, so they'll find a way. People do.

Still, it's a lot. Is it too much?

That thought surprises her. She has been desperate for someone to take care of for years now. That's all she's ever wanted, and now she has it. She has Seb. It is frustrating, frankly, how couples and people with families have no idea, no conception as to what it is like to be someone like her. They blithely go about their business—no, that's not right. Blithely suggests happily. In Fiona's experience, all these people do is whine. First about the expense of weddings, the inflated price tags on flowers and champagne, and then the difficulty of getting reliable childcare; next they are grumbling that they have to invite the in-laws for Christmas, moaning that an extended family is so much work. They are forever complaining that they are exhausted balancing everything—running a home, looking after kids, pleasing a husband, succeeding in a career. On and on they grumble. Instead of seeing that having everything is the dream.

Of course, Fiona knows women who are one hundred percent happy with being partnerless and childless. They call it partner-free and child-free. They usually have a lot of friends, pets and interests. They often have great careers. *She* has a great career. She should have got a cat. Of course she can see the value in their worlds, these partner-free, child-free women. She admires them. Envies them a tiny bit for their self-reliance and contentment. But it just isn't what she wants for herself. She wants connections.

The sea is a lonely place. She is never good when she's on her own; she thinks too much. She pinches Seb's ear in the hope of rousing him, but it doesn't help. She longs for his eyelids to flutter.

So when she notices that the old man's boat is getting closer, she welcomes it. She has nothing to fear from being spotted by the salty old sea dog. He won't be able to see Seb lying on the floor of the boat; just in case, though, she covers him with the blanket again.

"Hello," he yells, waving one arm high in the air.

She waves back. "Hello."

"You're quite some distance out."

"As are you, in that case," she says with a laugh, but it's a little forced. Having welcomed his company, she is almost immediately irritated by it. People are always in each other's business now, especially since COVID. It's annoyingly intrusive. He'd be shocked, no doubt, if he knew she was planning on going to France. Over these past few months, people have been reporting one another for going to the park for more than an hour.

"I'm turning back now," he says. "You?"

"I think I'll push on a little further."

He nods. Apparently willing to accept that she is free to do as she pleases. She's glad. Just what she needed, a brief polite encounter and not an overbearing busybody after all. But then, she can't believe her eyes. For a moment she thinks she must have fallen asleep and is dreaming, or that she's hallucinating because she's under such pressure and hungry. Her eyes are playing tricks on her. Because right here in front of her, Kylie rises like a kraken out of the hull of his boat. Back from the dead. Loud and living. Vicious and vital.

"Give me Seb, Fiona. You can't have him. He doesn't belong with you."

58

KYLIE

I just couldn't stay concealed in the hull of the boat. I've been hidden and lost for too long now. It's a great moment, even in among all this fear and chaos, I take pleasure in seeing the shock on her face as I stand up.

"What's the matter, Fiona? You look like you've seen a ghost."

She stares at me in shock and awe. "How is this possible?" she asks. "How are you alive?" Then she throws back her head and lets out an almighty howl of frustration. Her face is taut and twisted. I've seen Fiona angry on a fair few occasions—irate with ex-boyfriends, or bosses, or even a shop assistant who refused to exchange a dress with a faulty zip—but I've never witnessed anything like this. She is consumed with anger; her entire body is wracked and writhing in crude fury. Her loathing toward me is palpable; I can touch it, taste it. "You should be dead!" she screams. "You should be dead. You should be dead."

I want to yell at her that no, I should not be dead. I want to taunt her and point out that I'm not that easy to kill, but I resist. I keep my voice low and try to stay calm so I can reason with her. "Please, Fiona, give me Seb."

"You are not getting him," she spits. "You can't always have your own way. You can't always have everything."

"Okay, not for me. Think of Mark and Oli," I plead. "It's

dangerous out here. You won't make it to France. And even if you do, what then? The authorities will be waiting for you. It would be better if you give up now."

Our boats are very close. While I've been talking and holding her focus, Kenneth has quietly edged toward her. We are now near enough that I can see the shape of Seb's body on the floor. He's covered by a blanket and not moving. The sight catapults any sense of calm I was trying to cling to far out of reach.

"Oh my God. Seb! My God, Seb!" I yell. "What have you done to him?" I lurch forward, ready to leap into her boat and snatch him out of her grasp.

I feel the impact before I understand what has happened. While I was caught up in the horror of seeing Seb's still and lifeless body, Fiona jumped to start her engine again. *Wham.* The sound is loud and echoes through this empty expanse. Changing everything. She has rammed her boat against ours. I don't know if her act is one of thoughtless frustration, malice or desperation, but it's ill-considered, as she's risked both boats.

It is the longest moment of my life. The two small craft seem to jump into the air, nose to nose. Fiona's boat flips, ours lurches. I am knocked off my feet, as is Kenneth. As I slam into the side of the boat, I see him fall forward over the stern, slip over the edge into the water. I reach for him, but roll backward, further from him. Dizzy, I quickly scrabble to right myself. My head is bleeding, or maybe just wet. It's not clear. It doesn't matter.

Fiona's boat is smaller than ours, and her stupid act of aggression has backfired. I watch as Seb is flung out of the boat and up into the air. Up, up, too high, he flies, as though he is bouncing on a trampoline. I expect him to react, to move, to dive. He doesn't. He soars in an arc and then drops like a stone. He splashes into the sea and is swallowed. He doesn't gasp and start to swim as I know he can. He doesn't push up to the surface. He simply sinks. I watch in horror as his head disappears, then his hand. Then there is nothing. Nothing.

I yank off my life jacket and immediately leap in after him.

With the jacket, I wouldn't be able to follow him underwater. I dive down. The water is black and freezing. I gasp. My instinct is to push back up to the top. I remember the nightmares about drowning that have haunted me these past months; nightmares that I now know are memories. Everything is blurred and blunted. Once again my clothes are heavy and bloated. I kick hard, but this time I need to go deeper and not head for the surface. My lungs scream in protest; survival instincts instruct my body that this is counterintuitive, but maternal instincts rule my heart and soul, and there isn't a moment's hesitation.

It's hard to see anything underwater. I've always been the sort of person who closes their eyes when swimming below the surface, and it feels unnatural prying them open, but how else will I find him? Something floats down next to me, and for one glorious fleeting second I think I have him, but as I reach out and grab at the object, I realize it's just a rucksack. I panic and gasp, take in water. I swim up to the surface, coughing and spluttering. I fill my lungs once again. I hear Fiona and Kenneth shouting. I don't care, I don't listen to what they have to say. I have one job. I dive down again.

Then, I see him. Drifting, unconscious. I stretch toward him, propel my body in his direction; my fingers briefly touch his hoodie. With every ounce of physical and mental strength I have, I reach to grab him and haul him upward with me. Kicking and spluttering I break the surface for a second time. I hold Seb's head above water and half swimming, half drowning, drag his limp body back toward the boat. Suddenly Kenneth is next to me. He takes part of Seb's weight from me, and somehow, between us, we manage to manhandle him back onto the boat. Kenneth shoves me from behind so that I can get a purchase to clamber onboard too. I turn and hold out my hand to him.

"See to the boy," he instructs.

I take hold of Seb's shoulders and vigorously shake him to see if I can rouse him. Nothing. So I lie him on his back and tilt his chin and head to help clear his airway. I lean over him and place my cheek near his mouth, hoping with every fiber of my soul to feel his breath. Nothing. I look along his chest, longing to see it rise and fall. Nothing. I pinch his nose, and keeping his head tilted back, I breathe into his mouth. I do this five times. Still nothing. I put both hands together, one on top of the other, and firmly push down right in the center of his chest. I press and I pray.

59

DC CLEMENTS

"There they are, over there, to the right."

Of course it is bloody action hero Daan who spots the boats first. It's a good job Tanner isn't on the chopper; he'd be very annoyed. Clements is just so bloody relieved. "Can you get lower?" she asks the pilot. Her stomach is in her mouth as the helicopter immediately drops. She doesn't acknowledge the lurch; at least the pilot recognizes her authority. The sea below quakes in response to the gusts made by the whirling propeller, although the water is already agitated, because there has been an incident between the craft. That much is obvious; one boat is upturned.

"Whose boat has flipped?" asks Daan, obviously alarmed. None of us know.

The light is beginning to fade, but the helicopter is equipped with search beams. Clements quickly assesses the scene. She needs a count of four. One child, two women, one old man. "Someone is in the sea," she reports.

"Is it Kai?" Daan demands.

The DC sort of likes it that he can't keep his cool, that he shows how much he cares. She must keep her cool, though. That's her job. "It's a woman," she confirms.

They watch as the woman tries to right the upturned boat. She makes a number of attempts; again and again she heaves and strives, but to no avail: the boat slaps back onto the water, still the wrong way up. She must hear the helicopter approach, but this doesn't seem to reassure her as Clements would expect. She seems more frantic, not less, and starts to swim away from the boat. An irrational move.

"Fiona," says the DC with a sigh. "She can't think she's going to outswim us when we're in a helicopter, can she?" She watches the woman flail about in the sea. A woman who fell into hate and horror, self-righteousness and entitlement. She's seen so many criminals who've basically stamped their feet at the world and yelled *it's not fair*, then tried to make it fair by stealing, fighting, cheating or killing. Idiots.

"Where's Seb? Where's Kai?" Daan demands.

"Are they in the other boat?" suggests the DC, pointing to the second boat, which is drifting further from the upturned craft.

"Get more light on the other boat!" Daan yells.

The pilot turns the chopper to shine the search beam into the second craft. There is a woman crouched in the hull, but she doesn't look up and start signaling to them; instead she is focusing all her energy on something underneath her.

"That's her, isn't it?" Clements can't believe she is finally clapping eyes on the infamous, elusive Kylie Gillingham. Her heart lifts for a fraction of a second, and then plummets. "She's trying to revive him."

"Who, Seb?"

She nods sadly.

"Let down the rope ladder," Daan instructs.

"Are you going to shimmy down, then fling them both over your shoulders and climb back up again?" Clements asks with a note of sarcastic incredulity.

"If I have to," he says firmly, his mouth set.

60

DAAN

He's seen this stuff in movies, but now he's discovering that it's a lot harder in real life than they make it look. It's terrifying. Not because of the sway of the lightweight rope ladder, or the thunderous roar of the propellers, or even the fact that the stable webbing of the ladder, designed to aid climbing, is slick with spray from the waves and therefore hideously perilous—it's terrifying because he might not succeed. He might not save the child's life, or his wife's life, and that thought is horrific.

He has spoken to her. Well, yelled instructions, gestured for her to climb the ladder, but Kai has refused to leave Seb in the boat alone. She can't carry him; she's not strong enough. He knows that the DC was being sarcastic when she suggested he fling one of them over each shoulder, but he was totally serious: he'll do anything he has to. Everything he can. Obviously he can't carry them both at once, but he descends the ladder with the intention of persuading Kai to ascend first if he follows with Seb.

Their reunion is a strangely sharp, practical exchange. He tells her that the pilot assured him that the ladder is designed so that just about anyone with any ability can use it to ascend or descend from a helicopter.

"I'm not scared of climbing the ladder, Daan. I'm just not going to leave him alone. You carry him up first and I'll follow when I know he's safe. We have to get him to safety. He has to be okay."

Daan doesn't argue with that.

61

MARK

The nurses like Mark; he can sense as much and he basks in it. It's nice to feel approved of, after everything. Considering everything. They have been so gentle and sympathetic toward him this past week as he's sat on the skinny hardback chair by Seb's bedside, surrounded by tubes, trolleys and a faint smell of disinfectant. He tried to be self-contained and self-controlled as Seb lay unconscious because of the near-fatal amount of drugs Fiona had administered, and he was suffering from hypothermia, as well as the effects of nearly drowning. Mark never once gave in to hysteria or depression. He held his son's hand and silently and sincerely put all his energy into willing him to get better, as well as reassuring Oli that that would happen. He listened to his child's breath rasp and lumber through his small chest, his skin waxy, the same color as the bedsheets, his eyes closed. Mark was oblivious to the other sounds of the hospital: a nurse's feet clip-clopping along the corridor; an orderly talking to a patient in a squeaking wheelchair; the teen girl in the bed opposite occasionally laughing at the podcast she was listening to. He was deaf to everything other than the ping and hum of Seb's machines. He didn't allow himself to roar, or blame, or catastrophize. He simply hoped.

And it worked. Seb is on the mend; he will make a full recovery. He will be going home soon. He'll be back to shouting excitedly at his video game kills, moaning that Mark's cooking is pretty awful and leaving muddy football boots in the kitchen. Mark can't wait; he's never been happier. He finds himself being boisterous and playful; after months of feeling doomed and depressed, he luxuriates in feeling effortlessly up. One or two of the nurses have commented that he's nice to have around, that he lifts the mood of the ward, cheers up the other sick kids. He's talked to the teenage girl about her podcast now, as has Oli, at length. It seems Oli quite fancies her, which Seb is delighted by, as he considers himself an official matchmaker.

"It isn't always easy for parents to shake off their kids' ill health, even after they've been lucky and recovered," comments his favorite nurse, Dawn. "Many are left with heightened anxiety. You are doing really well."

"Life is for living. I'm not going to waste another moment," replies Mark.

The nurses don't like Leigh much, though. That's apparent. Mark has seen the faces they pull when she calls the ward to ask how Seb is. She isn't here at his bedside as much as he is, although that's not her fault. Due to COVID rules, they only allow one visitor in at a time. He and Oli take the lion's share of the available slots, naturally. Anyway, she has spent a fair amount of this past week answering police questions, giving statements, explaining where she's been these last few months.

They have been ships passing in the night. It's probably for the best.

The papers are still wild for info about the case. The police are trying to keep a lid on the details, at least until Fiona comes to trial. Her lawyer is saying the jurors will all be prejudiced against her, even before they hear the facts. Frankly, Mark can't imagine it matters whether the jurors have read the sensationalist and salacious details. It seems to him it's open and shut. Finally, something about his life that is categorical. Fiona has confessed to everything. He doesn't know if her near-death experience in the English Channel finally shocked some sense

into her and made her take responsibility for the pain and horror she's inflicted, or whether it's more the case that she can't
avoid the blame any longer. There's a difference. Anyway, it
doesn't matter to him: a confession is a confession. The list of
her crimes is long. In no particular order, he reels them off to
himself in his head: kidnapping, abduction, false imprisonment,
attempted murder, illegal drugging, assault. Other charges may
yet come to light. They will throw away the key.

Leigh has asked if she can talk to him. He's not sure whether
he's ready for that yet, or, honestly, whether he ever will be.
What should he say to her? What does she want to say to him?
He is sure of one thing: he doesn't want any more drama,
categorically no more tears, scenes or rows. There has been
enough of that to last a lifetime. However, Oli and Seb have
pleaded for him to hear her out. She's spoken to both of them
a lot this past week. Whatever she said was what they needed
to hear; both boys call her Mum again. So for their sake, he's
agreed to meet her.

62

KYLIE

It is pouring. The needles of rain fall with relentless determination. People speak of it being good for the gardens and a relief from the long, hot summer days. No one seems ready for it, though; people are wearing flip-flops as they splash through puddles in the hospital car park; summer dresses are barely protected by flimsy raincoats. A hire car that smells strongly of antibacterial spray isn't an ideal place for a reconciliation, but we're both conscious that we don't want to leave Seb's side for any longer than we have to. He's not on his own, of course, Oli is with him, and the nurses are vigilant, but nonetheless, the idea of driving even to the closest café is out of the question. We both feel anxious if the boys aren't being guarded. A café would have been unsuitable anyway; we need privacy.

As we get into the car, we both check over our shoulders. We're behaving like an adulterous couple sneaking about trying to see one another in secret, but in fact we're not on the lookout for suspicious or irate spouses; we're trying to avoid journalists with long lenses. The air inside the car is overheated and stale; I open a window and rain immediately pours on my arm and lap, so I close it again quickly.

"Can we take our masks off?" I ask. Wearing them is a totally understandable requirement in the hospital, but I feel there are enough barriers between us right now.

Mark must think the same, as he comments, "Literally or metaphorically?"

I sigh and remove the little blue mask. "Both, I suppose."

He nods and takes his off too. It's the first time we've been up close and personal with one another for months. He's still immediately attractive to me, but I'm struck by how tired he looks. I can see what he has endured. He's obviously studying me and is probably shocked by what he sees too. I wear my ordeal. He tactfully comments, "You suit the pixie cut."

"It's not a fashion choice." I grin, shyly touching the back of my bare neck.

"Yeah, I heard some of that crazy stuff. The old man who abducted you did that to you, right? He wanted you to think you'd had chemo or something. The DC told me." Mark shakes his head. "It's a lot to take in."

"You believe me?"

"Yeah, of course. Even you couldn't make that up."

"Thank you." I'm relieved, glad of that at least. I have been wondering how much he'd trust me.

"I heard he drowned," he adds. I nod, tears stinging my eyes as they do every time I think of Kenneth's death. "You're not upset, are you? The man abducted you."

"He saved my life too. Twice. And he helped save Seb's, I can't forget that." My feelings toward Kenneth will strike other people as odd, I know that. But then again, I don't have a track record of conventional emotions. I loved two men simultaneously and equally, although differently, for years. People struggle with that. And Kenneth, well, I think of him with a strange mix of love and regret, sadness and gratitude. For a brief time he was the father I wanted. He loved me in a way that made me feel valued, whole. Although I realize now that he didn't really love me, he loved his dead daughter, but still, for a time I benefited from that. I'm grateful that I experienced it. He wasn't well. He was grief-stricken and desperate; his behavior was eccentric but I find not unforgivable. People are complex. "He was only on the boat because he was trying to help. He ultimately sacrificed himself for me and for our son. Is there a greater love? I don't think so."

Mark blushes. I knew he would. He's always had a propensity to color up. The boys do too. I've missed this comfortable state of knowing a person so well you can predict how they might respond. I've missed it and I've also destroyed it. I might be able to guess when Mark will blush, but I'm not confident I can predict his responses, feelings or actions on a wider scale anymore.

"For a few months I really thought he was my father. I believed I was someone else, a much-loved daughter who had been cosseted and adored. It was nice." I shrug. That's gone now. It was never true. Never mine. "Kenneth helped me and Seb into the boat, and I was so concerned about reviving Seb I just forgot about him. Can you believe that?" I murmur. The guilt and shame burns behind the back of my eyes. "So it's complicated, how I feel about him."

"I get it. I understand. It's sort of how I feel about you." The color in his cheeks deepens. "I mean, you ruined my life, cheated and betrayed on a colossal scale, but you did risk everything to save Seb."

"Of course. Seb should never have been in danger and never would have been if it wasn't for me."

"I agree," he says shortly, his tone scolding.

"What are we going to do, Mark?"

"Do?" He seems surprised that action is required. That a plan must be made. That's very like Mark. He waits to see what happens to him. Normally I do the planning, but now I am in his hands and he must decide what happens next. A role reversal that makes us both uncomfortable.

"I'm their mother."

He draws his mouth into a thin line. I know he holds all the cards. If we go to court, I won't have a chance of winning visiting rights, let alone custody, not considering everything. I never officially adopted them; we never felt the need. I regret that now, as I have no legal claim. If we divorce, I'm their ex-stepmother, nothing more. I understand that Mark has filed for divorce. I think there is a chance that Oli and Seb would still want to see me; we've talked a lot these past few days, and they both still love me, I'm sure of that. But they are also angry and confused. They have questions; a lot more talking is needed. I must win back their trust and I'll only be able to do so with Mark's help. If he works against me, the boys will suffer. They will be torn. He could easily nurture their resentment and mistrust. I need him to work with me, but it's a lot to ask.

"The thing is, I don't need this," he says. I take a sharp inward gasp. Shocked and frightened that he's said the opposite of what I was hoping to hear. "You drain me." I want to deny it, but I look and see that his skin is gray; there's gray in his previously raven-colored hair too. He seems bleached and faded by everything that has happened. He needs to find life's color again, and I hate it that this man I once loved so deeply is less because of me. "I don't need all this that you've brought to us," he goes on firmly. "So much mess and pain. I can't cope with it. It's all too much. *You* are too much. I can't forgive you."

I nod, because his position is understandable. We both stare through the windscreen. The rain drums down, blurring our vision.

"Why wasn't I enough for you?" His voice scratches, husky with emotion.

It's a question I have asked myself, often. Was I greedy? Was he lacking? Could I have resisted Daan? Should I have? Who is at fault? I wonder how I can most honestly answer him, because he does deserve that, finally, my honesty.

"You always gave the impression that ever since Frances died, you spent your life making do."

"What do you mean?"

"You behaved as though you didn't feel entitled to good things, the best things. Or you couldn't be bothered to reach for them. I don't know, but I don't believe you ever really wanted *me*. You married me simply because I was handy, and to have someone to co-parent with."

"That's bullshit, Leigh. I loved you."

"Maybe, to an extent, but I was second best and we both knew it. You didn't *choose* me. If she hadn't died, you'd never have looked at me. You married me to shield yourself. You didn't want to raise the boys alone."

He drops his gaze to the floor. "I didn't think I could do it." His confession is heartbreaking. It is the crux of our marriage and of his own lack of self-worth.

"You could have," I say, gently. "But you hid behind me at parents' evenings, at doctors' appointments, at family dinners. You didn't want to get involved." I laugh sardonically. "In the final analysis, I think you married me to avoid the hassle of playdates."

"No, Leigh, that's not it. I loved you, but... Sod it, why am I the one justifying myself? You were the one who secretly married another man." He has a point. My actions are indefensible. "Besides, even if there was an element of convenience in my marrying you, you loved being their mother. The role I handed you was one you wanted."

"I did. I do. But what I'm trying to explain isn't about me and how I felt in relation to them. It's about you and what you expect from life. And you don't expect enough. I think I was make-do and I'm certain your brief dalliance with Fiona was the same." He blushes again at the mention of Fiona. Embarrassed? Angry? "It's sad. It's a pity. I hope you learn to do things differently with the rest of your life. I hope you begin to think you are entitled to the very best and that you have the courage to go out and get it."

"What do you mean?" He raises his voice. I notice an old couple paying for parking nearby cast a glance our way.

"When you're hungry, you go to the nearest newsagent and buy a slightly stale sandwich that has sat on a shelf for too long, because it's the nearest thing to hand. You mindlessly swallow it down, not expecting taste or even nutrition."

"And I suppose Daan would find a Michelin-starred restaurant." His comment is snippy. I don't respond, because the answer would hurt. Yes, Daan would find a restaurant. "Look, Leigh, I want to be clear. You are not choosing him over me, because I'm not giving you the choice. I don't want you." He thinks he's hurting me by rejecting me, and of course he is, but I'm pleased he's got this level of clarity and self-respect. It's what I want for him. Besides, the idea I might still choose between them hasn't even entered my mind. Mostly I've been concerned with staying alive, and during the police interviews, I've been busy with the thought of staying out of prison. The only emotional matter I've allowed myself to consider is whether I have a chance of retaining my boys' love. It's an audacious thought that there might still be a choice between my husbands; a chance with either of them seems out of the question. The thought is served up and dashed in the same instance.

"Of course," I murmur. I'm glad he's not settling. In this instance, I am the slightly stale cheese sandwich.

"We're done," he says. "Understand? We're at the end of everything. Our family, our history, your lies and certainly the fanciful analogies about sandwiches. I don't need this crap."

"The boys?"

He stares at me, his eyes so deep they are black. "You are their mum, that doesn't change."

I let out a sigh of relief. The air leaves in a rush and I feel light-headed. My heart races.

"Thank you."

63

KYLIE

Mark gets out of the car and heads back into the hospital. I watch as he puts his mask on, turns up his collar and then forces his hands into his jeans pockets. He drops his shoulders, pushes forward through the rain. It's a stance I recognize from the hundreds of times I've seen him step out the door, hunched against the elements, as he's set off to work in the rain or wind. I keep my eyes on him as he shrinks and then disappears through the hospital doors, then I rest my head on the steering wheel. I'm alive and I am going to be able to see my boys. I'm going to be able to mother them. It's a lot better than I could have imagined for a while. I am so grateful. So lucky. Yet a part of me still feels like hell. My marriage is over. I destroyed it. The air feels clouded with failure.

I nearly jump out of my skin when someone knocks hard on the passenger window.

"You okay?" It's DC Clements. She isn't holding a brolly or wearing a coat, but nor is she hunched against the rain; she seems completely unfazed by the fact that it is still pouring. She looks concerned but capable, as ever. Such an interesting woman. Over these past few days when she's been interviewing me, I have come to respect and admire her. She's bright, thorough, tough and yet compassionate. I found it easy to be completely honest with her, to unburden myself entirely of all the secrets I have kept for years and the ones that have been thrust upon me recently. She patiently listened to my backstory but obviously wanted to concentrate on the investigation.

I've told her everything I can about Fiona and the first abduction. I gave a detailed account of the night Fiona brought me to the coast and pushed me into the sea. I've told her everything I can about Kenneth: how I trusted him, but that I was mistaken, because he tricked me, held me against my will; and how he finally helped me. She didn't rush me or dismiss me. She didn't roll her eyes and make sarcastic comments about me meeting my match in duplicity the way the younger, male officer did. It was her calm ability to absorb that meant I even told her that Kenneth had confessed to me that he'd killed his daughter. "I don't know if it's true or if it matters now that he is dead too, but that's what he said."

She said she'd follow it up.

Right now, she is exactly the person I want to see. I lean across and open the passenger door. She climbs in, raindrops falling from her hair and nose. She shakes herself like a dog.

"You all right?" she asks.

"Tough day," I admit.

"Do you ever have any other kind?" She roots in her pocket and pulls out a package. "Will chocolate help?"

"Always." I take it from her and open the packet, bite into the sweetness.

"I wasn't sure if Leigh or Kai ate chocolate," she muses.

"They both do. *I* do. I'm not separate people. I just had separate lives because it was the only way," I say with a hint of impatience. "It's not like schizophrenia or dissociative identity disorder or anything like that."

"Just teasing. Don't take offense." The DC looks out of the window, scans the gray parking lot. "I saw Mark heading back into the hospital. He looked upset."

"We're both upset. I cause upset. That's my forte."

She's not going to allow me to be self-indulgent. "I agree

it's one of your many party tricks." She grins at me and it's impossible not to smile back.

"You know, it was really wonderful for a while," I confess. I don't think I've ever admitted that to anyone. It's too scandalous and selfish, but I flatly lay the truth out for her to examine. Clements invites confidences. She must be brilliant at her job.

"I can imagine," she says carefully.

"They saw the best of me. I was a near-perfect woman for both of them."

"I think women try too hard to be perfect. Men not hard enough," she comments with a sniff.

"Well, now they both know the worst of me. Everyone does."

"It can't be easy. It's a bit like going on a date and them discovering you wear Spanx." She nudges me in the side with her elbow, smiling sympathetically.

"Mark said I can still see the boys. I think that's pretty generous of him considering everything."

"Well, that's good." She pauses. During my interviews and debriefs, I've got used to her rhythm. I can recognize when she needs to tell me something important.

"What is it?"

"We followed up on your hunch."

"And?"

"Yes, Stacie Jones was buried under the sea-glass bed."

"Oh Christ," I gasp.

"We've identified her officially. Dental records and such. We're trying to find the mother. There are people in the village who will want to bury her properly."

"Will you let me know when that happens?"

"You're going to go?" The DC is incredulous.

"I think Kenneth would want me there."

She nods. I get the sense she's an old-school sort of copper who understands duty and is devoting her life to responsibility. "What are you going to do next?"

"Well, a lot depends on if I go to prison or not." I raise my eyebrows.

"I don't think anyone will be pushing for that. You'd make a good private detective."

"You think?"

"Yeah, with your twisted mind. You could even join the force. If the Crown doesn't prosecute your bigamy, which I think they may not—there isn't much hunger for it. Technically, you'd have a clean record."

"You think I'm suited?"

"Mind of a criminal. Attention to detail. Tough as old boots. You'd be perfect." I can't tell if she's joking.

"I'm meeting Daan next. We didn't get to talk the night of the rescue. I asked to speak with him because I owe him my thanks and apologies."

"How do you think he's going to react?"

"Well, obviously he must hate me."

"There's nothing obvious about Daan Janssen," says the DC with a soft smile. I realize that she too has fallen for his irresistible charm. It smarts, knowing that this man who everyone desires on some level or other was once mine.

"He's very proud. I've taken a sledgehammer to his ego, publicly. He'll never get over the humiliation. He'll never forgive me."

"Well, there is a school of thought that says if you get all your shit out in one day, at least it's over and done with," says Clements.

"Do you believe that?"

"No, not really. I think every day can be pretty shit, and it's impossible to get it all out ever." She looks at me with curiosity, or pity, or something else that makes me uncomfortable. I must seem very frivolous to her, a woman who spends her days tracking down society's stains: drug dealers, pedophiles, murderers. "Well, good luck. And goodbye for now. There will be paperwork, family liaison officers. We'll be in touch."

The DC opens the car door and dashes out into the rain, off to make the world a tiny bit better.

6 4

KYLIE

Daan messages me and says that he won't meet me in my car in the hospital car park; it's too depressing. He says he'll be at the Pig Hotel in Combe. I'm not due to visit Seb until tomorrow, so I drive to the Elizabethan manor house that has been converted into a luxurious hotel with a relaxed twist on a private members' club vibe. It smells of lilies and roses, and there is a long, glamorous bar behind which bottles of every color and shape imaginable shimmer temptingly. He's arranged for us to have private use of the salon that is known as the library.

"Coffee or cocktails?" he asks after politely kissing me on both cheeks. I know this is not a sign of any particular affection, just an automatic greeting that he rolls out for everyone. Still, I take advantage of the moment; I breathe him in, lean into the essence of him. Drink it up while I can.

"I'll have an Americano," I tell the smart, earnest young man who is hovering close by, keen to take our order.

"I'll have a Bloody Mary, and don't be shy with the Tabasco," says Daan. He glances my way, his eyes communicating the fact that he thinks my choice is lame. He always thinks he can make a savvy guess at what a person might like or need, better than they can themselves. "Are you sure you won't join me?"

He's right, I do want a Bloody Mary. "Make that two. Cancel the coffee," I tell the waiter.

We sit in silence waiting for the guy to return with the drinks. I stare at the open fire. As it crackles and pops, I realize that the silence isn't awful. It's surprisingly comfortable considering the magnitude of the conversation that is brewing. Somehow, the familiarity between us trumps the awkwardness at a profound level. Being comfortable has stayed out of reach for me this past week; I've shuttled between hard visiting chairs in the hospital and the lumpy bed in my B&B. Now I fall back into the deep sofa, allow the warmth of the fire to soothe me, and choose to wallow in Daan's company for the last time.

I allow myself to remember our beginning. A lean, tanned, blond stranger. A slow smile from a coiled, ready-to-spring man wearing a crisp white shirt, a dark blue tailored suit. He offered me a roach and I took it, my first time. The rules were thrown out of the window. Tall and powerful, he was easy to follow. There was a glamorous rooftop bar and an instant, urgent sexual attraction, the sort that is as uncommon as hen's teeth and as coveted as the elixir of eternal life. He sparkled. He climbed inside me mentally. Then physically.

The drinks arrive, snapping me out of my reminiscing. We clink glasses, the automatic gesture of people who have been familiar with one another's company for four years. Neither of us is stupid enough to ask what we are drinking to. He waits. He might have chosen the venue, but I called this meeting in the first place, and naturally he wants to hear what I have to say.

"I wanted to thank you." My voice scrapes in my throat. It's not reluctance—I want my thanks to be full and sincere— but I'm struck once again by how awfully everything could have ended.

"What for?"

"You came to find Seb and Oli. You were prepared to be arrested to save them. You are fearless, and your fearlessness saved them and me. Thank you."

He waves his hand nonchalantly, as if to say it's nothing, but I see pleasure shoot across his face for a fraction of a second before he manages to pull it under control. He loves being praised; he just doesn't like anyone knowing he needs validation.

"I simply wasn't prepared to go to prison," he says. "I did scramble around for alternatives and I pursued those avenues as ruthlessly as it was possible, remotely through your sons. I didn't plan to come to the UK. If I could have avoided it, I would have."

"You were fearless and I'm grateful," I insist.

"I was driven; don't confuse that with fearless. I was bloody terrified. Initially terrified that I would go to prison for your murder. Then terrified that I had embroiled a pair of kids and put them in danger." He takes a sip of his drink and then adds, "They're good kids."

"They are." His refusal to allow me to flatter him acts as a solid wall that repels intimacy. "Well, thank you anyway. Whatever the reason, the fact is your unremitting determination won the day. I've always loved that about you."

His eyes dart to meet mine. They are challenging, accusatory. Bringing the word *love* into our conversation is a pushy move. I didn't plan on doing so. It just slipped out. He stares at me for a second, and then throws his head back and laughs.

"You're the fearless one, Kai. I've never met anyone so damned plucky. I can't say that I've always loved that about *you*, though."

"Oh." I fight the pinch of disappointment.

"I've only just learned it about you." That is so Daan. I was hoping that he would throw a compliment my way to match the one I gave him. I thought I wanted him to say, *I've always loved that about you too.* But his revelation that he's learned something new about me is a bigger and better response. He is always in some way bigger and better than I can imagine. That is why I ache for him. And probably always will.

It hurts too much to give space to my longing. Instead I decide to ask his opinion on something I've been wondering about. "Why did Fiona set you up? It seems especially spiteful and complicated. Wouldn't she have been better just leaving the case open? It would have been less risky. By trying to frame you, she provoked you into discovering her guilt."

"She hates me."

"Because I betrayed Mark for you?"

He laughs out loud again. I'm surprised at how joyful he seems. "It's not always about you, Kai. She hates me because *I* betrayed her."

I burn a little. "What?"

"I had sex with her when you and I were married."

"I see."

"She didn't know I was married and was not pleased when she found out."

"Right."

"Sorry." He shrugs.

I take a big gulp of my Bloody Mary. "Erm, just processing, but sorry for which bit exactly?"

"All of it. I'm sorry that I was part of what made her so fucking mad and sorry that I wasn't faithful to you."

"Okay." I wasn't expecting this.

"There were a couple of other women. When you were away supposedly looking after your sick mother." He rolls his eyes at this. "I didn't have a harem, but you know…" He breaks off, preferring not to have to articulate his need for variety, or simply his lack of discipline.

"And here I was thinking our sexy phone calls and access to porn might be enough," I say. He shrugs. He doesn't think I'm owed any further explanation, which I suppose is true. "It's almost a relief," I admit.

"What?" Now it is his turn to look surprised.

"Well, I'm no saint. Obviously. This sort of evens the score a little bit."

"You are unbelievable."

"Good unbelievable or bad unbelievable?" And I can't help it, I look at him and I know my eyes are glinting with a hint of flirtation, a hint of hope. Because there is, isn't there? There is something here I didn't expect or even dare hope for; there is the faintest murmur of a possibility.

"I don't know yet," he replies carefully. "Okay, so it's your turn."

"I did come here to apologize."

"Obviously." He waits.

"I'm sorry."

He takes a big, theatrical gulp of his Bloody Mary. "Erm, just processing, but sorry for which bit exactly?"

I can't help it; I laugh out loud too now. Despite all the pain and suffering, the fear and danger that I've seen, hearing him play my words back to me is just funny. Life is marvelous that way; there is always hope. "All of it," I declare. "I'm sorry for the whole damn messy business and yet for none of it, because I wouldn't have missed out on my time with you, not for the world." This comes out in a gush.

He stirs his drink with his celery stick and considers what I've just admitted.

"You are the most complicated person I have ever met."

"I'm sorry about that too."

"I'm not. Well, I am a bit. I mean, I'd like a somewhat quieter life, but I'm not entirely averse to your complications. I'll say that for you, Kylie Gillingham, you are never dull."

Am I hearing this properly? I hardly dare ask, but it would be the biggest mistake of my life if I let this possibility of a possibility disappear. "Is there anything still?"

"Yes. There is something." He leans forward and tilts my face to his. "You know, point of interest: you haven't asked my forgiveness."

"I didn't want to ask in case you don't give it," I admit.

"Very wise. You can get the next drink in, though. You do at least agree you owe me a drink?"

"Yes, I agree with that, but we can't drink and drive. That's dangerous."

He nods. "It's lucky I booked us a room then."

And there it is, this thing we have. Whatever it is. His confidence, his expectancy, my complexity, my spirit, our desire, our compatibility. It's all right here now. Every time I have ever been with him, I have thought it was the last time and I valued it all the more for that. Then I came to accept that we have always been together, even when we were apart; the presence of him stayed in my head when I was pushed off that cliff, when I was given a new identity, when I nearly drowned. He is with me on my hips and breasts, between my legs, in my soul. Throbbing, pulsing like life itself. He doesn't go away. He doesn't fade or leave me. So this time, I don't think it is the last time. This time, I think it is the first.

★ ★ ★ ★ ★

Hello! Well, if you have read *Woman Last Seen*, you will know that *Two Dead Wives* picks up the story of Kylie, Mark, Daan and Fiona. If you didn't read it, the exciting thing for you is that you can now go back to find out what led Kylie to marry two different men in the first place, which is a whole other story...

I never planned to pen a sequel to *Woman Last Seen*. I rather liked leaving the ending ambiguous. I thought my readers might have some fun deciding whether Fiona's plan to frame Daan would work, or whether they thought she'd trip up and be found out by clever DC Clements. I purposefully did not write a scene where there was a dead body washed up on the shore, or for that matter, a live one, because I thought it was an interesting play with my readers. Depending on their level of optimism, they could choose to believe whether Kylie had survived or not.

My sister read an advance copy of *Woman Last Seen* and called me to say she thought it was my best book ever. This was such a lovely, gratifying call. However, she was outraged that Kylie had been through so much and had not survived. I was surprised by this. I thought she would be in the camp that believed on some level that Kylie had created her own mess and had to be punished for it. I said, "Well, you can decide if she is alive or not."

"No, I can't," my sister snapped, somewhat irritated. "That is *your* job."

My sister, who is a careful reader, noted that Kylie had dropped the wine bottle on the cliffside. "Maybe Clements can find that," she commented excitedly. "When you write your sequel." Hers was the first of about a thousand requests I received to write a sequel. Of course, I didn't know that then!

I was extremely lucky that people responded so deeply to *Woman Last Seen*. It's the biggest compliment a writer can receive: readers feeling the need to engage, message, discuss in book groups and write reviews because they can't quite let go of the characters. It's often noted that I write challenging characters, inasmuch as they may not all be likable—but I promise they will be fascinating! I insist on my characters being realistic and therefore, sorry to say it, flawed. Most of us are flawed (although to a lesser extent than my characters, I hope!). We are complex, irrational and sometimes unreasonable. Good people do bad things and bad people do good things. I hadn't quite anticipated how much sympathy Kylie would galvanize, but I was so delighted to find she did.

I started to receive emails and messages on Facebook, Twitter and Instagram. Some people begged me to tell them Kylie wasn't dead, others wanted to be reassured that at least Fiona would be punished for her crime, still others were concerned for Oli and Seb, and most women expressed a preference for one husband or the other. My mother commented that it was a shame that the "much-enjoyed man" had been framed for something he hadn't done. "I'd have picked him," she confided to me with a little giggle. There was a lot of feedback, which I delighted in, I so enjoy engaging with my readers. Everyone seemed to have a different viewpoint, but all the messages were saying the same thing: "This story isn't over. We want a sequel."

I love my readers. Where would I be without them? So the more I thought about it, the more I realized they—you—were absolutely right. I did have more to say and it is my job to offer answers. I understood why people were uncomfortable that I had created an ambiguous world, where vengeful people got the upper hand, perhaps got away with murder. I decided I wanted to create a world where everyone gets what they deserve. It may not always be the reality we live in, but it's a positive narrative that I want to promote. Kylie did a terrible and deceitful thing, but I don't believe she should die for it.

I decided I had to write *Two Dead Wives* after all. This was not as easy as it sounds. Whilst writing it, I often yelled from my office, "What fresh hell is this?" as I tackled the complex challenges of developing a second plot when so many things were dictated by what I had written in *Woman Last Seen*. My task was to write a book that was a satisfying sequel but also a compelling standalone. It was quite the intellectual and creative challenge. However, it turned out that writing *Two Dead Wives* was possibly the most deeply rewarding experience I've had in my career. I felt so attached to the characters and I wallowed in the extra space and time that I had unexpectedly given them.

So thank you, dear readers, for encouraging me to write the sequel. Thank you for all the messages you send; it's a pleasure entertaining you.

Love,
Adele

PS: If you want to get in touch with me to talk about this book, or any of my others, then you can find me through these channels.

www.adeleparks.com
Twitter: @adeleparks
Instagram: @adele_parks
Facebook: @OfficialAdeleParks
TikTok: @adeleparksauthor

ACKNOWLEDGMENTS

I want to start with saying thank you to Kate Mills, my utterly fabulous editor and publisher. We have so much fun working together, don't we. And if I say it myself, I really think we are a killer team! I'm so incredibly lucky to have such a committed, creative and clever Publishing Director. The same goes for the wonderful Lisa Milton, Executive Publisher, who sails the good ship HQ with such passion and sincerity. It is an absolute joy working with you both.

I believe the tone of a team is set by the leadership, so thank you Charlie Redmayne for being a dynamic, motivating, innovative CEO (who also happens to throw the best author parties!).

I wholeheartedly appreciate the talent and dedication of every single person involved in this book's existence. I know there is a huge team of people who work with energy, enthusiasm and expertise. Thank you Anna Derkacz, George Green, Joanna Rose, Vicky Watson, Sian Baldwin, Rachael Nazarko, Rebecca Fortuin, Angie Dobbs, Agnes Rigou, Aisling Smyth, Emily Yolland, Fliss Porter, Angela Thompson, Petra Moll, Halema Begum, Kate Oakley and Anna Sikorska. This list is not finite! Thank you to everyone who plays a part.

I want to send massive thanks across the seas to the brilliant teams who publish my books worldwide. You really are making my dreams come true. Thank you, Sue Brockhoff and all of the team in HarperCollins Australia; thank you to the North American team, Loriana Sacilotto, Margaret Marbury, Nicole Brebner, Leo McDonald and Sophie James; and to my many other global publishers including Carina Nunstedt, Celine Hamilton, Pauline Riccius, Anna Hoffmann, Eugene Ashton, Olinka Nell and Rahul Dixit. There are many other publishing teams who I have yet to meet, but I am grateful that so many incredible professionals across the globe are giving my books their love and attention. Thank you.

Thank you to all my readers, bloggers, reviewers, journalists, retailers, librarians and fellow authors who have generously supported me throughout my career. Your wonderful endorsements and recommendations are invaluable. They are never taken for granted and each positive review, excited tweet or kind shout-out is noted and massively appreciated. I love reader feedback and endeavor to respond personally to every comment, email and message I receive. Even if I don't respond instantly, know that I am listening. Indeed this novel came into existence because readers demanded to know what happened next after reading *Woman Last Seen*. Further, I was inspired to use the name Stacie after an unexpected, lovely act of kindness from a reader.

Thank you to my mum, dad, sister, nieces, nephew and other family and friends who are always so supportive and proud.

Finally, thank you to my son and husband. Thank you, Conrad, for finally reading one of my novels this year, and emerging from the experience not only apparently unscarred, but with a positive review! Love you. You make me so proud, I'm thrilled I can make you proud too. Thank you, Jimmy, for always listening to my plots, doubts, fears, hopes and finally the finished version as I grapple with creating each novel. Your patience and support is stupendous and, some might say, heroic.

In addition I'd like to acknowledge the amazing generosity of Naomi Thomas, who was the winning bidder in a charity auction that raised funds for Freedom from Torture. Naomi won the dubious honor of naming one of my characters in this novel. I have never met Naomi so the Naomi Thomas in this novel bears no resemblance to the real deal who is no doubt a compassionate, kind and wonderful being and would never over-linger in a library when people are hoping to take out a book!

Freedom from Torture is dedicated to healing and protecting people who have survived torture. They provide therapies to improve physical and mental health, they medically document torture, and provide legal and welfare help. For more information visit www.freedomfromtorture.org.